A Collection of

UNCOMMON BODIES

ISBN: 0983876940
ISBN-13: 978-0983876946

Fighting Monkey Press

TABLE OF CONTENTS

We is We by Michael Harris Cohen: "We is We" follows a day in Mary and Millie's life, traveling sideshow freaks who've lost touch with the outside world.

All the Devils by Keira Michelle Telford: It's 1889, and women are being killed in the East End of London. They've become the targets of a deranged sexual killer, but why? Because they're prostitutes? Sapphists? Or something else entirely?

Skin by Brent Meske: After constant bullying in high school, Patricia vows to change her name and her entire being. When she gains the ability to mold and sculpt flesh, that vow very quickly becomes a terrifying reality.

Mermaids by Robert Pope: Recently graduated from college, with no work prospects, Aqua-boy—so called because of the webbing between his toes—watches and listens to a group of musicians at a bar/restaurant when he notices the woman playing a diminutive red accordion has six fingers.

Phantom Pain by Philip Harris: Phantom Pain follows amputee, Mariana Jacobs, as she visits a man who claims to have information she needs. But that information comes at a cost.

Unbreakable Heart by Rebecca Poole: A cyborg must escape her creators in order to survive.

Saltwater Assassin by Samantha Warren: Syren has spent her life as a sideshow freak, caged in a tank of saltwater and gawked at by hundreds of normal humans. She has a secret, though. At night, when the lights are finally off and the fair goers leave, she turns into a human–a mermaid assassin.

In Her Image by Vasil Tuchkov: An English PHD student arrives at the scenic but haunting countryside of Matera, Italy, looking for answers. His translator introduces him to a crippled local painter who claims to have depicted the impossible. As the three men converse near the ancient settlement's caverns, a mystery unravels.

Undead Cyborg Girl by Kim Wells: When she wakes up undead after receiving a cyborg assassin upgrade surgical procedure, Undead Girl's life is forever changed. Is it for the better? She has all the skills, but she needs a job, she needs some friends, and she needs to remember who she is. Part 1 of the Cyborg Story trilogy.

Don't Touch Me by Bey Deckard: Fighting is what Beau does best, because the very thing he dreads is exactly what lends him the extraordinary strength to defeat even the worst odds. And he does it all with the help of his angel, the woman he longs desperately to hold... but can't.

Three Poems by Deanne Charlton: Brenga's Body, Eternity in a One-night Stand, It Runs in the Family

Ruby by Bob Williams: It's nineteen thirty-six and the town of Ransom, Oklahoma is barely functioning after the "Dust Bowl" storm of the year before. Michael Wootten sits upon the porch of his dilapidated house and watches a caravan of trucks pull into town. Melvin Mitchell Presents: Ruby and her

Amazing FreakShow Friends. Maybe this is just the thing to pump a little spirit into the near-dead town. But everything comes at a price, and Ms. Ruby always takes her cut.

UnTamed by Laxmi Hariharan: Wolf girl Leana Iyeroy, the first hybrid in her family, only ever wanted to be 100% human. An unexpected encounter with the Hugging Saint of Bombay forces Leana to face the wolf inside her. Will she finally make peace with herself?

Made for This by Sessha Batto: On the heels of unimaginable loss comes reinvention. Sometimes the gain is worth going through hell.

From the Inside by Daniel Arthur Smith: Strange, wondrous things happen when weeks of rain, fever visions, and anxiety, compel a young traveler to journey across Central Europe in pursuit of a uniquely talented artist.

Rudy and Deidre by Robb Grindstaff: A shorter than average man admires a taller than average woman from afar.

Daedalus' Daughter by P.K. Tyler: After her father's death, Isha begins sprouting feathers.

The Zealot by Christopher Godsoe: Six months ago, Tobin Maldovan was in charge of a manhunt for an enigmatic hacker named ATLAS. He lost his man near the Canadian border after a high speed chase, but not before ATLAS pulled strings to transfer the woman Tobin loves across the country, hampering any chance at reconciliation. With ATLAS having escaped his jurisdiction, Tobin had nothing left but to follow his wife to California, seeking reassignment at the West Coast cyber-terrorism field office. His reputation precedes him, and he has drawn the case pursuing a man the media has taken to calling "The Zealot." As usual, Tobin pours himself into his work, but the work becomes personal in ways that he never would have imagined.

The Well-Rounded Head by Sally Basmajian: A woman is smitten with her husband's big, entirely round head. One day she notices that his temples appear to be slightly indented, so that his head is no longer a perfect sphere. This revolts her, and she moves into their guest room in order to avoid him. When he breaks in, she kills him, in a most bizarre way.

Reserved by SM Johnson: It's been five years since the accident that killed Pete Spencer's younger lover and left him grieving, bitter, and broken. He's tired of his lonely world, but the kind of young men he's attracted to dismiss him the moment their eyes land on his cane. Pete's learned to hide behind the safety of his reserve, but he's never met anyone like Rory.

Scars: First Session by Jordanne Fuller: It takes years to beat a strong woman into submission. It has to start somewhere. After a life of abuse, Abigail made the decision to cover her scars with tattoos. What she didn't expect was to confront her emotional scars in the process.

WE IS WE
BY MICHAEL HARRIS COHEN

We're moving again. Doesn't matter where. For us, in our trailer, one place is the same as the last and the last and the next and the next. One place is all we know. We'll move 'til we don't then Cyrus will sell tickets and you will come. I grasp this future easy.

You'll walk by and gawp us. You'll stare or maybe you won't be able to look that long. Some can't. Some turn away and don't look back. Others sneak a peek when they think we is not looking. But we is always looking.

We got eyes in the back of our head, Millie likes to say.

We see you all. You'll stop and walk by. You're alone or together with your lovey ones, holding hands, laughing, covering faces. We'll watch you drag your scared child down the dark hall of our trailer. You'll fashion ugly faces at our ugliness but we is used to it. Being ugly is what we is good at. That's what you'll have paid for. You might take pictures, ignoring the sign that tells you not to.

Millie gets mad about the pictures. *Bang the glass and shake a finger. Rules is rules*, Millie says. She says they're the law, like Mama's Bible Book or the rules Cyrus made, though I've been wondering about Cyrus' rules more and more. Doubting if they're right and true rules.

Millie doesn't like it when I question things.

We is we, she says. *God stuck us together and we gotta stick together. 'Two are better than one, because they have a good reward for their toil.' No questions, and for sure no pictures.*

The truth is I don't mind. I sometimes even smile for the pictures. Millie says that's vanity and against the rules too, but I'm not vain. How could I be? I guess I just like that some piece of we makes it out and into that world, the world Millie thinks we don't need and won't never know, though I think different. I got plans.

"You're lucky," Cyrus says. "The outside world is a dark and wicked place. Thorns fill people's heads. Their hearts are graveyards."

But our world is dark too. All day and everyday and our world's got nothing to fill it. Our world is black box with a hard chair and mirror behind. It's a hot light bulb that shines and sweats our ugly head.

Or it's this room behind the room, the one we're in now. The other half of our world: bed, toilet, and dresser. There's Mama's Bible Book on the dresser. There's the drawer I found the tiny knife in, under peanut shells and clothespins. Cyrus disremembered it and now it's mine.

Millie said, *Thou shalt not steal*, and I said, *Finders keepers*. But she kept bugging and hassling and niggling, for days and days, 'til I finally told her, *I'm gonna give it back to Cyrus*, and that's the truth. Though not yet and not how she thinks.

Cyrus tacked a poster on the wood that covers the window. It's a picture of a mountain that touches the clouds. It's the only mountain we've ever seen. Picture Mountain.

Millie says it's the Lord's mount, Sinai, where God's rules were handed down, but I say it's something else. I stroll my finger up the mountain, feeling the tears in the paper, all the way to the clouds at the top. I say, "Things don't always mean what you think, Millie. Sometimes things mean something else." Like the man who spoke through the glass. Or the plans I got.

Millie doesn't know the plans. I reason those plans in a way Millie can't hear. I make them small and jumbled, like I'm stirring alphabet soup, and only I know what the letters spell.

Our trailer lurches to a stop and rolls me on Millie's face. I say *sorry* and stand up. It's maybe morning because we stopped moving. Though it doesn't matter when and it doesn't matter where. One place is the same as the last and the last and the next and the next, and we got our things to do.

We gobble the bread and cheese Cyrus brought last night. I brush our black hair so Millie looks ok. We pee and amble from the back room to the front, closing the painted door you can't see. We perch on our stool and wait.

Let's play a game, Millie says. *Word Swap? Bible Lines? Tag?*

Millie loves games but I tell her I'm not in the mood. I feel her pout on the back of my neck and cram my thoughts with a storm of letters so she won't know what I'm really chewing. I scramble the words "plan," "knife," and "Cyrus" in our head.

You don't come for a long time and then you do: a man and a woman.

You stop in front of us. The woman gasps. We see it though we can't hear it. We can't hear much through the glass. She gawps like a mother over her sick child, rainy eyes and raised brow, hands laced. I don't move a muscle except to blink, not until the man squeezes her shoulder and they move on to see the others. The ones we've never seen.

Millie wants to gaze back and think about mama but I don't let her. I'm gazing forward, to the coming.

All day you and yours come and I don't move but to blink. I make my plans and we watch you stop and walk by, stop and walk by. I sit on the stool and let your eyes march over us. I let you sneak your peeks and snap your pictures. Cyrus taught me how to sit still so people see us—me in front, Millie in the mirror. So they could see we. That was rule number one.

"Don't fidget, Mary." Cyrus said. "Just move a mite so they know you're real. Mostly, be a painting."

Cyrus will come tonight like he always does. He'll bring us dinner and breakfast for tomorrow. He'll arise through the other door, the one we can't open. He'll say something like, "A face most find horrid can be beautiful if one looks long enough. If one really studies it, they'll unwrap the beauty."

He'll tug out our dinner from the paper bag. Millie likes French fries and I don't so we don't get those. We both like burgers so that's what Cyrus mostly buys and will likely bring tonight. Millie likes pickles and I don't, but I leave them on the burgers and ponder something else when I eat them for her—though, truth is, I taste vinegar and garlic no matter what I'm thinking about.

Cyrus will unbag our dinner and then he'll lean in to kiss our cheeks and that's when I'll stab him in the face. I've been practicing on the wood in our back room, training on the paper mountain so my hand won't slip when the time comes.

Cyrus smells like pine trees. I remember pine trees and their whiff, or Millie does. She remembers better as she's always looking back. She retains more things of the world but I recall some. I recall the touch of sun on our faces, the wet feel of a bath. I remember grass between our toes. I still dream of those things and my dreams are mine and mine alone.

We don't really remember Mama. All we have left of her is what's in our blood and her Bible Book. She cried when we was born because mothers want a baby that looks like them and not a nature's mistake. We don't remember much but we know it's true because she told Cyrus and he told us. How she cried and almost drowned us in the bath and what mother states a thing like that if it isn't true?

Cyrus saved us. He set us free, Millie likes to say but I think about it different, though I wonder if it's gonna be hard to kill him. Will he fight? Will I cry? Will I later grieve for his pine smell, his rough lips on our cheeks? Will I miss his voice saying my old name? I look forward but I can't know. A wall stands between the forthcoming and me.

Cyrus calls us Mary because he says that's the name our Mama gave us, though we can't remember if it's true. We were too little. But it's for sure true that Mama garbaged us so I garbaged her name. I named myself and to hell with mama and Cyrus.

Millie doesn't like it when I swear or reflect about the name. She frowns and our scalp tingles. She says, *It's a sin not to keep your birth name, even if it's from a woman who forsook us. 'A good name is to be chosen rather than great riches.'*

I cross my legs and smooth our skirt on the stool. I tell her, "Who named you Millie? You weren't even born with a name." She doesn't say nothing to that because she knows it's as true as can be. I christened her and not mama, not Cyrus. I chose Millie like I chose my name. I titled myself Janus because of the man who spoke through the glass. The old man I could hear.

Between you and we is the wall of glass. Cyrus says it safeguards us. If it wasn't there Cyrus said you might chuck things or hurt us. The wall was new once but now it's forever smudged and scratched. Cyrus' rule number two is: don't touch the glass.

"Don't want to hurt yourself," he says. "You're my darling. My favorite."

All day people slip past. Brave children mush faces on the glass, tiny lips and noses pushed in like Millie's. You sometimes put a single fingertip on it to point at Millie in the mirror. Must have been a million you and yours fingers pressed on that glass between us. We can't count that high.

I've imagined walking through that glass a thousand times. I've imagined thinking so hard, I make it disappear. Then I'll stand off this stool and follow you out into the hall. I'll finally see the others in their rooms, then walk to the EXIT and whatever is beyond.

Millie quit trying to stop me imagining. We is we except for what is mine and what I imagine is mine and mine alone. Her face scrunches up tight when I imagine the glass gone. I can't see her but I feel Millie like you feel your fist tighten, with a mind of its own, when you're wrathful at something or somebody.

It's a funny thing that the thousands of you and yours can see Millie and I can't, because she's behind and I'm front.

I got your back, Millie likes to joke.

But when you are not watching us, I sometimes make the trick. I hold a mirror to a mirror to see her, though it's not a mirror at all but the knife I found. I witness fuzzy Millie in the reflection of the reflection on the blade. On the back of our head, sticking out of our hair, she's exactly me only with the air took out of her face–mushed nose and sleepy looking, as she can't hardly open her eyes. Sleeping Beauty. Her skin is pale, sun robbed like mine, white against the black of our hair. Snow White after the apple. The truth is she's not sleeping. She thinks all the time and talks almost as much as she thinks. Often I just long for quiet and peace, nothing more.

Right now she's thinking about our secret. We love our secret. What we know that you don't, what even Cyrus don't know. That Millie is Millie and not just a face on the back of my head, not just a twin I tried to gobble in mama's womb but couldn't finish because I was too tired from growing legs, arms and ribs, or maybe just not starved enough. She is me but not me and we is we.

We've been we since I can remember. When I learned to talk she learned to talk. *Hello Mary, full of grace*, she said like she'd just arrived and was introducing herself. Though she was always there. Always and forever. We'd play and sing and argue and she was always there–sleeping when I slept, waking when I woke.

We sometimes think how lonely it must be for you who are not we. All alone in your head, that must be a terrible thing. I wonder again if that old man was lonely in his head.

Millie doesn't like me thinking about the man. She says, like always, *He was just crazy* and this time I don't say anything. I just remember the story despite her.

I recollect how it was a slow day with not so many of you. We squirmed on our chair, restless and hot, legs stuck to wood, the air like sand. Then he came. Like a child, he pushed his face right up to the glass.

But he wasn't a child. He was the oldest man ever. For a weird moment I felt we'd paid to see him, the most ancient man in the world, and not the other way around, the way it was and is.

I froze like we're supposed to and watched him watch us. I tallied thirty blinks and waited for him to move on down the hall. But he didn't. He ran a hand through what little hair he had. Thin and white as cobwebs, it scarcely roofed his head. Brown, mud-like spots speckled his face and hands. His cracked lips mouthed words and I did something I'd never done. I slipped from our stool and stepped to the glass.

You stay put, Millie said. *Rules is rules.*

But I didn't care about the rules. I craved to hear his words. I brought our face up to the glass. Up close, I saw the blood traffic beneath his paper skin. His eyes reminded me of blue sky and clouds as I turned our head and pressed our ear to the cool of the glass.

"Janus," the man said, his voice a whisper from the sea, though he must have been roaring to get his words through to us. "You're Janus. You look to the future and the past. The god of beginnings."

He smiled, baring teeth like rotten corn, then bowed his dappled head and was gone.

Millie said, *The old got straw for brains*. But I took that name and made it mine and mine alone. I threw Mama's Bible Book back in Millie's face. *Respect your elders*, I told her, and that she was Lot's wife, looking back, while I eyed the future and new beginnings.

Pride goes before a fall, Millie says.

Better to fall than never run, I say and she doesn't say nothing to that and I smile because I know it's one of those things that means something else, too.

It must be closing time. None of you and yours has come for a while. I grip the knife in my hand and wait. Cyrus will come soon.

This is not the first time I've meant to do this. There's been more than 20 burgers since I found the knife and made the plan. But tonight I'll shove that tiny blade in his face, a face I've studied so long it's grown ugly to me, no matter how handsome Millie thinks he is.

His nostrils are too big and his ears stick out like wings. His breath smells like gasoline. Tonight I'll stab his ugly stinky face. I'll stab it and take his keys and run.

To make Millie happy I clear my jumbled head and we play a game, Picture Paint. She chooses dog, so we paint that. She chooses the breed and I add the ears and fur. I make it white with black spots. I make its tongue pink and wet. Then I choose mountain. She shades the trees and the rocks and I add the clouds and the birds atop. We paint and wait for Cyrus.

He's slow to come so when we tire of painting we play Imagine the Others. Millie styles a Crow Man, like always, with wings that touch both walls of his room. I make Fish Girl in her own pool of a room and The Eyeball–a man with a face that is nothing but a blinking eye. Millie laughs and I think how maybe I'll set them all free, all the others, whatever and whoever they may be.

When Cyrus finally shows I can tell he's well oiled. He fumbles with the keys and drops the food bag on the floor. He nearly falls over trying to pick it up. I clasp the knife so hard it becomes part of my hand.

Drunk, he'll be slow. *He'll be slow and I'll be quick*, I think.

Quick at what? Millie says. *What are you doing, Mary?* And I panic because I didn't alphabet soup my thoughts, I'm too nervous and now Millie knows, she sees the plans and future I gaze toward. Everything.

She doesn't say what I imagined, Thou shall not kill or Cyrus saved us. She just screams.

She screams and screams, like those sirens that pass us when we're on the road only louder and never passing, she screams so loud our head will explode. It'll splat all over the glass wall.

I try to tell her how we'll be free. I paint all the things we'll see that we've forgotten, and all the things we've never seen that we'll see: the sun, the moon, the stars, the sea, television and chocolate, dogs and horses and cats, grass between the toes, other books and laughter and... but I can't go on with the endless list because she just keeps screaming and screaming.

"What's wrong, sugar?" Cyrus says, his words slack from the drink. "You look... lost."

And I am lost as we collapse off the stool and I know the plan won't happen tonight, won't ever happen, because of Millie and how she's always looking back, back even to the

Garden and man's fall, and never forward and I can't think and won't ever think again from her screaming–a million crow caws in our head, the laments of the burning sinners in hell–and I jab the knife up and into Millie's sleepy eye, and it's a flame in my own, and she screams even louder, and I stab again, again, again, 'til finally the screaming softens and I whisper to her, *It's our only way*, and, *For no one who has a blemish shall draw near.* I stab 'til she says nothing. She'll never say nothing again and I marvel at the new quiet and stillness in our head, like I'm on top of Picture Mountain hearing the soundlessness of clouds.

My head grows wet from mists and lighter, as if I'm turning cloud. There's hurt but sleep and calm too, because I know Cyrus–who's by me, gripping my hand, though I can't hardly feel it, taking back the knife–he'll let me go because I'm not a freak, not like the others, and no more will you stop and gawp because I don't have Millie and we is not we but just I.

***

ABOUT THE AUTHOR:
Michael Harris Cohen is a recipient of the New Century Writer's Scholarship from Zoetrope: All-Story, a Fulbright grant, fellowships from the Djerassi Foundation, The Jentel Artist's Residency, The Blue Mountain Center, and the Modern Grimmoire Literary Prize as well as Mixer Publishing's Sex, Violence and Satire prize. He is a graduate of Brown University's MFA program where he received the Weston Award for best graduate fiction manuscript. He has published numerous stories, both online and in print, and his first book, The Eyes--A Novella and Stories was blurbed by Brian Evenson, Robert Coover, Stephen Graham Jones and Stephen Wright. He lives with his wife and two daughters in Bulgaria and teaches writing and literature at the American University in Bulgaria.

All the Devils
by Keira Michelle Telford

September 9, 1889

Pain shoots through the tip of her middle finger, piercing under her bitten-down, brittle nail and tearing into the quick. Another splinter. Cursing her clumsiness, nineteen-year-old Lizzie plucks out the jagged wooden sliver and sucks her finger into her mouth, tasting a foul, bitter mixture of her own blood and the astringent cleaning fluids she's been using to scrub the floor to no avail. No matter how hard she scours the warped boards with the cheap wire brush, the bloodstains won't be washed out.

Exhausted, her back and knees aching from kneeling on the hard floor for over an hour, she slumps against the bed frame and sobs. The heat isn't helping. Her clothes are sticking to her chest, tiny beads of moisture trickling down between her breasts and soaking into her chemise. Seeking relief, she unbuttons the bodice of her dress, peeling the fabric back to expose a thin cotton camisole worn over her corset. Too many layers for September.

Ready to call it quits, she stares glumly at her efforts. The wall is blackened in streaks where the former tenant's blood spurted after the blade of a knife was run across her neck, severing her carotid artery. She bled out in seconds. Crimson fluid flowed profusely from the wound, saturated the palliasse, and pooled on the floor. The cut was so deep her head was very nearly detached, but that was by no means the worst of the atrocities committed upon her.

After death, she suffered the worst indignities imaginable. Her breasts were cut off, her thighs denuded of flesh. Her organs of generation were cut away and placed on the bedside table, along with the lumps of meat removed from her thighs, so forming a heaping, slopping pile of fat and tissue. Her abdominal cavity was cut open, her uterus removed and placed on the pillow beneath her mutilated head. Her face was gashed beyond all recognition. Only her eyes remained, staring lifelessly at the doorway, the lids cut away.

Lizzie read of the murder so often in the papers that every detail of the crime is etched into her mind. The poor woman's innards were all displaced, her intestines deposited at her right side, her spleen at her left, and her liver between her spread feet. Her heart was never found.

By all accounts, she was a beautiful woman before she was hacked up. She was tall, possessed of considerable personal attractions, and had many friends. Several of those who knew her are still residents of the tenement-lined court in which this single-room rent is situated, and since Lizzie moved in two days ago, she hasn't been able to speak with any of her neighbors without hearing them profess profound sadness for the poor unfortunate who met her end here.

It's been some ten months since the slaying, but fear still abounds in the East End. No woman is safe. Certainly not those of a particular profession. The man responsible—ought he be called a man at all?—was never caught, and this was not his only crime. He claimed the lives of six women in eighty-eight, and though he fell dormant for a time, this summer he again picked up his knife.

A woman was stabbed in the throat not far from here. As she lay dying, her attacker threw up her skirts and mutilated her abdomen, gouging her privy parts with his blade. What his purpose is in the work, no-one is sure, but that he loathes women of a certain class seems irrefutable. He is the Whitechapel Fiend. A butcher of women. A maniac, some say. Others call him a devil. He calls himself Jack.

Eyes wet with tears, Lizzie picks herself off the floor and pats down her dirty white apron. In stepping away from the stained wall, she catches her foot on the chamber pot she's been using as a makeshift bucket and tips it, sending a gush of ruddy, slightly sudsy water surging over the sloping floor. At one spot beneath the bedside table, the water is funneled through a thumb-sized hole in one of the floorboards.

Intrigued, she drags the table away and inspects the hole, poking her finger through and hooking it around the lip, testing to see if it moves. Sure enough, with a gentle tug, the board comes loose and lifts away, revealing a hidey-hole beneath. In this hole, a small bundle of possessions have been secreted.

A coin purse containing a half-crown, a sixpence, and a few farthings.

A two-thirds empty bottle of laudanum.

A bundle of letters, tied up with a ribbon.

Reckoning them to belong to the former tenant, Lizzie plucks them from the hole. Some are from Ireland. Some are from an address in Cable Street, Shadwell, near the docks.

Dearest Mary Jane, the most recent one begins, it relieves me to hear you speak of leaving London. It's no longer safe for women of our kind, and I should rather like to think of you far away from here, prospering in new environs...

Lizzie sinks into a chair at the table and lights another candle. For all that it's daylight, the two grimy windows looking in on her dingy room do little to illuminate the dank old parlor, with its sagging ceilings and peeling walls. It reeks of death. The palliasse was replaced—it had to be—but everything else in the room is as it was ten months ago.

The bed frame.

The cheap etching above the mantel.

The spider-cracked porcelain washbasin.

The rusty tin bath.

She owns nothing herself. Not even the bedclothes.

Ignoring pangs of hunger—for she hasn't eaten since suppertime yesterday, and it's now past noon—she settles down to read, noting that the Shadwell letters are all penned in the same feminine hand: a woman named Kate. A friend? A sister? A lover? She works her way through the stack, poring over every word. And what words they are!

Without exception, the letters are intimate. They speak of love and affection, every sentiment rooted in deep concern and a sadly prophetic mortal dread. Knowing not what to do with them, Lizzie turns her focus to the coin purse. Though tempted to make use of its contents for her own needs, her conscience won't let her. It's not much, but it ought rightfully to go to someone who knew Mary Jane. Someone who cared for her. Someone who undoubtedly loved her.

It ought to go to Kate.

***

Dangerously out of her element, Lizzie wanders down Cable Street: an area notorious for vice. Guarding against the predatory glances thrown her way by any man she passes, she hugs her shawl tightly around her shoulders, covering herself as much as possible.

It's barely mid-afternoon, but already the women of these parts are out in droves, flaunting themselves in pub doorways, their skirts too high and their necklines too low. They're the lowliest class of whores, Lizzie's been told. Cheap, intemperate, often old and stricken with disease, they cater mainly to the hordes of sailors continually making port at the nearby docks. It's surely no life for any woman.

Whereas the prettiest, cleanest girls get to work in the West End, spending their days in the finest bawdyhouses, counting their earnings in shillings and pounds, the worn-out bunters of Cable Street count the sale of their flesh in pence, or enough gin to get drunk on. This is the last stop before inevitable debility and the workhouse. There is no place worse.

Repulsed by the rampant immorality of this iniquitous quarter, Lizzie walks quickly, acknowledging no-one. Afraid of what she might find within, she locates the address on the letters and steps inside a rundown tenement where single rooms are let to all and sundry—bad characters and all.

Upon making a few inquiries, she's directed up a rickety wooden staircase cluttered with rag-clad children. On the third floor, she knocks on a wonky, tobacco-stained door and strains to listen for a reply, the air thick with the din of crying babies, wailing women, and the execrations of angry, drunken men.

"Who is it?" a soft, groggy voice calls out from the other side. "It ain't rent day."

Lizzie hesitates, unsure of how to introduce herself. "You don't know me," she says at last. "But I have something what belongs to you."

No reply.

"You knew a woman called Mary Jane," Lizzie forges on. "She lived in Miller's Court... was murdered last year."

That proves sufficiently rousing, and Lizzie waits with bated breath as bare feet pitter patter across the wooden floor in the room beyond, followed by the click of the latch.

The door opens a crack and a dark-haired woman peeks out, her brow puckered with a frown. "Who are you?"

"My name's Lizzie." The teen beams a warm smile. "Are you Kate?"

The frown deepens.

Lizzie opens her mouth to say more, but the woman— undoubtedly Kate—grabs her by the arm and drags her into the smoky, candlelit room beyond, slamming the door behind her.

"You were a friend of Mary Jane's?" she asks, almost accusingly.

"No..." Lizzie backs out of Kate's reach and bumps into a washstand, the basin filled with stagnant, dirty water. "I live there. In Miller's Court," she explains. "I rent the room where... well, where it happened."

"What brought you to me?" Kate's tone doesn't soften.

"I was cleaning the place up... or trying to." Lizzie pulls the bound stack of envelopes from the deep pocket in her dress. "I found these..."

Kate snatches them from her. "You read them?" Her jaw tightens.

"It's all right. You needn't be ashamed." Lizzie supposes the reason for her tetchiness. "I've got a cousin what's that way inclined, and I don't see as there's anything wrong in it."

Kate holds the letters to her chest. "I guarantee she ain't nothing like me." She turns from the door, retreating to a slanted table on the other side of the narrow, windowless room.

Evidently, Lizzie's knock woke her from a deep sleep. She's wearing only her underclothes: cotton stockings, chemise, and corset. Her hair's tousled and disheveled, spilling from a loose braid and tumbling over her shoulders. Her eyes are puffy and dark, yesterday's eye powder still smeared on the lids, smudged onto her cheeks. She could be in her twenties, but she looks older. Still, she's a fine-looking woman. She has well-formed, healthy curves. Her bust is full, bulging from the confines of her corset, and her legs... long, shapely legs.

"Do you really sleep there?" Kate spins around, catching her staring.

"In the very bed." Lizzie nods.

"Why?" Tears prick Kate's eyes, her mood subdued, anger and annoyance dissipated. "Why would you live in that place? However can you bear it?"

"I can't afford nowhere else." Lizzie hangs her head, stealing a furtive glance at more of Kate's undergarments strung up to dry on a curtain wire across the ceiling. "The landlord gave it me cheap 'cause no-one else would take it on." She fishes in her pocket for the coin purse. "I also found these." She empties the coins into her palm. "It didn't feel right to keep 'em, and I thought, since you was her friend, she'd want you to make use of it."

Kate accepts the meager offering. Their hands graze as Lizzie turns the coin into her palm, and much to the teen's surprise, Kate's hands are soft. They're not the hands of a woman who's ever done any hard labor, and her nails are neat, buffed and colored a pearly pink.

"Would you like something to drink?" Kate dumps the coins on a shoddily-constructed mantel above a disused hearth and sets about looking for booze. "Help yourself to a seat."

Lizzie would, but there isn't one. For lack of anywhere else to alight, she perches on the edge of the bed, the palliasse sagging under her weight. She hopes there's no vermin. Shifting uneasily, she watches Kate work her way through one abandoned liquor bottle after the next, in search of one that isn't empty. Upon finding some rum at the very back of her ramshackle cupboard, she spits in two cups, gives them a perfunctory wipe with a bit of old linen, and pours two generous measures.

"God bless you for being so sweet." She hands one cup to Lizzie and sinks onto the bed beside her. "Ain't many as would've sought me out the way you did."

"It was the proper thing." Lizzie picks a dead ant out of her drink. "It means one less risk you have to take tonight at least."

Kate regards her carefully, one eyebrow cocked. "Concerned for my safety, are you?"

Lizzie shrugs. "Don't it put a fright in you?" She nurses her cup, disinclined to drink from it. "Working the way you do, what with Jack n'all."

"What other way is there?"

That's the truth of it, and Lizzie knows it. Since coming to London, she's tried to make her way as a flower seller, but London has thus far proved to be a wild and untamable beast.

Nevertheless, "Aintchu afeared of him? What he did to your friend..."

"Friends," Kate corrects her. "I knew them all in varying degrees, for we were of the same sort." She downs her rum. "He found out what they were. That's why he chose them."

"Sapphists," Lizzie supposes, having inferred as much from the letters.

"Not all of us." Kate shakes her head, staring into her empty cup, longing for the materialization of more rum.

"What, then?" Lizzie fails to fathom what else could possibly trigger such hatred and violence. "How is he provoked into such madness?"

"I ain't sure of the proper name for it, but I can show you." Kate places her cup on the floor and reaches for Lizzie's hand, drawing it up, under her chemise and between her parted thighs before any objection can be made.

Her firm grip prevents Lizzie from recoiling, and the teen gasps as her reluctant fingers make contact with Kate's core, feeling first the lubricious furrow, then higher. Where she knows there ought to be the seat of a woman's pleasure, there is a protrusion. A lump. Something soft and fleshy obtruding from her groin at the apex of her slit, sprouting from a dense thicket of pubic curls.

"This is why he cuts them." Kate loosens her hold. "He cuts all trace of it away, then he takes their wombs—the very essence of their femininity. When he's done with them, they're nothing. Not man or woman. Only flesh."

Thinking it to be some hideous deformity, Lizzie wraps her fingers around the thing, examining its shape. At first, it fits snugly in her palm, but under her continued ministrations, it begins to swell. It gains length and thickness, stiffens, and her breath catches in her throat.

Panicked, she wrests her hand free and scoots to the end of the bed, her back pressed to the footboard. "Whatever is it?!"

"Do you wish to see?" Kate pinches the hem of her chemise between her fingers and lifts it up, revealing a perfect replica of the virile member. "It's all right to be curious. Plenty people are."

"Oh, lummy..." Lizzie gulps down her rum and edges closer, her eyes riveted to Kate's peculiar anatomy. "I ain't never seen such a thing." She ducks down for a better look, her hot breath arousing the sensitive flesh of those parts.

"I'm sorry." Kate pulls her chemise back into place, covering her priapus as it rises to full rigidity. "I ain't that well in control of it."

"Why does it do that?" Lizzie keeps her eyes pinned to the bulge in Kate's lap.

"Because you're beautiful."

Intrigued beyond all logic and reason, Lizzie teases Kate's chemise up again, rucking it over her belly and fully exposing her southern regions. "It gets such a swelling." She admires the length and girth of the thing and wraps her hand around it once more, feeling it at full stiffness. "So hard n'all."

"Ain't you never felt a prick before?" Kate reclines, letting her feel where she may.

Lizzie shakes her head. "My mam says men ain't nuthin' but trouble, and that I'd best avoid the nuisance their pricks so often cause to a girl."

"Good job I ain't a man, then." Kate smirks. "Do you want to see more of me?" Without waiting for an answer, she strips off her corset and chemise, unveiling her ample charms and allowing Lizzie to feast on her nudity. "Explore me if you wish." She lies down, availing her body to Lizzie's inquisitive touches.

And what a body it is! Womanly in every regard... excepting one.

Lizzie ventures nearer and continues her investigation of Kate's priapic appendage. Awed by its weight, she flops it onto Kate's stomach and tiptoes her fingers up the shaft, counting the inches. She arrives at eight. Eight inches of firm, throbbing flesh, topped with a smooth, bulbous head.

"Are they all quite so big?"

"Not a bit." Kate laughs. "I'm generously proportioned. Some I've seen ain't no bigger than your little finger." She waggles her pinky in Lizzie's face.

Amused to think that Kate should be distinctly better endowed than many men, Lizzie swirls her fingertip around the fat crown, committing the sight of it to memory, lest she should never again have the opportunity to indulge in such erotic larks. In fact, she's so set on harnessing as much enjoyment out of this encounter as possible that when a single droplet of anticipation beads on the tip, she scoops it onto her finger and sucks it into her mouth.

That proves too much. Immediately self-conscious, her cheeks grow hot and she turns away. Alarmed by the force of her own precipitously revealed lusts, her cunt pulsing between her thighs, she shuffles to the side of the bed, ashamed that she should've behaved so lewdly.

"I feels all queer."

Kate nestles up behind her, diagnosing the problem directly. "Do you want to fuck?" she whispers, her breath tickling Lizzie's neck.

"I ain't never..." Lizzie whimpers, her head swimming.

"But do you want to?"

"I promised my mam I wouldn't." Lizzie swallows hard, determined to retain the last of her rapidly evaporating morals. "Not before marriage. It's a sin."

"If I were a man, perhaps." Kate eases up Lizzie's skirts inch by inch, tugging them over her knees. "But I ain't." She glides her hand up Lizzie's leg. "What sin can there be between two women?" She forces her way between the teen's tightly clamped thighs and fumbles through the opening in her split drawers, finding her treasure saturated with unrealized desire. "And you do want it ever so badly."

"It's so wicked," Lizzie mewls, doing nothing whatever to stop her wandering hand. "I'll be going straight to hell if I let you have the first of me. I know I will."

"This *is* hell, darling." Kate tickles her fingers over the hardened nub atop Lizzie's needy sex, making her quiver. "All the devils are here among us. We must snatch our pleasure where we can, before it's too late."

Rendered insensible by Kate's digital attentions, Lizzie surrenders herself. Kate's roving hands soon divest her of the layers: bodice, skirts, petticoat, camisole, corset, chemise, and drawers. Left in nothing but her white cotton stockings, she accepts Kate's kisses and caresses everywhere from her neck to her rump, delighting in the titillation.

Wound up to such a pitch that she then loses all sense of modesty, she rolls onto her side and crushes their bodies together, trapping Kate's priapus between them. Flinging a leg over Kate's hip, she draws herself tighter and grinds on the turgid instrument, generating a delicious friction until their bellies become slippery and wet. Perplexed by this sudden change in sensation, she peers down, surprised to see a profusion of mucilaginous goop oozing from the engorged pipe.

"It's leaking."

"I need to come." Kate guides Lizzie's hand to her erection. "Help me." She wraps the teen's fingers around the shaft, showing her how to move. "I'm so close."

Close to what? Lizzie isn't sure, but she wants to find out. She fists Kate's well-lubricated organ with clumsy enthusiasm, her hand gliding smoothly up and down the slick flesh, her pace increasing as Kate's breathing quickens.

"That's it," Kate encourages her. "Just a little more..."

Not a minute later, her hips flex and she bucks into Lizzie's hand, her priapus erupting with volcanic force.

Startled by several bursts of hot fluid spurting onto her stomach and breasts, Lizzie squeals. "You don't half make a mess with it!" She giggles, rolling onto her back, her semenalized torso shimmering in the candlelight. "Wherever does it all come from?"

"Damned if I know, but it aches to be released." Kate takes a moment to recover, then plucks a towel from the washing line above their heads and wipes her thick, creamy deposit off Lizzie's body. "It causes such a discomfort when it ain't tended to."

Her interest in the thing not yet abated, Lizzie glances at Kate's appendage, disappointed to find it withering. "The swelling's gone." She pouts.

"For a while." Kate discards the towel and wriggles between Lizzie's legs. "Until I'm stirred to passion again." She explores the teen's hitherto untouched body.

"How long might that be?" Impatience creeps into Lizzie's voice.

"Not long," Kate assures her, prying apart the folds of her sex. "Not if you let me kiss you." She admires the carmine slit, the entrance to Lizzie's body obstructed by a pink membranous barrier.

"Ain't I already let you kiss me?"

"Not like this." Kate dips her head between Lizzie's spread thighs.

The hot lashes of her tongue come as a surprise. Lizzie howls at the ceiling, her sex engulfed in heat, Kate's soft mouth kissing and licking, her tongue probing.

"Whatever are you about?!" She grips fistfuls of the bed sheets. "I ain't never known of a person to do such a dirty, filthy thing! You mustn't..."

The protest dies on her lips. Ever so gradually, a pressure builds in her abdomen and she begins to shake, her first orgasm coming upon her hard and fast, her voluptuous moans mounting in frequency and intensity until, fearing she might have a fit, she wails at the ceiling and convulses against Kate's mouth, her insides in spasms.

In the wake of her paroxysm, all the tension in her body dissipates. Her thighs relax, opening wider in full submission to pleasure, and she looks down, thrilled to see Kate's anatomy wholly restored. The straining instrument is mightily swollen and jabbing at her mound, the tip glistening with a fresh sheen of pearly excitement.

Sensing her want, Kate scoots forward, nudging the head of her weeping lance through Lizzie's plump folds and embedding it in her core, its progress halted by her intact hymen.

Feeling a twinge, her maidenhead stretching to accommodate the intrusion, a frown creases Lizzie's brow. "Will it hurt?"

"It might a little." Kate lays her hands on Lizzie's hips, preparing to thrust forward. "But only at first. Any discomfort will soon pass."

"Is it... safe?" The frown sticks.

Kate nods. "I shan't wet inside."

Her concerns suitably assuaged by that promise, Lizzie closes her eyes and holds her breath, preparing for pain, then Kate gives one firm shove. She lodges the bulbous head of her priapus completely within Lizzie's virgin body, obliterating her hymen, and at the moment of defloration, Lizzie stifles a yelp. Then it's over.

Kate plunges up her tight channel, fully impaling her. "How does it feel?" She hilts herself, her movements languid and unhurried, drawing out their pleasure. "Do you like it?"

Incapable of words, Lizzie clutches at Kate's back, urging her on, moaning with every upstroke, but their first coupling isn't destined to last. In just a few minutes, Kate's rhythm falters. There's a strained look on her face, almost pained, as if she's holding something back—which she is—and she starts to withdraw.

"I must stop."

"Don't." Lizzie grips her rump, pulling her deeper. "I'm nearly coming." She encourages Kate to resume her operations. "Have your spend in me."

Groaning with need, Kate remains embedded. "Are you sure, love?"

Ignorant of the dangers, Lizzie nods. "You ain't no man. What harm could there be in it?"

Ah, what harm indeed! Kate moves harder and faster, driving herself toward completion, her thrusts becoming ever more frantic, her inevitable crisis soon brought on by the exquisite tightening of Lizzie's climaxing sex, each contraction milking her priapus, delivering her libation deep into Lizzie's unprotected womb.

***

During the course of the afternoon and early evening, Kate and Lizzie are inspired to incorporate their bodies twice more, both couplings concluding with Lizzie receiving Kate's abundant and potent spendings inside her fertile body, the unsheathed tip of Kate's lance pressed firmly against the gateway to her womb. When finally sated—the starch well and truly gone from Kate's mighty organ, all attempts to rouse it resulting in failure—they fall asleep in each other's arms.

Later, waking in the small hours of the night, Lizzie rolls over to her bedmate, hoping that some rest will have had a rejuvenating effect on her parts, but Kate is nowhere to be found. Instead, there's a note left on her pillow.

Must work. Back soon.

Thinking it the natural course of things, Lizzie pushes away her paranoid fears and tries to go back to sleep. She fails. Nightmarish thoughts keep her awake, and just before dawn, she rises with the intent to hunt Kate down and drag her back to bed.

As she sits up, a torrent of Kate's milky sediment responds to gravity and evacuates her body, trickling down her thighs. Stupidly, she hadn't thought to wash. Before their second poke, Kate had confessed that she was more than capable of doing damage equal to that of any man, but by that time, Lizzie was too hot cunted to care.

Now, she brings a hanky to her sex and dabs up the spillage. How is one meant to guard against an encumbrance in any case? She doesn't know. She was never taught such tricks. Her mother only told her to stay well clear of men, and as far as that goes, she has. If she has to run home to her mother with a belly full, at least she can say that she never broke her promise.

Not having the first idea where to look for Kate, she pulls on her clothes and heads out into the gas-lit streets, beginning on Cable Street and wandering all around. Shortly after five AM, as she's about to give up and slink back to Kate's bed, a policeman's whistle sounds from beneath a railway arch on Pinchin Street.

"There's been another one!"

***

Between 1888 and 1889, nine women lost their lives in the East End. They were:

Emma Elizabeth Smith, April 4, 1888
Martha Tabram, August 7, 1888
Polly Ann Nichols, August 31, 1888
Annie Chapman, September 7, 1888
Elizabeth Stride, September 30, 1888
Catherine Eddowes, September 30, 1888
Mary Jane Kelly, November 9, 1888
Alice MacKenzie, July 17, 1889

The woman whose dismembered remains were found in Pinchin Street on September 10, 1889, has never been identified.

***

ABOUT THE AUTHOR:

Keira Michelle Telford is an award-winning author with a love for the gruesome, the macabre, and the downright filthy. She writes dystopian science fiction, erotic lesbian romance, and other lesbian fiction.

Website: www.keiramichelle.com
Facebook: www.facebook.com/keiramichelletelford
Goodreads: www.goodreads.com/keiramichelle
Amazon: www.amazon.com/author/keiramichelle

Skin
by Brent Meske

"If you repay me not on such a day,
In such a place, such sum or sums as are
Express'd in the condition, let the forfeit
Be nominated for an equal pound
Of your fair flesh, to be cut off and taken

In what part of your body pleaseth me."
 William Shakespeare, *The Merchant of Venice*

"Hey pig. Piggy pig pig pig."
    High school's a bitch. Most of us felt the same way. A
damn shame too.
    "Hey pig," someone laughed.
    "Oink oink." More laughter.

Streaks of red and yellow and darker hues colored her shirt, colored her face. Bits of dried food littered her crumpled expression. A chunk of brownie fell down her face and into her shirt. She lowered her eyes and kept moving, clutching her books to her chest, because her backpack was still somewhere in the cafeteria. Someone swatted her ample ass on the way through the halls. Somebody else did a surprisingly good impression of a pig squealing.

Tears divided the grime on her cheeks, but she wouldn't let any of them see it. She ducked into the bathroom and headed straight for a stall. Amanda Perkins and her friend Nina Calloway looked up at her through the mirror. Their giggles turned into laughter as she heard the door shut, and she was finally alone.

Her name was Patricia Swaine. Which was good.

Not good, it was perfect. It wasn't just that her name was totally perfect, to top it off she was five eight and a solid two twenty. It hadn't stopped being perfect through middle school, and it sure as hell didn't look like it was going to stop being perfect in high school. Piggy Swine the Porker. Hey Piggy. Piggy piggy piggy.

She didn't hate her name, not the last name anyway. Swaine was almost a gentle word, something graceful, maybe even pure. Swan, Swaine. Like drifting on a lake in the sunshine and feeling the cool water on your body.

Patricia, on the other hand, sucked it big time. You couldn't get anything pretty out of Patricia, not Pat (truncated and ugly, like an amputated stump), and definitely not Patty (which sounded like a kicked-around suburban housewife).

Piggy Swine didn't think of herself as a Patricia, not the other two either. They'd been tried, by her friends, but none of them worked. She couldn't have been stuck with a nice name like Katherine, or Katarina, which could magically transform her into multiple different people. It couldn't have been anything pretty either, like Violet or Amber or another color. It didn't help that her middle name was Tamara. Tammy, she wasn't.

It would be nice if you could get a name surgery. But Piggy couldn't. She'd tried before, cutting on her thick wrists with a steak knife. Her scars had faded to a dullish white-pink. You just couldn't incise your name out like a tumor. So the cancer in school, everyone else, had grown and transformed her name until it transformed her personality.

Piggy pulled on her flesh, wanting to rip it off. She actually dug nail marks into her arms, into her baggy stomach. Tiny bubbles of blood bloomed on her skin. The pain felt good enough to chase away her tears.

"It's all going to change," she told her skin, her fat. "It's gonna start with my name."

The name she eventually chose was Jenna. Jenna Swaine sounded just wonderful, thank you very much. Not to mention, the prom queen's name was Jenna. If Piggy couldn't do anything else, she'd at least gall that uppity, size two, six-foot blonde bitch.

"Patricia, are you in here?" Evan was a good enough guy, but he was ugly and fat, just like her.

She said nothing in response, just hitching sobs at what had happened in the lunchroom. So Physics was next, a useless class, and she'd miss it again.

"You're in here, aren't you?"

She was in here probably once every other week.

"Fuck off," she said, without any real conviction.

"Hey, come on, it's going to be fine. Fuck them. We'll set the school on fire after we chain all the doors closed." He stepped into the stall and hugged her. She noticed every single time his arms couldn't get all the way around.

***

"A pound of flesh," Mrs. Kirkenbaum said. She walked back to her desk and pulled up a scale, one of those with a little red pointer. It seemed to go from Empty to Full in no time, when their teacher placed her hand down on it.

"It's not much," their teacher went on. "Sixteen ounces. Less than half a Kilogram. Less than a quarter of what your Social Studies textbook weighs."

There were some polite snickers at this.

"Mister Shakespeare, the venerable lord of the written word of English, calls for it. His villain Shylock, whom Shakespeare portrays a nasty Jew with a grudge, makes a contract for a pound of flesh. No more, no less. He doesn't wish for his money returned, or any extra money on top for interest. He wants a pound of Antonio, from anywhere on his body."

With this Mrs. Kirkenbaum produced a lump of something the size of a tomato, but clear and squishy, like a stress ball. It was just larger than the size of their teacher's fist.

"Do any of you know what this is?" she asked.

"I know it's probably going to get eaten by Piggy later," someone muttered from the back. The class erupted, and Piggy set her jaw.

Mrs. Kirkenbaum frowned. "This, class, is a breast implant." It was shown to weigh a pound when she placed it on the scale. More snickers followed. "I present this because it is easier than trying to find a pound of real flesh, and because one should take a look at this, to realize the sheer silliness of trying to change one's self. Change always comes from the power of will, the determination to change."

"Someone ought to go on a diet of willpower," the whisperer went on, behind Patricia. More snickers followed.

"Thus the adage, beauty is only skin deep," Mrs. Kirkenbaum said.

"Not buried under layers of fat."

Their small teacher folded her arms under her breasts and stared at the class in disapproval.

"That will be enough. Now, to get back to the point: this entire play is about an evil money-loving Jew. Back then, this was a common theme: the Jews were usurers and moneylenders, and reviled all over Europe for that. It became a stereotype leading toward Hitler's line of reasoning that the Jews were wicked and ought to be cleansed from the land in order to give the right to rule back to the Aryans.

"Throughout the whole story, the characters ask Shylock to change his heart, to change his mind. But he's a stubborn Jew, and wants only his pound of flesh. It may become his undoing. We'll find out as the play unfolds."

The silicone balloon continued to sit lazily on the scale, ignoring the derision and horror and laughter directed at it.

Patricia flicked her eyes up toward the clock every few seconds, to see if perhaps ten minutes might miraculously pass without anybody noticing. After several eternities, the bell consented to end her torture.

***

Some whore sonovabitch tripped her on her way to gym class. The hallway erupted into half embarrassed giggling. Her books scattered to the four winds and she hit her chin on the tile, clicking her teeth together. The tears came like a reflex.

"Jesus, would you look at this big fat mess in my way?" This was Jenna Hawkins, resident prom queen and homecoming queen. The actual Jenna.

Patricia-not-Jenna lay at her feet, trying to pull together her dignity so she could stand up. It wouldn't work. If she'd had as much dignity as body fat, she could chase her problems away with hard stares.

"Hey, bitch," Jenna Hawkins leaned over her. Strawberry and cream scented blonde hair brushed her burning cheeks. It was shiny and perfect, not like Patricia's tangled mop of dirty brown. More than everything else about the past prom queen, her hair was just the right way every single day. "I heard you want to change your name to Jenna. I'm real flattered and all, but quit it now. People are going to start calling me Piggy, and I can't have that."

She stood tall. "I mean, it's not like anybody's going to confuse us. You couldn't fit a pair of my underwear around your ankle." Her thoughtless, idiot, hanger-on, Kardashian wannabe friends got a kick out of that one, and she went with them, laughing down the hall, perfect hair swishing.

"You'll always be Piggy to me," she called out.

***

She never cried in front of her parents. Of course they loved her, but their love always manifested with stuff. They wanted to give her more clothes that might not fit in months to come, more jewelry she'd never wear, and toys. They still gave her fucking toys.

The worst of it was the food. Both her mother and father enjoyed eating, enjoyed it prodigiously. They always cleaned their plates, at times wiping them clean with buttered bread so as not to miss anything. More than this, though, they stocked the house so full of food that the three of them could have eaten well for a month and not cleaned out the pantry. Whenever Patricia asked her mother about this, the excuse was always along the lines of:

"We eat it, don't we? It's not like it's going to waste."

Her mother had learned hard lessons from growing up poor. The Janislaski household saved everything. This practice was brought into the Swaine household when she married Patricia's father.

No, she never cried in front of them. It was sullen silence all the way.

She always ate in silence. Her computer time was spent in silence, during which she would clench her jaw and feel her throat begin to tighten, despite the Cheetos or potato chips or brownies by her side. Patricia, who wished her name could be Jenna, drowned these things in food. It was there, she was there.

The only one to see Patricia cry was her closet mirror. Or rather, the four full-length mirrors that made up her closet doors always watched her. She could not fit into just one of these, but it wasn't their fault. It was hers. They were dutiful; they only gave her the facts. The facts were thus: Patricia Swaine, or Piggy Swine if you were under eighteen, could not stop eating.

***

"May God look upon you with favor, and give you peace." Her pastor sketched out the sign of the cross in the air. Just the motion made her want to vomit.

Patricia didn't want to go to church anymore. She resolved to tell her parents how useless God was. If he could truly scrub cruelty from the world, he should start with the church. Her few friends went, but she just couldn't stomach the idea that God loved her. She couldn't fathom the idea that Jenna Hawkins and her prom date boyfriends came here every so often and prayed like good little Christians. That was a load of shit, to be honest.

Her faith wilted.

Watching Jenna sit there, with her blonde hair practically giving her a halo, made Patricia want to throw up again.

She walked out in the middle of the service that day, quietly turning her back on God, on the pastor, and her friends, even her family.

She left the church, swearing under her breath, and walked two miles home praying to Satan.

***

Piggy stood shivering in the school bathroom again, silently crying. The world of high school moved on outside, beyond her, distant and removed. Chocolate sauce spelled out her nickname on her chest in ragged letters: PIGGY. She'd sat there and let the fullback, a guy just about her size, drizzle the letters on there.

He took the dare, and she stared into his eyes the entire time, until his cheeks burned with shame. He'd never forget this day, for damn sure. His hands shook so bad by the time he finished that the Y was just a wonky scribble. It did the trick though. Somebody else had smeared a cupcake in her hair, then down her face.

Instead of lowering herself, she'd silently gotten up and left to the sounds of roaring laughter, and even applause.

Her chin crinkled, her bottom lip convulsed, and tears ate away at the frosting on her face. She held herself and cried, not caring to miss Physics with the rotten old bag that taught the class. Physics or Suicide 101, either one was okay by Patricia.

Once again she tried to steel herself against the pain. Failed. Instead, her stomach burned with hate and shame.

It was a battle, hating herself. Her fingers dug into her fleshy arms again. The pain was good, and she watched the little blood droplets form. Pain almost let you forget for a few minutes.

The pain disappeared, and the wounds closed, before her eyes. Patricia gasped, then looked outside the stall. No one.

She dug her fingers into her arms again. This time when she pulled, her flesh came with it, in big clumps of skin and fat. She opened her hands and found her body in her hands, on the tips of her fingers. She was too stunned to scream. Instead she looked down at her arms and found deep finger markings, where the skin and fat used to be. But no blood.

A tiny croaking sound came from her throat and escaped. It startled her. She held the fat out away from her, and shook it off her hands like it was manure. Gobs of it splattered onto the stall walls and on the floor. Mushy skin slid down with exaggerated slowness.

With her hands on her arms again, she poked at the marks in her arms. Then, feeling bolder, she rubbed over the reddish runnels and crevices. Her skin smoothed over like clay. A little more smoothing and she looked just like normal again. Yet there, spattered around the stall, were little pieces of her, blobs here and there stuck to the floor, the door, the walls, the toilet.

"Oh God," she moaned, and a stone fell into the center of her guts. It glowed hot and disgusting, and painful in her middle.

***

That afternoon, Patricia stripped off about a hundred pounds of fat in her bedroom, scooping and remodeling her skin as if she were a piece of art. It was actually kind of fun, once you got outside the butcher shop idea of what she was doing. She found that underneath it all, she had a surprising amount of smooth, strong muscle.

She kept her breasts just the size they were; only now they seemed huge on her.

She worked in a daze of satisfaction and determination, scooping off this or that disproportion and smoothing it here.

She worked herself down sixty, eighty, a hundred pounds, until she the scale read one twenty three. A massive lump of ruddy pink flesh sat in the corner, a strange snow that seemed would soon melt.

She even worked on her face, smoothing it down and scooping skin off until it was Jenna Hawkins-delicate and prom queen haughty. Now she looked herself over in the mirror, completely naked, and marveled.

For almost two hours she stared at it, the Piggy Swaine hill. And stared. And stared. Eventually the ability to think came back to her, and then plans began to form.

It wouldn't work, not for a few weeks at least, but she would end up back here. Like this.

She slapped most of her body back into place, making this and that adjustment until she was back to mostly normal. She left off ten pounds, which seemed pitiful in comparison to the behemoth she'd shed earlier.

But that was okay. She could scrape off a pound of flesh every day and be perfect in two months.

Patricia went out that night and bought a small postal scale, one that weighed up to two pounds. She hid it in her closet and fawned over it.

***

Patricia and her mother went out to buy her a new wardrobe two months later. She was a little awkward at it, as she'd never had to try on clothes to fit tightly before. They always had, whether she liked it or not. Whoever it was that made clothes for large people (plus sized, is what you would call the old Patricia) must have been a sadist of the worst kind. Every scrap of clothing produced by these fuckers was too tight in places she had no intention of showing, and loose elsewhere. She looked like a circus tent because of them.

No longer. They went into Saks and Abercrombie & Fitch, Hollister, Forever 21, and finally Victoria's Secret.

"Are you sure about this?" her mother asked, on several occasions, in a small voice. Patricia (Jenna Swaine, Jenna Swaine, she kept repeating) looked at her mother and held herself from rolling her eyes. In her reduced sized hands she held a pink tank top with the words 'Saturday Night Skinny Dip Club' in darker pink, with little bits of silver drop shadow.

"There are plenty of things at JC Penney that look perfectly respectable," her mother hinted. "Are you sure–"

"There are plenty of things at JC Penney that would get me laughed at," Jenna Swaine replied.

"And that'll fit you?" her mother inquired. She was quickly losing this little battle of wills.

Her parents had always been so conciliatory about her, apologetic about the fact that the bathtub was her enemy at eight years old. They would never come right out and say they were sorry about feeding Patricia so much food, but the worried glances and gifts and half-sorrowful tones were all there.

"It'll fit," Jenna-no-longer-Patricia Swaine said. Her voice felt stronger.

"Patricia," her mother said, then fell silent. After a few moments she piped back up, "The price tags on these things are outlandish."

Now Patricia/Jenna did roll her eyes. "If you don't want me to buy this stuff, or you're not going to pay for it or whatever, just say so okay?"

"I don't want you to buy this stuff," her mother said weakly.

"Fine," Jenna Swaine spat, and threw down the pleated skirt she was perusing over. She had been contemplating what size number she would end up at...perhaps a three? Wouldn't that be just like winning the lottery, to end up at size three?

"Let's just go then," Jenna Swaine said, "I'll find a way to pay for these, if dad's eighty thousand a year salary isn't going to cut a few hundred dollars for his daughter's first happy clothing purchases in her entire life."

She noted her newfound ability to pick through the tiny aisles without knocking clothes on the floor, while her mother had a much harder time. A good thirty feet away, and nearly out the door of the The Gap, her mother called her.

"Patricia, stop."

A muttered apology later, Jenna Swaine, now no longer the daughter that her parents had raised, walked out of the shop with two shopping bags full of clothes. They deposited these in the minivan, and came back for more.

***

Jenna-not-Patricia Swaine figured out that she could work bone just like flesh, only a little tougher. She considered switching into a sculpture class next semester, and smiled. With that, she bent her wrist bones back until her hand flopped at an awkward angle. She felt the tendons and ligaments stretching painfully. She lost the ability to use the hand, until she bent it back the way it'd been before. It wasn't as easy as skin and fat; you couldn't just slop it around like oil paint.

There was a little dog on Jenna Swaine's walk to school. It was a yappy little thing, and she had been sticking her tongue out at the thing for years. Since she lived in a tiny city, it was unavoidable that she was forced to walk by Prince Anthony every single day of her life since age six, when she began walking to school with Evan.

...No, the owners had had another evil yappy dog before Prince Anthony.

Patricia shook her head. "Doesn't matter," she mumbled to herself.

Prince Anthony, precisely the size of a large cat and with an attitude of a lion, would come flying out of nowhere every morning and surprise the devil out of her. The thing yapped and yapped.

Only, now she was no longer Patricia.

She was Jenna, goddamnit. So, one morning about three weeks (and over twenty pounds) into her weight loss/body sculpting program, she approached Prince Anthony's house with a sneer.

The little dog came rocketing out of nowhere, barking and snarling at her.

Jenna Swaine, who would never be Patricia again, knelt by the little beast. It barked and barked, in its lion wannabe voice. To think she had ever been surprised into jumping by this tiny, ineffectual thing. After all, with the digestion problems it had, it would be dead within a month.

Digestion problems, Jenna Swaine thought. Now how could she possibly know that? It didn't matter, she knew anyhow. She could almost see the blood running through its little veins, and feel its muscles protesting in certain places. It had injured its left back leg once upon a time, and it hadn't healed back properly.

"Come here, you little fucker," she cooed to it, as sweet as she could manage. Prince Anthony was already as close as the fence would allow. Jenna somehow squeezed her entire hand inside the little diamond of chain link. The skin from her forearm that didn't feel it wanted to slide through began to bunch around the small opening. She seized the offending Prince, and with a stroke of her thumb, erased its vocal cords. She smoothed the flesh of its windpipe back together before the dog choked to death, and put its fur back.

And she got ideas.

"I'll be back for you," Jenna Swaine whispered.

***

She was the talk of the school a week after silencing Prince Anthony. She found acceptance into new circles of friends in another two. Doors were opened and she walked through them, welcomed. Forty pounds down, she stopped hearing the Piggy comments, and watched people eye her in wonder. The cafeteria was no longer one of the circles of Hell.

She found that she was an excellent actress. She knew her personality had nothing to do with the friends she was making, or the popularity she was gaining. Rather, it was all just a merry-go-round, spinning and spinning with pretty lights and horses while everyone laughed and laughed. Yet it wasn't real. There was nothing meaningful to get out of the whole act.

Hatred grew within her; she traded sadness and suicide for fakery and flippancy as she peeled off the pounds. Every day started off with a few more ounces off her ass, a few from the chin and face, and some from the stomach, but it was done with a grim satisfaction that made her face into a mask of hate. The four full-length mirrors that made up her closet door stopped mocking her, and began to welcome her.

They started calling her Jenna Swaine, and it sounded beautiful.

***

"What are you up to?"

Jenna Swaine whirled and found Evan staring at her. She covered herself with a towel, and it worked this time. It wrapped around her easily.

"You don't even knock when you come over, do you?"

He shrugged. "I never had to wonder if you'd be staring at a mirror, half naked. Why are you staring into the mirror, Patricia?"

"Don't call me that."

He sneered. "Oh, okay, Jenna." He made the word a mockery. "Brand new Jenna, too good for her name and too good for her friends."

"Fuck you," she said. "If you just came over here to mess with me, you can get out."

"How did you do it?" he asked.

"What? Why does it matter? I feel better than I've ever felt."

"Pat–fuck. Your mom is like three hundred pounds. Your dad is big too. You've been a big girl all your life. Now this? What's up? Are you doing the bulimia thing again? Your parents are worried, and so am I. Jenna, please, I'm your friend. Please. That shit's not you. Come on, Patricia."

She'd stopped hanging out with Carlos and Dale and Evan now that people were asking her to hang out with them instead of her sullenly tagging along.

"Fuck off, Evan."

He went from comforting to serious in a heartbeat "No, you tell me just what it is you're doing to yourself."

She shook her head.

"You've never been like this. Tell me what it is. Tell me or I tell your parents you're throwing up every night after dinner."

Anger rushed through her. "You want to see? You really want to see?" She put a hand on her arm and pulled the flesh down like a sock. She'd never done this much before. It left her muscle and bone exposed, shining and blood-red against gleaming white. She dropped the skin to the floor and reveled in the pain that came with exposing her muscle to the open air. It hit the ground with a wet plop.

Evan's eyes grew very wide, and his skin went greenish gray.

"Oh dear Jesus," he whispered. Then he bolted for the bathroom and vomited everywhere. She heard the sickening splash from down the hall with a twisted grin painted on her otherwise beautiful face.

"What's the matter, Evan? Wishing you hadn't asked me now, huh? You pussy, you can't even handle a little skin. When you're done there, get out of my house. I don't want to see you around anymore."

***

Jenna pinched the fading amount of fat under her chin and took off a half ounce. It looked a bit like silly putty in her fingers, clinging to itself like bubblegum. Then she ran a finger over her stomach, collecting the flesh into a little ball. She worked primarily with her right hand, and kept the day's collection in her left. These days it was getting more and more difficult not to just scoop off a whole mess and toss it to the floor to watch it splatter.

She'd conducted experiments on it, but only a little. She wasn't a naturally curious person. She was a naturally defeated person, and had been since first grade when the teasing started. Still, she wondered how much life her extracted body still had. Would it bleed? There wasn't a heart to pump any of the blood around. It would die and decay after a little while, wouldn't it?

At first, she couldn't bear to look at it. She'd simply buried it at the bottom of the trash, or fed bits of it down the garbage disposal and tried not to gag. Afterwards, though...

She gave some of her flesh carpet burn, then punctured at it with scissors to see a little bit of blood leak out, at the behest of gravity. Somehow when she rearranged herself like this, her blood vessels corrected themselves, as did her nerves. She felt neither the razor burn nor the scissors, though in truth she would have enjoyed such pain.

A swipe of flesh off both of her butt cheeks, and some off the sides of her thighs nearly completed the pound ball. It sat dejectedly on the little mailing weight scale. At first it was all cellulite, all little dips and divots, but she took that off first. Now, whatever she took was smooth fat, a bit like Jell-o in that it wobbled precariously on the scale.

Last, but certainly not least, Jenna Swaine thinned out her ankles a bit. Men liked girls with thin, feminine ankles, especially the other Jenna's boyfriend, Jake.

Jake who had ignored her forever, until just last week. Jake who now pressed his lips together and looked away when he saw her, in an almost-smile.

Jake.

Through her experimental time, Jenna discovered that much of what made her was, in fact, muscle. She peeled her skin off and marveled how much dark red muscle there was to behold. After all, hauling herself around everywhere must take some sort of strength. In large part, she left the muscle alone, with one exception: her thighs.

She judged her thighs to be too muscled (who could bear to have thunder thighs, unless you were on the swim team?), and instead discovered that she could even pull off the muscle. This she redistributed, a bit to her shoulder area, a bit to her pectorals for those high, firm breasts the boys loved.

With her day's work done, Jenna peered at herself in the mirror and smiled. It was solitary work, but rewarding. She even discovered that she enjoyed doing it, toying with herself as though she were a doll.

She gathered the ball up, it was a bit like a ball of pizza dough, and put it in her purse. She glimpsed her parents as she passed the living room, where they sat, mesmerized, in front of the television. She headed into the kitchen, and down into the basement.

The Swaine basement was not a wonderful place. The
low ceiling, possibly conceived of by midgets, filled her father
with fear of hitting his head on a nail and ending up dead
without anyone bothering to come look for him.
Consequently, none of them ventured here very much. Extra
shelves for food lined the walls, and lots of winter clothing
packed into waterproof plastic boxes. Mostly it was odds and
ends, only necessary around the holidays, or never to see the
light of day until it ended up in a garbage bag. Jenna enjoyed
it because her mother never came down here, and her father
only rarely.

Plus, it had a little closet.

She opened the closet, and peered inside. There, attached
to the ceiling and back in the corner behind her father's
unused hunting jackets, panted Prince Anthony.

"Well hey there, you little fucker," she said affectionately.

Prince Anthony only looked at her, as dogs do. Did she
have food? No? Might she have food in a minute?

Its fur was almost completely gone. She'd discarded that
a long while back. The fur only got in the way of the
additions. Prince Anthony was, by this point, composed
almost entirely of Jenna's old body mass. It bulged and hung
obscenely in places. Its stubby little legs were all but lost in
the folds of flesh surrounding the head.

It hung from a little mesh hammock, the kind with hooks
and bungee cords for all kinds of inventive uses while
camping. Its little legs hurried to nowhere, and the hammock
bobbed a little. The bungee cords strained to hold up the
weight of the new and improved Prince Anthony.

Jenna got the pound of flesh from her body and began to
smooth it onto the silent dog's bloated body. She could no
longer feel the digestion problems within it; she had taken
out and spliced together those parts when she'd brought
him here. Then she fed it some water, and a bit of dog food

from a big bag even deeper in the corner. It was probably getting hungrier and hungrier, with all of the old Patricia attached to it, but she fed it the same amount every day regardless.

"That's a good boy," she whispered to the dog, and petted its tiny, pathetic head.

***

The fullback with the chocolate sauce was Greg Alvarado. These days, when she hung out with Jenna Hawkins (the real Jenna, Jenna Hawkins persisted) and her friends, Greg apologized for the chocolate syrup thing every day.

"It's cool, Greg," she'd say every day. One day, they were sitting around eating lunch at prom-queen-Jenna's house when Greg must have felt the need to apologize again.

"Jenna, I'm really sorry about that chocolate sauce thing," he said in that deep, rumbling voice that comes with being six foot six and two-forty. "I know I say it every day, but, you know, it was really stupid, and I'm really, really sorry."

She noticed how his eyes were usually downcast when he gave these heartless, pointless, tedious apologies, day after day. But sometimes his eyes would travel up her legs, over her stomach, and up her boobs until they reached her face a long time later. It didn't hit her until one day when she watched Greg's eyes travel over Jenna Hawkins, as she sashayed out of the room in one of her tiny pleated skirts.

She'd never had any sort of sex appeal before. Now though... it had possibilities.

They were in the kitchen, scraping off their plates, when she turned to Greg.

"Hey Greg," she said, looking up at him. She was still five foot eight, although perhaps not for much longer.

"Yeah?"

"You want to come over sometime and hang out after school?"

He flinched. "Wha...you mean it?"

"Yeah, swing by today, maybe we can catch a movie."

"Shit, yeah, cool. I'm glad you're not mad about the thing, you know."

She laughed in a perfect Jenna Hawkins imitation tinkle. "Quit beating yourself up over it, Greg. People can be assholes sometimes."

He smiled, and it pushed his broad face into an awkward shape. "Yeah."

***

She was in his arms, in his front seat. He could almost put his arms around her twice, and that was just awesome, when you came right to it. A steering wheel pressed against her fashionably spongy little butt, and Greg's face pressed into her fashionably sized breasts.

She stared down at his face, pressed into her smooth, perfect skin, and grimaced.

She reached behind her and smoothed the skin of his forearms together. They were touching, it was easy. With her hand against his forehead, she slithered out of the loop of his arms, and he started to panic.

"What? Jenna, what? I can't, my arms," he stammered. She shook her head and sighed. His voice rose in pitch, and he started to pant, to hyperventilate.

Jenna Hawkins still called her Piggy sometimes and though those times were becoming rarer, she still hated the bitch for it. Did he honestly think she was ever going to forget?

"Shut the fuck up," she hissed, and punched him in the face. She could feel every nerve ending and bone in his face, and her palm where the punch connected. She didn't pull his flesh. She could control that now. Instead she beat the hell out of him while he cried like a little girl. She punched him until his nose broke, and she could feel it, like an instinct. She could heal it too, smooth it over. It might take a while, but it was a possibility. A possibility she would never enact. She punched and punched while blood flew from his nose, his lips, and the bashes on his face. His cheekbone broke, along with his jaw. His crying stopped, and his consciousness faded. That was another strange instinct that popped into her head. She knew he couldn't take much more.

"Listen to me Greg," she said, her voice calm. "You're not going to say a word about this, or I'll rearrange every part of your body. Understand me? You got beat up at a restaurant defending me from some jackasses. They were trying to hit on me. Alright?"

He nodded drunkenly while a bubble of blood popped out of his nostril.

"I'm sorry," he said, but his voice was thick with half-consciousness and blood.

She hitched his shirt in her much reduced hands and hauled him close. "You'll never understand how you humiliated me. I want you to understand."

He was still nodding, one eye swollen shut, when he passed out. She pulled his arms apart and smoothed his skin back to the way it should be. Then she got out of his pickup truck and walked three miles home.

***

The scrape and clink of silverware on tableware were the only sounds. The Swaine family didn't have the television on today, which was strange in and of itself. Instead, they ate in complete silence, glancing at one another every so often. It was driving Jenna Swaine more or less out of her mind.

"So," her father said around a giant chunk of roast beef. Jenna looked at him.

"So?" she asked, trying not to sound as irritated as she felt.

"How was school?" he asked, and forked in a dollop of mashed potatoes with gravy and butter. Even when she'd been Patricia, she had never really thrown up on purpose. Now though, watching her parents eat, she was almost tempted.

Jenna Swaine shrugged and mumbled some nonsense syllables. She picked at her food and stared at the peas moving around on the plate. She destroyed the pea pyramid, and watched them invade her mashed potatoes.

"What's that mean?" her father asked.

"Answer your father," her mother snapped immediately, without giving her an opportunity. Jenna looked between them, back and forth, then back again.

"It means nothing really happened," she said. "Am I on trial or something?"

"We uh..." her father said, and scratched the back of his neck. If the answers were there, he hadn't scratched enough to discover them.

"We're concerned about you," her mother said.

"Well, I'm fine," she replied.

"We want to know what you're doing to yourself," her mother cried.

"Honey, please," her father said.

"Tell us!"

Jenna screwed up her face in disbelief. "Wait, you mean now you're all concerned, because I'm not fat anymore? Is that what the problem is?"

"Patricia!" her mother cried indignantly. "You weren't–"

"Oh, don't give me that shit," Jenna Swaine said. "Don't try to coddle me with that 'you weren't fat' line. I was fat, now I'm not."

"We weren't going to lie to you," her father said, with a glance toward her mother to tell her exactly what she shouldn't say. His tone was soft, not ingratiating or accommodating at all. "This is a radical change for you and we just, we want to know if it's healthy for you."

"Healthy for me?" Jenna all but screamed. She jerked back in the chair, as though her fat were suddenly back and pushing her away from the table. Then she was on her feet. "Healthy for me? I haven't missed a meal since I started losing the weight. I swear to fucking Christ, I've never felt better than this, and you want to ruin it for me!"

Her mother's mouth was open in a wide 'O' of surprise, while a bit of the flesh around her cheeks and jowls jiggled with fury. Color had appeared there, twin splashes of red wine on her pale, pale skin.

"Young lady, you sit down this instant," her father whispered.

"I'm not doing anything you say!" she shouted, "I hate you, both of you!"

And she, being a barely contained nuclear blast, left before the tears welling up could have a chance to humiliate her. She was done with humiliation.

***

"Hey Jake," Jenna Swaine said. She was down to one-twenty now, a nice weight that still left her rounded in the right places. She didn't have an ounce of fat in the places she didn't want it. Three weeks ago her mother had taken her clothes shopping again, but said nothing. Jenna knew her mother was still furious and confused over whatever happened that night at dinner, and dismissed it out of hand. She wasn't starving herself or doing the binge/purge thing, so why should her parents care? Sure, the little scraps of clothing she bought almost cost more than the plus sizes from those other stores (ones Jenna Swaine now thought of as 'fat people places') but Jenna didn't care. If her parents cared about her, they should be showering her with gifts, and more than just the clothes she should have been able to fit in all along.

"Hey Jenna Two," he smiled.

All that was past now, and she was hanging out at lunch with the other Jenna's boyfriend, Jake Graves.

"You're on the prom committee right?" she asked.

He nodded. "We've got the final arrangements on just about everything."

"Awesome!" the bright and cheery was easy now. Jake was hot. More than hot, he had a tattoo his parents had allowed him to get when he turned sixteen. Everyone in school knew about it, but only his circle of friends had seen it. A few weeks after Greg the Fullback got a hero's welcome for defending Jenna Swaine, the tattoo had been shown around again. It was a dragon, sort of, composed of spiky little blocks of black all arranged the right way. It seemed to rise up his shoulder, spread out its wings, and turn a speculative eye on whoever might be looking over his shoulder.

When he showed it off, Jenna Swaine fell in love with his smooth, tanned skin and muscles moving and bunching with his every movement. It had been lovely, feeling his heartbeat and sensing the blush of health in his body, until Jenna Hawkins had glided up and put her arms around him from behind, stroking him all over. Jenna Hawkins (who was not being called Jenna One) had looked over her shoulder and smiled derisively.

"What kind of tux are you doing?" she asked, with the pre-girlfriend-wrapped image of Jake fresh in her mind. Now he was like a paper doll, and she could dress him however she pleased. Or undress him at her leisure.

"Probably a double breasted, dark purple vest. Jenna's got purple picked out. Jenna One, heh." Jake drew out a little photo of the dress, printed out from a website.

"That is really pretty," she beamed. "Leave it to Jenna to pick out the most beautiful dress ever. How could anybody compete? Hey, can you share this on Facebook so I can order my dress off this site?"

He shrugged. "Sure, no problem." He grabbed out his phone and was tapping when Jenna Hawkins appeared.

"Piggy, oh, I mean Jenna, what're you doing with my boyfriend?"

"Nothing," Jenna Swaine said, looking at the grass of the school's courtyard. Why the fuck did the goddamn prom queen keep calling her Piggy? The rest of them had forgotten it, or at least stopped calling her names. They were all talking about her in hushed whispers, about how good she looked. Even the social circle of Jenna Hawkins had taken to calling her Jenna Two. Why couldn't she let it fucking go?

"We were just talking about prom, you know," Jake said.

"Oh, who are you going with?" Jenna Hawkins asked, and her voice was full of amusement. It seemed to say 'I've got Jake, so whoever you're going with can't possibly compare.' She looked from beautiful blonde Jenna Hawkins, with her perpetual strawberries and crème scented hair, to her beautiful boyfriend.

"I don't know. I've had a few guys ask me, but I haven't decided." It was a lie. Nobody had asked. She hadn't turned anyone down. She didn't understand why. The possibility of asking a boy, or perhaps her old cache of friends, never entered her mind. She sat alone most nights, after her homework and body reduction were done, and wondered. Hating the guys for not asking.

"Who?"

"Don't worry about it, Jenna," she said, standing up, "You worry about Jake and your purple dress and I'll take care of myself, all right?"

Jenna Hawkins seemed to float above the grass, to glow with overpowering teenage sexiness, and that perfect strawberry and crème scented blonde hair glimmered like divinity.

***

Jenna Swaine felt the triumph, not hers, sure, but how much could that matter? All eyes were on her, and Jake was in the middle of crowning her. Later she'd let him do whatever he wanted, because it wasn't her reputation she was ruining. This perfect mask was going to serve her well. Her shining, styled, stolen strawberry and crème scented hair gleamed in the spotlight. Nobody knew the difference. She was Jenna Hawkins right down to the stolen scalp grafted onto her head.

It had been strange stroking her bare, wet skull before replacing her mousy brown head of hair with Jenna Hawkins's own.

Now, the purple dress fit her Jenna-Hawkins-sized body. She had Jake on her arm, radiating manliness like a Greek god. They matched. So what if she'd had to borrow the real Jenna's hair to do it?

Somebody gasped from the darkness. Somebody screamed something, but the sound of gagging drowned it out. There was a sickening, unmistakable splash of vomit striking tile floor.

A hulking shape lumbered into the hall, and Jenna Swaine squinted into the light. The silhouettes of the other students parted into an aisle, like the Red Sea. A spotlight went to the figure, until someone screamed.

"You bitch," came a cold voice, the voice of the real Jenna. Jenna Hawkins. "You cunt. Come out here, Piggy."

"What?" Jake said from beside her. "Jenna?" He turned towards Jenna Swaine. "That sounds like you. Wait..."

"No! I'm Jenna!" Jenna Swaine almost shouted at him in her desperation, "Give me that crown, do it now."

Jenna One, who was no longer herself either, screamed from where the crowd gave her a wide berth. It was high-pitched, with a lost edge of sanity. The scream turned into a few gibbered words, then trailed off into laughter.

Jenna Swaine took the crown out of Jake's hands and put it on her head. A light was back on the other one, the monster she'd made. The spotlight trembled against the echo of flab and flesh she'd sculpted out of the prom queen bitch. Jenna Swaine hopped off the stage and went straight for it.

"I'm queen now, I'm queen! No more Piggy, not ever again!"

The massed form of fat and skin loped towards Jenna Swaine. It reached out with an arm that had too many joints and caressed the stolen hair. Somewhere in there was a load of the old Patricia, and somewhere in a dank basement the head of a dead dog lay amongst pools of dark, vile liquids. This monster had only stumps for legs; Jenna Swaine had stolen the feet and thrown them away. She'd used the shins for extra forearm joints. Apparently she'd made it stronger than she thought. Set in the middle of the ragged scraps of purple dress and skin and flesh sat a pale, perfect face.

A quick swipe of the disjointed looking arm later, and the little diadem was skidding across the floor.

"This is mine, you stole it," the monster said. "You'll always be little Piggy. You were nothing and you're still nothing, that's all you are, don't you see that?"

The monster was ripe with the smell of decay and richer, more potent reeking. Its Jenna One face turned into a mask of pain and rage.

The whole evening was totally screwed. Jenna Swaine, Patricia/Piggy, looked at Jake, who had wet his pants and slowly backed away now. She looked at her beautiful friends, who stared with horrid fascination. She looked at Evan, and at her old friends. Evan shook his head, then moved into the crowd and disappeared.

"You ruined everything," The Jenna-face said, then latched her elongated fingers around Jenna Swaine's pretty neck. She noticed the ragged flaps of skin at the wrists, where she'd bound them, bleeding onto the prom dance floor.

"What am I supposed to do?" Jenna screamed at the monster.

"You're supposed to totter around and squeal," the monster rasped. "Forgetting your place." Jenna's face nestled between mounds of flesh held a strange mocking tone.

Jenna Swaine stared into the horrified crowd. Most of them were lost in darkness, but those faces she could see confirmed how she felt. Nothing mattered now.

She dove at the thing in the center of the gym floor and tore it apart.

No one moved to stop her.

Jenna screamed and pulled off the monster's flesh, handful by handful. She screamed, and that was the cue for a chorus of other screams. The hands disappeared first, skidding on the waxed floor, then the forearms, the arms at the shoulders, then gobbets of fat and organs and skin. It went on for minutes, where the only sounds were the sloshing and ripping of the monster she'd created. Blood poured rapidly onto the floor, soaking everything.

When it was over, Patricia-Jenna-Piggy Swaine was soaked with gore and knee deep in piles of skin. Everyone still left in the hall watched silently as she left the building with Jenna's pretty face in her hands, cradling the mask like a doll. Tears dripped from one Jenna's cheeks to another.

***

ABOUT THE AUTHOR:
Brent Meske writes to find out how it ends. He currently lives, teaches, writes, designs, and does the dad thing near Seoul, Korea.

Come back for more:
Brentmeske.com
Facebook.com/bmeske
Email me at: meskebrent@gmail.com

Mermaids
by Robert Pope

Aqua-boy sat at the bar sipping a beer, listening to the three women of Mermaids making music on a low stage. The one front and center in the fedora, a little older than the two behind, held a guitar on one knee, leaning to the microphone, producing random sounds that almost formed words. Behind her, on the right, a fat girl played a mournful fiddle, and to the left, in a puffy hat, a blonde played a red accordion. He couldn't see her eyes, just the dirty blonde hair hanging out from under the, a small nose, and full, wide lips. She had on a loose vest so he couldn't see much of her figure, but he did notice her right hand resting on her knee.

The way it glowed in the dim stage light troubled him in some ineffable way. When he saw the reason, it frightened him a little. He counted several times to make certain. Six fingers lined up on her knee, against brown corduroy, the thumb longer than normal. The hand rose, latched on the keyboard side of the accordion, her fingers moving against keys as the piece swelled to conclusion and applause.

At a nearby table, several women smiled as if reliving pleasant memories. Of two bartenders, one nodded at him. A desperate basketball game ran up and down the court silently on a television behind the bartender. A cook peeked through the window in the door below the television and disappeared. When Mitch looked back at the resting accordionist, the strangeness of the hand spread through her whole person.

The guitar player sat sideways, talking quietly and searching for some tune. The violinist smiled hopefully—the only one smiling. The accordionist hadn't moved, head down, waiting for the music to emerge sufficiently that she could join it.

"Have you decided on something?"

The bartender had a thin jawline beard, which made his skin look pale. His brown eyes were professionally inquisitive, his mouth set in a smile made to carry easily. His shoulders looked painfully narrow, his body insubstantial in white shirt and black pants.

"Something I can get you?"

Mitch nodded, overcoming his desire to leave this restaurant entirely. "Do you have a hamburger?"

"We don't have beef, but veggie burgers and a bison burger."

Mitch thought a moment. "Bison isn't beef?"

The bartender shrugged. "That's how it's listed. People want to know what they're eating these days. It's good, I hear, though I'm vegan."

A shudder went through Mitch, and he had to lower his head a moment to control it. But then he nodded and said, "I'll have the bison."

"We have sweet potato fries with that."

As the bartender went back through the door to the kitchen, Mitch turned sideways, to watch the group. The music began quietly, slowly, everything normalizing for him—just a restaurant, set on a balcony over a natural foods grocery store. A woman in a long blue sweater danced in front of them. Three young girls, eleven or twelve, stood to one side, like they wanted to join. Each wore shorts over black tights, all three had long hair: a redhead, a blonde, and a brunette—coincidence? The music paused briefly, by design, and started again. The hand on the keyboard of the red accordion still had six fingers.

He knew a guy in college who had a large forehead. A little Frankenstein the first time you saw him, it jutted over his face like a cliff, a normal face inset underneath. It was physics, and Aqua-boy wondered if the big head gave him any advantage. Not everyone noticed anomalies like he did. In high school, he lost every hair on his body, even his eyebrows. Other guys on the swim team shaved the head and legs to reduce resistance, so they thought him crazy enough to have done it to himself. That and connective skin between his toes earned him the name Aqua-boy.

No one would have noticed if he hadn't been a swimmer. Rivals accused him of taking unfair advantage but couldn't disqualify him for what he was born with. Teammates laughed, but he had dreams with scales involved in the shape of his head, slightly blue-green, where he swam an ocean strange with sea monsters armed in claws and fangs. Other times, he swam higher: as if air became water, he breast-stroked through the sky.

Late after school, waiting for his mother to pick him up from practice, he stared through the glass front doors as sky transformed into airy ocean. He imagined opening them and swimming out over the town in which he had grown up.

Otherwise, everything about Aqua-boy was normal. Five-ten when he graduated high school, acceptable even to girls who preferred someone taller, he grew two more inches by the time he graduated college. He had short brown hair, light green eyes, and considered himself just good looking enough not to constitute a disadvantage. He dated a girl in high school, a couple of women in college, but nothing lasted so far. He hoped this would come in time. He quit the job that had gotten him through college, on top of what his parents contributed, with enough saved to last a few months. He moved back in with his parents to look for a job. He thought about grad school, but he wanted a paycheck now.

Life was in the air. He had recently become anxious that it all work out.

When the burger came he went at it in a way which didn't allow thinking. He hadn't eaten since breakfast–oatmeal, banana–and that gave out hours ago. He had mixed emotions about eating the buffalo. He thought they had been hunted out by frontiersmen, but there must be some left. Did they roam free, as when they were the sustenance of some Indian tribe whose name he forgot though he could recall studying them in school?

The music stopped and the woman in the puffy hat sat at the bar a couple seats from him and ordered salad and a cup of tea. He glanced, but still could not see her eyes. He sipped the beer.

"That was nice," he said, thumbing the stage.

She smiled and said thanks, but when the bartender brought tea, she gave it her undivided attention.

"Do you play here often?" he asked.

She shrugged and said, "Off and on. This is our first time in a few months."

She blinked more than normal. When her meal arrived, she said, "Excuse while I snort my seaweed."

"Are you vegan?" he asked, but she was forking greens into her mouth.

"Well," he said. "I guess I'll be shoving off. My name is Mitch."

He offered his hand and, after a moment of hesitation, she took it. When he felt the six fingers, liquid fire ran up his arm, down his back, into his groin, where it stayed like a glowing lump. He forced himself not to look at the hand.

"Melody," she said.

He laughed a little. His face burned. "What a great name for a musician."

She nodded, putting away another enormous forkful of salad.

He pointed at the stage again. "You rarely see someone playing accordion these days," he said, "never a red one."

She nodded back toward the stage. "It's my Cajun Cordy."

He could see her eyes sparkling dark green or hazel, some yellow in there. Her hair that looked so stringy onstage hung in shiny strands like plastic. Her nose wasn't as small as he had thought, and she made him think of a marionette, the way she moved, smiled. The wide mouth looked plump, especially her lower lip.

She might have been five or ten years older than him, no slip of a thing, as his father used to say.

She had breasts and hips, enough size to make her real. He was probably more slender than her. When the bartender came, he tapped the empty glass. "This time with a shot of Jameson's." A vein in his forehead throbbed.

"A little of the Irish?" she asked. "You must be staying for the last set after all."

He looked into her blinking eyes, her funny mask-like face. "Wouldn't miss it for the world," he said. The ends of her mouth hoisted enough he could see the little space between her front teeth. She got up and sauntered to the stage. Shiny, like vinyl.

When she took up her accordion, a little blonde girl ran to the low stage, standing on tiptoes to speak to her. "Go ahead," she whispered, and played softly as the girl sang

"Twinkle Twinkle Little Star" in a pure, shaky voice.

He sipped the shot, felt a burn reach through him once again.

Everyone clapped when the little girl finished and ran to her table. Mitch thought she might have been Melody's daughter, four or five years old.

The weird wail of another original song wound through his head as he watched Melody's wide hand play across the short, vertical keyboard of her accordion. Her voice kept up a soft vowel chant that made him dizzy. He applauded with the others when the song finished, grinning in her direction, though he couldn't be sure she saw him with her eyes lost in shadow. He touched the shot glass and nodded at the bartender, who brought the bottle with him.

The woman in the fedora spoke into her mike—he couldn't hear words, just a sound like the wind, indistinct, secret as a whisper. He had this sensation after hours at swim practice, moving underwater in a trance while pictures not words blossomed in his mind. The Mermaids weaved before him like sea fronds. He imagined Melody swam beside him, her little girl running beside, breathless with things to say, her worn teddy dangling from one hand by a leg.

He downed the shot, chased it with beer. Would it matter she was older or had a child? It would be blissful, sometimes she would sing. He took a long drink of beer to feel cold down his throat. Something had happened to him since stepping in the bar. This morning, at a coffee shop, poring over want ads—that had been the dream, fading into an acceptable future.

When he woke from a daydream, he was pissing at a urinal.

He glanced down—not exactly flaccid, pretty decent actually. He had seen enough in the locker room to know. He shook, zipped, and then studied himself in the mirror while he washed his hands. He looked fit, kept up with weights, swimming, younger than she would be used to. He wouldn't be her first, that was obvious, but he could be her best. His green eyes floated free in a flushed face. In his entire time on the earth he hadn't gotten used to his own eye color, almost aqua, luminous. Freckles across his nose, a dozen with a brown tint that picked up the color of his close-cropped hair. His ears were too small. He never liked how much nostril he showed—he slanted his head for pictures. And he had little teeth and too much gum for his liking.

When someone came in the bathroom, he started washing all over again, to cover how much time he spent looking at himself. A shock jolted him as he watched the reflection of the newcomer move behind him in the mirror.

She had not noticed him, but he recognized her immediately. Melody stepped up to the urinal, her head ducked to watch herself. If that wasn't enough, she hung a wrist over the narrow wall that abutted the side of the urinal, affording him a full view of her hand, much larger than he thought, the knuckles swollen, the fingernails sharpened to points.

He fled to the bar before she noticed him, ordered another shot and beer, turning himself so he would not have to watch her return. The music had ended. They were packing instruments when he got the nerve to look again.

Melody had her back to him. He wasn't certain he wanted to see her face or hand again, ever. Still, once he paid up and headed to the stairs, he glanced back, checking her out, but some damn fool had spilled a drink at the top of the stairs and no one cleaned it up, which was why he slid on his heels and dropped off the first step.

He didn't just drop off the first step–he kept going with a balance that came from his athletic past. When that petered out, he pitched headlong into the wall at the landing, banging his head, slamming the heels of his hands against an object so immovable pain shot up his arms. He didn't want to do anything but let them hang as he leaned on the wall to let the pain subside.

He hit the wall so hard he didn't feel the full impact on his nose right away–it went numb. Blood dripped on his shirt. When he saw it on his hands he took off down the stairs and through the store.

Customers watched, a few called out, reaching for him as he flew through checkout. He stopped at the glass doors.

It had been cold when he went in, now snow spun in the dark. When he glanced back into the store, a skinny counter clerk with large, dark eyes stared at him, and further back, the Mermaids came toward him, bundled in their coats, carrying their instruments. Throwing caution to the wind, he pushed open doors and swam out in the swirling sky. He gasped and thrashed until he found the long, dark current that carried him against a smooth, slick body he could not see.

It circles back beneath him, all its sea-green length, the beaklike mouth and orange eyes turning up to him. He strokes with effort, toward a glow ahead. A giant squid slides past. Shadows circle the distant light like sharks. Slippery creatures with fleshy breasts and dragging genitalia move along the ocean floor. He hears the sounds that swarm him now, not words, not squeals or whistles, but voices in a language never heard by men. They weave him in the frothing of their wake.

***

ABOUT THE AUTHOR:

Robert Pope has published more than sixty stories in periodicals including Missouri Review, Kenyon Review, and Alaska Quarterly Review. He has published a novel, Jack's Universe, and a collection of stories, Private Acts. He teaches at The University of Akron. He and Art Director Chris Bentley recently put out the third issue of a so-far mostly regional magazine called Insomnia & Obsession: http://www.magcloud.com/browse/issue/971483?_r=491 718&s=w.

Phantom Pain
by Philip Harris

They say the pain fades, but it doesn't, not even a little. I know that now.

***

Rain clattered off the tin awning above the narrow door, almost drowning out the sounds of the busy street behind me. But I could hear the tuk-tuk driver chattering away, wishing me a pre-programmed farewell that seemed too happy, too optimistic for this mud-draped city. The tuk-tuk beeped its tinny little horn twice, then hummed away down the street, searching for the next wanderer in need of a ride.

I reached towards the buzzer, stopping when I saw I'd instinctively moved my right arm. The sight of the stump and the criss-crossed scars triggered a fresh wave of pain. My hand, the one that's no longer there, itched and burned. The sensation made me want to grind the stub of my wrist against the metal grille above the buzzer. Maybe I could shred it, tear away whatever nerves were still firing. Instead,

I pulled back my sleeve and stuck my arm out from under the awning, letting the rain soak the skin. The raindrops were cold, almost sleet really. The burning began to fade. Whether it was because the rain eased the pain or because I expected it to I didn't know. Or care.

I pressed the buzzer with my left thumb.

A voice from the grille, as tinny as the tuk-tuk's horn, asked me what I wanted.

"It's Mariana Jacobs. I was told you had-"

The door clicked and whirred.

"Come in, come in," said a voice, the words barely audible above the rain.

***

Barely any light illuminated the shop, and it took my eyes a few seconds to adjust. Like most back street surgeries, it was small, and the air smelled of formaldehyde and burning flesh. Dozens of shelves lined the walls, crammed with jars and tanks. I tried not to look at them as I walked through the gloom towards the counter at the back of the room. Still, I caught a glimpse of pale flesh, gray organs, bloody liquids. One of the jars contained a hand, and the itching and burning returned. Gritting my teeth so hard they hurt, I forced the sensations back down into my subconscious, focusing instead on the steady rhythm of my boots on the concrete floor.

An old man stood behind a steel counter at the end of the room, watching me as I made my way towards him. His skin hung limply around his face, and dark creases underlined his eyes. A few wisps of hair clung stubbornly to his otherwise bald head. But his hands looked strong, nimble, up to the task. He was grafted, of course, all the best dealers were. But then so were the bad ones. It's supposed to show faith in their merchandise and reassure customers they're in good hands.

The man had replaced his ears and his nose, the smooth, pale grafts stark against the leathery skin surrounding them. The work was reasonable–the lines puckered but clean with no sign of infection, now or in the past. But noses and ears are low-end grafts. The worst that can happen is the client ends up looking a little bit uglier, and that can be solved by another graft if they can afford it. It's not until you start playing with nerves and arteries that irreparable damage becomes a concern.

"Miss Jacobs."

"Dr Taylor?"

The old man nodded. "Welcome to my humble store."

I placed my hands–my hand and my wrist–on the counter. "You said you'd be able to help me." I have no interest in idle chatter these days.

Taylor looked down at the counter and sniffed. Then he raised his head and sucked a breath through gritted, yellow teeth. "Price has gone up, I'm afraid. Just a little."

I'd expected this, the quote was too low and grafters know you need them more than they need you. No one visits a grafter by choice–they're a last resort for the sick. And the desperate.

Still, I considered leaving, just for a moment. But we both knew I wouldn't.

"What do you want?"

The old man rubbed at his chin, ragged fingernails scraping across graying stubble. He looked me up and down for a moment, then settled on my eyes. When I was younger, they were my best feature. Now they're just tarnished sapphires nestled in sagging, weather-worn flesh.

Taylor smiled.

***

I lay back on the operating theatre's cold metal table. The smell of formaldehyde was even stronger here but it was mixed with a bitter, medicinal tang that was almost comforting. Taylor shuffled around the room, retrieving scalpels, a syringe and a pair of tongs from drawers and placing them in a kidney shaped stainless steel dish. I tried to ignore the patches of red that speckled its surface.

Taylor flicked a switch and five ceiling lights sputtered to life, the glare bright enough to force me to close my eyes. They hummed and sputtered and something to my right popped quietly. Taylor made a wet hacking sound then spat into something metallic. Water ran for a few seconds, and I heard him rubbing his hands together.

A shadow appeared over me, blocking out the harsh lights. I opened my eyes to find Taylor peering down at me. His face was scrunched up but the expression didn't quite affect his grafted nose. Up close, the rough pores of his cheeks contrasted sharply with the smooth skin of his second hand nose. His breath was rank, a mix of rotting meat and blood that made me want to gag. Doubt gnawed at me. I had to force myself not to push him away and run from the room.

Taylor raised the syringe, examining the clear fluid within, then pressed his fingers against my cheek. I closed my eyes again as he slipped the needle beneath my skin.

***

I let the door snap shut behind me and ran my fingertips across the leather patch covering my left eye socket. It was soft, almost pleasant to touch, but the flesh beneath was tender. Soon, the anesthetic would wear off, and the pain would begin. I could already feel a dull, throbbing ache forming deep in the socket. I thought of my missing hand and wondered what phantoms this new absence would bring.

It was almost dark, and the street was getting busier as the city's inhabitants came out to spend their hard earned cash. A tuk-tuk slid to a halt opposite me. This one was covered in neon lights that flickered and hissed as the rain hit them. I got in without bothering to check the safety record pasted to the side of the cab and spoke the name of the hostel into the mic dangling from the ceiling. The mechanical figure in the front of the cab chirped enthusiastically. The tuk-tuk darted into traffic, wheels spinning in the thick mud.

I reached into my pocket and retrieved the plastic bag Taylor had given me as payment for my eye. My heart sped up as I reached inside and pulled out the photograph.

I stared at it for several long minutes.

The girl in the picture was ten or eleven, the right age. The hair was right, long and blond, and a scattering of freckles decorated her cheeks. She had a slight smile on her face, but I couldn't mistake the fear in her eyes. And it was her eyes that were wrong. They were green, not blue.

The photo was a year or two old with a tear in one corner. It had faded slightly. I tried to convince myself that really her eyes were blue, that the age of the photograph made them look green. But I knew the truth.

I would recognise my daughter and this wasn't her.

An address had been scrawled across the back of the photograph. I knew the area–a run-down collection of brothels, drug dens and black market dealers. I slipped the photograph back in my pocket as a familiar ache settled within my heart.

Even if the girl is still there, I can't help her. I have my own phantoms to chase.

**

ABOUT THE AUTHOR:

Philip Harris was born in England but now lives on the west coast of Canada where he spends his days developing video games and his nights writing speculative fiction - anything from horror to science fiction to fantasy.

His first published story, Letter From a Victim, appeared in the award-winning magazine, Peeping Tom, in 1995. Since then he has been published in numerous magazines and anthologies including Garbled Transmissions, So Long, and Thanks for All The Brains and James Ward Kirk's Best of Horror 2013.

More of his work, including the dystopian science fiction novella, The Girl in the City, and his pulp science fiction novel, Glitch Mitchell and the Unseen Planet, are available from Amazon and other book retailers.

He has also worked as security for Darth Vader.

Unbreakable Heart
by Rebecca Poole

The harsh wind blew tiny pieces of silica into her eyes, scratching her optical implant. She glared morosely at her right leg as she crept slowly across the loose desert sand, desperately attempting to pick up speed and make her way to a haven. In her haste to escape her captors, the heavy automatic doors had slammed shut unexpectedly, crushing her ankle. She regretted that her timing of the alarms had caused her injuries. Her calculations had been off by only a few short seconds, but that was enough to cause the damage. As she walked, she could hear the crunching of her weight pressing down on the destroyed joint. Unfortunately, she had to use the leg as it was, and she reflected that at least she couldn't feel anything. Pale pinkish gray liquid seeped from her artificial veins, leaving a trail that would make it simple to track her. Nothing could be done about that at this point in her journey. She'd been able to reroute the fluid coursing through her body away from the damaged ankle so that all wasn't completely lost, but a small trickle escaped as she made her bid for freedom. If she could find cover, she could repair or remove the broken foot at the ankle.

The sand flying around her head and invading the right eye didn't cause her pain, but it scratched the delicate membrane coating the inner machinery of her optical implant. She still blinked as a force of habit, which allowed the invading grains even more opportunity to damage the membrane's surface, and caused hell on the readings sent to her brain from the implant. Thankfully, her left eye was untouched and entirely organic. While the sand bothered it, her tear ducts still functioned. The liquid discharge left tracks in the dust on her skin and kept her eye clear.

She marveled at the colors of the outside world. She LOATHED the color white. Everything in her room (or prison cell, as she thought of it) was white, including the grout between the tiles. The only time her gaze was graced with another color was when she caught the reflection of her eyes in a shiny surface or when they drew her blood for their countless tests.

She'd lost track of the many surgeries and tests she'd undergone. Ennui had set in during her loneliness and isolation. At first, she'd been apathetic to her situation, believing that "this too shall pass," but she finally realized they weren't going to stop. Ever. She'd already lost most of her memory, including her name. She answered to Subject 86-75-309 and most of the time, was reluctant to use her idle vocal chords unless necessary.

Her flight for freedom was certainly a shock to the scientists as well as herself, she supposed. They'd installed experimental implants into the back of her head to enhance her thought process. It was also supposed to give them full control of her physical and mental faculties. Unfortunately for them, the operating scientist had forgotten an essential part: flipping the switch.

Her self-preservation instincts were activated when she realized that she'd completely lose her self-awareness, which made her still remotely human. One very strong opinion she still held was that she did NOT want to give up herself. She didn't know who she was, for the most part, but she did know she was pretty damn tired of them playing around in her brain and body. She remembered sleep and dreams, even if she'd not had any for a very long time.

All of the modification and fiddling had left her without a need for sleep and, because she didn't need it, she couldn't force herself to unconsciousness. It wasn't for a lack of trying, however. She wanted to be able to lose track of time and her surroundings instead of constantly analyzing the information coursing through her brain and a stream of numbers and data flowing across her vision due to the implant. Once the brain surgery had been completed, she'd overheard the operating scientist speaking with his assistants. The conversation filled her with a sense of dread because she realized that their plan for her was not going to end with her as a happy and well-functioning member of society, so she'd devised a plan of escape.

She'd calculated it would take them several minutes to get organized and give chase, so she'd disabled the tracking device implanted in her organic arm. She had to bite into her skin to rip out the tiny bead that lay just beneath and crush it. She'd welcomed the pain because it had been such a long time since there had been any sensation.

She wasn't so naive as to think that they'd not come after her. Several billions of dollars were invested in her creation. Intact, her value soared, and even higher if they harvested her artificial heart, the catalyst to set her escape in motion.

The heart they'd given her was, in a sense, unbreakable. They'd discovered the breakthrough when her body did not reject it. Anti-rejection drugs weren't necessary and the excitement felt around the lab when the tests came back was palatable. The scientists wanted to take back that which they had given, and she realized that once they'd removed it, her part in their experiments would be over. She could function without her limbs, but without the heart and her brain, she'd cease to exist. She knew they'd want to take her brain and tinker around with it to see if it had anything to do with why her body didn't reject the implanted organ.

Scanning the horizon for anything that would provide cover or even tools or metal to do repairs currently ranked high on her priority list. If she could restore her leg, she could run instead of the shuffle walk that she was presently using. After continuing for several miles in this manner, she spied a group of buildings clustered together and made her way to them. Her lips curved into a satisfied smile upon reaching the pavement surrounding a small housing complex. A small paved road led into the remote neighborhood, and she marched down it with renewed purpose to her gait. The grinding of her broken ankle was much more audible on the pavement than the sand, and the vibrations more pronounced as they staggered their way up her leg.

Many of the houses she passed had an unfinished look to them and were vacant, but she finally found one with an attached garage. There were curtains in the open windows that moved with a slight breeze. Removing the exterior portion of the ocular implant, she blew into it in an attempt to remove most of the debris that had collected. She didn't want to chance scratching the membrane beneath, so, very carefully, she replaced the external device and rotated it 20 degrees to activate the infrared sensors within. Seeing only the heat signature of a small animal inside the house, she entered the nearest open window, the sill groaning under the weight of her surgically modified body.

Rotating the implant to its original position, she took in the new surroundings. An open floor plan showcased a modern living space. A large television monopolized most of the space in what she considered the living room that also held a tiny bistro style table and two chairs. There was a rather worn love seat and a bookshelf containing pictures of a man with a dog.

She frowned when she realized she was in the living space of one of the scientists who performed many of the experiments on her. Doctor Keller was the cruelest of them all, refusing to see her as anything except sub-human when he was the reason for all of her modifications. Noticing another picture hidden behind Dr. Keller's, she picked it up. It was one of her and him, together.

In the picture, she smiled into the camera while he did not, and his arm was wrapped around her possessively. She stared at the familiar couple as unwelcome memories flooded her consciousness. The onslaught of so many emotions in rapid-fire succession nearly brought her to her knees as her breathing became short and rapid. She remembered being an impoverished college student and signing up with The Neural Society. They promised to pay her tuition and expenses in exchange for participation in various experiments and research.

The moment she met Doctor Reese Keller flashed vividly, and the course of their relationship ran through her mind like a movie on fast-forward. She recalled falling in love with him and secretly making love in the laboratory at night, unaware that he was recording their trysts. When she discovered he didn't reciprocate her feelings, it was devastating, but not as crushing as when she realized he was not only using her to fulfill a physical need.

He had kept notes on her emotional state of being when they began altering her with their mechanical parts. He wanted to know if her reaction to his cruelty would be lessened as she became more cybernetic and less human, at least in his mind. Discovering his notes about their relationship was the pivotal point during the experiments when her memory had broken, in a manner of speaking. The pain of the mechanics coupled with her emotional distress shut her mind down. She'd compartmentalized her feelings and forced herself to forget their relationship until now. The moment she discovered the photograph of the two of them together, it all came back.

The restoration of her memories played havoc on her electrical sensors, and she struggled to regain control of her wayward emotions. She needed to figure out if anything inside the house might be of use to repair her leg and eye. She would have to worry about her broken and misled heart later. Taking several deep breaths to regain some semblance of control, she blinked to clear her organic eye of the tears streaming from it.

Quickly locating the door leading into the garage, she scrounged for anything that she could use. After a frustrating search through a toolbox that yielded nothing helpful in reconstructing her ankle, she noticed the garage was too small to hold a vehicle. She pushed against the wall and then used her weight to move the built-in shelf, which swung open into a small chamber with just enough height clearance to accommodate her without having to bend. Feeling her way along the right inner wall, she located a light switch and turned it on, the illumination revealed rows of instruments, including an extra exterior ocular prosthesis.

After sliding the extra device into her pocket, her first concern was the ankle. Once repaired, she could work on the optical device and hopefully clear the membrane over the socket. Reaching up to her eye, she rotated it counterclockwise 45 degrees to activate the x-ray protocol and examined her damaged ankle. She'd have to look at the leg in several stages due to the scratches interfering with her vision on that side. The head-up display that appeared showed her what had broken, and she began working on reattaching the severed vascular hoses first. With shaking hands and rummaging through the set of instruments Dr. Keller had in his hidden room, she put together the parts like a puzzle. Making swift work of the leg, she moved onto the eye, using aerosolized air to remove the dust particles, then she looked through the remaining supplies for a solution. In her haste and nervousness, she almost dropped the outer portion of her eye. She was becoming increasingly worried that she wouldn't be able to fix it. She'd never realized just how much she'd become dependent on the implant. Huffing in irritation and anger when she couldn't find a replacement membrane, she replaced the outer device and examined the instruments she wasn't familiar with.

One, in particular, caught her attention and she gingerly picked it up with thumb and forefinger. Gazing at it with her cybernetic eye, the head-up display revealed a circuit board, one much faster than currently installed in her circuitry. There were a few things on it that the display didn't recognize, and it gave her pause. The connectors were oddly shaped, and she was unable to find a power or reset button. The lack of an on/off switch bothered her. She liked having a failsafe in place and the idea that there possibly wasn't one made her extremely uneasy. She thought it prudent to upgrade, if possible, especially in her current situation, but that would require disabling her systems. What if she couldn't work through the agony sure to follow once the circuitry allowed her pain receptors to work again? What if the upgrade gave the scientists exactly what they wanted: control over her mind and body. Her memories had just returned, and that was another risk she wasn't sure she wanted to take for fear of losing them again. Her sense of self was important to her and, regardless of how inhuman she felt, she was still just that: human.

Knowing that once they found her she would be so many spare parts, she eyed the circuit board to see what she could understand of its mechanics. The new circuit board had a processor that was much faster than her current one, which would enable her to force her organic and biomechanical parts to move in sync at a closer speed to each other. The advantage of that was something worth considering, and her mind reeled with the possibilities. Taking a calculated risk and holding her breath, she quickly opened her scalp flap and removed the board inside. Excruciating pain filled her mind and washed over her newly awakened senses. For several seconds, all she knew was agony, and she suffered in the silence that followed. Her eye bulged with the shock of it, and a scream escaped her throat before she could silence herself.

Removing the circuitry had stopped her cybernetic parts from functioning, save her heart. Her cybernetic limbs floundered around on the floor of the chamber. After what felt like an eternity, she regained enough of her faculties to slide the new circuit board into place with a soft click. Nauseated and gasping in pain, she waited impatiently for her systems to reboot.

Once all systems were on-line, the pain faded as quickly as it had come. Nausea, however, did not, and she spat on the floor when her mouth flooded with saliva. She scanned through the new features in the installed hardware and noticed a new option for enhancement.

Upon investigation, she was pleased that she could upgrade without doing significant changes to her organic body. Once finished, she gathered the instruments and placed them into the small unused tool box for carrying, and left the garage.

Searching the rest of the house, she discovered the bathroom and washed up a bit before heading out. Dust coated her exposed skin. Glancing up into the mirror, she sucked in a horrified breath as she took in her appearance. Her once glorious mane of white blond hair was now sheared from her scalp, giving her the appearance of dandelion fluff. Her face was gaunt, almost skeletal, and her skin sunburned by her trek. Her eyes...oh, her beautiful blue eyes. The right eye had been completely removed, and a visual prosthesis placed there. The black plastic and steel stood out in sharp contrast to the crystal blue of her remaining eye, from which tears streamed uncontrollably.

She allowed herself a few minutes to wallow in the shock and disappointment of her lost beauty before running lukewarm water into the sink. She used a white washcloth hanging next to a towel to gently scrub her skin clean. Once finished, she looked at herself once more in the mirror, squared her shoulders and went in search of clothing that could cover up her cybernetics. Luck was on her side when she found the closet. There was a ball cap she could steal along with a pair of sweatpants with a matching tee. They hung on her loosely, but tightening the drawstring in the waist kept them from falling off.

Snagging the toolbox on her way out, she decided against following the road to a populated area and left the cluster of houses to continue her travels through the desert. Her leg moved well, and she moved at a much quicker pace than before. She didn't want to run and alert anyone to sudden movements or plumes of dust, so she elected to walk briskly through the desert.

Her heightened senses helped her avoid detection, looking and listening to everything around her. Save for a lizard and the roadrunner hoping to make it supper, she passed several miles without incident. Hearing a vehicle, she focused sharply in their direction and heard a familiar voice.

"Subject 86-75-309 is in sight and within range. I'll activate the protocol to unplug her." Dr. Reese Keller spoke into the radio he carried, alerting the scientists on the receiving end to expect them within the hour.

Her enhanced cochlear implant had no issue picking up the startlingly shrill tones of his voice. Fury and rage filled her mind. She relived the moments of cruelty she'd endured while under his control. Fear took her breath and, for a few seconds, she only heard the thumping of her heart in her ears. If he took her back, she'd die. She was going to live out the rest of her life on HER terms, not theirs. She might look like Frankenstein's monster, but she refused to be treated like one or cast aside once they'd gleaned everything from her they could.

With an anger fueled purpose, she whirled, and headed directly for him, crossing the distance at a far greater speed than he could have anticipated. They'd never let her test her upper limits of speed and strength in the lab, and her upgrades made her almost a blur crossing the desert.

His gasp of surprise became a slight hiss as her hand lifted him from the ground by his throat. Eyes narrowing as she watched a drop of sweat drip down the side of his terrified face, her lips contorted into a hateful smile.

"Hello, darling," she said mockingly. "Miss me?"

Checking to see if anyone else was in the SUV, she chucked him towards the vehicle with a happy realization that they were alone. His back and head slammed into the side, leaving a dent, and he crumpled to the ground, dazed and breathless from the impact.

"Oh, lover." She paused then said, "Remember when you used to call me that? I'm going to show you what your 'love' has done."

She studied him for several seconds while images of the many things she'd like to do to his defenseless body slid through her head. He was entirely coated in a sickly sweat, and she could smell the sourness of his fear and distress leaking through his pores.

Pulling the spare ocular device from her pocket, she grabbed his throat again to lift him up. He tried desperately to break away, his hands beating uselessly against her arm.

"Let me show you, lover," she said as she pushed the steel and plastic over his eye. He tried to jerk his head away but her grip was sure and strong, and the popping of his flesh was audible as the skin broke. He screamed in pain as his eyeball burst from the pressure of the prosthetic being forced into place. Dropping him again, she stepped back to watch him writhe and claw at his face, attempting to remove the foreign object, his fingers slipping uselessly. The blood flowing from the wound wouldn't allow him to gain purchase.

"Look at me," she said. "Look at me!" she screamed when he didn't do as she said. Her anger threatened to overcome her other senses, and she wanted to relish these final moments with him. She wanted him to know that his death, while at her hands, was entirely his fault.

Terrified, he looked in her direction and attempted to focus on her face. The agony was overwhelming, and he was nauseated with it. "Please. Please 86-75-309. You don't want to do this," he plead.

His refusal to say her name, even in his final moments, to give her back her identity, sent her rage over the edge, and her foot struck his throat, crushing his windpipe. Blood spurted from his open mouth when his teeth sliced his tongue. She leaned down to listen to the final beats of his heart as he lay dying in the sand.

Spinning her body away from his corpse, she stalked away in her originally intended direction. "My name is Jenny," she said, "not Subject 86-75-309."

***

ABOUT THE AUTHOR:

Born and raised in the rural South, books have always been a comfort and joy for Rebecca Poole, so it's no surprise that she's been bitten by the bug to create her own stories and worlds. She uses her artwork to help visualize the characters and scenes she creates digitally to bring them to life on the page.

She lives in Georgia with her husband and fur children. It would not be surprising to see her attempting to 'rescue' another stray cat, for she might have an addiction to the cuddly critters...

http://rebeccapoolewriter.com/

Saltwater Assassin
by Samantha Warren

"Step right up. Step right up. Feast your eyes on the lovely, luscious Syren–the only living mermaid known to man. That's it, my dear. Come on, don't be shy."

Syren watched through the crystal clear glass as a young girl with blond curls peered at her. She smiled and waved, but the child sank back into the arms of her mother. A small part of Syren's heart seized, but she buried the feeling down deep with all the others.

She was a freak. There was no denying it. Even at the orphanage where Master Opal found her twenty-three years ago--a mermaid child of barely five, living in a tank, cared for by a confused and scared nun. The woman had practically thrown Syren at Opal when he expressed interest in adopting the girl. He raised the strange child as his own, teaching her to embrace the uniqueness and use it to make money. For him, of course, but at least Syren had a home and was treated better than at the orphanage. And she learned to kill. Efficiently.

Syren's strange gift allowed her to change at night, only as the last rays of the sun faded from the sky. Master Opal had knowledge no one else possessed. He understood her species better than even she did, although he wouldn't discuss how, nor would he tell her if any others like her existed. When she asked, he would simply grunt and continue on as if he hadn't heard her.

He showed her how to change. Or rather, explained it. He was simply human and had no obvious deformities, unlike all those in his employ. His talent lay in recruiting oddities, running the show, and finding side jobs for his freaks to perform at night.

The freakshow wasn't the money maker for Master Opal. No. The real money came later, after the curtains closed. Davinia, the boneless wonder, earned top dollar as a special-order escort to the few who could afford her unique services. Jakob, who could walk through walls, made himself invaluable to those with something to steal – a habit he had before Master Opal found him and offered his protection. And Syren was a trained assassin with a concrete alibi. No one would ever suspect the water-bound mermaid of murder. She couldn't leave her tank, after all. Only those in the freakshow knew the secret of her nightly transformation.

"Party's over, kids." Master Opal clapped his hands and his assistant dropped the curtain doors. Nilla wasn't the dopey sidekick she pretended to be for the paying crowds. Her skills as a witch made her capable of scary levels of magic. But Opal mostly used her for security. She could seal a simple tent up tight and keep out even the nosiest of late night spectators. And those she couldn't keep out, well, they were never heard or seen again.

As the curtains closed and the lights flared, Syren placed her hands atop the water cage she spent her days in. Her fingers gripped the side and she hoisted herself up. She sat propped on the edge of the tank, her flippers dangling in the water just below the surface, and inhaled deeply. The air tasted stale, tainted, as it passed over her tongue.

Her unique body would be the envy of many a diver. Not only did she possess the normal nostrils and lungs of a human, but she had gills that let her survive under water. She could breathe in or out of the tank and transition smoothly between the two. Twice a day, she performed like a dolphin, doing tricks as demanded by Master Opal, awing the adoring crowds and growing more and more unhappy with being a sideshow freak and Opal's toy, to do with as he pleased. But she had no choice. She had nowhere to go, no place to run to.

She watched from her perch as Davinia slipped out of her skin-tight costume. The woman's body was perfect, of course. How else would she earn so much? Opal treated her well, especially when he took advantage of her services, and her clients were just as gracious, lavishing expensive gifts and dinners, but Syren saw the sadness behind her dark eyes, visible only to those who knew where to look.

Jakob, on the other hand, loved his job. He reveled in the awe of crowds and the power he had over them. But he craved his after-hours work even more. More than once, he bragged to the others that Opal wouldn't survive without him, that all their money came from the jobs he pulled.

Syren doubted that the show would collapse without him, but he did make their lives more comfortable, to say the least. And he kept Master Opal busy and away from the women most of the time.

Though she couldn't see outside, Syren knew when the sun faded. Her tail itched, so bad she longed to scratch her scales right off. Once she had tried. She had dug and pulled at her fins until the scales finally did come off, but she bled profusely. Nilla's healing powers had saved her from permanent deformity, but she hurt for days. Since then, she simply clenched her teeth and dealt with it.

Shaking off the memory, she swung herself over the side and gripped the edge with her hands. The itching grew as the scales withdrew into her. Her thick snake-like body separated into two distinct appendages. Her fins transformed into feet.

The itching subsided and Syren dropped from the edge of the tank. She landed smoothly in a crouch and rose. Her upper body was scantily clothed with the alluring clam bikini top that was her show costume. It revealed her patchily scaled skin. Even during the change, the scales on her stomach, chest, and arms remained, but everything below her belly button was completely bare. Smooth like a newborn babe.

Jakob let out an ear-piercing whistle. "Lookin' good."

"Blow me," Syren shot back. The man was one of her least favorite people. He was cocky and coy and she didn't trust him even a little bit. She did her best to avoid being alone with him.

He gave her a skeezy smile as he bowed before her. "I'm always open to a little kink."

Syren growled and walked across the open area in the middle of the tent. Master Opal refused to let her have clothes or a robe anywhere near her tank, no matter how hard she begged him. He argued that if anyone saw it, the gig would be up and they would think her a fake. She personally thought he just liked the power he had over her and wanted to make her uncomfortable on purpose. It worked.

She reached the small dressing room at the back of the tent and ducked inside. She shared the area with Davinia. Well, shared was a bit of an exaggeration. The boneless escort used 90% of it. Outfits she had tried on and discarded for one reason or another littered the space. Trunks and small armoires lined the walls, along with two different vanities, three full-length mirrors and a rack of costumes for her show. Syren, on the other hand, had exactly one small closet. Inside, she found more clam-shell bras, the only attire Opal allowed her to wear in the tank, and one other outfit. It was black and loose-fitting, a classic ninja outfit. She had repeatedly argued that another get-up would be more comfortable and efficient, but Opal liked being able to hire out his mermaid ninja and insisted she keep up the appearance. She slipped on the black clothes and grabbed the dual swords propped next to the closet before finding her way to Opal's office.

"It's an easy one," he said as she opened the door. "A disgruntled wife."

"Husband's a cheater?" Syren leaned against the door frame and crossed her arms.

"Sort of. Prostitute. Always the same one."

She gave a curt nod. "Yep. Cheater."

"It's not your place to make judgments." He held out a lumpy brown 9x12 envelope. "Just do your job."

Syren pursed her lips and took the envelope. She left without saying anything. She paused at the entrance to the tent to give the information inside a brief overview. She folded the envelope and stuffed it into one of her oversized pockets. The flaps parted to let her through and snapped shut behind her. The fairgrounds were empty aside from the random carney nursing his blues from the bottom of a paper-covered bottle. She kept to the shadows, passing unnoticed through the gates and up the streets to the hotel indicated in the file. It was dingy, worn-down from years of disrepair and less than reputable clientele.

A single light shone outside the row of doors that marked the rooms. The drawn curtains hid the view inside, but the noises indicated that she had found her target. She stayed outside the glare of the bulb and watched the cars pass on the street. She would let them finish their business. They may be slated to die, but they deserved at least that much. Opal wouldn't be pleased if he found out. He would relish her taking them in the middle of the act, but it was her choice, and she would hold on to any small bit of power she had.

Nearly an hour passed before the screams of lust finally faded into soft moans and happy chatter. Syren stepped from the shadows and knocked on the door.

"Beer delivery," came the excited cry from the female inside. The door swung open. The woman's smile didn't have time to fade before Syren's blade made its way to the back of her throat.

The assassin pushed the dying prostitute back from the door with the sword still buried deep in her neck and drew its companion from behind her. The woman dropped, along with the sheet that covered her. Syren advanced on the man.

He kneeled naked on the bed. For a baffled moment, he stared at her, then his hands clamped over his private parts and he snarled, "Who the hell do you think you are?"

Syren calculated the distance between them. If he fought back, it could get messy. Not hard, but messy. She didn't really want to have to take a shower tonight.

"Your wife says hello," she said and took a step forward.

He moved to his left to roll off the bed.

She flipped through the air. Her blade came down in a solid arc and sliced clean through his skull.

He dropped off the bed with a grunt and lay still.

Syren knelt on the bed and surveyed the scene. Blood pooled on the carpet under the prostitute and had begun to seep out of the man's skull, but none had gotten on her. She removed her blades from the bodies and wiped them clean on the bed's comforter before slipping them back into their sheaths. Then she pulled the little disposable camera from the envelope. This job required evidence. Definitely not her favorite part. Not anywhere close to it. She hated this sick display of power, this violation of the dead. Killing them was one thing. Mocking them with photographs was another. Half the time, she wondered if the photos were the client's idea or Master Opal's.

Syren snapped a dozen or so pictures and stuffed the camera in her pocket. She closed the door behind her and slipped into the shadows once again. The job had taken almost no time at all, a couple hours at most counting travel time. She had a good chunk of the night left at her disposal. She didn't need to be back to her tank until just before the first rays of sun came up. She used the time to do nothing but roam the streets in the dark, to use her legs, to stretch and explore. She leaned against a wall in an alley and watched a pair of prostitutes attempt to sell their wares on the corner. She sat in an empty park on a swing and stared up at the sky. She snuck into one of the carnival tents and stole a bag of cotton candy, one of her favorite treats. Her legs were beginning to tingle when she crept back inside her tent, returned her ninja costume to its closet, and slipped back into the tank to wait for her legs to finish changing as the sun rose outside.

There were no more jobs during that fair. No more excuses to get out and wander. She spent the time in her tank, forbidden to leave, despite the itch to get out and move around. She was Master Opal's property, and he wanted her in her cage until she had a job to do. It was easier for him to control her that way.

She was thrilled when the show packed up and moved on. They were slated to stay in the next place for two weeks, a town that hovered just under the size of a city, lined with streets and alleys and pretty parks she could explore, assuming a new assignment gave her an excuse to leave the tent. Full of old charm and modern conveniences.

"You have a job." Master Opal knocked on Syren's tank one morning, a couple days after they arrived. "Come see me when you're up."

The water muffled his voice through the tank and saltwater, but she heard him well enough and gave a curt nod. She refused to show her excitement, but her heart soared. She had been locked in that tank for over a week. She needed to *move*.

She ignored Jakob's comments as she walked across the tent. Davinia was already gone for the evening, off to please whatever client Opal had set up for her. Syren took her time getting ready. She enjoyed the peace, the privacy. Something she rarely got anymore. Her tank was open to the public and on display to her colleagues in private. Jakob's sneering visage ogled her on a regular basis. She had nowhere to hide, no place to retreat. Except the dressing room on the nights she had extra work.

"You're late," Opal chided when she walked into his office. He was texting someone on his phone and didn't bother looking up.

She stood at the door and waited. He continued looking at his phone while he held out another brown envelope. This one was flat. No camera.

She took it and began to walk out.

"This is an important job," he said as she reached the door. "Don't screw it up."

She paused, seething inside. She had never screwed up a job. Syren gave him a brief nod and started to leave.

"And don't die."

She spun around and stared at him, but he didn't look at her. He had turned around in his chair so his back faced her.

Don't die? Why would he say that? He had never, ever said anything like that to her before. Why now? Her heart raced as she walked through the tent. The flaps opened, thanks to Nilla's talents, and she found a bench where she could sit to examine the contents of the envelope.

Most of her jobs had at least a little background info, something to help her complete her task more efficiently. This one offered three sheets of paper: an address, a blueprint of a house, and a name. That was it. Three pieces of paper, three small details. She didn't even have a picture of her target. Master Opal's job was to do the research for her so all she had to do was kill. How was she supposed to make sure she had the right target?

She sighed and stood. She would have to figure it out somehow.

The house was farther away than she would have liked. It took her over an hour to get there on foot, eating into her valuable and limited time. A tall, barbed fence surrounded the property. What was inside? What was it protecting?

She walked the edge of the property, looking for something to clue her in as to what she was here for.

It was silent. Not a tree moved in the breeze. Not a dog barked. Not a bird twittered. Nothing. It was like the house was waiting for her to make her move.

She reached out and waved a hand near the fence, feeling for a spark of electricity or something to clue her into a charged barrier. Again, nothing.

She should have been pleased, but the unease growing in her gut made her ill. This was wrong. Weird. Had Master Opal set her up? Was this a test?

She grabbed the fence and monkey-climbed to the top. The barbs weren't an issue. She braced her small feet between them and surveyed the area below her.

A few bushes and trees here and there dotted a wide, flat lawn. A marble breezeway led to an in-ground pool that glistened in the moonlight.

She searched for something to tip her off, but heard nothing. No guards, no dogs, not even a spotlight anywhere on the yard. She jumped down and crouch-ran across the area, weaving a random pattern just in case someone spotted her and opened fire. Again, nothing.

She reached the house without encountering any resistance whatsoever. A single light glowed in the kitchen that opened onto the back patio where the pool was. The French doors swung wide, giving her free access to the inside.

Something was wrong. It was all too easy. Her gut screamed at her to leave, to turn around and go back to the tent, to crawl into her tank where she was safe. She yearned to tell Master Opal to stuff it, to do his own dirty work.

But that wasn't how she was trained. And he would surely put her out if she refused. Or kill her. With a grimace, she slipped a sword from its sheath on her back and held it out in front of her.

The kitchen inside opened onto a sunken living area. White leather couches were arrayed around a central fireplace. Despite the warm weather, the logs roared, releasing a peaceful crackling sound and a smoky scent.

A figure sat on one of the couches with its back to her. A black hood covered its head.

"You're thorough," it said. *He* said. His voice came out like a rumbling purr, but it was almost certainly male. "Opal taught you well."

Syren's hackles went up. She knew it. Opal had set her up. Why? What did she do?

"Tennyson Yeats?" she asked as she edged forward.

She could hear the smile in his voice. "Yes. My mother was a bit of a poet." He rose then, revealing a lithe figure dressed in the same attire she wore. Like her, a black mask covered his face, revealing only his bright green eyes.

Syren tried to hold her tongue, but she found herself speaking. "How do you know Master Opal?"

Tennyson laughed. "We go back a long way. Not a good way, but a long way."

"Why does he want you dead?"

"Because we disagree on things. Many, many things." He cocked his head. "Are you going to do his bidding like a good little girl?"

Syren bristled at the comment. "I'm going to try," she growled.

He gave her a small nod. "Very well, then." He leaned forward and picked up a sword much like her own from the couch. "Let's see how this ends."

He leapt at her before his sword was completely unsheathed.

The unexpected motion threw her off and forced her to duck and roll. She managed to get her sword up just in time to block his attack.

His blade slid down hers with a screech of metal-on-metal and slammed against the kitchen counter, taking a chunk of tile from the glistening white surface.

"You're quick," Tennyson said, "I'll give you that."

Syren gritted her teeth and sprang to her feet. She brought her blade to bear and spun through the air. He parried her as if she was a child. She found herself rolling across the floor in an unchecked tumble.

"But overeager." He jumped and flipped, completing a perfect somersault before landing on her other side. "You'll never win that way."

She barely had time to roll before his blade slammed down beside where her head had been. She screeched as a piece of her ear was separated from the lobe and clapped her hand to the wound. Her fingers came away bloody.

"Never pause to inspect a minor wound during a duel to

the death." His voice came right beside her ear, so close the fabric of his mask fluttered against her skin. The point of his blade sank into her back.

Don't die. Master Opal's voice echoed in her head. Had he known? Did he know how this would end? Did he orchestrate this? But why? To what purpose?

She jerked away. The sword ripped through her flesh and pain raced through her body. She stumbled back and held up her blade.

"Who are you?" she growled through gritted teeth. Her body screamed at her, but she kept herself upright.

Tennyson tipped his head. "I can be your savior, or your demise. It's entirely up to you."

Syren pressed a hand to the hole. Her legs were weak and she could barely stay upright. "Stop speaking in riddles."

He glanced at the floor by her feet and his smile faded. "Shit." The word fell from his mouth without any of the arrogance he had displayed before.

She followed his gaze. Blood pooled at her feet, more than should have if she just had a flesh wound. Something important had been hit. She was in trouble. She would never make it back to the tent, to Nilla, their healer, before she bled out.

She raised her gaze to him. The small movement sent her head swimming and she stumbled to the side.

He stared at her. "Let me help you," he said.

"Why?" Even as she questioned him, her knees gave out and she sank to the floor, her hand slipping on her own blood. She had been wounded before, but never to this extent. Never so bad she questioned her own ability to survive. She yanked the mask from her face as she struggled to breathe deep.

"Because you don't deserve this. You didn't ask for this." He knelt beside her, heedless of the blood soaking into his clothes. "You were born to be something special, Syren. You aren't like them. You aren't a freak."

She laughed and blood slipped from her lips. She licked it away. "Yes, I am. Clearly you don't know me as well as you think you do."

He used a clean thumb to wipe the blood from her mouth. "Yes, I do. I'm like you, in a way."

Syren's eyebrows puckered with disbelief. "Yeah, okay." She coughed and more blood came out.

"It's true." He reached up and removed his own mask.

She couldn't hold back the gasp. Suddenly, the purr in his voice made perfect sense.

He was a cat. Sort of. His body appeared human, but his facial features were very much that of a cat, minus the actual fur. He even had little whiskers on his cheeks, right by his nose.

"See? I understand your plight. For years, I've battled Opal over his abuse of our kind. Davinia, Jakob, Nilla, you. None of us should be used as you are. You're not freaks. You're people. Humans."

Syren laughed again, only this time it hurt so much it almost made her stop. "I'm not human. I'm a fish."

"No, my dear. You're still human. You're just part of a different race than most. Our species, our unique class of beings, we've always existed. We've been here since the beginning, just like they were. But humans tend to shun things they don't understand. It scares them to not understand something and magic is one of those things most humans simply do not get. It's beyond them, beyond their ability to comprehend and experience. And so they label us as freaks, deformities, abominations. But we're not. We're beautiful. We're mystical. We're magical."

Syren leaned back into his arms. She kind of liked the way he talked about her, about them. Like they were actually important. Like they were worth more than a few bucks to gawk at. But it didn't matter anymore. Her legs tingled. They were starting to change. Too early. Before the sun. She was converting back to her true form. She was dying.

She raised her eyes to his. "It doesn't matter anymore," she said, and she truly believed it. None of it mattered. She was done. The world would continue on without her. She would be blissfully unaware of any of it.

"No. I refuse to believe that." Before she could stop him, he ripped off her pants and underwear.

She slapped at his hands weakly. "Get away from me," she hissed.

"You can't change with your clothes on. The fabric would be trapped in your body. It could kill you."

She resented the fact that she was naked in front of this stranger, but he was right. The cloth between her legs would be sealed inside her skin and prevent muscles and veins from forming together as they should. She would be crippled at the very least.

He picked her up even as her legs began to fuse together. He carried her, blood dripping a trail behind them, out to the pool and set her along the side with her feet dangling into the water. He raised a hand and waved at someone in the shadows.

The woman who Syren knew only as Master Opal's meek servant witch separated herself from the blackness. Her onyx-black skin gleamed in the moonlight. "Nilla?"

She tipped her head to the younger woman. "Yes, it's me." She knelt beside Syren and pressed a hand to the wound. "You weren't actually supposed to kill her, Tennyson."

The cat-man shrank back in shame. "I didn't mean to. She moved too quickly."

"Sure. Blame the girl." To Syren, she said, "Hold still, dear. This will hurt."

Hurt it did. The pain that raced through Syren's body was almost too much to bear, but mingling with the pain was a magic more powerful than anything she had ever experienced before. It made her vibrate down to the very core of her being. She could actually feel the cells in her body moving, healing, fusing together. She knew Nilla could tend minor hurts, but this was something altogether different. This was beyond magic. It was a miracle.

"There. It's going to ache for awhile, but if you take it easy, it should stay closed. Don't change forms for a few days. Let your body heal. "

Syren took a tentative breath. It hurt, but she found the pain fading to manageable depths. She enjoyed the feeling for a moment before looking at Nilla. "If you're here..." She didn't finish the question. She didn't really know what it was she wanted to ask.

"The show is done," Nilla said. "It was time for Opal's reign to be over."

Syren's brow puckered. "I don't know what that means."

"It means you're welcome to stay here," Tennyson said. "I have numerous pools, and there is a room in the basement that would suit you quite well, if you prefer it."

"What if I choose to go back?"

Tennyson glanced at Nilla. "You can't," the woman said. She reached into her pocket and removed her phone. She tapped a few buttons and turned the screen to Syren.

The tent blazed.

Her tank exploded as the water boiled over, drenching Jakob in a flood. It would have killed him if he hadn't already been dead. The camera moved. Someone or something was obviously in there, recording. There, by the platform Davinia used, lay another body. A body Syren would never have mistaken. Master Opal. His eyes were wide. His mouth open in a scream. His stomach exploded out in a mass of gore and horror.

When the video reached its end, Syren looked up at Nilla. "You were there?"

The other woman shook her head. "No. I'm a healer, not a killer. Some of Tennyson's crew took care of the others and got me out."

Syren nodded and sat in silence for a couple minutes. It was a lot to digest and her brain still buzzed from the magic and blood loss affecting her body. She blinked rapidly as she attempted to comprehend what had happened in a mere few hours. The life she had known was gone, completely gone. Tennyson and Nilla offered a new one, but would it be better? She had no idea.

"Davinia?" she asked.

Nilla responded. "She chose to go her own way." She gave a wry smile. "She's going to try her luck in Hollywood."

Syren's lips twitched. Hollywood would be perfect for Davinia. "And I can stay here?"

Tennyson nodded. "Yes. For as long as you wish."

Syren nodded. It was a lot to think about. She needed time. Her feet turned to fins and she slipped into the pool just as the sun came up.

***

ABOUT THE AUTHOR:

Samantha Warren is a speculative fiction author who spends her days immersed in dragons, spaceships, and vampires. She milks cows for fun and collects zombie gnomes and colorful socks.

IN HER IMAGE
BY VASIL TUCHKOV

"Nine-thousand years old. His family tree goes back. Says his ancestors lived in this same cave, in Sasso Caveoso. Over there. He still lives there, too. Right on the edge of town...How to say..."–here the translator struggles, then lights up–"Not the edge of town but the edge of the world!"

Both translator and painter point in the same direction; heads turn, tan arms stretch behind their backs.

The Englishman traces their trajectory. His eyes follow the uneven path of buildings and terraces that climb up and down the hillside, each on top of the other, as the roofs of some serve as streets for the levels above. They all lead to caves, carved deep into the rock, millennia ago. The sky is lead; so low, it hangs over the town like it means to crush it.

Nestled on the edge of a ravine, the settlement would look somewhat ominous, were it not for the sound of life, the bright painted wood of the churches and the hotels, the cacti and shrubbery grown on the scalp of the rock.

The river below takes his eyes and carries them to the far side of town–no lights aglow, only murky sockets of prehistoric caves, barely visible in the distance and the waning afternoon. Sassi di Matera is still unacquainted with the full concept of tourism.

He'd only spotted two English-speaking groups since his arrival this morning. They wandered around, getting lost in this remote maze of Escher structures and paths, with their cameras, breathless sighs, and numb legs. As he would be, if he were not here after something else.

He turns back to the table. They are both waiting on him. The translator he'd picked up in the next village, or got picked up by.

And the painter.

"Tell him this is the most extraordinary place I've ever visited."

A series of nods and translator turns to painter. Word tennis in a language he does not understand past his travel dictionary; it sounds like they're arguing. But then the painter looks up at him and breaks a huge smile. The mouth reveals gunpowder teeth; among the bombed ruins, a single gold incisor shines like a sacred tower. The lips close and kill the flicker. The brush mustache settles in place. His face is back to stone, carved like the caves of his village.

"I've lived my life here. I paid little attention as a boy, looking at the valley and the caves as if they were drawers in my room. But with the years, I learned to appreciate it. The background. To see more things in it every day. Restless detail."–The translator delivers the painter's words in English.

Of the three, the Englishman is youngest but fatigue gives him weariness beyond age. Dark circles weigh heavy on his eyes; his skin once chalk, now a painful tone of pink, scaling, touched by a hundred days of Italian summer. Black hair falls on his face thin like a willow. A man in travel clothes, the head of a wet dog on his shoulders.

"Tell him I agree to his terms but on one condition. I get to record the conversation."

Both locals examine him as he places the tape recorder on the table and presses "play".

The painter slaps the table and bursts, metallic and sour, a smoker's laughter. He waves a hand like it's nothing. There's something wrong with it.

"17th of July. Sassi Di Matera, Basilicata. I find myself on the terrace of a local pub—*Ristorante Francesca*, nested high on the cascades of Sasso Barisano, across from the old town Sasso Caveoso—the prehistoric cavemen settlement, one of the oldest known in Europe. Topic: of myth and fable. My search has led me here, following the last trail I stumbled upon in the Vatican. Talking to a local painter regarding the..."–he mumbles low into the recorder when the painter interrupts him.

"Journalista?"–the painter mouths to the translator, a mere device to him, as he's locked eyes on the Englishman.

"Student. Anthropology. Tell him I'm writing a PHD on truths and fallacies in modern myth. ...Research,"–he says before the translator has a chance to respond.

More Italian, more nodding. All three of them now nod heads like dummy dogs on a car's dashboard. Synchrony, at last.

"Ah, Studente."–the painter concludes; his hair is long and white as factory smoke, combed back with wax or just unwashed.

He says something more and the translator announces: "He cannot continue without more wine. Says he can't tell a story on an empty stomach and a dry throat. Says he can't remember a thing like this."

The foreigner nods. First to the translator, then to the painter. Hails the waiter and orders a bottle to accompany the glasses present, and the wooden platter with cheeses, Prosciutto, Bresaola and whatever the rest of the smoked meat is called.

When drinks are spilt, the painter gives him again one of his broad black-and-gold smiles. Then he's back to serious, even grim. His eyes over the glass as he drinks, once blue perhaps, now pale and colorless as stale milk. No motion inside. Sad eyes. Beautiful eyes.

A man of sixty or seventy, he wears a white and blue striped linen shirt, and nothing beneath it. A sailor's outfit almost, framed by bracelets of wood and bone, and a necklace crafted from ceramics and minor gems, settled in a laurel of chest hair.

"You want to know about her? Ah," the translator delivers the message but he catches the painter's intonation and knows it is no question but a statement; he watches him closely, compensates for the linguistic hiatus with body language.

The painter's left hand is crippled; a withered spasmodic turnip, it shivers every now and then, like freshly dead. But there's nothing fresh about it, only the nails keep growing. It floats the air as he speaks. More than the other one, really. It doesn't seem to bother him.

"The elusive one. The ghost bride of history. The shadow time traveler," the painter continues, stuffing salami into his mouth and spitting; dried paint of all color on his fingers. He drinks with the same hand, the other one is for conversation emphasis solely. And he waves it like a flag of flesh.

In the midsummer afternoon, all three of them sweat bullets but only the Englishman seems to notice, wiping his forehead with a napkin every now and then.

"I hear you've seen her. First hand... Wait... Without that last part..." but it's too late, the translator is at it already, a verbatim robot; the painter's expression registers no change, so it is left unclear whether the bad humor carries over.

"I've seen her, all right. This much is true," the translator delivers.

"What is her real name?"

"Only one knows. She wears many names..."

"Can you describe her for me?"

Here the painter stops chewing, just stares. His face is a sandstone formation: wrinkles, bones, and spider veins. His eyes are about to melt. Then he grins again, wide as ever. Conclusion, he has two modes: dead serious and dead smiley.

"Impossible," he pronounces with an arc of food debris; the translator fills in the rest. "You cannot describe her. No one can. You cannot photograph, film or paint her."

"Yes, yes, I've heard the stories." The Englishman rolls eyes. "From here to Dublin. Stories of glitch cameras exploding in the hands of their owners, of overexposed photos, broken pencils, lost minds...But I need a description. Tell him it took me seven months to find him, to get here and ask these questions. Tell him I drifted through Italy, France, Warsaw, Ireland, and Hungary for many days and nights. Sometimes waiting weeks, months, for the next clue in this mystery. My stipend is almost done. Tell him I'm not leaving without a description. Anything will do. Eyewitnesses are reluctant to even try, except the obvious charlatans and loonies. First she's a Scandinavian blonde, then a Hispanic brunette, some say she had skin like milk and flames in her hair, others say she was a Nubian Queen, with flesh dark as chocolate and peacock feathers for eyes. I was told you had proof, Amico. At this point I'm ready to take a lie from you too...Feed me something. Anything..."

The painter listens, then drowns his bite in wine, and refills his glass. The other two are still, in silent expectation; the Englishman can't help but notice the translator's interest in the story, growing beyond the politics of translation.

The recorder keeps rolling.

"Then I cannot help you," the translator says in a newly developed narrative tone, as if almost imitating the painter's voice, and both men give him an odd look. "I don't do lies. And I cannot describe her for you. Description kills action."

"Fabulous! Why am I even wasting my time here! Lovely. Dead end." He turns to the translator, ready to get up from the table.

As he reaches for his coat on the back of the seat, suddenly the translator speaks to the painter, so fast the Englishman cannot catch a word. The painter responds with a word or two. His tone irritated.

At last, translator turns to him: "Forget this guy! He's crazy. I can help you find your wife, sir. Or fiancé. Prostitute? Looking for woman, no?" He holds onto his arm but the Englishman pulls it free; tall and scrawny, the translator sweats and adjusts his spectacles again and again, as if looking for the perfect angle. He licks his dry lips and makes the cracks glisten.

"Look..." the foreigner starts but the painter's voice cuts his word short.

He is asked to repeat.

The translator deciphers: "He says he cannot describe her. But he has the closest thing to a description of her in the world. Not description... How to say... Picture-description..."

"A depiction...?" the Englishman offers.

"Depiction! Yes! He has a depiction."

"I thought it's *impossible*. Thought she was beyond depicting. No picture, no scripture, only word of mouth." The Englishman sits back slowly, his leg half-way on the exit.

The painter extracts a sketchpad from an inner shirt pocket. Tattered leather, rubber-band strapped. Among the mash of postcards and sunsets, his finger selects a gray folded triangle; pushes it forward, stays on it.

"It is. But once in a lifetime, an extraordinary man can achieve the impossible."

"And, I take it, you are such a man. Extraordinary."

The painter is now rolling tobacco in rice paper; he uses only one hand but in a matter of seconds fumes crawl in his mouth.

"Or very lucky." He smiles huge again, lips apart, the cigarette bitten by his gold tooth, through a veil of smoke.

"Can I see it?

"He says you can see... But it will cost you another bottle." The translator winks at the Englishman, as if sharing an inner joke.

"Bollocks... He's not even done with this one... Ah, forget it. And don't translate! I wonder how many bottles he's won himself over the years with the *depiction* trick–probably his greatest work."

Both men wait on the Englishman, or perhaps just the translator, as the painter seems busy smoking and looking serious.

"Tell him...I agree."

"Why?" the translator drops but the Englishman's ears are deaf to his opinion.

Painter and translator quarrel again, so loud this time, every other table in the restaurant sets their eyes on them. For a moment, anyway. The place is too noisy and the view too sharp to steal attention for longer.

Finally, the translator faces the Englishman and sighs: "This man. He is crazy. We can find better...He wants me to leave. Says he'll only show it to you but not to me."

The Englishman frowns.

"Turn around," he says.

"What?"

"Turn around. Your back facing the table. I'll pay you extra."

When the translator obeys, shaking head and mumbling offended, the Englishman looks at the painter and nods.

The painter takes a long puff. Then nods, as well.

From here on the conversation adopts an even quirkier form. Two men face each other, take turns to speak and wait. The third, middle, man listens and delivers with his back.

"No one can draw or photograph her. Too big for canvas, she is. No one can repeat her image, one can only witness. If one tries to recreate or even remember too hard...Bad things happen. My grandfather would tell me of it but I wouldn't listen," the painter explains as he opens the notebook, unfolds an old raggedy paper, neatly pressed until then, then peers at the Englishman proudly. "I dare say it is the closest depiction of her in the world. It better be. For it cost me a hand. My good hand. Some luck, that is. Extraordinary."

The Englishman leans forward, unfolds the triangle, and studies the drawing inside.

A scribble, really. Pale charcoal circles repeated again and again as if by a child's hand. The circles are interrupted by a torn gash–the point where pressure had gone past what paper could take. There was no abstract art here. Just a madman's doodle.

The new bottle arrives and "pop" goes the cork. This time the Englishman drinks, too. He drinks fast, no savor to it.

"I see nothing of particular interest. Scribbles. Circles. A hole in an old paper." The Englishman speaks into the recorder on the table.

The painter presses his deformity against the scribbled paper. The uncut nails haul along, a dark mixture of paint underneath the shells.

"Look further... It is there... Look beyond the lines," the translator recounts, uneasy in his chair, a gloating to his tone.

The Englishman looks closely. His weary mind or the wine responsible, a form shapes in his vision.

"This... This curve here... This was the nose," the painter explains via the human device.

There, among the chaos, is perhaps, a profile–reminiscent of a nose but the line had curved and repeated aggressively over it. It could have been anything.

"Seventeen, I was, when I drew this. Until then, I was my family's treasure, a true progeny of the brush, they said. After that one day I became the black sheep, cast away, forgotten. You must understand, my father was a good man, harsh but just. I come from seven generations of painters, some very good, some mediocre, none truly great. To have had a true gift, and thrown it away...Or better say, allowed it to slip from my grasp, this was real crime against the family.

"I heard the story from my grandfather. He was a painter, too. A superstition that ran in his generation and before. Like sailors and women on board. Only, about what should be painted and what not. A story. Of her. The Woman. How she came from the caves, a vision not meant for human eyes, slippery like a jellyfish, unbearable like staring at the sun," the painter continues, his mustache red from the wine, his bad hand dancing to the rhythm of his words, at times to those of the translator, too, a sort of visual echo.

"I was young and boiling then. Everything a matter of life and death. Chased girls like a hound, and drank Absinthe with my friends. We adored not the local classics but a crazy Dutch painter, who cut pieces of himself in tribute to his love for a prostitute. And sure, I thought my grandfather was feeding me a fairytale, I could not get it out of my mind. In fact, it was all that I painted–a woman of mystical proportions, no two portraits alike, changing something every time, always trying to depict her the way I imagined her from my grandfather's story. Or what was missing in that story. The one no one could picture. I never succeeded in my mind but I sold a lot of paintings. My father was proud of me.

"Then one day, as I sat at a café, no different from this one, I saw something: a gorgeous lady I had never seen in town before. Back in the day we had even less visitors. Yet no one seemed to notice her the way I did. She stood out, gorgeous beyond comparison, but there was something else to her...I couldn't quite make out her features, couldn't avert my eyes. Before I knew, my hand was sketching. I only had a charcoal on me but it didn't matter. I had to put this fascinating woman on the paper."

The painter drinks two consecutive glasses of wine. Not without delight, either. His own story caresses his ears; repetition turns it into music lyrics. He rolls another cigarette.

"And then?" the Englishman breaks his ennui.

"And then she saw me. What else? She sensed my eyes on her. Felt the lines of the charcoal tracing her features, falling into shape, locking her down with a net. She gave me a smile like nothing I'd seen. But to this day, I cannot tell you what kind of lips or teeth it wore. If she had mascara, or the color of her eyes. I cannot tell you anything, in fact, not a single stroke more than this sketch you see, even though I claim to be a man of detail.

"What I can tell you is that the moment this smile fell upon me, I felt a tickle in my hand. It grew into a stiffness, and finally into the worst pain I had experienced until then. Until now, for that matter. A spike, all the way to my brain. When I regained consciousness, she was gone, like a bad dream or delirium. No one would believe me."

He waves the dead meat at the end of his arm and smiles victoriously, gold and decay on display.

"An alcohol-induced stroke, the doctors said. Devil, and traitor, my father said. I learned to paint with the other one but this was my talent hand, I lost something beyond a limb. That *something-something* we all crave to touch. Today I still paint but no one sees it."

"And you never saw her again?"

"Never. Only a blank image I could not forget but not quite bring either. A ghost memory that never goes away."

Good story, the Englishman thinks but decides to go along with it: "Along my travels, I met strangers, heard things. Things like she's a descendent of the foul copulation of Gorgon Medusa and a muse. Some said it was Adam's first wife, Lilith herself. The whore of Babylon. Bound to haunt dreams of the children of Adam. That in her image hides both mankind's knowledge and vanity. In her image, brilliance and madness linger, awaiting to be held in the eye of the beholder. True or false, just as you, I could not get it out of my mind. What a good myth will do to you, right?"

"Now it is my turn. Let me ask you this," the painter begins, back on the serious side of his coin. "All you artists, historians, why you want to capture a piece from the flow? Photographs cripple memories, portraits stiffen faces. Attempting to record is to ruin authenticity. To pause a river, to freeze a bird in the sky. It is like running a needle through a moth, pinning life down. If you did manage to put her down, her magic would be gone. The world has become a picture on display. A zoo. Some things are to remain uncaught."

The Englishman speaks through a sip of wine, gargle to his voice: "Someone's got to." He shrugs with a smirk. "Someone has to be the first."

As he lifts his glass to a toast, something flies by his periphery, almost hitting him but instead bouncing off the translator's head with a thud. Before the Englishman has a chance to react, the painter picks up another cork from the table and shoots again; the translator dodges that one.

The painter is back, returns to cold serious, eyebrows clutched, nearly touching.

The rest happens too fast but in the end the Englishman manages to prevent the brawl, hopping between the two

Italian men like a referee. The only casualties are a broken glass and the half-full bottle of Rosè, bleeding on the cement floor.

Amid the torrent of curses, it becomes clear that the translator had been peeking, trying to catch a glimpse of the sketch on the table. The Englishman stuffs a few more bills into his hands and the man is released from service, foul gestures and threats at his fellow countryman on the way out.

He and the painter now sit at the table alone, no Rosetta Stone between them.

The painter looks at the ground, says something about the wine, regret in his voice.

The Englishman orders another bottle, while trying to figure out how to proceed.

The recorder records, unconcerned. It does what it does.

"All those years. Why did you keep it?" he says to himself; then tries again but this time consults his travel dictionary and points at the "depiction" on the table. "Why? Perche`?...Salvo?

"Avevo paura." The painter lifts shoulders apologetically, gives him a brief gold-and-rotten.

"You were afraid to throw it. Couldn't bring yourself to do it," he says to the recorder or himself.

"How can I make you remember? Anything at all."

The sun is ready to descend, bathing the old Italian countryside in a tone of ochre, cinnabar, and magenta–as if taken from the dry oils on the painter's fingertips.

The painter sits mellow, smokes and studies the foreigner across the table. His face is calm, stoic, no sign of the golden grin. A feel to the air is present at the table, like the two of them were friends for years, silent because all has been said, simply sitting together, enjoying comradeship on a hot summer day.

Lips apart, the Italian is about to say something when his mind wanders elsewhere. His gaze averts, drifts away from the Englishman, settles on the background of the restaurant. The Englishman notices because it bears the sudden mark of change, like a wind that carries the smell of fire.

For the first time today, the painter's eyes clear; the same sharp wind chases away the miasma, and leaves behind clarity; the blue replaces the undefined. Across the table, the Englishman now watches a pair of young eyes.

Without a sign, the painter gets up from the table. "Toilet...Uno momento," he says and slaps his belly; gives the Englishman a signature grin. Then he turns and vanishes between the tables with such haste the foreigner is left with no chance for comment.

"Rare bird," the Englishman says to the recorder, his one true listener.

Moments later, looking down the terrace, he catches a glimpse of the painter descending the lower cascades of Matera. He takes two steps at a time, and never looks back. His limp hand whips low behind him like a tail.

The man turns to find the ghost that chased his source away but sees nothing out of the ordinary. Locals and visitors over simple wooden tables, talking, smoking, drinking, marveling at the view, waiters sliding between them, no hurry to anyone's move.

Still there, on the table, lays forgotten the "impossible" depiction.

The Englishman folds it carefully and pockets it away. A silly souvenir from a summer in Italy. He decides to frame the scribble to remind him of his own folly.

He sighs.

"It's time to go home," he says to the recorder but the little black box has nothing to say; keeps blinking red.

He stares at the floating, half-empty bottle. Gasps.
Smiles. He handles his liquor hardly as well as the painter.
Pours himself another, takes his time.

Suddenly, he feels a strong pull for the caves, as if drawn
to crawl back inside, deep into the Earth, never come out
again. Then his eyes extend beyond the caves and the river.
He is already sipping tea back in London, wrestling in despair
a PHD thesis hunt that led nowhere, ready to abandon it over
the next adventure.

With nothing more to do, the Englishman's attention falls
on a woman looking for a seat. He has not had his Italian
romance yet.

The woman, young or old, he cannot say from the
distance, is definitely attractive. Or attractively clothed, at
least. Something to her.

Before he knows it, boredom leeks from him like mercury
and forms words, adjectives. He describes her to his future
self; bent low, his chin touches the table, lips move a few
inches from the recorder's ear.

The "record" button pops up. Strange. He checks, and
there is still recording space left. He wraps fingers around it,
keeps it on.

Chinese shite...

... Aghm... Sunset in Matera...

Her hair is red... No... blond with red curls...

Red entirely...

Her nose...

...

Her neck. Like a swan's... A tiny mole... No, a tattoo... Or a
necklace....

The tape recorder is hot in his hand, almost burning. It
must be the battery. Torched as if he left it in the sun or in an
oven. But he continues, thumb on the "record" button, lips
pressing at every vowel.

Her ears are...

Her ears...

Damn...

Her ears are shaped like...

Focus. It's really hot... Must be a sunstroke. Note to self–wear a hat in Italy.

What is she doing now? What?...She's talking to a waiter. Tall young guy with long curly hair in a blue shirt.

Now she does something...Points at the menu...

As she speaks to the waiter she freezes a moment...Right there...Her mouth stops just mid-sentence. Her expression straightens. She rubs her neck like it is stiff or it itches. Her cheeks pull at the corners of her mouth to reveal a set of flashing even teeth. She must be a model.

Perhaps her hair is blond, after all...

Damn. Can't breath in this heat...

They exchange words...She nods. The waiter bows and takes the menu.

*Her nose is slightly curved but small...Familiarly curved...*He coughs into the recorder; his tongue feels somewhat swollen, perhaps an allergy to the local wine.

She takes a table on the far side of the restaurant. Sits down and...Turns this way. My way.

Her eyes are on me now...

...She smiles...

And what a smile it is.

The recorder cycles one last turn, chews on tape and stops.

***

ABOUT THE AUTHOR:

Vasil Tuchkov is a graduate from the American University in Bulgaria. He writes fiction primarily in English, though he is a full-bred Bulgarian. Vasil is a professional self-employed multi-media artist – practicing in the areas Guerrilla Marketing and conceptual design under the brand Studio Rubik (www.studiorubik.com)

He spent time abroad as both emigrant and traveler; was lucky to live in San Francisco, LA, Las Vegas, Odessa and Kiev – the Ukraine, Scotland, and Amsterdam.

His first novel Trumping Fate, Vasil wrote in Bulgarian at age 15, which at 17 he published with a major genre publisher in the country – Bard (www.bard.bg). At the time he was into fantasy, and so was his work - a fantasy trilogy, later translated into Russian and published in the Ukraine.

Tuchkov has just finally been able to get back to the rhythm of completing longer work. He is a recovered gambler, a weakness, which took him years to overcome through his writing.

He is also the founder of "Living Museum" and "Living WEB", a dynamic platform for installations and festival, fusing art and technology (www.enterlivingweb.com ; http://www.youtube.com/watch?v=kflBzHcwghI – his TedTalk for more clarity).

His novel Cyan was short-listed for Rethink-Press' New Novel Competition 2014.

In addition to Cyan, Tuchkov has a completed novella, a bunch of short stories, and two novels in progress.

Undead Cyborg Girl
by Kim Wells

"Though both are bound in the spiral dance, I would rather be a cyborg than a goddess." ~Donna Haraway
"Why not both?" ~Sean Wells

The girl woke in complete darkness. She licked her lips, felt them sting with a frosty sensation, like the morning after a snow. She wondered, "Where am I?" She felt weird, lacking something indefinable. Not expecting an answer, she asked herself, "Am I dead?"

She had been swimming in a dark sea of stars, warm and salty. Alone. She remembered a loud beeeeeeping tone that wouldn't quit, and agitated voices. But that was gone now. Just the darkness. She turned her head, still seeing nothing. Then, a single red blip of light. She focused her eyes, which felt intensely sharper when she thought about it, and saw a digital readout, heartbeat and blood pressure machine.

Oh. A hospital. No. Clinic. THE clinic, and the cyborg assassin implant.

She remembered going in for the operation, but not much after. She looked at the blips on the machine for a long time, feeling sleepier each time the red pulse appeared. They beat slower than she thought they ought to. She didn't feel herself breathing very often, either.

Maybe I'm dying, she thought.

"No," said a voice in her head, tentative, as though it had never spoken before. The voice, which must have been herself, but somehow separate from thinking, spoke with a surety she didn't want to think about. She surrendered to the sleepiness and dove back into the warm sea of stars. She'd figure it out later.

The next thing she knew, lying still but awake, she realized she heard voices.

A woman said, "She's technically dead. But somehow alive. The doctor called it undead. I call it a freaky zombie."

That sounds weird, the girl thought. *Who are they talking about?*

She opened her eyes to a room filled with light. The voice belonged to a woman standing next to her, who startled when she saw the girl's eyes open. Another woman stood across the room, moving gadgets around. They both stopped what they were doing when she opened her eyes.

Haltingly, the woman said, "How are you feeling?"

Remembering the questions of her sleepy ride through the darkness, the girl found she didn't care to answer, but instead everything struck her as incredibly funny. Instead of answering the nurse, she laughed. Hysterical tears dripped from the corners of her tired eyes.

The nurse looked startled, then angry, then both nurses left the room abruptly.

The first nurse stage-whispered as the two women left the room, "She died on the table just as they were putting in the chip." The other, with a sound like shivering in her voice, responded, "What is she?"

This exchange made the girl laugh more. Everything was hilarious. The voice in her head, the one that had given that gentle but tentative *"No"* informed her that she was, *"...creeping everyone out."* She laughed again, and decided to go back to sleep. Undead. She giggled. What did that even mean?

The cy-tech already installed in her brain–tech that allowed for access to strategic combat databases–only brought her halfway back. As she squinted at the readout in front of her, the red 50F highlighted an alarming blue-green flashing color, the girl thought 50 sounded kind of low. She wished the nurses hadn't left so she could ask them.

The heart machine from last night still blipped at the corner of her bed, slow, steady, but more halting than she remembered, like it had to think about it each time it started a new beat. She thought of the nurses calling her "undead" and "zombie." She found she didn't mind the undead part but the zombie part seemed pretty rude. The voice in her head informed her that her temp, heart, and respiration rates were significantly below the standards for human definitions of "alive."

"Well, that's cool."

After accessing the various new systems, and pulling up the menus she had been outfitted with, she found she didn't miss breathing. Every now and then she would remember to take a breath, but it wasn't automatic. Her heart still beat, but it pulsed at a slower rate than she was used to, the persistent throb in her ears, that bass line to life, was gone.

She felt fine. A little tired, but not in any pain. This seemed to her a significant improvement from what she'd expected–days of painful recovery from multiple surgeries.

She rose and went to the bathroom, the way one does, but found she didn't have to go. In the mirror, she studied her new reflection. Her skin, which had always been fairer than most people's, was now platinum-y white, with a grayish tinge. Her hair, which had been a boring brown shade people called dishwater (which she'd always found insulting) had also gone completely platinum white. There wasn't much of it left because doctors had shaved the side they put the implants into, but what remained looked shocking and different. Kind of a white side mohawk. She turned her head and found she approved of the new hairdo. It made her seem like a new person.

Her eyes had also changed from their previous mud-brown shade to a grayish-white, ringed in black. Dark circles that could have been mistaken for thick goth eyeliner (but that she could not wipe off even when she tried) entirely skimmed her eyes. She examined her lips, which were now tinted a grayish blue. Rubbed them to see if that color came off, and...

No. Still blue.

Inside her mouth, her tongue was now dark, almost black. She liked the way it made her teeth shine whiter. Sharper, as though the canines had been filed to a fine point. Deadly, like a large cat. She surveyed her face from side to side and calculated that her appearance was now beautiful. She gave a little "roar" and smiled.

Well, this is fun. Kind of cool–never been brave enough to try this, she thought.

She mused, *This new look won't make it very easy for me to blend into the crowd, which could be a drawback for an assassin.*

Then the tentative voice, which she guessed was the analytical AI software in her brain, offered a few videos of combat scenarios where such a distinguishing appearance could be turned into an asset, instead. She had been briefed that the AI would sound like someone else at first, but would eventually merge with her own thoughts until it felt seamless. Stream of consciousness, but better. It ran simulations where being the most unique looking person in the room allowed one to disappear in a way that being average didn't. No one expected the strange to do anything, apparently.

These lessons from a newly booted cybernetic AI within her own head would take some getting used to. Gaining confidence, the voice of the AI rambled, a stream-of-consciousness kind of thought which was going to be there all the time now, making suggestions.

She decided to climb back into bed. There wasn't much else to do in the hospital room and she didn't know how long she'd be here. She lay quietly, accessing the new technology that had been integrated into her system. The combat software and Alegis 7.1 system in her head far exceeded her expectations. She hadn't, after all, expected to wake up dead.

They should add that to the brochure.

Still here, she thought as she surveyed the hospital room, and then turned her attention back to studying her new alterations.

The other upgrades she had purchased included bionic arms, and she pulled the hospital gown loose to try them out. They were thin and gray, shiny. She had planned for flesh-colored skin grafts to cover the metallic surface, but that would happen in a second stage of the process, and now, she thought she might skip the grafts.

The sleek silver surface worked with her new platinum-gray skin tone; the dark line between the organic and mechanical split her upper arms right at the bicep, a sharp cut framed by shimmering optic circuits that wove an intricate and delicate pattern around her arms, but two inches higher. She poked at the line and felt no pain. She had expected the surgery to hurt more, had been briefed on post-surgical recovery and pain killers and the drawbacks for this systemic change.

These arms, this skin color, this state of being alive yet not suggested the essence of better. She kept looking at the silver and black tech in her arms, which were smooth and elegant. She could see blue pulses where circuits of electric energy showed the connections worked. They pulsed again when she flexed the fingers, touched both hands together. Her arms felt strong, and she decided they were one of her favorite things about the upgrade. Before this, she had usually felt so common, normal, bland.

Now, she felt like she was one of a kind.

She kept wanting to laugh. For some reason, waking up dead seemed to be the funniest joke ever. A nurse came into the room and looked startled that she was laughing again. The nurse gathered herself, smoothed her scrubs in front, and asked, "How are you feeling?"

The girl assessed her systems, "Fine. I've been mostly dead all day, though." She smiled.

The nurse laughed, "Oh yeah, I get it. That old movie." She didn't seem to think it was funny, though.

Undead Girl found that she could tell what the nurse was writing by the sound the pen scratched out onto the pad. Her AI translated the scritchy-scratchy noises into text:

Odd sense of humor. Indicator of brain damage?

Below-average heart rate, lack of identifiable pulse, and hypothermic body temperature of 67 degrees F.

Next the nurse wrote a note in the chart:

This patient should, for all intents and purposes, be dead. Was clinically dead for a total of ten minutes during surgery.

Undead Girl, assessing the cynical nature of the nurse's notes, began laughing again, and the nurse did not stay long.

This really would have been a great time for someone from the Clinic to discuss what had happened to her, but the nurses all ran away as soon as they could. Instead, Undead Cyborg Girl sat in her room, not needing to heal from a surgery that hadn't left her in any pain, no need for rehab or OT, and listened to her AI spool out its secrets to her in a palimpsest of facts, old urban legends, fleeting feelings and sensations, and stupid jokes.

**

Wetware: One Month Later

Creative activity could be described as a type of learning process where teacher and pupil are located in the same individual. ~Arthur Koestler

Undead Girl was home. She had worked for weeks with the doctors and techs and PT personnel they brought in to train her on how to use her new upgrades. She figured out pretty quickly that they knew less about the systems than she already did. At night she dreamed about the upgrades, and in the dreams, a voice would explain how to use her arms most effectively, or why she could hear the heartbeats in the nurses from all the way down the halls, could know things about them she shouldn't.

For example, she once heard a tiny heartbeat deep within one of the nurses' bodies, and when she asked the nurse why that would be so, "What was that tiny fluttering racehorse heartbeat?", the nurse had blanched.

She stuttered, "How can you hear that?" and ran out of the room.

The AI informed her that the tiny heartbeat must have meant the nurse was pregnant, but that the faint quality of the sound meant it was still very, very early. Possibly she hadn't been sure herself yet.

"Why did that bother her, though?" Undead Girl asked the AI.

Silence that hissed like the gap between songs on an old vinyl record filled her thoughts. She almost felt like the AI had shrugged in her head.

She found that she didn't need to sleep for rest, but still, her AI dreams were essential to understanding who she was now.

She had left the clinic because the look in her eyes when she talked to the nurses, doctors, and other patients scared them. This happened more and more after the incident with the pregnant nurse, who refused to come in her room anymore. The nurses recorded in her charts a clinical detachment, an emotion of icy nothing. They made special notes about Undead Girl's bouts of hysterical laughter, and the vital signs that never changed to being, well, living.

What the hell was she, anyway?

When she didn't think it was hilarious, she felt detached about everything, not generally analyzing emotions. She could remember emotions, but they were far away now. She knew that she ought to care that the nurses hated her, avoided her, and that the doctors had only cursorily explained what had happened. But the feeling of empathy, the sense that she should yawn when someone else did, was only a fact on a piece of paper. Not something she actually felt.

She didn't need to eat, either, and her undead body seemed simpler than it had been while strictly alive. She did, however, keep dreaming of pomegranate seeds. On her first shopping expedition she had loaded her refrigerator with packages of the seeds. They made her happy. She liked the way they turned her lips, which had lightened to a medium blue color, dark purple again.

She also craved noodley soup, salty and the hotter the better, and she would order out once a day for a delivery. Other than those two desires, the old intensity of focus she remembered of eating and sleeping–maintaining your wetware meat body–seemed pointless. She felt sorry for people trapped in the conformity of life.

The nurses had called her "undead." And "zombie."

Trying to figure out what that meant, she watched a couple of zombie movies she remembered from before and decided of the mindless hordes of living appetites, "Wow, those guys are stupid."

Her AI seemed to agree, flashing an image of a zombie chewing on its own arm, and the sound of laughter.

She certainly wasn't a werewolf or a ghost or mummy, either. She researched vampires, too, but the whole Goth European aristocrat vibe was so not her thing. Also, she didn't crave blood, having the dirt of her homeland in her bed, or seem to need anything other than an occasional nap. So she deemed any "undead" she had ever heard of before irrelevant, at least as far as the "What am I?" question was concerned.

The AI software in her head, which felt like its own separate personality, still fed her images of combat scenarios in which she was killing hard targets–especially world leaders and heads of large corporations. One time, she zoned out to a scenario where she was stalking and assassinating a famous European pop star through a concert venue, and when she woke, she couldn't get the tunes from an incessant playlist of that singer's music out of her head. It generally made her **WANT** to assassinate that singer. She kind of hoped the contract would happen.

Basically any target someone could want assassinated, she knew how to make that happen. Getting used to the upgrades and scenarios in her head was helped by not having a real life; no one ever visited her. She vaguely remembered family, her sister crying with her after her parents died, but since none of them ever called or came by, she assumed everyone she had known all thought she was really dead.

Who cares? Killing targets seemed fun. She wanted to get to do that. It was her dream job. Literally. As she thought of the truth of that, she snorted laughter and soup out of her nose. Which only made her laugh harder.

Every night she dreamt of multiple moments when someone was standing in front of her and she assessed their weak points. Snap their throat here, plunge a knife there. It was fascinating how many ways existed to kill a person in an instant. Now that she was undead, she found that she didn't care very much about that tenuous grasp humans have on life. It slipped away so easily; why should it be so valuable?

The chip in her head delivered the goods she had been promised. It was integrated with combat knowledge from thousands of years of training, from early martial arts to Greco-Roman combat and all the way up to close-quarters-combat styles of the trench warfare of the 20th century such as Defendu and Krav Maga. The AI demonstrated video of the best defensive knife versus sword positions, how to turn a battle where you were knocked to the ground into your upper hand rather than your loss. Everything available about firearms, every kind, was detailed in yet another video.

But it wasn't just images; she could practically hold them in her hands, stroke their shiny grips. Touch the people she simulated killing, feel their fear.

Fascinating.

The AI in her head filled every thoughtful moment with another detail, and she felt she must have the most comprehensive assassin's database on the planet. She would enjoy trying it all out. But society (the AI informed her; she personally was getting pretty fuzzy on the details about why it mattered) would frown on her actually making someone else fully dead or undead without permission. She had no real-world practice, and so far hadn't found a paying gig, either.

The impulse to get the assassin upgrade had come one day out of the blue when she was watching old movies about fighters trying to make their way out of a strange dystopian arena. The girl in the movie was amazing at using a bow and arrow. Undead Girl had wanted to learn how to do that without having to train for years of her life. She thought of the savings account full of money from her inheritance, and she used it to pay her way into what was supposed to be a new life.

Now that her unlife was entirely different from expectations, the teacher in her head seemed almost destiny-driven, as though it had always been there, just woken up by the surgery.

She found a website where guns were for sale and sometimes she fell asleep as she scrolled through the pages, scanning them, tasting copper in her mouth and feeling the pulse and shock of a gun's report. There was one AK-47 bedazzled with rhinestones and a kitty cat with no mouth. It was pink, girly. That made her laugh, and she entertained what she would look like holding it for a moment, but dismissed it because it would draw too much attention.

When she woke, her hands felt empty, itchy, the way a missing limb could have phantom pains. Even though she had fully functional nanotech bionic arms with the strength of twenty men, she knew she was missing some last piece. After one of these naps, she woke with the image of the gun she wanted: a square laser-based shock pistol, pulsing green energy, coiled heat. A single blast to the right spot would render a target incapable of movement when set on the easiest setting, fatal if set higher.

Turn it up to eleven, she laughed. Her AI was also equipped with all the pop culture references a cyborg assassin could want. Either that or she had been a nerd before. She couldn't quite remember. It didn't seem relevant.

She ordered a simple, black, squared-off gun from the website, chose three- to five-day shipping. She had money saved up but worried that it would run out before she found work. Also, since she was undead, she had no idea how long that money needed to last. How long do the undead "live?" The AI program, that was supposed to be non-judgmental but sometimes reminded her of a favorite surly teacher she had in middle school, informed her that the gun she ordered was a great choice, especially at that price, and used by many law enforcement agencies and the military. The chip offered more opinions lately, and fewer dispassionate virtual lessons. Everyone else had hated that teacher but now, with a version of him in her head, Undead Girl realized she had missed him.

She needed a job. How did one get a job? The AI had no suggestions. In the accident that made her an undead cyborg instead of a simple living one, the job-finding tutorial part of its coding had been corrupted. It seemed super weird that this big life-change upgrade hadn't considered adding that aspect to her programming, but she was stuck thinking about it all in terms of her old life. Or maybe she should research it.

She looked it up on the Internet, found cyborg professional organizations, résumé help, forms to fill out. It took her about a week, and the cans of pomegranate juice piled up next to her monitor. After filing the last application form, she looked around her loft apartment and felt lonely. She thought maybe she should get a cat, but then wondered why she thought that? Cats were interesting, but they were alive. Being alive seemed an awful lot of maintenance. Was it worth the hassle?

***

Hardware

You can mass-produce hardware; you cannot mass-produce software–you cannot mass-produce the human mind. ~Michio Kaku

Reading computer manuals without the hardware is as frustrating as reading sex manuals without the software. ~Arthur C. Clarke

She walked down the street with the color red foremost in her mind. It was as though in finally deciding to buy the gun, the one she envisioned in her hand, her arm outstretched and ready, her mind had freed itself for dreaming of other things.

Red was everywhere: fruit, lips, blood.

Her apartment lacked the color and she decided she must have it. There should be soft red surfaces everywhere. She didn't know why her life had been so beige–beige blankets, a brown couch, white walls. She began to wonder how her body, so fragile and simple before, had survived death on the surgical table. What was special about her?

She was still trying to figure it out, still lying in her bed lazy with dreams of apples, and red grapes, and red fuzzy starfish she had seen somewhere (*Where? When?*) when her computer "pinged" an email's arrival.

You could be undead, you could be a cyborg out-of-work assassin waiting for delivery of your new gun and you'd still get SPAM and newsletters you hadn't actually meant to sign up for.

Some of them would write every day, letters addressed to her but which she knew were from some kind of automated email address field. An AI selecting her because of a cookie on her computer's web browser. "You read an ad for these kinds of boots; other people who like ugly boots also enjoy reading about these things!"

Targeted marketing doesn't care if you're undead.

She sighed, which was odd because she didn't need to breathe anymore but she did still make that gesture when annoyed. She got up to her computer and opened her email, which she had set up, bored and planning big things, a few days ago. She didn't know who could be emailing her because she hadn't shared her new address with anyone.

But maybe this was a job offer! Or a note about her gun's shipment status!

undeadgirl@email.com

Dear undeadgirl:

Did you ever wonder why you have been dreaming about the color red? Did you wonder why you died and came back from wherever we go? Did you even ever wonder why you wanted to get a cyborg upgrade in the first place?

Reply with your phone number to this message and we'll tell you where to find the rabbit hole. (Yes. Just like in that movie.)

Love,

The Ghost in the Machine

Interesting. The rest of her inbox was filled with random adverts from the job seeking websites she had signed up for in a binge of enthusiasm two days ago, nothing specific, all emails promising big results but no actual jobs. A few of them offered to teach her all the secrets of getting a job at the low low cost of only more than her bank account could afford with this helpful web-based time-share seminar!

But no job offers. Not even any nibbles.

The AI offered up a picture of a stark desert landscape. Undead Girl silently agreed. She realized she'd come to think of the AI in her head as a different person, almost a roommate. Strange, but then again, maybe not.

Still feeling as though there was a lack in her life, she thought about setting up a dating profile but who would she choose, and how to explain her look? Plus, the thought of any kind of romantic encounter left her wondering exactly if her undead parts would still work the right way, and then that felt wrong. She felt like she was missing some kind of OS software update: Undead Sex 1.0, available today! She couldn't imagine any of the hunky guys on the website's ads kissing her.

Frankly, it was depressing.

She worried: as someone undead, she didn't know what kind of legal status she had. The manuals in her AI had no help to offer. They were all for living cyborgs.

Do the undead have any civil rights?

Cyborgs did. The Three Laws of Robot Behavior, and the Robotic Life Convention hosted by the UN a few years ago had guaranteed them protections. Robots and AI of all kind had lobbied to be included in a new, very specific bit of legislative legalese about the place for sentient life on the planet. Heck, that treaty included dolphins! And whales! And strangely enough, pigs!

But undead cyborg girls–well, what was she? She had to wonder whether she fell into the category of sentient AI, given that an AI computer chip was what "woke" her back up after she had been dead for a legally acceptable time, and after her heartbeat raced at 30 beats per minute, when she was excited. Her body temperature had leveled off at exactly 78 degrees F. She didn't know if there were any others similar to her (the doctors, worried about potential class action lawsuits, had not shared any information about that), but she had her suspicions.

Keyword searching "undead groups in my area" only brought up a bunch of cosplayer groups which looked fun, but weren't exactly what she needed to know about.

As she sat there, pondering the impossibility of her existence as an AI, her email box pinged. She idly opened the e-mail, thinking about red silky blankets and cold fruit, and found:

To: undeadgirl@email.com

From: UFAIL-U (Universal Federation of Artificial Intelligence Labor-Union)

President: JS 2000, AI, Robotics Commission, Sebastian Industries

Re: your recent application to join the UFAIL-U chapter of New City (chapter #42asff) as a "Cyborg Assassin, Grade B"

Dear Ms. Deadgirl:

We regret to inform you that your recent submission of an application for membership to your local Assassin's union has been <u>denied</u> based on <u>the death certificate on record at the Liberty Hospital and Surgical Center.</u> Membership to the UFAIL-U is only granted to human living and/or sentient intelligent robotic life forms. If you feel this decision has been made in error, the attachment to this notice will provide a list of steps to take to correct the application process. Thank you for your interest in the UFAIL-U.

Cordially, JS 2000

Attachment: FAQ.pdf

CC: Sebastian Industries

She stared at the email for the longest time, sitting there looking at the words "death certificate on record" on the computer screen. How and why would there be a death certificate? She was breathing (well, a few times every once in awhile, when she remembered). She was sort of alive. Granted, she had never met anyone similar to herself before and the doctors and nurses at the Clinic had not been able to explain to her satisfaction what had happened to her. But she wasn't dead.

Compounding that was also the detail that since her "death" in surgery a month ago her hair had grown back at an amazing rate. They had cut most of it off for the brain surgery but now it hung well down her back, the longest her hair had ever been. Pure white, and softer than she remembered it being before. (Although to be honest, those "living" memories were fading. She had to work to remember her own name sometimes). Did a dead person's hair grow? But that wasn't a good argument to make against a bureaucratic, arrogant AI.

She was going to have to dispute the death certificate. Somehow. She couldn't work without belonging to the Union. No way she wanted to be a (she queried the AI: *what was the word?*) scab. She did not want to piss off The Assassin's Union or she might wake up even deader than she already was. The thought made her laugh. She laughed until her stomach hurt.

She resolved to get a cat after all. All this laughing alone in her apartment was too emo, even for an undead out of work cyborg assassin.

And those dating profiles were disturbing.

***

Two Weeks Later
Every revolution evaporates and leaves behind only the slime of a new bureaucracy. ~ Franz Kafka

Bureaucracy, the rule of no one, has become the modern form of despotism. ~ Mary McCarthy

She still hadn't heard back from the Union on her appeals letters, which she had filled out meticulously three times because the computer kept crashing the instant she submitted the forms. The relative instability of computers, which she had never noticed before, made her worry about her AI cy-tech.

After checking her email obsessively for the fifth time in the last ten minutes, Undead Girl decided to go out. The shiny assassin's gun was tucked away in her bedroom closet, away from the curious and sharp claws of her new black girl kitten, whom she had named Conjurer. The name seemed appropriate, although Undead Girl couldn't remember why. Her past, before she had died, was fading more every day. She didn't miss it.

But today, she felt a longing for something. Maybe it was the lack of a job, maybe it was human contact. She didn't know.

She did, however, remember liking coffee.

Black, rich espresso with steamed milk and two real sugars.

She made her way to the shop down the street, the one with the green sign. Its mermaid logo's siren-song blasted loud and clear. The AI offered selections from various movies about mermaids, three short audio fairytales, and a YouTube of a group of professional performing mermaids in bright colors. Undead Girl dismissed the offerings with a subvocal "Shhhh." The AI sent one last picture of a cat sticking its tongue out at her before quieting and she smiled.

Standing in line to place her order, she was enjoying the present-tense feeling of being surrounded by the smell of freshly brewed coffee, the bustle of people chatting, writing, meeting each other and doing those weird air kisses next to each other's faces.

Lost in her thoughts, she didn't notice the line had moved until, from behind her, she heard, "Hey, Zombitch, move your skinny ass!"

Zombitch? Really?

Undead Girl looked side-eyed at the woman behind her who glared back. The AI offered up a picture of a tree with lots of shaded area underneath, and that didn't make any sense to her.

So used to her own pale-gray pallor in her mirror at home, it shocked Undead Girl how red and puffy the woman behind her seemed. Also, she was offended. She wasn't a zombie, thank you very much. She re-examined her inner cravings and found that there was nothing at all about the culinary delights of braaaaiiiins in there. Only an intense desire for coffee and the beginning of a headache.

She scooted forward in the line, placed her order, and heard the woman behind her muttering again about, "Skinny gray emo zombitches with too much eyeliner."

Well, that was the last straw.

"This isn't eyeliner."

"What?" The woman seemed taken aback that she had been heard. But really, she didn't need super assassin AI skills to hear someone muttering right behind her.

"I said this isn't eyeliner. And calling me a Zombitch is rude."

The woman sputtered, "I didn't say anything." She stepped a few steps backwards, almost bumped into the person behind her.

The line was restless, and the cashier waited for the next order, clearing her throat to encourage the budding altercation to move along. Undead Girl wondered...squinted her eyes and looked at the now-even-redder-faced woman.

Then she heard: *Shit. How did she know what I was thinking?*

But since she was watching now, she saw no lip movement, though the woman was freaked out, eyes widening when she realized that Undead Girl could still hear her thoughts.

OH. *So now my undead powers extend to mind-reading,* Undead Girl thought. *That's new.*

Undead Girl turned back to the cashier, trying to ignore the woman behind her who was still freaking out as she thought, *Did I say that out loud? This emo bitch is going to hurt me...*

This is why I don't go out, thought Undead Girl. *I'll get my coffee and go back home.*

They both pretended nothing had happened and Undead Girl paid for her coffee and shuffled–not zombie like though. Just, customer like–over to wait for her coffee's delivery.

The cute barista, a petite girl who had a small hoop earring in her nose, skin naturally brown (a soft-touch, young fawn-color) dark eyes, and dark spiky hair winked at her and handed her the coffee order. She'd written "Zombitch" on the cup in Sharpie, along with a smiley face, but with a tongue protruding and two "X"s where the eyes should be. A little dead smiley face. She must have heard the altercation at the cashier desk.

Great. A nickname. How did this kind of stuff happen to her?

But to be honest–if she really thought about it–she liked it. And the cute heart... What did that mean?

Oh...Wow.

Undead Girl pondered what she was feeling about the whole situation. She felt kind of, tingly? Excited?

Her memory of the past before she became undead was pretty hazy, and the AI chip kept suggesting ways that she could have snapped the line lady's neck (swift flexion, extension with rotation, brutally strong quick force). It argued with itself the force required was really a lot, it would be easier to slam her head against the counter...or maybe just crush her windpipe...

Great. Now the AI in her head was arguing with itself.

But she slowly walked away from the counter, stirring sugar into her coffee, and she remembered, thinking of the barista's amazing smile, that she liked girls.

LIKED girls.

She felt butterflies in her stomach, which she couldn't remember happening to her since the surgery, and she glanced back over to see if the barista was looking at her. Then she had to look away again because yes, she was, and yes, she was smiling. It made parts of her she hadn't thought of in a while wake up. The AI offered video–which Undead Girl quickly rejected. *Stop that,* she subvocalized.

Undead Girl sipped her coffee and shuffl–*NO*–strolled, out, into the waiting afternoon.

The AI sent a picture of birds and bees, and flowers, and waves crashing on a beach.

This morning was ever more interesting. Perhaps there would be an encouraging email from the UFAIL-U to top it all off.

A Zombitch could hope, she thought, her step turning into an almost-skip. The smile on her face, which was both happy and scary, like a cat who had cornered a tiny mouse, made a few passersby skip a step, doubletake, and then rush away.

When she got home, the kitten was playing on her desktop, batting off all the things that had been on there and were unattached to anything else, onto the floor. Undead Girl moved her gently over to the bed instead and removed the tiny kitten claws from her hand. After situating the kitten with a toy, she went back to her desk and loaded up her email. Sure enough, finally, there was an email from the UFAIL-U.

To: undeadgirl@email.com
From: UFAIL-U (Universal Federation of Artificial Intelligence Labor-Union)
President: JS 2000, AI, Robotics Commission

Re: your recent appeals letter

Dear Ms. Undead Girl:
We have reviewed your recent appeals form regarding your attempts to join the UFAIL-U Assassin's union for your city as a "Cyborg Assassin, Grade B." Unfortunately, our guidelines clearly state that you must be a sentient, living, non-robotic, cybernetically enhanced and/or modified human being to join the union. Since you are classified as "undead" on the official documents that we received, you do not qualify for membership to the Union as current conditions continue. You should consider joining one of the non-Cyborg Assassin unions, or one of the Undead unions.

Please note that we reviewed your situation carefully and consulted with the experts in the field of your minority status group and did not reach this decision lightly.

We simply do not feel that, at this time, your special needs would be served by our group. Membership in the UFAIL-U is a coveted, very specialized status and we must protect our members, as well as ensuring that you are properly served by a group with your needs in mind.

We know that you have many options for your Union needs and are thankful that you have chosen ours for your job-seeking needs.

We cordially thank you again for your application,
President: JS 2000, AI, Robotics Commission

Well damn.

It was a barely customized form letter, as though someone couldn't be bothered to take the time to reject her personally.

Undead Girl removed the kitten, who had abandoned her toy and currently gnawed at her ankle, tiny needle-sharp teeth not really hurting but causing black nicks in the flesh that experience had already taught her would take forever to heal. And would linger with an oozy blood a much darker shade than she remembered her blood being before. The kitten fought with ferocious strength and hurled herself back onto the bed where she proceeded to pounce the pillow and do battle with the covers, left untucked and messy.

Undead Girl was tempted to crawl back into the covers. The letter was that disheartening.

It had taken her hours to figure out where to find the death certificate filled out by an overworked nurse at the clinic. And more to convince the nurses at the records department that she was, indeed, authorized to have a copy. Then it had taken hours fill the forms out, upload them to the requests division of the UFAIL-U. This refusal meant she still couldn't list her membership in an official union on her job application profiles on any of the job seekers websites.

Dammit! She had searched for undead unions. It seemed that her demographic was so very small, or possibly non-existent, or trying to lie low and not attract unwanted villagers with torches and pitchforks, that any organizations related to her "minority status" were completely hidden. Impossible to find.

Undead Girl leaned her head on her hands and pondered the problems of proving her humanity. Dead, living, and sentient, AI, cyborg--you name it, she needed the category. All of these things seemed easy until you combined them. Then it became a big old keywording mess.

All she wanted to do was get a job, travel, see the sights of the world and known universe and perhaps kill a few deserving heads of state here and there. Take in a movie afterwards, or drinks with friends. But here she was, instead, watching a tiny fuzzball of a black kitten rip a paper bag to shreds. So she sent a frustrated, ranting reply, on a whim, back to the Union.

Afterwards, she realized that it probably wasn't her best idea.

So-called President: JS 2000

I can't believe you have denied my application again. Do you realize how absurd it is to be told you don't qualify to any of your own demographic groups? And you're supposed to be an AI. I have an AI chip in my brain that would tell me how exactly to destroy you were you to be someone I was hired to do so, and this is documented by the exact paperwork you're using to disprove my membership! Who did you consult with in "my status group?" Because I haven't been able to find anyone who is an expert on me. Not even me!

How about a little solidarity? I can't apply for jobs without one of these memberships! For the record: there are no undead unions. I don't know if there are any other undead humans, let alone enough of them to create and fill out a whole union roster!

You are the least Intelligent AI that I have ever met.

Sincerely, but not with regards,

Undead Girl

She hit send and immediately regretted the decision.

Why is there no "Take Back" button on an email?

She didn't know how long it would take but she had the distinct feeling that something bad was about to happen.

Great. Now not only am I an unemployed undead hit woman, I have just pissed off an AI who is in charge of hundreds of certified Assassins.

I should go back to bed.

The kitten, however, settled the decision by pulling over a pile of clothes that had been folded at the end of her couch since she got back from the Clinic. She rarely wore anything other than the black bodysuit they gave her when she was discharged from the hospital. It was comfortable, and the needs and goals of fashion struck her as stupid now. She didn't know why she still kept those old clothes. It felt as if they belonged to someone else. But now they were in a mess on the floor.

She was OCD about messes, so as she was cleaning up, debating throwing away a floral sundress that would clash terribly with her current skin tone and pretty much everything about her life now, the "ping" of an arriving email pulled her back to her computer.

undeadgirl@email.com

Dear undeadgirl:

Oh boy. Now you've done it! Did you know that the JS2000 holds grudges you wouldn't believe, and has a real inferiority complex about the designation 2000? It feels it should have a much higher number and hates being called stupid.

You still haven't asked me how I know how you became undead. Or even about the color red. Still craving it?

I know all about you. Remember, I am: The Ghost in the Machine

p.s. that barista IS cute.

She looked carefully around her apartment for signs of surveillance. A camera, a bug. Looked at the window and opened and closed the shades, to see if anyone was watching from nearby apartments.

As far as she could tell, there was no one peeping at her. So who kept sending her these "ghost" emails? And how did they know what she had been thinking about the (admittedly cute) barista? Or was it the same way she had been able to "hear" what that woman at the coffee shop was thinking? Mind-reading?

This ghost in the machine: could it be another undead?

She was about to write a reply, her hand hovering the mouse over the arrow on her email, when another incoming message stopped her. It was from JS 2000. If she had moisture in her mouth before, it would have gone completely dry at this point. Her heartbeat at an almost normal 50 BPM felt as though it was racing. Her cheeks felt hot, in what she remembered was a "blush."

The subject field did not look promising.

Re: What the hell did you just say to me?!!!

The number of exclamation points was worrying. Not to mention the fact that an AI in charge of the very union she needed to join had cursed at her.

Was she going to have to assassinate the president of the union in order to get someone to give her union position? The AI in her head sent her the plot of a novel called Catch 22. She scanned it, but wasn't sure which character she was supposed to be. The AI then sent images of a man called "Gregor Samsa" and suggested she read a book called *The Metamorphosis*. It didn't look very much like something she wanted to read right now. So the AI sent her a book called *The Very Hungry Caterpillar*. She was starting to think her AI was over-programmed for sarcasm.

She sighed and clicked the email open. All that it said was:

"Dear" Undead Girl:
You. Are. Finished.
JS 2000.

This was followed by a bunch of rather insulting tiny cartoon images. Emoji? She had no idea how the JS 2000 had found an emoji of someone with their head up their butt.

Almost immediately, hundreds of emails began to flood her inbox from SPAM sources, including explicit porn advertisements, diet remedies, "Increase your Member Size," and "You'll Never Believe What Secret This Celebrity is Hiding" clickbait.

It wasn't exactly nuclear war or a hostile takeover, but the emails filling her inbox would need to be deleted, and she could miss something important. The emails kept coming. By the time she clicked the "x" on the corner of her email program, the number of new emails shot up into six figures.

So it was a bad idea to insult an AI with micro-processing time to kill and the ability to multitask.

I must be on every spammer mailing list on the planet by now, she sighed.

It was going to be so hard to get a job when this bogus designation of being "minority status" meant her application wasn't being considered. She couldn't get into the union, she couldn't get an appeal of a clearly discriminatory practice. Official documents had been filed that she had no control over saying something not exactly true about a state of being that did not have any effect on her potential job performance. She was highly skilled! The assassin's cyborg upgrade had completely done its intended job! Yes, there had been a few side effects, but they were mostly cosmetic in nature and easily overcome.

Now her computer was, of its own volition, downloading massive programs and viruses, and she had no way to stop it. Her mouse wouldn't move and when she tried, a big laughing clown face popped up on the screen.

She unplugged the machine and went to bed. The kitten followed, pouncing on her feet every time she moved. At least she wasn't alone.

**

REDD

Your lips betray the secret of your soul,
The dark delicious essence that is you,
A mystery of life, the flaming goal
I seek through mazy pathways strange and new.

Your lips are the red symbol of a dream,
What visions of warm lilies they impart,
That line the green bank of a fair blue stream,
With butterflies and bees close to each heart!
~from "A Red Flower" by Claude McKay, 1922

In the morning, everything felt hopeless again. She dreamt all night of the color red and wondered what the heck that had to do with anything. She especially wondered why some random email person who kept calling itself "Ghost in the Machine" would know what she dreamt about? The AI kept trying to get her to watch some movie by that title but she had thus far pressed pause. She didn't think a movie from 1993 would help her.

She checked her computer and it was still completely hacked by JS 2000. Now, the clown that had been laughing at her last night was replaced with an animation of a clown systematically cutting the head off of a cartoon version of her. Over and over again.

She still couldn't get her mouse to do anything.

She set her internal Alegis system to synch with the computer when she fled the house but was afraid to log into it, and subvocally disabled the commands. She worried about JS 2000 somehow hacking her brain. She really, really shouldn't have sent that email. Pissing off a bureaucratic and possibly sociopathic AI was probably the dumbest thing she had ever done, and that included the upgrades that had landed her (un)dead, out of work, and apparently the only member of a minority group of one.

The kitten slept in a patch of sunlight by the window and she hated to disturb it, but she was also feeling pretty lonely again so she figured she'd head back to the coffee shop, get a hot drink and a breakfast snack and perhaps use one of the public computer terminals they had there to . . . what? She didn't need to check her email–it would be full of junk from JS 2000. She wouldn't have any job offers because of the same bitchy AI.

Surely, having chocolate with coffee would solve some problem. And she kept thinking of the dreams she had–the color red, in all kinds of repetitions, *flowers, fireworks, silky sheets, birds. Lips.*

She was also thinking of the beautiful barista. Couldn't (and didn't want to) stop.

So she walked to the coffee shop. The street wasn't busy–she lived in a section of town being converted by people with lots of money from a slummy old block of Depression era houses that had been left to decay into expensive remodeled houses with lots of fancy upgrades and stainless steel appliances. Rent increased as the neighborhood improved, but it meant most people in the area were young, urban, unmarried types who got up late if they weren't already at work by now. The AI sent her a joke about "The sound of gentrification" buzzing in the air. She smiled weakly.

The coffee shop bustled with activity, though. It made her wonder if people actually ever used those fancy stainless steel appliances in their houses.

Couldn't they make their own espresso? But she supposed she wasn't one to judge.

No one was sitting in the chair at the moment, but someone was logged in to the computer. She worked her way over to the snaky line; she could see a cup of coffee steaming to one side of her preferred spot, and a muffin with a few crumbly streusel bites out of it. The someone logged in must have stepped into the bathroom or gotten a phone call. They clearly intended to come right back. Well, she didn't need a computer anyway. She wondered idly what kind of policy the corporate coffee place had on hiring undead cyborg-assassins.

Everyone studiously kept their thoughts to themselves today; maybe the psychic thing she had with that crazy woman was because the woman was specifically directing the thoughts at her. When she got to the front of the line, she placed her order and craned her neck to see if the barista who had flirted with her yesterday was working. Sadly for her lack of love-life, the guy behind the espresso machine was cute (short, natural, fro haircut and intricate tattoos snaking up his right arm) but wasn't her type at all. She still smiled at him, causing his sudden-loss-of-nerves fingers to drop the container of milk he was steaming. She placed her coffee order, paid with her rapidly becoming maxed out credit card, and waited for her name to be called.

It seemed to be taking a long time and she stared at the one claimed but unoccupied computer, mentally willing the user to log out and leave it for her use–Maybe some happy cat videos would cheer her up–when she heard someone call out: "Zombitch... coffee for Zombitch."

People in line tittered. A few looked her way; apparently they figured out it was her. Maybe they were here yesterday?

Remembering that this ought to be embarrassing, but not particularly caring, she went up to the spot where the baristas handed out the coffees and saw her white cup with the nickname scrawled on it, and the cute picture of the zombie with xx eyes again. Then she looked and saw the dark haired, fawn-toned girl standing behind the counter and smiling a ridiculously sexy, wicked smile at her. Her stomach did an entire flip. Or at least it felt flippy.

"Sorry," the barista said, not looking very sorry at all. "I know that's kind of rude of me, but when I saw it was your coffee, I had to do it. Scott let me, even though it's not my shift anymore." She gestured at the now smiling guy and moved out of his way for him to get back to work.

"My name's Danni." Undead Girl took the coffee and felt butterflies as Danni followed her to where she could add her sugars (two) and grab a napkin.

"Do you come in here a lot? I've never seen you before the other day."

Undead Girl felt her voice crack as she said yes, she was new to the area. Which was kind of true–though she had been coming in here for years. The mousy, brown-haired girl she used to be wasn't someone this barista would have noticed. She found she was forgetting what her name had been back–was it really only two months ago?

"Do you want to join me at my table?" Danni gestured to the table with the computer terminal, hot coffee and blueberry muffin she had noticed earlier still waiting. "I had to get up to grab the spreadsheet I needed," she explained, smiling at Undead Girl's look. The smile looked hopeful.

They sat down together and Danni smiled again, making Undead Girl need a sip of her coffee, which wasn't too hot or too cold, perfectly foamed, perfectly sugared, to gather her composure. There was a look in her eye, the same one as when she handed her the coffee with Zombitch written on it the first time, a sparkle, like she was going to do something sassy.

"So....you're an undead cyborg, aren't you? Like Deathlocket?"

"What?" The question threw Undead Girl off balance. She spilled her coffee, mopped it up with napkins. It kept her hands busy, and that was good because they were increasingly jittery.

"You know, the Marvel comic? Oh sheesh, was it 2012 when she first appeared?" Danni looked at Undead Girl like maybe somehow she might actually know the answer. For some reason, everything she said was a question. It occurred to Undead Girl that maybe the Barista Girl was nervous, too.

Undead Girl felt her AI, so far completely silent from its usual whirring stream of consciousness of combat images, stir, and then pause, as if thinking. It had been offering up suggestions more often lately on things other than what it was supposed to be programmed for (combat). It sent books, suggestions of what to watch on TV. (Mostly Sci-Fi). Perhaps it, too, was going through a personality change.

After that brief pause, the AI sent a flash-image of a pretty girl, younger than herself, African-American. Short, adorable. *This must be Deathlocket.* Her face was half robot, half human, with a few other robotic looking accessories. The image was unexpected. Why would a comic book character be in the combat database? Her AI did seem to tend to like odd Popular Nerd Culture. What that had to do with being a Cyborg-Assassin, she had no idea.

Maybe Danni was talking about that image. She tentatively said, "Um, yeah? Comic-book super hero? Or is she a villain?"

Danni looked thrilled that Undead Girl seemed interested in talking about it, and went off on a tangent about the issues she'd appeared in, and another character named Deathlock who was older, apparently. (Her AI offered up a pretty impressive picture, unbidden.)

So this was what an out of work cyborg assassin's AI did, she thought, *act like an internal Google database.*

Undead Girl wasn't paying much attention, she was more interested in Danni's eyes, and the way she dropped her eyelids in a way that meant "smoldering heat" every now and then. While Danni pulled up images of her favorite Marvel comics on the computer, Undead Girl caught herself playing with her long, white blonde hair. She squashed the idea that came to her that she'd rather run her fingers through Danni's. Even with the gaps in her "Sex 1.0 OS manual," that seemed a little fast.

It seemed ridiculous to be suddenly thrust into a teen after school movie having a crush on the barista down the street. Undead Girl finished her coffee and thought about going home.

She just–didn't want to.

The kitten had eaten and would sleep all morning, resting up to attack her feet all night. And she had never meant to be home this much. She was supposed to be this big deal cyborg assassin chasing all over the planet to kill the bad guys and have martinis with James Bond before swooping off to the next adventure. Pop song swelling over the speakers while the credits rolled.

And then Danni said, "You've heard of REDD, right?"

That got both her and her AI's attention. Images in red–

Strawberries

Flowers
Stars Exploding
Satin Sheets
Blood
Pomegranates
Fireworks
Ladybugs
Kissing lips

–flashed through her head. Undead Girl wasn't sure anymore who thought this–the AI or her. "What?"

"REDD. The group. You know, surReal Existences Dead and Divine? The local undead and supernatural chapter. I do their bookkeeping. I can totally introduce you to them; they can help with the problem you've been having with JS 2000. I think they also sometimes go by the catchphrase Ghost in the Machine. There used to be a flyer on the cork-board..." Danni looked around, to see if that flyer was still there, but didn't seem in a hurry to jump up and look for it, either.

"What?" Undead Girl repeated. Not exactly original, but it was all she could think of. (She didn't process that she hadn't told Danni about JS 2000, yet.) Here, this... this gorgeous woman was telling her exactly what she had been looking for. There was someone else like her! Some group that had an acronym and everything!

"REDD?"

Then her AI or her brain or whatever the hell suggested that maybe that's why she kept dreaming about the color...somehow this Ghost in the Machine had taken control of her dreams...scary but exciting.

Was it hacking her AI? Is that why it told her things other than the designated combat protocols of the Assassin's upgrade?

Danni looked at her expectantly. She had asked some kind of question while Undead Girl's mind whirled through thoughts of demonic possession by a cybernetic ghost hacker.

Could you call an exorcist for that? *Shit.* Usually people called an exorcist for things like her.

"Could you repeat the question?" Undead Girl asked. Her heart beat so fast it felt almost alive again, and her face must have looked different too because Danni said, "Are you okay?"

She reached out a hand to where Undead Girl fluttered her fingers, nervous and agitated, and gently held on. It was the most soothing yet hottest thing Undead Girl could remember.

The AI reminded her that she couldn't remember much past a month and she told her—it—to shut the hell up. The AI sulked. How could it sulk?

Too much was going on in her head and Danni still looked concerned, but smiling-concerned.

"Ohhhkay. Ummmm. If you're alright, then. If you'd be interested. I hope you'll be interested in going...with me."

Undead Girl smiled and said something stupid back, rambling about trying to get a job, and her new kitten, and a gush of all the things that had been happening the last few days.

Finally, someone who not only seemed to really like her but who had information she had been looking for. Danni wasn't a heroic rescuer and it was an intro to some resource group; it was unlikely to save her life. She also wasn't a damsel in distress. Far from it. But this was a connection.

Undead Girl couldn't stop talking, and the gush of words coming out of her mouth amazed her.

Danni still held her hand, and then reached up with the other hand and touched her face to stop her from talking.

It worked.

"Oh, your skin is cool. I thought it would be. I love that."

Undead Girl's heart actually stopped for a moment.

Danni, unaware of the effect and also completely unembarrassed, said, "Is it okay if..." and leaned forward. It was clear she meant to give Undead Girl a kiss.

Her heart started back up. She said, "Yes," so softly anyone nearby wouldn't have been able to hear the whisper, but Danni did.

And so she kissed her, the first kiss, a little early in their courtship, yeah, but still innocent and sweet. A gentle, soothing kiss. She lingered for a moment, eyes still closed, the empty coffee cups between them on the scarred wooden tabletop. The sun shone crazy-hot through the window and the computer had been ignored so long that the screen lock had come on.

Danni opened her eyes then, and said, "What's your name, by the way? I would call you a goddess but that would be a little crazier than even I am. I can't believe I kissed you before I asked that question, but it seemed..." she let the comment hang, the ending obvious, and Danni pushed the long white bangs out of Undead Girl's eyes.

My name?

Undead Girl thought for a moment. Then she smiled. Danni smiled back; the kind of smile you have to respond to, and the energy between them arced back and forth, endless waves building upon each other. She couldn't believe she had just been kissed in the middle of a coffee shop, and all of her dreamy fantasies were on the tip of her fingers. So she said the first thing that she could think of. The thing that had been on her mind every time she'd dreamed lately.

"My name is Red."

***

ABOUT THE AUTHOR:

Kim Wells has a Ph.D. in Literature, with specialties in American Lit, Women Writers, Feminism, Sci-Fi/Fantasy & Film Studies but please don't hold any of that against her. She used to teach academic writing and how to read literature at a university in her hometown and tried to convince college students that it really is cool to like poetry. She has written two full length novels, both Magic Southern Slipstream and several shorts which will find their way into longer stories eventually.

She lives in the South, has twin children (one girl, one boy) and a husband who is the model for all her best romantic heroes. She also has two cats–one black and sassy, one stripey and fat, and also kinda sassy. Check her out at http://www.kimwells.net/ or on Facebook at https://www.facebook.com/kimwellswrites

If you enjoyed Undead Cyborg Girl, you'll be pleased to hear that there will soon be two more installments to Red and Danni's story. They'll meet her tribe (the appropriately acronym'd REDD group) and get to know more of the local Cyborg Assassins in "Red," and then go on some pretty fun adventures in "Tribe".

Don't Touch Me
by Bey Deckard

Breathe.
> *Remember to breathe.*
> *Keep eye contact.*
> *Breathe.*
> *Keep moving.*
> *Stay out of reach.*
> *Protect your head.*
> *Breathe.*

Those are the thoughts going through my head as I bounce on the balls of my feet even though I'm so fucking exhausted and in so much pain I'm not seeing straight. The man I'm up against always gives himself away before a move, and I'm watching for the sign like it's my last hope. Lean and mean, he goes by the name King Cobra because they say he strikes like a snake, quick and deadly. I think the name's bullshit. He's just tall. Taller than me. It's the only reason he's in my weight class. But it means he's got a helluva reach—

that's why he downs so many guys. Nothing to do with snakes.

I take a quick jab to the abdomen, but manage to send him back with a kick. I clamp down on the pain. Bury it.

Breathe.

There's a drop of sweat on the end of my nose. It moves every time I take a breath, tickling me. I shake my head and send the drop flying. *Focus.* I gotta stay out of range of those long arms; otherwise he's gonna pin me against the cage. Worse, grapple me down to the floor. The thought of him pushed up against me makes me want to puke. The surge of adrenaline shoots me forward for a bit of dirty boxing. I'm in and out before he can do more than slam his elbow into my shoulder.

Breathe.

I bite down on my mouth guard. My breathing sounds like static. I hurt everywhere, but I'm wearing him down. I gotta wear him down.

Then I see it. He's about to lash out. My body moves on its own before I register it. I jump back, dodging one fist but still take a hard punch to the side. Can't be helped. The sound of him bruising my meat is like a wet slap, but his fist ends up out there like a spent bullet. Before he can pull it back or use the other, I spin around and back-fist him as hard as I fucking can.

The mat shakes with force of his fall. I dance back, heart pounding.

A risky move. He could've got me. He could've grabbed me with those big sweaty mitts and covered my skin with a mountain of flesh.

Breathe. Hide the terror. He didn't get you.

The roar of the crowd is a tidal wave of noise. King Cobra's not getting up.

Fear. My secret weapon. That's why *I* down so many guys.

The ref reaches for my arm, but I growl at him and he steps back. I see him recover, remembering what he was told *not* to do. He just lifts his own arm and I mimic. The crowd is a sea of howling faces. Like animals. Patting each other on the back for my win. Fuckers.

Then I see her. My angel. A spot of pastel color in the swarming dark. Hands clasped under her chin, I can almost make out the tears in her big blue eyes. My Suzy.

I always tell her not to come. She never listens. Stubborn as I am. She's the only one who knows what fighting does to me. I hate it that she watches me, but I'd be lying if I said it don't make me feel better knowing she's there.

***

Another night, another fight. This one's in a warehouse. It smells like tar and metal, and it's cold as a witch's tit in here. Illegal fighting is risky, but I see at least two cops slumming it in the crowd. I figure my ass is covered.

I jump around on the balls of my feet. Throw a few practice punches at the air. The mat is cracked in places, and instead of a cage there's ropes. Fine with me. Easier to get away from ropes.

Out of the corner of my eye, I see something bright against the grimy black coats of the men. My angel. She shouldn't be here, not around these assholes. Suzy meets my eye and gives me a little nod. She's so pretty. So fucking pretty.

That old sadness comes crawling back, and I stuff it deep into my guts. No point in thinking of *that*. Not when there's a fight to be won.

Head in the game.

The guy who ducks into the ring is a huge fella, and I lock eyes with him like I wanna tear his throat out. Sometimes it's the big guys who are easiest to take down. They're also the ones who can pin me under their weight. This is dirty fighting. No weight class. No rules except "try not to kill your opponent."

You can do it. Just get through the fight.

Don't let him get you.

Breathe.

He doesn't blink, just stares at me, lip curled like he knows something I don't. The ref is a new guy, and he slurs through our intro like he's had one too many. Then it's show time.

Immediately, I know I'm in trouble. No matter how I bob and weave, jump back and spin, his fists find me. Each one's a sledgehammer of pain. I can't escape. He's everywhere at once, and when his skin meets mine, it's like there's a ratchet tightening the fear and disgust around me like a belt, choking my breath off. Nausea sits like a cool puddle of grease in my belly.

Breathe.

I try for a risky move: a sweep even though he's solid on two feet. But it's all I got. Though it catches him off-guard and makes him shift, I'm not fast enough to land a punch before he recovers.

I made a mistake. I'm too close. Instead of swinging those clubs again, he ducks and grabs me around the waist, slamming me down to the mat.

The wind's knocked out of me for a second and my senses are *screaming.* He's on top of me, his skin suffocating mine. Fear brings on fury, nausea becomes rage. Every part of me is so hell-bent on getting away from him that I could probably lift a car in this state. Berserker power feeding off terror.

With a crazed howl, I flip him over and elbow him hard in the face. Once. Twice. I've almost managed a third time before he gets his knee up high enough to shove me off. Then, like a rabid dog, he comes after me again, dragging me back down. My forearm snaps under his knee, and I yell through clenched teeth. His fist flattens my nose, my head bouncing off the mat. What I've gotta do goes against all my instincts to flee, but it's the only fucking way I'll win. Or survive.

I pivot my hips, my strength like a drowning man's, and cage him between my thighs. Skin to skin, it's a fucking nightmare, but I hold on. Locked together, I crush him while he bashes my face in, the punches barely registering.

Breathe. I can't breathe.

Is it my fear that's making the world go dark, or the pain? I think I'm gonna retch. But then I see my chance, and I take it. One quick shift that leaves me open to another brutal punch to the face, but I got him by the neck...and I *squeeze*.

It's over.

Lying on the mat. Voices. Eyes half-closed, I watch them drag the guy away. Someone touches my arm and I have a spasm, curling in on myself like a pill bug. Doesn't matter who they are or what they want, my bladder's gonna give because I can't take no more.

But then I hear *her.*

"No! *Don't you fucking touch him*! Jesus fucking Christ will you get out of the fucking way? Back off!"

Suzy. My angel. She's got a mouth on her. It brings me out of my shell a bit.

"If you're gonna touch him, the least you can fucking do is put on a pair of fucking gloves!" As if everyone knows about it.

She kneels next to my head, still swearing at the men to stay away. I hate being like this. Suzy can help. Suzy always helps.

"Beau, you okay honey?" She makes it sound like we're the only two in the room. "Can you get up?"

I nod. If she wants me to get up, I'll get up. I'll do anything she says. Weak as a kitten, I sit up, holding my broken arm against my chest. They're gonna have to sedate me to get a cast on it. I can't go through it awake. I pull out my mouth guard and scowl at the men standing around us like the big rocks at Stonehenge. They're annoyed. I can tell. Probably lost some cash, but it's not my fucking problem.

Besides, by the time the next fight ends in blood and pain, they'll have forgotten me anyway. I'm just another gladiator in the ring.

Finally I'm on my feet, and even before Suzy and I get to the door they're calling the next match.

I crawl into the backseat of Suzy's Civic and lay down.

"I wish you'd give it up," says Suzy, like she always does. But the wad of cash in her pocket probably feels good, and I'm glad I put it there. She just starts the car and gets going. We'll be at the hospital soon.

"You gotta tell them to knock me out," I mumble. My voice is all weird because I can't breathe out my nose. I know I'm getting blood on her seats, but she never seems to mind.

"I know. Don't you think I know?" She sounds annoyed. She's just worried about me. I hear a click and then a crackle when she lights up an American Spirit. The smoke finds me in the back. She wishes I'd stop fighting; I wish she'd stop with the cancer sticks. "Jesus, Beau, I thought that guy was gonna do you in good this time."

Me too.

"He didn't."

She takes a few drags, corners too sharply, and jerks the car to a stop at a light. Suzy's a terrible fucking driver, but I'd rather be here than with anyone else in the world. She's my guardian angel, even if she drives an automatic with both feet.

I know we're at the hospital by how steep the road gets. Another slam on the brakes jostles me back hard against the seat, and I wince at the fucking pain in my arm.

Worse than that, though, is the fear. It's building up again. The waiting room. Too many people. Nurses and doctors, swarming around.

"They can't touch me until I'm out. Promise me, Suzy."

"Don't worry, big guy. Promise, cross my heart no one's gonna touch you."

"You got my papers?" I got a bunch of scribbles from some shrink saying I need special treatment because I got PTSD from my tour in Afghanistan. It's bullshit, of course. What I got ain't nothing like that.

"I have your papers. How many times have I done this for you?"

"Okay." My heart's going at it again. Picking up speed. I can't help it.

"Really, Beau," Suzy says, looking over the back of the seat at me. She's got eyes like you see on a doll, huge and baby blue. "Everything'll be okay. Just relax."

I nod, but we both know that's impossible for me.

***

I'm watching Suzy through the little kitchen pass-through while sitting in the old La-Z-Boy with a beer in my hand. Her blonde bangs are damp and sticking to her forehead from the heat of the stove. She's making spaghetti. Suzy makes three things: spaghetti, fried chicken, and shepherd's pie. Spaghetti night's my favorite. She always mixes in a can of mushrooms with the store brand sauce I like. Makes it special. I smile when she notices me looking at her, and she smiles back. But it makes me hurt a little inside.

Suzy and I've known each other since we were kids. We grew up three doors apart in the same shitty slice of the city, playing together in the back alley behind the row houses. I think she's the only person left alive who really believes me about my condition. Well, at least she's never said anything that would make me think otherwise. Not like those other kids who always teased me and called me a liar, even when I was crying like a baby from them laying their hands on me. She just accepted the truth and made sure that I didn't get bumped in our games.

I think I've loved her all my life.

The doctors don't know what's wrong with me. They all seem to think it's in my head. Or from getting shot back in '04. But I've been like this for as long as can I remember. Mama said when I was born, the first thing I did was push her away, screaming like my skin was on fire.

It doesn't hurt. Nothing like that. Just seems that all those nice things that folks talk about, all those gentle, loving, fuzzy feelings, are turned inside out when I'm touched. I get the nightmare version: fear, disgust, and anger. No matter who's doing the touching, it's always the same. My pop tried to beat it out of me when I was barely out of diapers, thinking that if he held me down long enough, I'd come out the other side cured. All it did was make me get sick all over the carpet and then black out. That was the last time I saw the bastard. Mama kicked his sorry ass out.

Plain and simple, there's something wrong with my skin, and it's getting worse every year. Bare contact is bad. Wet contact's worse—which is why fighting pushes me to the very limit, what with all the sweating and grappling. If someone's got on a pair of gloves to touch me, I can stand it for a little while, but whatever it is that causes the terror and sickness always seeps through and gets me in the end. Me being dead drunk's another way I can block it out for a bit, but the contact's gotta be rough and quick. When I can get it up, I pay the whores extra for any bruises I leave behind when I crash into them like a head-on collision. It's always the same two, and those girls are damn good sports even though they don't believe the reason why I use them so hard. They think I just like it that way.

My condition's why Suzy and I can never really be together. I don't wanna be with her like that, all drunk and harsh. Suzy deserves a helluva lot better.

I really don't know why she's stuck around all this time. Maybe she feels sorry for me. Maybe she actually loves me like she says she does, but I wouldn't blame her for a second if she left. I'd miss her something terrible, but I know I'd find another way to get myself to the hospital after a solid beating.

I like that Suzy's here though, living with me. When I came back from the war with my guts all bullet-riddled, she'd just buried the little girl she'd had with the fella she married. Came to see me in the little house I grew up in when she heard I was home. Kicked the useless nurse out, and took over. The only thing she said when I asked about her husband was that there was nothing left there for her. I never asked her again.

Suzy frowns at me from the kitchen. I've probably got that look on my face that makes her worry for me. I always tell her that worrying over my fool head's gonna give her wrinkles, and she always laughs, saying that wrinkles can't make her any more plain. She's got no idea how pretty she is.

Normal folks don't know how nice they got it, being able to touch. They take it for granted. It's the little things that I can't do that hurt the most. When Suzy comes home from her cashier job, sore from standing all day working a double, I'd love to sit on the couch with her and rub her feet to make her feel better. And she's got the daintiest feet too. I'm sure they'd disappear in my big mitts. But I can't fucking do that.

Who in their right mind would want to touch the lady they love and feel only fear and disgust? Not me.

So this is what we got.

Suzy playing housewife for a man who can't ever love her like she deserves. Being my guardian angel and making sure I get put back together right after a match.

Me stuck fighting because that's the only thing I'm good for. I've been fired too many times over the years. My special needs get in the way, and I'm not smart enough to do anything but warehouse or factory work. Illegal or smoker fights when I can't get into a real match. We need the money. These are tough times, and only getting tougher with my arm in a cast like it is.

"Want another beer before supper?"

I just shake my head and go back to smiling at her as she strains the spaghetti over the sink. My angel. Sometimes I think I love her so much it'll kill me.

***

I ball my fists and box at the air, annoyed at the ache in my arm. I cut the cast off a week early, but I couldn't pass up this fight. It's good money. Just gotta keep my left shielded.

Breathe.

Relax.

I'm gonna keep a little of the cash aside and take Suzy to the fancy Italian place down the street. The one with the real tablecloths and candles stuck into wine bottles. I haven't told her yet, but I know she'll love it.

The alleyway is dark, and the crowd's a little rowdy. A few guys are obviously drunk. I don't like it. Suzy shouldn't be here. I take a look over my shoulder and see her standing there in her pink coat, smiling at my ugly mug like I'm something special. But she looks a little pale, and I think she's worried about the crowd too. Still, she gives me a thumbs-up, and I grin.

The restaurant's the kind that puts a basket of bread on the table. I like that. If I don't get hurt too bad, we can probably go on Friday after her shift.

There's a commotion and I turn, bouncing in place. I take a look at my opponent and I'm laughing inside. I know him—we shared a few shifts at the docks a year back. He's a wiry little guy with great hairy paws that can probably pack a wallop, but I figure this one's in the bag. It's a bareknuckle fight. Five rounds at a minute and a half each, and I can take a helluva beating before I'm knocked out. I nod to him and then pull my shirt over my head and toss it out of the ring. There's no barrier to speak of, just a bounding square in chalk on the pavement. It's freezing out and my skin steams a bit from my warm up.

There are two refs for a fight like this. Mine looks like he's been in a few good fights himself. Bastard puts his hand on my shoulder before I can dodge it, and I end up shoving him back a step. Not a great beginning to the match, what with him staring daggers at me. Means he might miscount the punches I land. Swearing to myself, I try to shake off his touch, but it's put me on edge. The feeling in my guts has gone from bad to worse.

Think about Suzy.

Breathe.

Fists up, head down, protect your arm.

As soon as the fight starts, I begin to feel a bit better. Breathing hard around my mouth guard, I'm almost able to ignore the bursts of panic I feel every time my knuckles slam into his flesh. My fists are the only ones doing damage, and by the fourth punch, he's blinded with blood and needs a minute to rest.

By the time the fifth round's halfway through, I'm nursing

a few bruises of my own, but nowhere near the damage I've caused.

Then I hear it. I'd recognize that sound anywhere. I spin around and look for her. Suzy's a few feet from where she was standing before, pushing at some men who I figure are trying to cop a feel. She's cursing them out the way she does, but that sick, bad feeling is back in my guts. I just walk out of the fight. Glass crunches under my shoe and one of the assholes looks up in time to see my fist connect with his face.

"You stay the fuck away from her!" My shout pings off the walls of the warehouses to either side.   .

The biggest of the guys messing around with my Suzy gives me a look, and I recognize him. He beat the living tar out of me once. My stomach takes a dive just remembering the way he held me down.

"What makes you think I care what you gotta say, you sack of shit?" His voice is low, and I can see ugly things in it. "Mind your own fucking business. We're just having a little fun here." Suzy yelps when he grabs her backside hard. I see another guy has her by the shoulder.

I'm frozen like a statue. My heart's like a rat trying to claw through my ribcage. I can't breathe. The fear has hold of me. I don't want him to touch me. The nausea begins to rise. Just being a few inches away from him is enough to make my skin crawl.

Suzy lets out a yell and stomps on someone's foot hard. All shit breaks loose. I'm still staring like a dumb fuck when the first guy clocks me in the jaw and the second hits me in the ribs. But everything falls away when Suzy flies backwards from the hard backhand dealt to her.

There's nothing in my world but red. Fear can't touch me. Pain is meaningless.

My fists connect with skin, breaking cartilage and fracturing bone. I'm a whirling demon, not even feeling it when they lay into me with their boots. I barely register the knife that slices into my bicep, or the bottle that shatters and opens my scalp.

But the bullet that rips through my chest stops me.

Not because it hurt, but because Suzy's scream is so loud in the narrow alleyway that it breaks through my trance. I stand in a daze, staring down at the blood pouring out of me. Someone yells something about cops coming.

In seconds, Suzy and I are alone under the buzzing street lamp.

"Beau... oh shit... Here." She hands me something. I think it's my T-shirt. Even now, she's so careful not to touch me. I push it against the bullet wound, but that's not gonna stop the blood running down my back. Blood everywhere. In my eyes, in my mouth. My arm's busted again.

I fall to my knees and keel over. Suzy presses a hand to her lips for a second. She's covered in blood too. Afraid, I reach for her.

"You...hurt?"

The laugh that bursts out of Suzy sounds deranged.

"It's your blood, you asshole."

"Oh."

It takes a second for me to realize I'm holding her hand. Her too. We both stare at our gory fingers linked together.

"Beau." Her eyes wide, she looks up at me. "You don't feel anything?"

"Yeah, I do," I mumble. The cold pavement is drinking up my warmth, one heartbeat at a time. "Just you, nothing else."

Tears are running down Suzy's face, and she squeezes my hand. I can hear sirens. They're too late, though. I lift my other hand and put it on her cheek. She's trembling.

"My angel."

"No...Don't talk like you're leaving me, Beau."

"Mm." Even though my hand's sticky, I can't help but think how soft her skin is against mine. What a fucking way to die. I always figured I'd get done in the ring. But at least I get to touch her without fear before I go.

"Beau! Oh baby, open your eyes. They're coming. We'll get you all fixed up."

I think about how just how much I love her.

"Touch me." It's barely a whisper, but that's all I can spare. Suzy understands though. She knows what I need.

Her fingers stroke my face, slide down my side, and run through my hair.

I drift away to the feeling of her hands on my bare skin.

***

ABOUT THE AUTHOR:

Born and raised in a small coastal town in northern Québec, Bey spent his early summers on his uncle's boat and running wild on the beaches of the surrounding islands, lighting fires and building huts out of driftwood and fishermen's nets. As an adult, he eventually made his way to university and earned a degree in Art History with a strong focus on Anthropology. Primarily a portrait painter and graphic artist, Bey sat down one day and decided to start writing.

Bey currently lives in the wilds of Montréal with his best buddy, a ridiculous, spotty pit bull named Murphy. www.beydeckard.com

THREE POEMS
BY DEANNE CHARLTON

ETERNITY IN A ONE-NIGHT STAND

She gave her body to an astronaut
but was allergic to moon dust,
she, the velvet loop to its many jagged hooks.
The scratches bloomed, tiny protoplasmic peonies
in all her private places. Doctored
all wrong, they grew, bonded shards
of sand, limestone, feldspar, ash
and cosmic minerals not intended
for human flesh. Invading her viscera,
eyes and beating heart, their task
near completion, they lovingly encrusted
her ivory skin. Fiery opalescent now,
she gazes at stars, missing her siblings
flung across the teeming void.

BRENGA'S BODY

Brenga internalizes everything but nobody
knows why she grows so thin from
fat experience. Left alone, she secretly
laps life like a cur at the gutter,
ever watching as

she cuts her hair, her eyebrows, her
nails to the quick, slowly turning.
Punctured everywhere, she
twists each hardness like
a worry stone:

one for mum; four for dad; bro the pro
had six before she cast him off,
part of her purging routine,
unpurified. She always binges
on the same boy,

although he has different bodies. He
likes the moving pictures sprawled
across her heartache by the
thousand unnatural shocks
her flesh is heir to, then

something shiny always catches him and
he's gone and pain, not enough, sends
her alone to slit her skin yet again and
insert her tears into the now newest gap
that never quite closes.

IT RUNS IN THE FAMILY

Deep South deep woods,
nineteen hundred and fifteen, white kids,
not albinos, fuzzy hair colored
like boll fruit. Not all of them
cottonheads; just the middle three.

People stared, of course,
pondered the why. School
was perplexed; church, askance.
Born that way, they finally decided.
Not a problem. Clap the chalk erasers,
pass the collection plate.

~   ~   ~

Deep South deep woods folks,
a hundred years on. Two white mothers
living wrong with their uncommon bodies;
two damn daddies holding hands.

People stare, of course,
wonder why. School frantic; church rabid.
Not born that way, they decide.
A problem, sure. Delete enrollment,
pass the collection plate.

ABOUT THE AUTHOR:
Residing with a view of the Great Smoky Mountains, Charlton
has visited 49 U. S. states, including North and South Denial;
moved over 50 times; traveled in 7 foreign countries,
including San Francisco; and prefers eating sorbet to being
drawn and quartered or complimented. She enjoys editing
books, short stories and magazine articles.

Ruby
by Bob Williams

1

Michael Wootten sat on the front porch of his home on an already blistering Sunday morning in Ransom, Oklahoma. Michael and his father had completed the decking a couple of years before and planned to start setting the posts for the overhang when Michael Sr. suddenly died of a heart attack. Michael never could force himself to finish the project. On mornings like this however, when the blazing sun seemed to hand pick him out of the world's population to torment, he sure wished he had.

There were still significant repairs that needed to be completed on the house but he just didn't think he could bear it today. He'd been slaving away on the damn repairs since the "Black Sunday" storm had decimated the Oklahoma Panhandle, then traveled south all the way to Amarillo.

The gale force winds had caused significant damage to not only the roof, but structural damage to the house itself.

Michael honestly didn't know how he was going to fix the cracks which had shown up throughout the home. All but one of the windows were boarded, and it was unclear when Billingsley would be able to order the glass from El Paso for the replacements he was building.

Michael had spent the better part of two months sweeping and removing what felt like thousands of pounds of dirt and debris. *The Ledger* had reported that particular storm from April fourteenth, nineteen thirty-five had displaced over three hundred million tons of topsoil by the time it was all said and done. Another man referred to the storm as the "Dust Bowl." Michael couldn't deny that name was appropriate. He often thought all three hundred million tons must've landed in Ransom.

The city itself was in squalor. About three quarters of the town had fled in the weeks and months following the storm. The utter devastation the "black blizzard" had inflicted on the panhandle itself had been historical. Ransom had been sucker punched.

The aftermath left the town crippled, with no clean drinking water for weeks. No electricity for a month. It was chaos. Currently, not a single elected official served in office. Brent Peterson was sort of the Sheriff. Mr. Billingsley stuck around to keep his hardware store open–granted, he was closed for several months before reopening. The Clements stayed to operate the grocery but it took great effort to reopen. A very small group of townsfolk were present but that barely made an acceptable infrastructure. The truth was, Ransom was dying.

It wasn't difficult to see. In fact, everyone left in town wore it like a badge of defeat upon their daily dressing. You never saw a smile anymore, not even on the faces of the few children still sprinkled about. It was like they'd already been taught to say, "Fuck it," by their parents and given up. Then again there weren't many, or any, reasons to smile, to be honest. Michael never smiled himself because he could feel the dust coating on, and in between, his teeth. And not a soul alive needed to see that.

Michael took the thought one step further. *We're not only not smiling, we're not talking to one another. Ransom, I can't...hear...you. Your heart used to beat with such passion and vibrancy! Will you ever return to the city you once were?*

Michael stood from his rocking chair, removed the hat from his head, and used it to wipe the sweat gathering in his furrowed brows. "I don't know," he said aloud, mostly to hear the sound of his own voice. It had been too long. He turned, with hat in hand, and strode towards the door. It was time to get inside where it was only slightly cooler. His hand on the knob, he saw something off in the distance: a cloud of dust, and it was heading towards town.

2

No more than forty-five minutes later, a small collection of trucks pulled right into the heart of Ransom. Michael had never quite made it inside, but stood and watched the entire time it took the small convoy to arrive, at his doorstep.

Next door to Michael's house was an open field that had once housed the Allendoerfers, but their home had been all but destroyed by the storm. They had packed up quickly and headed for Texas, and the house had been demolished in the hope that eventually someone would build on the land. Suffice it to say, that never even came remotely close to happening.

A finely dressed man of about six feet or so exited the passenger side of the lead Ford truck with much fanfare. He had a very fine walking stick with a gold knob handle. Cupped between his forearm and hip was a black top hat with a blood red band circling the brim. His pressed pants

were made of the finest material Michael had ever seen.
Velvet? And the polish on his black shoes was of the finest
quality.

Once comfortably out of the vehicle, the man placed his
hat upon his head and surveyed his direct surroundings in
three hundred sixty degrees. That done, he placed his hands
on his hips before barking orders in rapid fire succession.
There were twenty-two people in all mingling around the
trucks. He quickly became animated, pointing and waving his
walking stick wildly in all directions. After that, he walked
excitedly across the street and right up the walkway to the
Sheriff's office. Turns out the walking stick provided more
than just effect, as one of his legs was significantly longer
than the other. He wore a special boot that matched the other
in style but had a much thicker heel.

The well-dressed man knocked for several minutes but
the "occasional" Sheriff, Brent Peterson, never answered. He
tried the door in that manner of "once you determine it's
locked the first time you believe it simply can't be true so you
shake it violently several times to confirm" kind of way. The
man showed no kind of frustration as he threw on a wickedly
huge smile and made his way back to the cavalcade.

Michael was in complete awe of the situation. Even
before the storm, Ransom just wasn't the place carnivals and
sideshows came to. The top attraction in nineteen thirty-six
Ransom, Oklahoma was a mouth full of dirt.

Two extremely hairy men pulled a rather large sign out
of the back of the third truck and carried it over to the main
entrance of a massive, candy striped tent and pounded it into
the ground. The tent was truly stunning in both its size and
brilliant white and red stripes. It had been quickly and
efficiently erected. About the same time the sign was being
tacked up, a rather scaly looking man with a sheen to his skin
sort of slithered up to the side of the second truck and

released two knots, dropping a canvas mural of phenomenal color and design: MELVIN MITCHELL PRESENTS: RUBY AND HER AMAZING FREAKSHOW FRIENDS!!!

Ruby... 'freakshow friends?' Michael began to seriously inspect the crowd of visitors congregating around the truck. There was a lady with a beard. Another man who was easily eight feet tall. Little people, a woman with weird eyes and pointed tongue, even a man who looked like a tree! A few other unique individuals, along with the man who must be Melvin Mitchell, mingled with a few of Ransom's inhabitants who had come out of the woodwork.

Michael, however, kept his distance. Michael was looking for Ruby.

Michael had never known a Ruby before. He felt that the name Ruby carried with it an air of nobility. *Anyone*, he thought, *named Ruby would certainly stand out.* When his eyes finally landed on her, he would say to himself, Ah ha! There she is! That is Ruby!

But that never happened.

What did happen was a late-as-usual appearance by Sheriff Brent Peterson. He sauntered up with a perturbed look on his face. His face, which wasn't the most dashing, had a rather distinguishing scar across his cheek from a childhood scythe accident.

Michael watched him enter discussion with Melvin Mitchell which wasn't exactly heated, but also wasn't exactly cordial. Sheriff Peterson pointed and flailed while Melvin Mitchell simply smiled and nodded at carefully orchestrated times. In the end, the two begrudgingly shook hands and the Sheriff went on his way as Melvin Mitchell returned to his friends.

Michael wanted to engage the strange gathering of folks next door to his house but couldn't seem to make himself leave the front porch. In fact, after several hours of gawking at the "Freakshow Friends," he'd gone inside. The mystery of Ruby and who she was had begun to take hold on Michael. He sat alone at his kitchen table. Waiting. Patiently. Later that night he would go and see RUBY AND HER AMAZING FREAKSHOW FRIENDS.

3

Melvin Mitchell didn't give a fuck about people. He barely gave a shit about Ruby, and he supposedly loved her. Melvin especially loathed the pathetic townies he took to the cleaners in every city that allowed him to set up his tent. Personally, Melvin wouldn't pay a dollar to look at these filthy freaks. Fuckin' doctor should've put the birth defects out of their misery. But time and time again, the blind mice would fall in line, dropping a dollar a head, even for the kids, when they could barely afford the water to take a bath. And in this godforsaken dirty asshole part of the country, a bath could mean the difference between life and death.

He did have reason to smile, though. Although they barely made it out of...of...shit–Melvin couldn't remember. All the jackhole towns blended together after a while. Anyway, the crew had barely gotten out of town after Ruby had gotten her cut. The kid had made a stink and before you knew it there was auth-or-itays after them with torches and rifles. They eventually outran them but at great personal detriment.

He had wanted to keep going well into the afternoon but Ruby put a stop to that, saying, "The performers can't stay cooped up in these small trucks in this heat for so many miles, Mel. We have to stop."

Melvin thought, *You fucking bitch, Ruby! If I wasn't tied to you, I'd kill you myself.*

"I guess we don't have too much to worry about," he said. "We've been driving all night. Maybe we can squeeze in a show, get some quick cash, and get the hell outta Dodge."

Ruby said, in her majestic voice, "Don't forget about my cut, Mel."

"Always, darling."

"Fuck you, Mel."

And so it went. Mel and Ruby's eternal dialogue. They'd been together for over fourteen years. The castoffs were interchangeable. But Mel and Ruby, well, they were the constant.

Almost on cue, the caravan passed a sign for Ransom that said fifty-five miles. So it was decided by senior management, meaning Ruby and Melvin, that an impromptu show would be added to the schedule in Ransom, Oklahoma.

4

The convoy pulled into Ransom and began to immediately set up shop. Melvin always insisted that erecting the tent quickly before anyone could show up to ask what they were doing was the first stake in the ground to eventually striking the deal. Melvin always said, "What kind of asshole would make us tear down the tent once we already put it up?"

It had always been part of the "show" as a whole to never let anyone see Ruby before the entrance was pulled back and the first dollar paid. Ruby waited inside a custom constructed crate that was incredibly comfortable and transported from the truck to the tent. That was, of course, Ruby's idea, and Ruby always got what she wanted. Melvin may be the face, or the manager, of this traveling clusterfuck, but Ruby...Ruby was the brains. It was in your best interest, if you wanted to be part of Ruby's crew, to go with the flow. Word got around quickly to any new performers. And even the long timers were reminded from time to time: don't even think about pressing your luck, or Ms. Ruby's gonna take her cut.

Ruby O'Dell was a sprightly thirty-four years old. Born in nineteen-oh-two with a devastating birth defect, she spent the first ten years of her life completely reliant on others.

Her words.

She couldn't eat on her own. Couldn't drink a glass of water. She couldn't even use the restroom alone. Ruby couldn't accomplish a single act of nearly any nature that normal people completed daily without a second thought.

Ruby would often catch herself thinking about what happened at age ten that caused her shift in philosophy. It wasn't an event. No, nothing...happened. Even after she turned ten years old, she remained reliant on family and friends for those same basic needs. However, she began to look at how she asked for that assistance in quite a different way.

And then, well, from there, in one way or another, Ruby always took her cut.

There was no sense in lying, neither to an inquisitor or herself. She was angry. Bitter to the core. Why would God commit such a heinous act of cruelty upon her? She was innocent. Well she had been. She had accepted her "deformity" as it had been called by doctors and the life it meant for her with innocent, childlike grace. For many years she was, of course, greatly limited but happy. She was loved by her family and a few close friends. But eventually love alone wasn't able to fill the void in her heart.. As she grew older, she wanted more. More from life, and more from the people in her life.

Ruby lay in bed one night, even now she would never forget it, and a thought came to her. That thought, like a seed it planted in her mind. And there it grew. A weed or poisonous vine that slowly corrupted her mind, then her soul, and finally her heart until it turned black and villainous as the night. She asked herself, *I wonder what else I can get them to do for me?* The question was answered soon enough. A mere six months later, Ruby politely asked her primary caregiver to jump from the open window of her family's twelfth story apartment.

When she complied, Ruby screamed and burst into tears. Tears of unimaginable joy.

She spent the next several years acting bewildered and unable to provide any explanation for the growing number of accidental falls, maimings, burns, and deaths that kept happening to her caregivers, friends, and even family. Finally, a solid connection was made and, despite the protestations of the very deformed and quite literally helpless Ruby O'Dell, she was committed to an institution for the mentally handicapped.

The year was nineteen sixteen.

Ruby would go on to spend eight miserable fucking years in that institution without hurting a soul. That is, until the year nineteen twenty-four, when a new maximum security orderly by the name of Stuart Brown joined the staff. You know him better as Melvin Mitchell.

A fellow resident of the institution, while visiting the institution's infirmary for an emergency medical procedure, claimed he saw Stuart Brown carry Ruby out the front door of the hospital in the pre-dawn hours one early winter morning. When pressed about why he hadn't said anything or alerted hospital staff he merely replied, "Ms. Ruby asked me not to."

The follow up question, ironically, for it should've been the first, was, "What the hell happened to your hand? Where is it?"

The patient, who shall remain nameless, looked at his newly sutured right stump, shook his head, and calmly answered, "Ms. Ruby always get her cut."

The two were never heard from or seen again.

5

The time was six-thirty p.m. The sun had clocked out on another soul crushing day, and the night time sky was creeping in to throw a bandage of stars over the open wound of Ransom.

Melvin Mitchell had walked up and down Bilbrey Street with a megaphone barking, "Melvin Mitchell Presents: Ruby and Her Amazing Freakshow Friends will be open for business this evening at seven o'clock! Come one, come all! Fifty cents at the door gets you a world of visual wonders!"

Michael Wootten had waited all day for this. Yes, he was curious about the other participants, but he wanted to meet Ruby. Michael wasn't crazy. In fact, the town generally regarded him as a well-respected craftsman and handyman. If you needed him, Michael was always willing to pitch in to help. Especially after the dust blizzards. But this was something altogether different. He was captivated by this cast of characters and the mystery that surrounded them. Something about RUBY AND HER AMAZING FREAKSHOW FRIENDS beckoned him to this tent.

He couldn't figure it out. Maybe it was simply the fact that Ransom was dead in the water, *Ha!* and this tent show was the only thing going.

He turned off the lights, locked up, and headed over. It was a beautiful night. He wished the caravan had parked a little farther down the street. He'd have enjoyed the walk. However, it was a quick jaunt to the previously empty lot next door and he was in line.

Michael's curiosity had wanted him to come much sooner but he'd waited. He hoped he didn't seem too eager. He didn't know why. He spent the next thirty minutes mingling with Mr. Billingsley, whose excitement for the show made him quite animated.

Billingsley could probably be in this show, considering

his missing eye. They'd likely want him to lose the patch, though.

At precisely seven o'clock, the line of over a hundred people (not a great crowd by any stretch of the imagination but still most of the remaining residents of Ransom) went silent with growing anticipation. Rustling came from behind the tent entrance and the overly large flap was untied from within to reveal Melvin Mitchell holding a flaming torch.

"Welcome!! Thank you all for coming this evening on such short notice. Ms. Ruby and all of our performers are very excited to be here in Ranson tonight. You're in for an unforgettable evening. Before we begin, why don't we shed a little light on the subject?"Melvin walked past the line of spectators and towards a pike in the ground about ten feet away.

Once Michael noticed the first pike, he noticed a row of them encircling the tent.

"All of us here at MELVIN MITCHELL PRESENTS: RUBY AND HER AMAZING FREAKSHOW FRIENDS sincerely hope you enjoy the show. Five dollars a head for everyone. Please take your time. There's no hurry!" He made a production of waving his torch around before finally touching it to the pike.

Michael was amazed to see a chain reaction of all the torches lighting in succession, one after the other with no visible method of lighting.

6

Michael noticed as the line progressed towards the dwarf taking money that everyone, at least everyone he'd seen who worked for this "show," was in fact a "FreakShow Friend," regardless of whether they performed in the show or worked for it.

"Ladies and gentlemen!" Melvin Mitchell clapped his hands a couple of times, then spoke robustly to the entering crowd. "Ladies and gentlemen! Welcome once again to our show. As I said earlier, we are very pleased to be with you here this evening. You may be wondering what such a motley crew of individuals get out of this. You may secretly be hating yourself for coming. That's okay. Morbid curiosity pays for gas!"

This drew a hearty laugh from the customers.

"What we are really doing here, truthfully, is celebrating. Not a soul among us feels sorry for ourselves. Nor do we hate the way we look. We are all very proud of who we are. We love ourselves and each other for our uniqueness. We are a family. And we welcome you into our traveling home.

"Now, it is true, each of us has suffered horrendous indignations and ridicule at the hands of those who refuse to understand. Those who think that if you don't have two eyes, a nose, a mouth, two arms, two legs, and ten fingers and toes, you don't belong. If you are one of those individuals who have come here tonight with intentions on shaming us or disrupting our home, kindly turn around and please leave. If you'd like, you may have your entry fee returned. All we are attempting to do tonight is show you that, even though we may be different, we are all beautiful."

Once Michael entered the tent he immediately started scoping for Ruby.

There! He saw her booth and attempted to go straight for it. Before he'd taken three steps, the Bearded Lady called to him from her booth. "Please, sir. Show every performer in the show equal respect and follow the natural progression."

Her request was really a demand and her poorly rehearsed politeness fell flat.

"I might be offended if I thought you didn't want to spend a few minutes with me, Mister."

Michael was caught off guard by the woman, now that she was so close. He stared at her so intently, like he told himself he wasn't going to do at all, much less the first person he saw, he swore he saw her mustache grow a quarter inch.

"I..uh..." He stammered. He couldn't bear to look at her. Why doesn't she shave? A woman shouldn't have a beard. "Yes, ma'am," was all he could muster.

Next up, standing stoically in his booth was the "Tree Man." He stood about six feet five inches, wore a blue t-shirt and gray shorts. He couldn't wear shoes as his feet were literally two separate root systems that spiraled outward from where a normal person's toes began.

Michael stood behind Bob Crosley's two young boys and smiled as their mouths hung agape. "Do you have to trim your toes?" one of the boys asked innocently.

"Why, yes I do young man. It only hurts for a second before the ends heal right up." Tree Man's voice sounded...old. Ancient even.

That's weird but he just feels old. There is no way a man is also a tree! Is there?

Tree Man's skin was coarse and crumbly. It was definitely supposed to look like bark. "You there, my friend. What's your name?" he asked.

"Me? Uh...Michael Wootten."

"Michael Wootten, my name is Scott. I'd like you to have something of mine. A gift."

"Well, I couldn't-"

"Please take it." He reached across his body and peeled a piece of bark–*skin!*–off his arm and handed it to Michael. "Now don't say I never gave you nothin! Okay?"

"Okay." Michael felt more than a little disturbed by the encounter. He debated internally about leaving but moved on to the next booth.

There, Michael had a pleasant but brief conversation with Five Fingered Albino. Two fingers on his left hand, and three on his right. And he could juggle! From there it was the Eight

Foot Giant, and then on to The Lizard Woman. She spoke with a very sinister hiss that accompanied a forked tongue that shot out of her mouth about every minute or so. She was pleasant enough, though.

Michael relaxed and began to enjoy himself. There were many more performers to interact with and seeing Ruby last would most definitely be the icing on the cake of a really fun night. He took a few moments and looked around the tent. Smiling faces greeted him, and some insecure looks, but mostly a lot of laughing and fun.

Families were out together, music played, although the band had no arms and all the instruments were strummed by feet, and, at least for one night, Ransom had a pulse.

We'll take it.

He didn't know about anyone else, but Michael felt a great deal of gratitude towards Melvin Mitchell and his cavalcade of unique and special individuals. They had truly done a great kindness to the city by stopping here this morning.

7

Melvin Mitchell could physically taste the shit coming up from his asshole when he had to spew that crap to these people. It had taken years of work, serious work with Ruby, before they were able to put this venture together. Going around and glad handing these losers was bad enough, but he could feel the layer of dirt on his clothes, in his teeth, and in his eye. *One of these days I'm gonna pull the plug on all this freakshow bullshit and Ruby and me, we're gonna run away with the cash. Sooner than later.*

The shows typically ran anywhere from seven to ten, or eleven if it was still lively. It was nine now, and they weren't breaking down the doors, so it looked like ten it would be. He hadn't been paying attention, he didn't really, most often, but they were closing in an hour and it was time to start looking for Ruby's cut. James the Tree Jerk had probably already given his bark to the "lucky winner," and now Melvin had to scurry around like a rat, looking for the cheese.

That tree asshole NEVER tells me who he gave the marker to.

About ten minutes later, by sheer luck, he saw the young man carrying the bark in his hand.

He probably doesn't even think it's real bark, the idiot.

Melvin quickly crossed the distance between him and the young man and came to stand directly in front of him. "Good evening to you, Sir!" He said with completely false excitement. "And how are you enjoying the show this evening? Is it what you were expecting?"

"Well, yes," said the man who appeared to be in his early twenties. "More so. I'm glad I came. I'm very interested to see Ms. Ruby. After all, her name is on the marquee. But she's the biggest mystery."

"Oh you do have a very keen sense, don't you young man. Eh, what is your name son?" asked Melvin.

"Michael Wootten."

"Well, Michael, are you in for a treat. You say that Ms. Ruby is a mystery? Well, maybe you can solve her when you meet her tonight after the show in a one-on-one private meeting!" Melvin bellowed with delight as bile danced wickedly in his stomach.

"Wow? Thanks, Mr. Mitchell! What do you need me to do?"

"No need to thank me Michael! The pleasure is all ours. If you will just kindly follow me, Ms. Ruby is waiting in a small private tent for just this very occasion."

Melvin asked Michael to follow him down the row of performers whom he'd probably not get to see but he didn't care, past Ruby's empty booth, from which a sign hung saying, "Ms. Ruby's performance will begin promptly at 9:30," and out into the night.

Michael saw four large torches burning brightly in the distance, casting a stunning ripple of shadows on the tent where Ruby waited for him. For a private meeting, the tent did seem rather large, though not in contest with the tent housing the carnival. He more followed Mr. Mitchell then accompanied him, and, honestly, since they'd left the main tent, Mr. Mitchell had gone silent. When they finally reached Ms. Ruby's tent, Melvin Mitchell turned back to Michael and said, "One moment please," then entered the tent.

8

Melvin stepped into the tent and wasn't immediately able to locate Ruby. This was not uncommon. She was adept at moving freely within the shadows.

How does she do that? It's not like she can get up and walk.

"I can hear you, Mel. You know I don't appreciate it when you talk about me that way." Her voice was like the sweetest song he'd ever heard. It never raised and it never lowered. Melodic in sound but deadly with intent.

Melvin had known her a long time. Longer than anyone else had managed to. The key was to listen without listening. He would hear what she said but focus on any other thing possible. He knew, he wasn't naive, one day she'd take her cut, again, but, Fuck it! I'm gonna ride this bull 'til it kills me.

"Mel!"

"Yeah, Yeah! The moke is outside. His name is Michael Wootten. Try not to kill him, okay?"

"My, my, Mel, why do you suddenly care? You never have before."

"I don't. Trust me. Do I need to remind you that just yesterday we got chased outta who knows where we were by pissed off people with guns and torches? Just saying we might need to lay low for a bit."

"Don't you fuck this up for me, Mel. We have a good thing going here. Don't piss your pants now."

She was right. Ruby was always right. "Nah, I know. It'll be fine. Okay. I'm getting outta here. Have fun, babe."

"Thank you, Mel," she said. The whole conversation played out like he was playing a soft tune on the piano, while she leaned up against it singing. It was, after all, how she did what she did.

9

Melvin Mitchell shot abruptly out of the tent. He stopped, pulled his vest down sharply, bowed and gestured towards the opening of the tent. "Ms. Ruby awaits! Thank you for coming tonight! Thank you in advance for your gift." Melvin prattled on as he stumbled down back towards the main tent.

Where is his walking stick? Wait. What gift?

Michael cautiously approached the entrance to the tent. He pulled back the flap and peeked inside. Quickly taking in the scene from his view at the rear of the tent, Michael didn't see anyone. But once his eyes adjusted he could see a very fine, high-back parlor chair that sat next to a small side table with an oil lamp in the center. Was there someone in the chair? He stepped all the way inside, and even took a few unsure steps before he called out, "Hello."

"Hello, Michael. I'm so pleased to make your acquaintance. My name is Ruby. Ruby O'Dell."

"Nice to meet you Ms. Ruby. I can't see you."

"Oh, you can dispense with the formalities, Michael. Just Ruby will be fine."

"Oh, okay. Ruby."

Michael turned when he heard the sound of a match striking and a small flame appeared. The flame grew within the glass globe of the lamp and emerging from the darkness was simply the most beautiful woman he'd ever seen in his entire life.

Ruby.

The face of a goddess, with the most stunning red hair, and sapphire blue eyes. She was an angel. She had neither arm nor legs but sat stoically in the chair. She commanded his attention. Michael couldn't look away.

"You're staring Michael," said Ruby melodically.

"Yes, I am. But not for the reason you may think. You are the most beautiful woman I have ever seen." Michael hoped he wasn't stuttering. He didn't want to look like a child in front of this woman. Michael thought her smile could tame the wildest beast. Considering her current company, it probably had.

"And what reason is that, Michael?"

"You're so beautiful. The most beautiful I've ever seen."

"You flatter me Michael. Or are you overcompensating for my deformity?"

"Deformity? No. Not at all. If I may say, in the presence of your beauty I see no deformity, but a set of circumstances of which you have made the best." Michael had no earthly idea where those words came from, but he sure hoped he could continue.

"Oh dear, Michael. Do you think I was born this way? If God had made me in this manner, I might be able to accept it. But my fate was a cruel one, at the hands of a butcher." Ruby closed her eyes and turned away from him, but Michael knew well she had nowhere to go and no way to hide her shame.

Michael felt a pang in his heart for her.

"I'm...sorry. I don't know what to say Ms. Ruby. Why would someone do such a horrible thing to you?" Michael felt like he was sinking in a pool of humiliation. That's probably the last question she wanted him to ask.

"I've asked that question of myself for years. Michael, I was in the capture of a madman. He surgically removed my arms and legs and kept me alive out of pure malevolence. I begged him to take my life as well. This man, he refused. He told me 'Now all you have is your looks. See how far that gets you.' After he discarded me like a piece of useless garbage, it took me years to see that he was wrong. I am much, much more than looks. I am intelligent. I am creative. I am intellectual. I am pain. I am joy. I am deception. I am harmony. Michael, I am whatever I choose to be. This is what makes me smile."

"You are an inspiration!" exclaimed Michael.

"No, Michael, I am just Ruby. A woman who chooses to share her experiences with those who can take something positive away from it. We are a very giving group of travelers, Michael. We give our time, we give our stories, and we give...ourselves. But do you know what amazes me every time we stop in a wonderful town like Ransom?"

"What's that?"

"Each and every time we embrace a city or town. We are embraced in return. There are always good hearted, generous patrons that want to give back. Do you smoke Michael?"

"Yes."

"Would you be a dear and enjoy a cigarette with me?"

"Of course Ms. Ruby. I'd be delighted," Michael said genuinely.

"Thank you. Would you so kindly pull out that drawer and retrieve my cigarettes and matches?"

That question caught Michael a bit off guard as he clearly recalled a match lighting to engage the lamp. "Is something the matter Michael?"

"No, I...I'm sorry. It's just I thought I saw a match strike to light the lamp when I first entered the tent." Michael said unsurely.

Simpleton ,thought Ruby. *He thought he saw a match light? Damn fool already doubts what he clearly saw. He deserves what he gets.*

Ruby chuckled. "Why, clearly you are mistaken, Michael. How on Earth could that've happened?"

Michael looked to the ground, grateful the semi-darkness shadowed his blazing red face of embarrassment. "Yes ma'am. That's correct. The lamp was lit when I entered the tent. Let me get those cigarettes for you."

Michael approached the small side table and pulled out the drawer. He picked up the pack of Lucky Strike smokes and the matches. There were only two left in the pack. Tapping the pack against the inside of his palm, he slid one out. Holding out the cigarette awkwardly towards Ruby, Michael hoped desperately for direction.

"Just put it in my mouth Michael," she said with a wry smile.

"Yes ma'am." Michael flushed bright red again before placing the cigarette between her lips, then taking the last one for himself.

He opened the book and struck a match. The small blaze of the match catching reminded him again of what he saw...or thought he'd seen. He wasn't sure anymore. He offered the flame to Ruby who took a drag and exhaled.

Michael popped the cigarette between his lips, struck a fresh match, and lit it.

Ruby said to Michael, "Could you take mine please."

"Yes, ma'am."

"I suddenly don't feel like it. Sometimes they hit me just right, sometimes I'm just not feeling it."

"I think that's everybody, Ruby. These things are little nuts," Michael said, taking another drag.

"But really, Michael, what are we without our vices?"

"I don't know as I can rightly say," said Michael.

"I have my vices. Things I crave. Things that may be to the detriment of others, but I just can't help it."

"I...uh...what?" Michael suddenly felt ill. His vision was losing focus and his legs felt as if they couldn't support his weight.

"Michael, are you alright? You don't look so good. Should I call for help?"

"What...kind...cigarettes..?"

"Why, Lucky Strike, you saw the pack. Oh my goodness!!"

Michael collapsed to the ground. His eyes rolled back and he wet his pants.

"Michael! Michael!!" Ruby screamed as loud as she could. She knew, however, that nobody would come. Both of the Lucky Strike smokes were dipped in Ruby's special solution. Laudanum and a few other key ingredients. Ruby had been at this for quite sometime. Even if she had to light her cigarette, she would be just fine. Michael would not.

"Dear Michael, don't go just yet. There's something very important I need you to do for me. Declan, help Michael, please dear."

Declan, who was the equivalent of a human chameleon, walked out of the shadows and around to where Michael lay. Declan went everywhere Ruby did. He was her private bodyguard.

He cast shimmers of a form but nothing concrete.

To the human eye it looked like Michael Wootten sat up sharply, and lazily scuttled in front of Ruby's chair.

A small amount of drool made its way out of Michael's mouth, and down his chin.

Declan placed an item next to Michael and disappeared back into the shadows.

"Michael, sweet Michael. I need you to do something for me. Something very important."

Michael was in his final moments before his life would change forever. As he slipped away, the most sinister and horrifying laugh he'd ever heard echoed in the ether.

10

MELVIN MITCHELL PRESENTS: RUBY AND HER AMAZING FREAKSHOW FRIENDS was long gone before Ransom woke up the next morning. Some towns are harder than others, but this crew of performers and roadies made an absolute art form out of tearing down and hauling out under cover of night. Besides, it was never in their best interest to be around after at least one particular individual came to.

Ruby and Melvin drove for hours without saying a word. Ruby chose to break the silence. "Thank you in advance for your gift?" She couldn't help but smile as she looked across at Melvin.

Melvin, in response, doing his very best Ruby impersonation said, "Michael! I was the capcha of a madman." They both laughed hysterically.

"Where to now, my dear?" asked Melvin sincerely

"Wherever the next dollar lays my love."

11

Michael awoke slowly and was very disoriented. He knew he was in his house. He wasn't sure how he'd gotten there. He knew instantly he needed to vomit. As he attempted to push himself over on his stomach...nothing happened. He was able to partially sit up before he vomited all over the front of his shirt and pants.

What the hell? Damnit! My head is killing me.

Beads of sweat collected in his brow and he tried to wipe them away. Except he couldn't. Michael looked to his right arm...it was gone.

He immediately vomited again over the side of his bed.

On the floor next to his bed was a blood-stained hack saw. His head swirled violently and he threw himself back into the bed. Tears streamed from his eyes as he screamed.

Ruby always gets her cut. Always.

***

ABOUT THE AUTHOR:

Bob Williams lives in Nashville, Tennessee with his wife Sara and daughter Kate. When Bob isn't writing he works for Habitat for Humanity of Greater Nashville. Bob has two previous short story titles "Smoke" and "Magenta," both currently available in the Amazon Kindle Store. Bob hopes you enjoy reading his words as much as he loves writing them.

http://bwilliams.thirdscribe.com/

UnTamed
by Laxmi Hariharan

Sept 30, 2060. 4pm

"Your stories are very amusing, old man, but now that you know who I am, I have to kill you." I pull grandmother's sword out from its sheath. Everyone in this new world has been looking for this sword and I inherited it a few weeks ago. *Me,* the first half-human descendant of the woman who destroyed Bombay.

She was impulsive and hotheaded, my grandma. She'd never meant to cause such havoc and yet, she'd gone and touched the sword to the altar in that little temple and set the tsunami free. The storm had leveled the city and for this my family has never been forgiven.

Pulse racing, I rush forward, bringing the blade down on him; but he moves aside and I slide past and bang my head against the railing of the boat. I spring back to my feet and waltz around him, ready to leap.

He's looking at me, arms hanging by his sides. He seems not in the least surprised. Then, he raises a hand and beckons, one side of his lips quirking in a smile. Blood thudding in my ears, I jump towards him, and again he steps aside; only this time he puts out his foot and I stumble over it and crash, face down, right at the feet of the other two, who burst out laughing.

"You sure fight like a *girl*," the fisherman snickers.

What the—! Is he making fun of me?

Anger blasts through my head, filling the space behind my eyes. The hair on my forearms stands on end, bristling like spears; my nostrils quiver, leg muscles tense and I grip my sword.

"Came to learn from the master swordsman himself, did you?" the baker chuckles.

"What do you mean?" I growl, already swinging to face the old lamp seller.

"He's Aki, the best swordsman in the islands; perhaps in all of this new world. And he's been waiting for you," the fisherman replies.

"Oh! Yeah? Has he now?" I sneer and, pushing the fisherman aside, I lunge once more at the lamp seller. One step, a second, a third, and I leap through the air–Didn't see that coming did you old man?–and fall head down against the wooden floor.

The breath whooshes out of me and my nose slams against the wooden boards. I hear the sickening crunch of it breaking and pain shoots through me, screeching through my nerve endings, so I almost black out. My hands are flung out, the right gripping the sword and I scream as a heavy weight crunches on my palm, forcing me to loosen my fingers.

"No! No! No!" He's wrenched my sword from my grasp and is holding it aloft.

"Don't you dare!" I grind out through clenched teeth.

He grins and, still looking at me, tosses the sword up in the air.

What the–? I follow the blade as it whirls around and up and up and up, 'til it is silhouetted against the sun. It drops down, hilt up. Grabbing the sword by the blunt side, he swings the handle towards me.

A scream boils up, then everything goes dark.

***

An hour earlier

My thoughts are in tumult when I arrive at the pier. This is the only way to the island with the temple where it all started. My mother had been hunted and stayed on the run most of her life. But not me. No, that's not me. I am here to face my past. To find out about my origins in the city of my ancestors.

Soon, I am joined by a man carrying empty fishing nets, that distinct, dried fish smell clinging to him like a jealous lover. Then, a young baker, dragging along a metal casket full of various local delicacies. A third man joins the queue.

He's carrying metal and clay lamps of various sizes in a large basket on his head. With a sigh of relief, he drops it to the ground and seats himself next to it. He pulls off his hat and fans himself. He's older than the others. At least fifty. He's probably the oldest person alive I have seen. Definitely is.

He smiles, showing stained teeth, and his eyes crinkle at the corners. His eyebrows rise slightly. A tattoo in the form of a third eye between his brows moves, as if it's alive. It's watching me, even when he is not looking. It's following my every move.

I tear my eyes away from him.

The others chatter about the local market where they are headed to sell their goods. I don't want to talk to the locals.

Best to keep to myself. I shrink into my skin, and step away, touching the hilt of the sword tucked into the back of my waistband. It's hidden by the long shirt I wear; at least I hope so.

The ferry arrives, gears churning in the water. I walk onto the upper deck past the rows of wooden benches, seating myself on the one right upfront. All three men follow me on board.

The fisherman–taking his smell with him, thankfully–and the baker sit at the back. The lamp seller settles across the aisle from me. The boat toots its horn and pulls away from the pier.

"I've always wanted to get as far as possible from where I was born," he says aloud.

Eh? Is he speaking to me?

"One belongs to the entire universe, not just one part of it, don't you think?" he continues.

I ignore him, looking across to the shore. I can just make out the triangular shape of a building in the distance.

"Been to the temple of the Hugging Saint yet?" he asks, following my gaze.

I look at him properly. He's wearing a thin, cotton shirt carrying a tiger skin pattern. His loose, white trousers fray at the hems.

"I don't believe such stories," I reply, while wriggling around and trying to make myself more comfortable on the narrow seat.

His bushy eyebrows shoot down over his eyes. "A myth. Is that what you think he is?"

"Isn't he?" I sneer, "Mr. Hugging Boy, the one who can cure you of all your sicknesses, who can help you find your path. All with just a hug."

My voice comes out all cynical, and I hate myself for it. I'm just sixteen, but already I feel tired. Tired of being world-weary. Soul-weary. Sad and lonely. Yes, yes, go bury your head in self-pity.

To my surprise, the man chuckles, "Hugging Boy. Hug Boy. Boy Hug...hmmm," he says aloud. "You should tell him that's what you call him. He'd enjoy it too."

Yah! He's kidding right?

There's a smile playing around his lips, but his serious eyes never leave mine. His matted hair is wound in a braid around his head. The intricate coils resemble the pattern of a cowrie seashell; yellowish-white and all held in place with a pin in the form of a crescent moon.

"So, are you going to tell him, yourself?" He raises his hand to take a drag from the hand-made pipe.

There's a second tattoo in the shape of a trident on his right lower arm. This one's dark, almost black, and stands out on his light skin. The sun bounces off his gleaming, teak-colored skin. It's as if he spends as much time polishing himself as he does the lamps.

The silence stretches.

He's waiting for my answer.

"Uh! No," I say. "I doubt hug boy can help me. Help with what I have." I mutter the last in a low voice, but he hears it anyway.

"And what is it you have?" He takes a drag from his pipe and offers it to me. I stare at it then back at his face.

"Really?" I hear the surprise in my voice despite trying my best not to show it. "You're offering me, a teenager, your pipe? To smoke?"

"As if *you* follow the rules?" He is about to take his pipe back, when I lean forward, grab it from him, and put it to my own lips, taking a deep breath. And promptly cough. My lungs are on fire; my throat feels like it is being smothered in clay and little white puffs of smoke roll out of my nostrils.

"What the–what is in this thing?" I say between splutters.

He takes the pipe from my trembling fingers and puffs at it again.

"Not as grown up as you'd like to pretend you are, now, are you?"

I don't reply, and he asks again, "So you were saying... something's not quite right with you? An ailment?"

"Uh, no. Not exactly." I laugh aloud. It sounds so fake, my laugh. I swear to myself. Now he's going to know for sure I'm hiding something. Something no one must guess. Certainly not this...this old man. "And even if I did," I say, "as if I'd tell *you* in our very first meeting?"

He lets out a bark of laugh, "You sure this is the first time we've met, Leana?"

I swear inwardly. "You know my name?"

"As if I am going to tell *you* all my secrets, in our first meeting?" He raises his eyebrows.

"Aha! You admit it then, this is our first meeting."

"Quick you are." He nods. "It is our first meeting, in *this* life, in *this* skin that we wear, yes."

"Oh, please, don't give me a story about reincarnation and the like," I say, trying to sound as if I don't believe him, but my heart begins to beat faster.

"You know you really should put facts to the test before dismissing them this way," he says.

Yah. Whatever. "Interesting tattoos," I blurt out, my gaze drawn once more to the spot between his eyebrows.

"Nice sword," he counters, and I start.

I was so sure no one could see the sword, thought I had hidden it well. I want to cover it up, want to get a large blanket and throw it over myself and hide from the world. I pull out the sword and cradle it on my lap.

Its touch is still new to me, almost as foreign as the beast I carry within myself: my other half.

"Looks ancient, your sword. Where did you get it?" he asks, a quizzical expression in his eyes. A slight smile plays around his brown-with-age lips.

It's as if he knows...No, that's not possible, he can't recognise this sword, can he? He knew my name, though...

"It belongs to me," I say and, unable to stop myself, I bunch the fingers of my left hand and touch the sword, then bring my fingertips back to my lips and kiss them.

"Superstitious, are you?" he asks.

"Not particularly," I reply.

Yes I am. Of course I am, especially right now, when I'm looking to escape my past, to reclaim my future. To reclaim myself.

There you go again, getting philosophical. Overthinking everything. You're so going to tie yourself up in knots.

I blink, take a deep breath to calm myself and try not to shuffle under the lamp seller's piercing scrutiny. It's as if he can read my thoughts, as if he knows me already. Knows me in a simple easy I-see-you-as-you-are-now way.

Clearing my throat I ask, "Are you headed to the market to sell them?" I nod towards his lamps.

"Yes," he nods, "it sprang up after the tsunami; a place for the survivors to barter what they had. When all else fails, we have only the old ways to fall back on."

"Did you see it, the tsunami?"

He laughs at that, "I survived it. Just me and a handful of other kids."

Huh? I've never met a real survivor of the tsunami. Someone who lived through it.

"And you've stayed here since?" I lean forward.

"Where else would I go?" he asks. "This is home." His eyes snap onto mine suddenly. "Now you, you are far from home aren't you? And you're not one of us, either," he says, a canny look coming into his eyes. "You are half-human."

The muscles of my back go rigid. How does he know that?

"Yes," I agree, surprised that he can so quickly tell the delicate difference between a human and a hybrid. We walk more heavily than normal people. There's something not quite human about our footprints. But very few know this.

My eyes narrow and a low growl wells up in my throat. I swallow it down and my fingers graze the sword.

No, don't do that, don't pull out the sword. Not yet.

I tuck my hands back under my thighs, then say, "I don't know where my other half comes from."

No, you lie. You do know what your other half is. You just don't want to 'fess up. Not even to yourself.

"We in Bombay don't have that problem. We are all fully human in this city."

"Really? Everyone here is totally human?"

"Fully, one hundred percent!" he nods.

100% human? No way. My neck muscles go rigid with tension. How had I not known that Bombay was a 'humans only' city? How did I miss that? Do they even welcome hybrids here? All my life I've wanted to be completely human. And now I am surrounded by them. Except I'll never be like them. If I could, I'd tear my skin off my bones and dig into the cells below, and pull out that animal DNA running through me, the one intertwined with my own genome. I would–

No, don't go there. Don't go wishing for something you can never be. Just keep him talking; keep him distracted so he doesn't guess who you really are.

"So was it just the bunch of you kids who survived the storm?" I ask.

"There were others, grown ups too, but we didn't meet them 'til many years later," he says.

"How did you grow up, then? Who took care of you? And all this...?" I gesture to the land we pass by. Land filled with low-rise buildings, children playing by the beaches. "How did all this come about?"

"It's all thanks to Brahma, the founding father of this new world."

"Brahma?" Of course I've heard about him, whispers of how he had helped rebuild the city. But I've never heard the story first hand.

"Tell me more," I say. "How did he save the city?"

"A few months before the tsunami hit, Brahma, then a young soldier in the army, was on a leave of absence, in Bombay. One day when washing his hands in the Banganga Tank—" seeing the question on my face, he explains, "It's an underwater spring at the Walkeshwar temple in Bombay."

"How many temples are there in Bombay, anyway?"

"Too many." He chuckles. "We love our temples, it's where we come together to not only pray but to reassure ourselves that we are together on our shared journeys. That we are not alone." He pauses as if gathering his thoughts. "Anyway where were we?"

"Brahma," I prompt him.

He nods. "Oh, yes. So Brahma is strolling by this beautiful spot. He is in a contemplative mood, wondering what's the point of all this combat? He is gazing into the water, sitting by the edge of the pool, soaking in the quiet, when he feels really thirsty. So, he cups the water from the pool and drinks from it. The water is fresh and sweet, and he's returning for one last sip, when he sees a tiny fish in his cupped palm. To his surprise the fish talks to him.

"It begs him to save it, saying that it would return the favor.

"Brahma asks the fish how something so tiny could save a man like himself?

"The fish replies that there is a great storm on the way, bringing with it floods which will wash away all living things, and it was here to save Brahma from that.

"Despite his misgivings, Brahma takes the fish home and puts it in a pot."

A talking fish? It's just an old story of course, but

somehow I almost believe him.

"And then?" I urge him.

He continues. "Within a day, the fish outgrows the pot, and he has to move it back to the Banganga Tank. The fish keeps growing, so he takes it to a lake. Soon the fish outgrows the lake so he takes it to the open sea. Within a week, the fish is large enough to fill the entire shoreline of the city, and it asks Brahma to build a boat, for the flood is coming. By this time, the skies have darkened with angry clouds, building up, churning crossly.

"Brahma calls all the recruits in the city to help build the ship. When the waters rise, the ship rises with it. The fish advises Brahma to find three women who he thinks he could spend the rest of his life with, and bring them to the ship.

"It tells Brahma to choose such women as represented by the three worlds–heaven, hell and earth–for together they would be creating a new city for future generations. And so he chooses Gayatri the prostitute, Savitri the chef, and Vidya the schoolteacher. When he brings them back to the boat, he finds that the massive fish has reached out to women in the city, asking them to bring their children to the boat to be saved.

"And thus Brahma finds himself with three women and twenty-one children, all born the week before the apocalypse struck."

"Three humans, twenty one babies, and one ship!" I exclaim. "And then there's you and the other kids."

"Twenty four of them and nineteen of us kids made it out alive," he agrees. "Not to forget the big fish, now," he chuckles.

"And did it survive the storm too?"

"Oh! Yes, the fish tows them to safety, away from the city, toward the middle of the ocean where all is calm. And when the tsunami blows itself out, they return."

"To a destroyed city?"

"To the original seven islands that made up Bombay. All through the nineteenth and the twentieth centuries, the city had grown unchecked to become one of the most populated urban areas–and among the richest–in the world. Overnight, all that craving, all that thirst for money and power, was washed away. Nature had taken revenge for the centuries of greed the citizens had indulged in. By the end of 2014, when the waters receded, there was no more maximum city. All that remained was Bombay as it had been in the beginning."

The boat lurches and I jerk out of the images his words have trapped me in.

"Not far now," he says, beginning to gather his lamps.

"Wait, what happened then?" I am holding my breath now; I want him to complete his story. I need to know how it ends. Have to find out.

"What happened to what?" he teases me.

"The children, and Brahma and his women?"

"When the waters settle back, the fish tows them back to the islands, letting them off on a small hill at the southernmost tip of the city. It was the only space with enough fresh water and food to sustain them over the next few years."

"How did Brahma provide for all of them?"

"Brahma knew how to survive. Being in the army had taught him that much. So there, with his new tribe, he stood next to the ancient temple of Lord Shiva, a thousand feet above sea level."

"Was that the only thing to survive? That temple?"

"That, and the temple of the Mother Goddess, Mumbadevi, after whom the city of Bombay is named, emerged unscathed from the tsunami."

"So, at least in destruction, nature had balanced out the masculine and the feminine?"

I don't realize I have said that aloud until he says, "Wise, aren't you? Yes, you can look at it that way too. As you well know, the post tsunami years weren't easy, for it was as if the storm was only the start. Soon after, the effects of global warming accelerated."

He pauses and I take up the story, "The survivors of the storm had to face up to something much bigger; the threat of human extinction, for the sun's radiation grew in intensity, rendering many sterile."

He nods and continues, "Some died without progeny. Others began mating with non-human species, the only way to propagate their bloodlines. All of this happened only in the last decade."

When he stops, I know it's my turn. It's as if we are trading words in a twisted relay race, each of us reading from a puzzle that has already been solved.

"And yet," I swallow, "yet, Bombay managed to keep its blood-lines pure." My voice tapers off but my mind is racing with questions. How had they done this? Unless, unless they have a way of keeping us hybrids out.

But if they did, why haven't I heard about it before?

My lips curl back and I want to snarl and demand he stop playing games with me, but instead I ask, "And how did the people of this city keep the purity of their genes? How did you stay 100% human with so few left?"

"We are selective about who we let into the city, and who we take on as partners and spouses." He pauses, looking at me thoughtfully, "In fact it makes me wonder what you are doing here. What are you up to, Leana?"

He stares at me, and there's this expression on his face, a wise, knowing look that sears through me. I blink, but can't look away. I am trapped in that all seeing stare of his.

The hairs on my forearms stand on end, and I know then that he knows what I know. He knows who I really am.

No, he doesn't. He has no idea. Him and his tall stories.

And if he does know, if he has guessed that so quickly, then he can't live. Not if he's guessed my ancestry, my true identity, or where I am headed with the sword.

I pull the blade out of its sheath and leap at him.

***

Sept 30, 2060. 7pm

Bam. Bam. Bam. Those drums are so loud. Who's beating them so?

I stir and pain shoots through my skull, bouncing off one side, swinging to the next and back to the other side, and back again.

BAM. BAM. BAM. The beating intensifies, sparking red behind my eyeballs, knocking against my ears with such violence, everything goes quiet for a second before the sounds from the outside world rush right back, smashing straight into the bottom of my skull. I groan.

Die. Die now. Anything is better than this horrible, horrible pain that's tearing me apart.

A touch to my forehead, and something cool flows over my head, over my hair, down my feverish cheeks, splashing over my chest and taking some of the pain with it.

Then there's a pause during which the pain rushes in again, greedily, taking over, and then the water flows in again.

Pain.

Water.

Pain.

Water.

The ebb and flow is killing me. The lack of pain only makes the return of the throbbing so much worse. The contrast hurts much more than being bathed in one long stream of pain. All. The. Time. I push myself up to my feet, swaying, dragging my legs, one step. Two. Three. Four. Five. Six. Seven. Eight. Nine. Ten. Keep counting. Keep going. I walk up the beach. Half way up the shore and I am sinking down and falling slowly.

***

I open my eyes and blink a few times to clear them. In front of me, all I can see is black and brown and gray. No, it's sand. Sand. I'm on the beach.

Darkness has fallen and the tide has crept in after me, lapping at my feet now. I bring a hand up to touch my forehead, and a spark of red and yellow shoots through my skull. My hand falls to the side. There's a throb at the base of my skull.

Getting up to my feet, I walk slowly up the rest of the beach. Reaching the low wall skirting the garden behind it, I lower myself against it, leaning my head against the bricks. Ah! That's better. My neck's not strong enough to support me yet. I close my eyes and drift.

A dog barks in the distance, the palm trees rustle from somewhere overhead. The waves come in with a swoooooosh and pull back with a swaaaaaash.

I breathe in and out. In and out. Flow in with the wave and out again. In and out. In and out. The rhythm calms me, lulls me a little, and sleep creeps in on the wings of the next wave. Then a laugh peals through the air. A girl screams with surprise. More laughter and a boy yells, "I am so gonna get you."

I turn slowly and, by the time I look over the wall, they have run past me and towards the outline of a building in the distance.

There are colored lights outlining a small minaret, pyramidal almost. A temple? Now that I focus on the scene,

I'm not sure, but I think there are stalls stretching out from the main building and moving figures milling around it. A warm breeze blows the faint notes of music towards me.

What's this? A celebration of some kind?

The building ahead looks vaguely familiar. Where have I seen it before? I get to my feet, ignoring the knock of pain against my temples. Out of habit, I feel for the sword nestled against my back and then swear. It's not there. Of course not. He took it. Why, that old conniving bastard.

Anger bubbles up under my skin, pushing aside the last vestiges of pain, so my nerve endings all snap to attention. I turn back to look at the yawning darkness behind me. Aki, the lamp seller. The most skilled swordsman in this new world. He'd been waiting for me. He knew who I was, where I was going. He hit me, injured me, took my sword and pushed me overboard.

Now, I'm furious. The blood rushes to my head and I swear aloud. You stupid, stupid girl. That doddering old man got the better of you. Okay, so not that doddering, and he was pretty good with a sword. But he was old, one-foot-in-the-grave old, and yet you couldn't defeat him. He was better than you, way better than you, and he kicked your ass, all right. Now, what are you going to do? You sad little girl!

I growl aloud, adrenaline rushing through my bloodstream.

Every individual hair on my body stands on end. My eyes refocus, searing through the dark. My night vision readjusts and I take in the scene. Every. Little. Detail. I make out the carvings of the temple; the red-brick colored minaret shooting up; the individual statues scattered in the courtyard, colored in lurid blues and greens; and around it, people. I look down and see the hair on my arms stand up, and grow longer and thicker.

No. No. No. Don't give in. Not now.

A burst of energy has me leaping over the wall and I jog towards the temple.

Keep moving, keep going.

I know where I am, now. It's the temple I had seen from the ferry, the temple of the Hugging Saint. Hug boy's temple. Apparently the lamp seller dropped me off here. But, why, why would he do that?

I'm not sure. I don't know why I'm going to the temple either. But it's like the animal inside–the wolf–is taking over.

No, I cannot. I will not let that happen.

I fist my hands at my side and will the nails to retract. To my relief, they obey me. For now.

Take a deep breath.

Another.

Another.

Keep going.

I walk past the brightly colored stalls along the perimeter of the grounds. My nostrils quiver as I smell freshly made snacks. My mouth waters, and I swallow down the pang of hunger that leaps up into my mouth.

I reach a stall selling small mounds of sweetened cheese shot through with saffron threads, sprinkled with cardamom powder, and slivered with almond and pistachio. I can't move further. Have to eat. Have to get my hands on the food.

I stand there watching the cupcakes. The man behind the counter picks a few of the perfect treats, wraps them and hands it over with a smile. When I don't take it, he says, "Go ahead. It's free for the pilgrims."

I grab it and dart out.

The first one is crunched, gone, swallowed. And the next. On the third I finally taste the honey pouring out of the cake into my tongue and gasp at the sweetness. I shut my eyes and let the sugar-high shoot through my veins. A shriek of delight pulls my eye to the amusement rides.

I pass children waiting their turns on the joyrides. So well behaved they are. Almost as if they are too scared to be happy. That if they are happy, then sadness can only be round the corner.

The food fills some of the yawning darkness inside me. It's calmed me enough for me to follow a slowly moving line of people. An inscription on the outside wall of the temple reads–

'The Ganesh Orphanage & Interfaith Home, 2016.'

And below that in, smaller script, 'Built on the site of the original Ganesh temple that was destroyed by the tsunami of 2014.'

Ganesh–the elephant headed god. The queue circles around a small idol of him in the outer sanctum. Many bow their heads in prayer; some stretch out in front to seek his blessings before they continue.

It must be amazing to believe in something bigger than you. A power you can't see, only feel sometimes as it leads you along. And then we are in the inner perimeter of the temple. A hush falls over the already silent crowd.

I can make out a figure on the dais in front of us. It's a boy seated on a large armchair.

The man at the head of the queue kneels and touches his forehead to the ground. Then, getting to his feet, he walks up the steps towards the figure, and bends down so he is at eye-level with a boy who opens his arms and hugs him and whispers something in his ears. Then, the man is ushered to his feet by the boy's helpers.

Without pause, the next woman in the queue first bows to the boy, steps onto the stage, is hugged, whispered to, and ushered on.

And the next person is hugged.

And the next.

And the one after that.

And another.

That's a lot of hugs coming from one young boy, hell, coming from anyone really. Just watching him makes me tired and dizzy.

As I get closer, I see he doesn't look tired, though. In fact, he's smiling slightly. And his pale skin glows like ivory. He has long hair, almost blue-black in color, that flows down his back. His eyes are lined with kohl, so they stand out against his pale skin.

I tap the young girl in front of me and ask, "Guess that's the Hug Boy–uh, I mean the Hugging Saint?"

She nods and a smile lights up her face. "Yes," she says, "that's him."

"Why does he do that? Hug people?" I ask.

She looks at me in surprise, as if I should know, as if everyone in this city is in on the secret but me.

"Well?" I prod her.

"He takes care of us," she says.

"So, this is an orphanage?"

"We are orphans," she smiles, "and this is our home. Are you going to let him hug you? You should; it's really wonderful."

"So, he's a professional hugger?" I chuckle a little, but there is no answering grin on her face.

Her forehead furrows, "I suppose you could call him that. It's simple really; many of us don't have any family. No parents or aunts or any other grown ups to take care of us. The orphanage provides food, clothing and shelter. But he," she looks towards the figure on the dais with adoring eyes, "he makes us feel safe, even if just for a little while. Just providing the basic necessities in life is not enough. It's also very important to be hugged, you know?"

"So, food, clothing, and hugs? That's his magic formula?" I try to sneer but actually I agree with her.

It all makes sense, in some hidden, forgotten part of me. That wild restless part of me. The one that wants to be set free and be close to earth and nature and the spirits. The part that can't be cowed. The beast in me that I have never managed to tame. That animal half of me that's simple and basic and sees everything in black and white. The wolf in me is content, and accepts what I am hearing.

Of course, it's nice to be hugged, isn't it?

And then, it's my turn, and he's opening his arms.

I drop to my knees on the cushion in front of him and lean into his embrace. A musky scent of rose mixed with cinnamon rises up to push at the space between my eyes. It's as if he has reached inside and touched that inner essence inside of me. The one that has no shape, no form, no color. For a few seconds, my eyes close shut and everything stops. Then he releases me, and I look at him stupidly.

"But aren't you going to whisper something to me?" I ask.

He smiles then and leans closer, "Do as you will, I will not stop you," he says.

And then his helpers are taking me away and I don't want to go.

I want to stay and be hugged once more. I want to be held and to feel like I belong somewhere. I want to stay, and the words just burst out "That's not fair. You can't send me on my way like this. You can't. You can't."

But his helpers get me off stage and take me halfway back to the exit leading to the open perimeter and then they leave me, and return to the dais. Back to the Hugging Saint and the next person to be hugged.

I stand there, unsure of what happened.

How dare he just send me on like that, and with nothing to help me? Nothing to actually tell me what to do next? And then I realize I had come here looking for guidance, for help. I need him to tell me what to do with my life. Here I am alone, stranded, many, many miles from home. And I have lost the only thing that linked me to my roots: the sword. And all he can tell me is to do as I will? Well then. That's exactly what I'm going to do now.

I shut my eyes, take a deep breath and let myself fall into me. Breathe out and fall deeper.

Breath in. Go deep.

Breathe out and go deeper.

Deep, deep, keep going further.

Into that well of darkness inside, in that hidden part of me, tucked away since before I was born.

Breathe in and let go.

Breathe out.

Let go.

Go.

And let that arrow of gold shoot out, streak through the darkness, and follow it, up, up, up, through my eyes and out. I crouch down, push back on my hind legs and leap forward. Forward. Forearms thrusting out. Strong, muscled arms, hair bristling, standing on end. And leap, over the heads of the crowds, above the people screaming, yelling, scattering around me. Terror lights up their eyes. I know that fear. The kind I saw when I had first transformed at thirteen and discovered the wolf inside me. I had been unable to control it then, had to give into the animal. Had to let it take over. My wolf had killed my ma.

All she said before she died was, "You are so like your father."

The human part of me had heard and remembered that, of course. Remembered it vividly. You could have said something about that earlier Ma.

All those years I wanted to know about my father and you'd refused to even talk about him, and tell me that the animal inside me was a wolf. And I had to find out the hard way, and look how well that went. Now, I'll never forgive myself, not my human self. Never. Ever.

My wolf had been happy, though. Quite pleased and sated with the kill, too, she had been. She had quenched her thirst with my mother's blood. But now, that doesn't matter.

My wolf wants more. More of the thrill of the chase and the pleasure of another kill. And now, there's nothing to stop it. To stop me.

I jump onto the dais and remain there, quivering and restless.

I can smell the boy's helpers; a familiar scared-helpless-adrenaline-charged stink leaps off them, bathing me in anticipation, sparking off little lights of delight in my brain. My stomach rumbles. I have been hungry for so long and I can't wait any more. Blood thumping in my ears, breath heaving through my lungs, heart pounding in my chest, I jump and bring them both down.

Burying my jaws into the throat of one, I tear out the flesh and drink his blood. His scream echoes in my ears, sharpening that edge of expectation even more. My teeth grind through his veins and drink of his blood while my front paws carve out a healthy chunk from the side of the other guy. His entrails hang out; sausage-shaped small intestines that I yank out and heave aside. But it's not enough. I want him. Him. HE who set me off. He who is responsible for my finally giving in to my baser side. For revealing the beast inside. I spring, muscles heaving and rippling under my skin, and then I am on the boy.

That soft, cushy armchair of his topples and I am straddling him, standing over him and holding him down. My breath rushes out, hot and furious, caressing his cheeks; crimson colored spittle hanging from my jaws streaks his shirt.

The rose-cinnamon aroma of his skin mixed with the salt of the sea air rises up and flows around me, over me, seeping into me.

My front paws dig into his chest and I look into his eyes. His dark, blue-black eyes. And in them I see myself for what I am. An animal. A lost, confused, senseless-with-grief girl. A confused, half human half wolf, in girl's clothing. A hungry wolf girl so like her father. Hungry for food, for love, for attention. For my place in this world.

The boy holds my gaze and, raising his arms, he puts them around me. He hugs me. And I begin to cry.

***

ABOUT THE AUTHOR

She had an awesome time launching TV channels for MTV and NBCUniveral (Syfy) around the world, when a near death experience convinced Laxmi Hariharan that she had to get writing. A one-time journalist with The Independent, she has since published fast paced, action thrillers, such as the multi award winning RUBY IYER SERIES. She blogs for the Huffington Post, has written for The Guardian and been featured in many publications including The Times of India. Married to a filmmaker and fellow author, her life often resembles a dramedy of errors film script. She is also the proud owner of a mononym

Receive a free copy of THE RUBY IYER DIARIES when you sign up to her newsletter: http://bit.ly/NewsletterLH

@laxmi : https://twitter.com/laxmi
Instagram: https://instagram.com/laxmiwrites/
FB: https://www.facebook.com/laxmihariharanauthor
Blog: http://www.laxmihariharan.com/
Amazon: http://www/amazon.com/author/laxmihariharan

MADE FOR THIS
BY SESSHA BATTO

The irony of his situation was one of its most pleasing aspects. He was, after all, a creature made for submission. To be tied to a master who desired domination almost made up for the past. Almost.

The incident itself was two decades behind him.

He barely recognized himself as the shyly snarky pseudo-intellectual who had so earnestly argued gender politics in an attempt to impress some silly coeds. That he had survived the psychosis his words inspired was, truly, miraculous. Or so he had been told. In truth, most days he considered his current life a cruel joke by an angry god. Personal vengeance, perhaps, for some grand transgression he had already forgotten.

His transit from cocky grad student to genderless thing had been swift, not subtle. He'd walked through that park a thousand times without encountering anyone. It never occurred to him that such seclusion might come at a price. To this day he still marveled that so much loss came so silently. He never even heard the shot.

Looking back, he hates how surprised he was to be confronted by a girl he had so easily cast aside. The trauma surgeon refused to try and rebuild the shredded lump of flesh, realizing that salvaging a gnarled stump of cock would be pointless. The bullet had merely nicked his scrotum, but there wasn't much point to balls without a cock, and the repair was simpler with a single graft.

The surgeon had argued the advantages of gender transition. Hormones would be a part of his life now, no matter what. But it was easy to arrogantly argue the benefits of such a thing when not faced with the reality of it. In the end he knew playing at female would be even less satisfactory than accepting his sexlessness. He still had the heart of a cocksman, even if he lacked the necessary equipment.

At the trial, she laughed when they handed down her punishment. Ten years against his life sentence seemed like a good bargain.

Afterward, he tried to go on as if nothing had changed, subsuming his anger in pain pills, liquor, and futile, chaste dalliances with women. In the end, he found himself neither wiser nor calmer. Even the debates on art and culture he had once so fervently engaged in lost their meaning. His facility with words had vanished with his cock. Listening suited his newly passive nature, until even that required more of himself than he had left to give. The thought that everyone knew drove him into seclusion.

A chance encounter led him to a place he never imagined finding himself. After all, what use is a sex club to the sexless? Five minutes was enough to confirm he longed to be the one wielding the whip. The fact that he was willing to dole out such pain sent him running for the exit.

"Are you leaving because you hate it, or because you despise yourself for not hating it?" The hand latched onto his arm in a death grip forced him to actually consider the question.

"I shouldn't even be here. This is no place for someone like me."

"On the contrary, I think this is exactly where you should be." The retort on the tip of his tongue melted away as he got his first look at man behind the voice. "Why don't we sit down and you can tell me why you don't think you belong here."

Ten years later that voice could still bring him to his knees.

"Aren't you a pretty thing." Such notice from the faceless crowd jerked him back to the present, to the role he was expected to play. It was a toss-up as to which was more unsettling, the crop in his hand, or the massive phallus studded with shiny balls of stainless steel protruding from the codpiece he wore. Both were symbols of how far he had fallen, or risen, he was as conflicted about that as everything else in this scene.

But, as always, that voice had convinced him to push past his conflict with an ease that baffled him. Had he been this easily lead when he was whole? But now was not the time for such philosophical contemplations.

Up on the platform his master shivered in his bonds, inked trails oozing out of the tight corset wrapping his midsection, leather pants jerked down to his knees to expose the pale, silky flesh of his ass for all to admire.

Master, the heart of his confliction. The man who had simultaneously saved and condemned him. The sun around which he now orbited, a wayward planet still tugging at its leash. Muscles tensed and twitched in anticipation as he traced idle patterns, afterimages burning a trail that flared into need.

"Are you ready?" As ritual demanded he broke his silent contemplation, more sure of the answer than his question.

"Yes." The husky tremor in his master's voice spurred his resolve. The crop snapped against porcelain flesh, leaving a mark, his mark, and the demon of rage slumbering inside him tore free.

When he finally stopped, every inch of exposed flesh bore the record of his madness, reddened welts mixing with tribal tattoos in a cacophony of frustrated desire.

Now came the part he dreaded. The beast inside him tamed, for the moment, leaving him without the will to finish this passion play. That his master was willing, prepped and waiting gave him no comfort. The murmur of the watchers spurred him into action, and he buried the ridiculous faux-cock to the hilt.

His fingernails dug ragged furrows into reddened cheeks as his mind trumpeted the futility of his actions. Pegging was a game for women, not men. His cheeks flamed as he realized all the silent watchers must know of his peculiar lack. In an effort to disprove that knowledge he redoubled his efforts, plowing into the writhing figure with greater abandon.

As with all good things, his frustrated rage couldn't last. Absent sexual satisfaction or the driving force of anger, their copulation became just another task to complete. He found himself counting the indentations on the soundproofed wall, picturing towering mammatus clouds in their place. When the figure beneath him began to whimper he breathed a silent sigh of relief. The sticky spray of his master's semen meant he could, at last, put aside this facade.

The transit from top to bottom was mercifully brief. The cruel cock discarded, he was stripped, spread, bound, and his soul absolved. Freed from the need to think, able to lose himself in sensation.

This was the instant he now lived for, his desire released from the cage in which he kept it securely locked up.

As the first cock slipped inside him, his breath caught, by the fifth he was panting, by the tenth, at last, transported. He shuddered through what passed as orgasm and fell into darkness. His last thought that perhaps he could stay cocooned in the soft richness of this moment.

His eyes snapped open, Master slumbered beside him, ointment-coated welts glistening in the dim light. And so it began again, the futile race to oblivion that trapped him in the present. His joy, his terror, his destiny fulfilled.

***

ABOUT THE AUTHOR:

Sword wielding Buddhist author of transgressive homoerotic fiction, Sessha turned to writing full time after a twenty year stint in video production editing, scripting and creating motion graphics. Her novels include Strength of Will and the Shinobi Saga – Geisha, Shadow Wolf and the soon to be released Ripples. Her short stories are included in the anthology Sex Ray Specs. Her Celtic fairy tale Amadan na Briona is part of eightcuts gallery's Once Upon a Time in a Gallery exhibit. Her short story The Poetry Game is included in New Sun Rising: Stories for Japan, an anthology for tsunami relief. Originally from Belfast, she lives in the States with her husband, son, three cats and too many swords. Read more about her work on her website http://sesshabattousai.com or follow her on twitter @SesshaBatto

Website: http://sesshabattousai.com
Facebook: https://www.facebook.com/pages/The-World-of-Sessha-Batto
twitter https://twitter.com/SesshaBatto
google+ https://plus.google.com/u/0/+SesshaBatto/posts
pinterest http://www.pinterest.com/SesshaBatto

From the Inside
by Daniel Arthur Smith

In those days, I was compelled to keep moving and I'd planned to drift in for a day, maybe two, see the renaissance sights, then journey back to the vitality of Prague, but my meanderings through the village's maze of worn cobblestone streets were darkened by cloud clusters and a relentless rain that failed to cease that day or the next. Within a week, the rising waters brought on by the endless downpour were being called the hundred-year flood, and I was riding out the storm in the shadow of a cupcake castle, in a hostel with the coincidental name of *U Vodnika*–the Water Troll's House– watching the Vltava river rage by, while Tom Waits sang of inebriated pianos.

At that time, the backpacker drunkards that Europassed station to station through Western Europe in their beer hall quest seldom navigated the complex train bus connection required to travel southern Bohemia, so the storied thirteenth century town of Cesky Krumlov remained a secret to true seekers. Appropriately and predictably, my fellow confined guests in the Troll's House were a cadre of eclectics, professionals on personal pilgrimages, overachieving entrepreneurs in search of themselves and spiritual adventure, dedicated trekkers and globe trotting travelers, those more interested in the history of the castle's gypsy caretakers, the enchanted baroque and rococo gardens, the mystic ley lines, and the stories of alchemists and the local Rosicrucian Enlightenment than merely drinking away their Grand Tour.

But, even self described new Bohemians can succumb to monotony. Adrift in the doldrums, the high-minded opt for high and we were as lost at sea as any motley crew. The spliffs floating around the hostel may've been many or one eternally lit, it was hard to tell and it mattered not because the gray U Vodnika days had become indistinguishable, repetitive cycles of journals, sketchbooks, and board games by the open window.

So it was that we entertained where we could.

I had plenty of LSD, which I was happy to share, but doses had to be spaced a few nights apart at best for full effect.

It was on one of those tripping nights, amidst of the worst of the rain, when the dark day before hadn't even lightened to gray and the sky had gone absolutely electric, that Kiwi Dave stumbled into U Vodnika, parka pouring water, a wide grin on his face, and a twinkle in his eye as if he was finishing a garden stroll rather than seeking shelter from the storm of the century.

Kiwi Dave, as his name suggested, was from New Zealand. He was Caucasian but he assured us that even though he went by the name Kiwi Dave, his ancestry was Maori. Nobody questioned, the travelers in the hostel weren't the questioning type. He was a naturally upbeat, high-energy fellow, constantly on the move, doing yoga, running errands into town for the group, and within days actually climbing U

Vodnika's walls. To do this he would scoot up between the sides of the hallway and rest for hours compressed between them, and other times he would suspend himself from the high wooden beams of the common area for the entirety of the afternoon. He'd even strung his climbing hammock up there so he could sleep suspended.

Quiet times in the Troll's House were punctuated by tales of travel—the outrageous and mundane—such as how long it took to secure a visa, who had to secure a visa, how lucky the Kiwi was that he could travel anywhere without one. Kiwi Dave seemingly had visited most everywhere and had the best stories of checkpoints and corruption, most consisting of a border guard and an empty bottle of vodka.

And then there were ugly tales of refugees from the Serbian waged wars and what we'd heard was still going on there—murder, neighbor against neighbor. Nancy, a girl from Johannesburg, spoke of modern Joy Divisions, girls rounded up from the local towns to be forced into the sex trade for the soldiers in the once busy ski resorts that peppered the Bosnian slopes.

Gray conversation for gray days.

But it was Kiwi Dave and one of those former conversations of the mundane variety that led me to Budapest, and her, the de-fingered woman.

He was up in his hammock when Peter, a twenty something Afrikaan of mysterious background and means, shared an article he was reading. There were stacks of travel magazines lining the wall and we'd all taken our turn flipping through the tattered pages, yet somehow Peter discovered an unread feature of particular interest within a National Geographic.

"Unbelievable," Peter said.

"What's that?" Rahm asked. Rahm was a modern hippie in a Henley. He'd confided in me that his parents were

upscale holistic healers in Woodstock, an interesting fella to
be locked in with. He and I were playing one of the countless
games of Go by the window. We'd moved the black and white
pebbles around each other for hours, sipping honey tea until
it grew cold and then adding more hot to keep the small
glasses full. At one point in the day the honey tea would
become grog, but we'd yet to add the rum.

Peter continued. I guess he decided we'd be most
interested since everyone else had huddled into a bunk with a
book or a partner–there was a lot of that during the rain too.
"It says here that the Aboriginal fishing women in New South
Wales tie coarse twine around their pinkies until the upper
joints die from blood loss and fall off. After the finger dies from
the twine tourniquet, they row out to sea and throw it into the
ocean to be eaten by fish. Can you believe that?"

That is where Dave cut in. "The twine is made of spider
web."

"No way," Rahm said.

"Big spiders," Dave said.

"That's what it says," Peter said. "They wind the spider
thread to make a twine. How'd you know?"

"I visited a tribe. Not in New South Wales, but close. Same
custom."

The three of us shrugged matter-of-factly.

Dave sat up in his hammock, bowing his head below the
ceiling, "They believe there's a link between the finger and
the hand it came from." He wiggled his pinky. "They figure
the finger wants to get back to the hand, and if it's in the fish,
that fish will come with it."

Peter walked over to share the photos. "Yeah, they're all
missing a finger."

As he described, the women in the picture held up their
nets with one hand and their pinky-less hands palm open for
the camera to see.

"They're highly revered," Dave said.

Rahm nodded, "Yeah, I've heard of that. The finger stump is a symbol of social standing." He axed his right hand down across his left pinky. "They're held in high regard because the same magic that brings the fish goes into every fishing line they make. The more digits the better."

I watched him, disturbed, as he continued to land his flesh axe first on the outer joint and then on the inner, as if deciding which he would cut.

"It's true. I've seen it," Dave said. "The fishing line is strong as all hell." His eyes went wide. "I've got some."

"You don't say," I said.

"I'll show you." In a single fluid motion, Dave slipped from his hammock, swung from a beam, then down to the floor.

"I get it," I said as he dug at his pack. "The devotion to the craft." I dropped a black pebble on the Go board grid and Rahm quickly placed a white one next to it to eat it away. "I mean, they must've realized long ago that the pinky was in the way of making the fishing lines and the nets. That's devotion. It's like Zorba in that Kazantzakis book."

"What book?" Peter asked.

"Nikos Kazantzakis wrote this book, *Zorba the Greek*."

"I've read it," Dave chimed. "It's good."

"Yeah, well, it's kind of a trope where the simple guy teaches the smart guy. Anyway, Zorba tells the narrator all of these stories, and one of them is that when he wanted to become a potter but every time he sat down at the potter's wheel, his thumb ended up in the way, destroying the clay." I wiggled my thumb in an odd fashion. "So his solution was to cut off his thumb."

Peter's face became a mix of dislike and disgust.

Dave returned to the table with a small coil of red, waxy line. "I know someone who really did that," he said.

"Did what?" I asked, examining the sinewy line. "Cut off their thumb for the potter's wheel?"

"Cut off their finger for art and magic."

"Yeah right," Rahm said.

"Check this out," Dave said. He pulled up the thin scrap of a blue tee he had on.

Now, Dave could support his own weight by his fingertips. He was fit, muscular, and toned. His six-pack belly was cut in high definition, as was his chest. He was a man in his prime. But what drew our attention was the fresh, mesmerizing ink, raised plump above rose red flesh.

It was a tattoo unlike any I'd ever seen before.

Perfectly set into the contours of his chest was a fist sized black disc, and stemming from the center, directly above his heart, the coiled tip of a silver fern that draped down across his midriff to his waist. I'd seen plenty of tattoos before, as well as what was new in the studios–ash rubbed carvings, silicone injected words and designs, hard plastic implants in the shape of sheep horns. I'd even seen the newest battery operated electric displays that slid beneath the skin and lit up any neon color you'd like. But I'd never seen metallic silver ink before, nor had I ever put eyes upon a tattoo that appeared to hover above the flesh and ripple with his breath. This wasn't a mere image–this ink was alive.

"That's amazing," I said. "Where'd you get that?"

"Thanks," Dave said. "This was inked freehand, no pattern, by an artist in Budapest. She had to cut two fingers off to get that type of precision."

"Like Zorba," I said.

"More than that," Dave said. "Like the Aborigines, this Tattoo Artist has a magical connection to her work."

Rahm's expression was one of not giving in, "That's an incredible tattoo. I mean out of this world. But magical?"

I wanted to disagree. The tip of the silver fern, the coil, appeared to spin, drilling into Dave's chest.

"The artist said she drew it out from the inside. It's like a shield, as magic as that fishing line." Dave bit his lip in what I guessed was a flash of thought. "I'll tell you what," he said, "let's go toss that line in the river and see how long it takes to catch a fish."

A fool's errand down to the rushing Vltava was far from my mind. "Why don't we boil some water and break out the rum first," I said. "I want to hear more about this Budapest artist."

***

Ruminations of Dave's tattoo and the mysterious de-fingered artist who had inked him became an obsession. I found myself shadowing the Kiwi around the hostel, absently glaring at his sleeveless tee, as if to pierce through it, and if by chance I did catch a glimpse, even a small portion of the rippling silver or black, a wave of euphoria would wash over me and all else in the room would fade until only I and that mark were alone in a void. More than once someone snapped me from the trance with a mention of my name. A joke would be made of the LSD or the walls closing in and we'd have a laugh. But that wasn't the cause of my daze; it was the ink, it was her.

The more I dwelled, the more anxious I became. The tattoo began to appear everywhere. The seductive ink manifested in the shadows beneath the bunks and the unlit rooms, in the grains of the old hostel's thick wooden beams, and through the open window I saw the swirling silver fern in the torrents of the rain.

I volunteered to run the market errands, to escape the confines of the hostel. She was there, past the corner of my eye. The image would come quickly, shimmering like the Kiwi's tattoo, a dancer in the rain, a gypsy perhaps, her long swirling skirt and her wide flung arms flowing up, leaving a trail echoing behind. My heart would beat fast and I'd spin to look, never catching the woman unseen. The visions had infected me and festered so deeply that there was no place in my waking state where they didn't appear, and when the time came to sleep, they were worse. Night upon night I'd wake to lightning and thunder, my knapsack soaked, hair matted with sweat.

One night I awoke standing on the bank of the Vltava, having walked into the storm and down the stony path in my sleep. Rivulets ran from my forehead to my cheeks, down my warm wet body, and the boxer shorts I wore, my sole clothing, hung drenched from my waist.

I was staring off to the southeastern horizon and must've been for some time because my bare feet were seated deeply into the mud. That's when the yearning to journey back on the road began. Not the wanderlust that'd first brought me to the Austrian border, and not the cabin fever of being held up in the Water Troll's House. No, this was something different. Somewhere out on that horizon the living ink called to me.

Two infinite weeks of fever dream delusion passed before the cerulean skies returned. I lusted to leave but the damage brought on by weeks of rain was far worse than I'd imagined. The nearby Austrians, those with access to what was happening across Central Europe, shared the new word for the storm, Jahrtausendflut: the Millennium Flood. I guess after the Poles and Bohemians tolled the death and destruction, they felt the need to up the Hundred-Year Flood by a factor of ten.

With the bus and rail lines yet to be clear, the picturesque village was destined to be my prison for a few days more.

But the ink continued to call.

To curb my anxiety, I ventured to the castle that'd loomed above us for the past month and, in the lush rococo gardens, gifted myself with a double dose of LSD. I strode out into the rolling hills, expecting the young nun Maria to come running across, singing of her life and the sound of music, and I gazed out over the red roofed town as murmurations of starlings formed atomic symbols, whirling dancers, silver ferns, and de-fingered hands.

The thought of her would not leave, and, back at the hostel, my distraction with the Kiwi continued.

If in all this time Dave noticed, he was kind enough not to say. But of course, he knew. And the morning of my departure, he sat beside me at the table and drew the map that would take me to her. He was calmer than I'd seen him before, almost somber. And I realized he was about to pass along a piece of information intended for me alone.

The map was simple.

Scrawled down the middle, a wavy line—the Danube— Buda and the citadel were to the west of the river, and Pest, the inner city, to the right.

As Dave filled in the tiny landmarks, he softly spoke. "These are the medieval Rudas Baths. You have to go here before you see her."

"There will be plenty of time for sightseeing after I see her," I said.

Dave gave me a stern look. "It's your opportunity to cleanse your spirit. The bath's thermal waters have medicinal and magical properties. If you don't go there first, she'll send you there."

I almost questioned his mention of the magical but swallowed back my words.

The novice in me must've shown through because Dave dropped the harsh glare. He traced his pencil over the bridge, "Take the trolley up the main avenue two city blocks in. Then go north." He scribbled an address in the corner. "You'll find her here."

"Will I need an appointment?" I asked.

"No. She doesn't work that way. She'll see you or she won't."

"Who do I ask for?"

"Her name is Anika. But you'll know her when you see her." Dave hesitated. "It's not just her fingers."

"What do you mean?"

"You'll see." He drew a thin rectangle back by the river. "Go here to the Marriot when you're finished."

"What happens there?"

"They have a fantastic view of Buda and the Danube and the best cheesecake I've ever had, excellent with brandy."

***

Before the storm, the ink, the visions, Prague was one of the few places I'd lived where each morning was a miracle and every time I set foot outside my flat I was astounded by my surroundings. The onion domes, sherbet facades, and Kafka's castle overlooking it all—the mother of cities was the new Left Bank and she never disappointed. Jazz horns played, absinthe poured, and love was free. But upon my arrival from the south, the golden city–newly washed and shimmering from the rains–was a pale, bland, monochrome town, and though my many friends were surely wondering what happened when my weekend foray became extended by the weeks long flood, the rapid beat of my heart compelled me to catch the first train Budapest bound. As it was, that train didn't depart until four in the morning.

Rather than be chased down twisted alleys and across wide squares by shadows only I could see, I found the only private space readily available, a slab of cold unoccupied cement in a stairwell of the Prague train station, and closed my eyes to muster what sleep I could until it was time to embark.

My cabin was compact, my seat a mere bench. The next six hours were a blur of industrial Slovakia, stark Hungarian fields, Aborigine fishing women, and their self-mutilated hands reaching for me.

When the train rolled into Keleti station, I was little more rested than when I'd left Prague. I hefted my pack onto a mustard yellow Buda bound trolley and the guesthouse I'd arranged. I arrived too early for my bed and was sent to wait in the backyard of the hostel on a carpet covered dais the guests used for meditation. I succumbed to the large incense infused pillows and collapsed until the evening. The dais may've been my first and only haven for the past weeks, for when I woke to eat and move into my readied bed I was met with more wakeful dreams of the de-fingered hand and living ink.

The next day, I followed Dave's instructions, went to the Rudas Baths, and did my best to lose myself in the spa. I donned a loincloth, let the heated sulphur smelling water of the octagon pool soak into me as I gazed up into the patterns of the ancient Turkish dome. But there was no losing myself. All the while, my mind was with the mysterious Anika. Phantom fog formations confronted me as I wandered through the depths of the blazing steam rooms, each one hotter than the last. The seething mineral gases seeped deep into my lungs, scalded my core, yet I pushed further, until I could stand the heat no more.

I never reached a point I was sure I was as cleansed but when my skin had soaked in all of the medicinal waters it could, I dressed and boarded a trolley to Pest.

***

I got off the trolley at the stop past the bridge and followed the Kiwi's map to the small arcade mall where he'd said I'd find Anika's studio. Like many European arcades, the enclosed first floor mall was an empty strip of glass facades. I'd seen the same layout in Madrid, Barcelona, and Prague. Some developer saw the future, threw a pot full of money into a build-it-they-will-come dream that never panned—the location was too hidden and tucked away for the vision to ever be real.

Tinny seventies rock resonated from the bowels of the failed retail tunnel and my boots clopped an echo off the high sheen floor. Hungarian newsprint papered the glass of all but a few storefronts–the types of places opened by the management's wife, girlfriend, or daughter. A tree of plastic wrapped lollipops adorned the entrance of a pink walled candy shop and two doors down was the token costume jewelry store.

The only other occupied shop in the doomed complex faced me from the end of the corridor, where the arcade turned to the right. Rather than newsprint, the stall's glass was walled with Hungarian concert posters and a red and blue neon tattoo sign.

Beneath my throat I felt a flutter, an urge to flee. I denied the anxiety. I was too close, my body resistant to entering Anika's studio but my mind willing. My steps became purposeful, forced.

As I went farther, the shaft of daylight at my back faded, the darkness encroached from the unoccupied wing to the right, and the neon glow grew more ominous.

The darkness only added to my anxiety. My chest grew tight and my legs sluggish, the mineral infused blood throughout my body thickened to sludge.

I stopped outside her door. The ostinato of Zeppelin's Kashmir pelted me from inside her studio. The thought flashed through my mind that I was alone in that under city. The Earth had swallowed me up. The idea of magic made sense to me, coursed through me with the rhythms and wails of Plant and Page. I was in an old city, in the womb of a village aged thousands of years.

I studied myself. My breathing and heart beat slowed. The darkness that surrounded me seemed to fall away and the soft orange light from within that room appeared to grow brighter.

The Kiwi had gotten to me. If there was magic, it was that freehand tattoo he had upon his chest, and that's all it was, really. It was no small thing to create such a magnificent work of art, but it was art.

I sucked in a deep breath and stepped into the studio.

Immediately, the sound of the music gained in quality. It was a small space, with peach colored walls and a few framed drawings I recognized as H.R. Giger but didn't know well. There wasn't much furniture. The chair was to the right of the door, hidden from the corridor by the concert posters, and beside it, a stool, against the wall, a Formica counter with a cabinet above and below.

And she was there, Anika, her raven hair draped midway down her back. She faced the counter and the patter of metal told me she was emptying the autoclave, dealing with her tools. She was svelte, wearing tight pleather pants, the kind that laced up the sides to reveal a strip of flesh. I'd seen this regurgitation of the eighties look all over Central Europe. The Prague discos were bursting with bright leggings and bangles, and headbands and Rock-and-Troll leather dominated the Slayer inundated underground nonstops— Central Europe was where the West had shipped the eighties shit surplus when they were through with it.

I'd bet her vest came from the same place, but it looked like real leather.

I searched for words, something to say, and then the image of the de-fingered hand rushed into my mind and I tilted my head to peek around her, to search for the uniqueness that I'd come to see.

She said something in the Hungarian tongue. The words were foreign, chopped, but her voice was familiar, strong.

The reaction of my throat was to close and forbid speech.

She spun to face me.

I want to say that the first thing I noticed apart from her hair was her eyes, because they were like few women have away from that part of the world, dark, direct, piercing and lush. Women of the west wear mascara to have eyes such as hers and tan to have her tone. But I initially missed this natural allure. I was magnetically drawn to her hands. I wanted to see the mutilation, where she had cut away. But she was drying them with a towel, hiding them.

Blood rushed to my cheeks. I was embarrassed to be so trivial, such a tourist, my eyes veered up to hers, kindly waiting for my reply.

"Hi," I said. "Anika?" Clever I know, but in all the contemplation of the last few weeks, I hadn't thought of what to say when we finally met. In my visions, our rendezvous was always voiceless, without conversation. She was more beautiful than I imagined yet I don't think I'd ever envisioned her face. There was only her silhouette, the dancer in the rain.

"Oh," she said. "English. You've come for a tattoo. Yes?"

Her accent was smooth, stunning.

And again I must've looked the fool because I remained without words.

"A tattoo?" she asked again, tapping her arm.

"Yes," I said. "Yes, I came for that."

Anika nodded, expecting me to say more. "Do you know what you'd like?" she asked.

"My friend said, I mean, I was told, you'd know."

I surely was the fool for saying that. But Anika didn't appear fazed.

"Okay," she said. "Sit in the chair. Let me have a look." And then as I sat she added, "Take your shirt off."

I did as she instructed, pulled my tee over my head, and sat back. My spine slightly quivered as it touched back against the cool vinyl of the seat.

I heard her moving about behind me, the music—Pink Floyd singing of the moon and a lunatic—bounced off the wall to my front. The framed Giger to the left of my chair was one I hadn't seen before but typical of his style—biological, mechanical, organic–it reminded me of a print titled Lilith, but this creature had more arms.

I squinted to absorb the surreal detail in the picture.

"You like H.R. Giger?" I asked.

"I studied under him," her voice came from behind. "In ink and in oils."

"No shit?"

"No shit."

"He's very famous in America."

"He's famous here too. I studied as a painter," she said, stepping to my left, "but Ruedi taught me about metamorphosis, completeness, and body flow. Now I prefer the living human canvas."

"Ruedi," I repeated.

Anika raised her brow, rubbed a lotion into her hands, and took a seat at the stool. She let her left hand glide over my torso. She appeared pleased, observant, and from my periphery I scanned her—her hands at least. I could see nothing off with her right hand, or her left. I looked more closely at the rings that she wore, for a hidden prosthetic, but if a fake finger was there, it was the best I'd ever seen.

"I smell the baths," she said.

"My friend told me I should go there before seeing you."

"He spoke correctly. You are cleansed." She pressed and prodded around my nipple. "I can see clearly."

In an effort to be more at ease I said, "You don't have any tattoos."

It'd only just occurred to me. Anika glanced away from my chest to make eye contact and I realized the blunder–no tattoos that I could see. But then I realized that brow-grin combination she formulated was designed to tease me, and after only a brief few seconds of taunting she coyly said, "No."

I was going to then ask if she had any piercings and decided the question was too forward.

She dialed her left index finger counterclockwise around my left pec, once, and then a second time. "I see something here," she said, and then she did it again. Sure of herself she ran the tips of her nails up and over my left shoulder, "and here, definitely you have a lot going on here."

Her touch was comforting, maternal, yet I still felt an anxious thrill, like when I was a boy and my young teachers would lean over me to run their bright red painted nails under the words Dick and Jane. They'd breathe on my neck and my body would stiffen, my breathing would stifle, and the back of my neck would tingle and quiver. Anika wore no makeup that I could see, and she didn't smell of perfume, but her touch triggered the sense memory of the floral fragrance of the compact powder those teachers used to wear, Miss Newhouse, second grade.

"Yeah," I said, clearing my throat. "That sounds good."

"And how are we going to pay for this?"

And I was the fool thrice. In my quest, I hadn't calculated the cost. I traveled on a tight budget, working when I could as I went along, and the unscheduled month's stay at the Troll's House had taken a toll. Clouded as my mind had been, I'd only thought to exchange for enough Hungarian forints for the baths, trolley, and a meal.

But I did have some US dollars.

I wasn't sure how many. I dug into my pocket to pull out what I could, and then my fingers came across something else–my chapstick.

I held up the small cylinder and said, "I have a few dollars, but I also have this."

"This?" she asked.

"American LSD. I understand it's hard to get around here." I could tell she was intrigued.

"Is it any good?"

"It's double dipped." I furrowed a brow, "paper dipped twice. That means it's potent, the best."

"Okay," she said, "two."

She watched while I removed the top and unscrewed the lip balm until it fell from the cylinder to my hand. "Why do you use that?" she asked.

"I cross a lot of borders," I said. "The chapstick tube is sealed in wax. What's inside can't be detected. And a lot of people carry it." I reached in and withdrew a small cigarette cellophane repurposed to hold a perforated sheet of LSD. "Do you have some tweezers? I don't want to touch it."

"Yes." She reached to the table behind and gave me what I needed to secure her pay.

When the transaction finished, she unceremoniously donned a pair of gloves and sprayed my chest with a foamy shaving cream. The foam was at first chilly and then warm. She went right to business, stripping away the hair from my chest with the quick short strokes of a disposable lady bic razor.

"So, your name is Anika?" I asked.

"Ahem," she said, but didn't ask me mine. Talking time was over.

When my chest was shaved she rose from the stool and went to what I guessed was a bathroom. I heard running water and then she returned with a metal bowl and a large sea sponge. The water was warm and soapy and Anika used the sponge to mop my chest and wash my arm.

My breaths went short with the intimate attention.

When she finished she set the bowl on the counter behind her.

"I will now take my top off too," she said, and, as if asking my permission, added, "okay?"

"Okay," I replied.

She began to undo her vest, and I admit I was aroused. The low v-neck of the leather revealed an attractive bosom and I was under the impression I was about to see her breasts. I remembered the haircuts I received in the dorms at college. One of the art students used to cut hair topless to make a little extra money, and the boys, and girls, would line up down the hall. Nothing funny ever went on and the haircuts were fair at best, but the excitement came from the nubile young lady's nipple slipping into your ear as she leaned close to trim the top of your head.

I wondered if that's what was happening here, if the Kiwi had set me up from the beginning with his tale of the two missing fingers. Again forgetting my manners, I chuckled openly at the idea of the ruse. The thrill was to have this beautiful woman create the fine work of art while nude.

Anika, mid-button glanced at me. "Are you thinking of something?" she asked.

"Oh," I said. "I'm just excited to get the piece. I've seen your work, the friend who sent me here. It's marvelous–no–spectacular."

"Hmm," she said, her dark eyes again teasing me as they had when I asked whether she had tattoos of her own. "And what did you see?"

"I saw a silver fer..." I hadn't meant to stop speaking, but what I saw before me took all my attention. It wasn't her breasts, I mean, they were round, full, perky, evenly toned with her dark apricot complexion. Perfect I suppose, as was her midriff and stomach. She was young and healthy, and youth in itself is perfection. No, it wasn't her body that left me speechless. The stone fruit curve of her breast, the sloping nape of her neck, those most attractive physical characteristics apart from her eyes would've elevated my voice, but not quieted me. What shut me down was her left arm.

Not the arm I'd seen before, but the second left arm that'd been hidden below, beneath her vest.

***

"You'll see," Dave had said. "It's not just her fingers." I've known Kiwis to be humble and understated, but this certainly was something more.

Anika had a second left arm that appeared as natural, fully formed and functioning as the one at the shoulder above, and a second right one as well.

Two sets of arms.

There'd been no giveaway with the vest on. Her second arms had been tucked under her breasts, and she simply appeared to be well endowed. But I hadn't really looked for second shoulders, and there weren't any in the same way as her arms above.

To see her four arms fluidly moving together as she prepared her workspace was dizzying. Were I standing, I'd need to sit down. Even sitting, my head swam, so I closed my eyes. When I opened them again, the four arms were still there.

I did my best not to show my intrigue, my shock. My mind raced to the obvious. There were many Hindu gods and goddesses with four arms. Their images were plastered all over the hostels. There was Vishnu on top, his gal Lakshmi, the goddess of wealth and wellbeing, and Parvati, the goddess of knowledge and the arts, even the Shantee House, where I had my rooms in Buda, had a wall sized Lotus and image of a four armed goddess.

Anika placed her swabs and cloths on a metal tray by the stool and then rubbed more lotion over the middle and index finger of her left hand–the second left, I suppose. This was the de-fingered hand Dave spoke of and I could easily see the stumps of amputation above the first digits of her pinky and ring finger. When the fingers were ready, she fit a sleeve over them–on top of which rested a coil tattoo machine.

The nudity made sense to me. Anika wasn't an exhibitionist, she was uninhibited. If she wasn't going to let two fingers violate her path, she certainly wasn't going to wear a bra, blouse, or vest.

When she had her electric pen in place and her inks lined up, she dropped her three free arms back and asked me simply, "Are you ready?"

With a near gasp I said, "Yes."

I don't know that I've ever seen a woman of such innocence and beauty. Intently, she directed her attention to my chest. Her head bobbled gently side to side, and then, birdlike, her head spun to her tray. She pulled some ink and returned to my chest.

With the electric buzz of a bee and a burn of my flesh, the ballet began. At different points, one of her free hands would press against my flesh to wipe away excess blood and ink, and another hand would position my body so that my form would contort, reveal itself, and with her de-fingered hand she fluttered the electric coil machine.

Adrenalin anointed the burn, and my flesh rapidly became numb, with exception of my areola, where the needle closed in on my nipple, there was no special place to hide from the agony.

By the time she finished my chest I was drunk with the pain.

She gave me water, and then the needle dance resumed up my shoulder, a burn and a tickle, a tickle and a burn.

At first I'd veered away, to hide, now I watched her, and the effortless flow of her mystical hand as it glided the hills and valleys of my muscle tone. When the needle touched my clavicle, another wave of intense pain washed through me. My head jolted up and I looked over Anika to the Giger. The image in the drawing was moving, alive, slowly hovering away from the wall, yet still behind the glass.

A bead of sweat formed on my forehead and then another and Anika mopped them away, and then the multi-armed creature in the picture was woman, and the woman was Anika, and that made sense, too.

Hours passed, and I was exhausted.

She must've been too.

When she finished, I was laden in sweat and so was she. Her breasts glistened, as did her cheeks, forehead, her eyes, and her arms—all four.

Absent the buzz of the coil tattoo machine, the silence in the room amplified and threatened to drown out the radio altogether.

Anika sniffled and grinned.

As she cleaned my new wound, she spoke in Hungarian, or in some other tongue. She didn't speak to me, nor to herself. I think it was a prayer, or a summons, because a wave of euphoric relief wafted through me. It seemed to ebb from my core and out through the images she'd inked onto my shoulder and chest.

From the corner of my eye, they appeared to writhe, as the visions in shadow, the dancer in the rain, the echoing trails behind her flowing arms weren't echoes at all.

"When you're ready," she said. "There is a mirror in the back."

I nodded in compliance, and then raised myself from the chair. The world was tactile in a way it hadn't been before, and not just on my shoulder. My entire body, from my scalp to my toes, was a buzz.

When I rose to my feet, the breath of air I took in was sweeter than any other I'd taken before. I stood taller. The anxiety that'd plagued me was gone, replaced by calm.

I walked to the back of the studio and slowly turned toward the full mirror on the backside of the open bathroom door. The entire upper left quadrant of my body was red raw. If a truck had dragged me a mile, my flesh may've appeared the same. On my chest was a sky blue lotus, and like the Kiwi's coiling fern, the lotus was blooming. And on my shoulder, something I can only describe as a living extension of myself, a dozen curling, black vines lashing and intertwining above my flesh.

"Amazing," I said, turning back to face her. She was already putting her vest back on, transforming back into a mere beautiful woman. Astounded by her creation I asked, "How did you --", but before I could finish she said, "It was always there. I drew it out from the inside."

Those were the words of Kiwi Dave. She drew it out from the inside.

No longer burdened by petty fears of social formality, I asked, "What happened to the finger?"

Her statement was quick and matter of fact, vindicating that all of the anxiety I'd built up previously was unnecessary, part of my antiquated self. "That was art for myself. You are now complete through your metamorphosis. Yours was drawn out. My metamorphosis was different, I had to remove something to feel complete."

"Ah," I said, and pondered her choice. "And what did you do with them? The fingers I mean?"

She gave me a face that I was so unsure of, a look that I've continued to question since. Playful, sarcastic, the plain truth, I don't know. "I ground them up," she said, "and used the powder to make my ink." Then she blinked both eyes, and it may've been the light, but I'm sure that for a split second, her orbs went black.

My chest and shoulder numb, I went to the Marriot as Dave instructed. I looked down on the Danube and watched the sun set behind the Buda citadel. I sipped brandy and ate perhaps the best cheesecake ever.

***

I've often wondered if the ink was drugged, if it contained some type of psychotropic that slowly releases a hallucinogen each time I set eyes upon it. Because the ink still writhes, the lotus still blooms, it still brings me calm, wellbeing.

I haven't been anxious since, about the world, traveling, about myself. Up to that point in my life, I was a wanderer in search of myself. Anika revealed to me that I was always in there, beneath the flesh. She drew it out from the inside.

I've often thought I'd return to that underground arcade in Budapest. But twenty some years have passed, and I never have, and I'd bet I couldn't find it if I tried. I don't have the map, and part of me believes that wouldn't matter. It seemed a place out of time, another reality.

So many have tattoos now but I've never met another with a tattoo of living ink. At a glimpse, across a crowded room, in a split second from the corner of my eye, I've thought I saw dark ink ripple. But it never moves on a second glance.

Other nights, when I've drunk more than I should, I scour the internet searching for her, Anika, others who may've met her, may have a similar tattoo. There are occasional mentions of living tattoos, but they're never like Kiwi Dave's or mine. And there is never a mention of her, by the name of Anika or any other, the artist with the de-fingered hand.

**

ABOUT THE AUTHOR:

Daniel Arthur Smith is the author of the international bestsellers HUGH HOWEY LIVES, THE CATHARI TREASURE, THE SOMALI DECEPTION, and a few other novels and short stories.

He was raised in Michigan and graduated from Western Michigan University where he studied philosophy, with focus on cognitive science, meta-physics, and comparative religion. He began his career as a bartender, barista, poetry house proprietor, teacher, and then became a technologist and futurist for the Fortune 100 across the Americas and Europe.

Daniel has traveled to over 300 cities in 22 countries, residing in Los Angeles, Kalamazoo, Prague, Crete, and now writes in Manhattan where he lives with his wife and young sons.

For more information, visit www.danielarthursmith.com

RUDY AND DEIDRE
BY ROBB GRINDSTAFF

Rudy reached to slip two quarters into the slot and pushed the button. He hated when the only dryer available was on the top row. Three dryers on the bottom row sat unmoving, full of dry clothes whose owner was probably at the pub across the street. He considered pulling out the laundry and tossing it on the folding table, but that would be rude and might attract attention from the clothes' owner. Perhaps some big guy who wouldn't take too kindly to having his clean clothes handled by a stranger.

Rudy's clothes slowly picked up tumble speed as the lower dryer stared at him. Full of pinks and powder blues and maroons, lace and frills.

Thank goodness I didn't handle some girl's stuff.

He'd just gotten comfortable–as comfy as you can get in a molded plastic chair at a laundromat just off campus at eleven p.m.–earbuds in, a Dr. Who episode on the tablet, when she ducked in.

Deidre. In a knee-length, modest but form-fitting black dress, make-up, jewelry. And white tennis shoes.

Rudy stared momentarily, then forced his gaze back to the tablet, but shifted slightly in his seat to keep her in his peripheral vision as she headed to the dryer. He pulled out the earbuds in case she spoke to him. A futile exertion, he knew, but hope springs eternal.

Hope had bubbled in Rudy for his three years at the university, ever since he'd first spotted Deidre standing out among the crowd of somewhat shell-shocked freshmen. She hadn't noticed him then or after. She wouldn't notice him in the laundromat either.

At six feet seven, a trim two hundred or so pounds, Deidre was what Rudy would call a big girl. Perfectly proportioned. Stunning beauty.

***

The three dryers full of her clothes lay still, taunting her with promises of wrinkles.

Deidre hadn't thought the audition would take that long. They never did. But tonight she had to wait while a dozen other hopeful Juliets read before her.

She pulled each article from the dryer and shook it twice, folded it neatly and stacked it on the table. Some were okay. Some would need to be ironed. If only someone else had been in the laundromat, some decent, honest person, an elf maybe, who would have grabbed her clothes the moment the dryer stopped and folded them for her. But no elves were to be found, so she shook the t-shirt three times before folding.

Deidre had always wanted to be an actress. She'd worked the stage lights for high school plays because she knew no teenage boy would want to appear on stage with her.

She majored in drama at the local university, where all the professors raved about her remarkable talents, the way she threw her entire being into the roles, the way her face transformed into whatever character she brought to life. Each time she sent in a video audition, she received a call. When she showed up, before reading a single line, the silhouettes one-third of the way back in the empty auditorium would gasp, sigh, and attempt to cough over an escaped chuckle.

"You're a lovely girl, dear," one would say, "but you're not quite what we had in mind for this part. Thank you for coming."

On her way off stage, the suppressed giggles would turn to guffaws. Even then, she wouldn't slump her shoulders.

"Stand up straight and keep your shoulders back," her mother always chided. "Keep your chin up and your eyes straight ahead. Look where you're going, not at where you are." Her mother's posture lessons made sure Deidre never hunched over in shame of her height or her breasts.

Deidre opened the second dryer and pulled out the delicate items, washed and dried on gentle cycle and low heat.

***

Rudy tried to act interested in his video or the news or a book–whatever was on his tablet that he wasn't seeing–while keeping Deidre just in his scope. If she looked his way, he would glance up and smile, maybe say hi, ask if she remembered him from first-year English composition.

Or he could just speak up and say, "Hi, Deidre. I'm Rudy. You were in my comp class a couple of years ago. It's good to see you again."

But she hadn't seen him when she walked in, so that might startle her. In this neighborhood at this time of night, her senses were likely heightened anyway. Only, if she was that aware of her surroundings, wouldn't she have noticed a guy sitting against the wall not twenty feet away? She might notice some other guy, Rudy grudgingly accepted, but she wouldn't notice him even if he was the only man in the room.

He was. And she hadn't.

He tried hard not to stare as she folded pink and powder blue and maroon bras and bikini panties.

***

With the last pair of jeans from the third dryer folded, she wiped a tear on her sleeve and set the stack of clean clothes in the plastic wicker basket.

"Good lord, but I'd like to mount that," she'd overheard the voice from the audience say as she left the stage. He probably thought she had left, but she stood behind the curtains, slipping off her high heels and into more comfortable shoes for the walk back to get her laundry. The acoustics in the hall were incredible.

"You'd need ropes and a grappling hook," said the female silhouette.

All she'd ever really wanted was to play Juliet. She'd memorized all the lines by third grade, but Shaquille was never available as Romeo.

She shifted her basket to one arm and opened the door, catching it with her heel and shoving it open wide enough to exit.

***

Deidre was out by the time Rudy thought to jump up and ask, "Can I get that for you?" He watched her elegant stride across the parking lot and down the sidewalk in tennis shoes and a not-so-little black dress, carrying a load of fresh clothes. He stared until she disappeared around the corner.

At five-three, Rudy wished he could throw Deidre in the dryer for a while to shrink her down to a size where she'd notice him.

***

ABOUT THE AUTHOR:

For the past three decades, Robb Grindstaff has managed newspapers from Japan to Germany, from Washington, D.C., to small towns in North Carolina and Texas. The variety of places he has lived and traveled provide the settings, people, and ideas for most of his character-driven writing. He has published two novels with Evolved Publishing, a dozen or so short stories in collections, anthologies, and magazines, including the award-winning "Desert Rain" in Horror Bound magazine. His fiction editing clients include traditionally published, agented authors as well as award-winning and best-selling indie authors. His articles on the craft of fiction have appeared in international writer magazines and websites, and became the basis for a presentation at the Sydney Writers Festival in Australia.

He now manages a publishing company with fifteen newspapers plus websites, magazines, and specialty publications. He and Linda, his wife of 30 years, live in the countryside not far from Madison, Wisconsin, along with their somewhat neurotic but lovable dog Cera.

Daedalus' Daughter
by P.K. Tyler

The first feather appeared the morning of my father's funeral. It sprouted on my shoulder, soft and white. Its appearance happened quietly, a slow creep of his past into my present. It grew to half an inch before I noticed and plucked it from my skin. It came out with a hard wiry quill which had been seated deep within my flesh.

A drop of blood appeared on my shoulder where I'd pulled it loose.

I tucked it away and left it behind, along with all my unshed tears. I couldn't bring myself to mourn for him, the man I'd only known as Father. Never Dad or Daddy. No kind words or paternal comfort had ever passed between us. I lived in the shadow of his loss, never knowing how warm the sun would feel on my skin.

When I arrived at the funeral home, I went straight to the front and sat next to my mother. Her hands clenched a picture in her lap and her chin tipped up, keeping the sagging skin of her neck taut, the fog behind her eyes was thick with tears.

"How are you, Mom?" I placed a hand on her knee to draw her attention, but she ignored me, lost in a maze of grief. The nurses from the hospice had brought her earlier, giving her time to acclimate before anyone else arrived.

"Hello, Isha," the funeral director held out his hand for me to shake. "I'm so very sorry for your loss."

"Thank you." I stood and took the man's hand, frustrated by his weak grip and sympathetic smile. His brown suit hung a little too loose and his tie hugged his neck in a perfect knot. Everything about him was orchestrated to put me at ease. But he didn't know I wasn't really there, just a mirage, a reflection on the water of my life. I soared above it all, golden and free, watching with uninterested apathy as my family shrank yet again.

"Is there anything special you'd like me to say other than what we discussed on the phone?" His tone attempted to sooth my rough edges, factory designed to calm.

"No, thank you."

Next to me, my mother whimpered, a single tear running down her cheek. "My boy, so young, so brave. How could I lose you?"

A nurse rushed over and placed a soothing hand on her shoulder, knowing better than I did how to ease her pain.

I ignored her.

The funeral hall remained empty until well after the time the service had been set to start. Finally, the director said a few non-committal words about life well lived and how all things have their time. A time for living and a time for dying and all that. I waited for the hours to pass so I could walk away and leave all this wasted time behind. Would anyone even notice? Would my mother remember my name?

No body rested peacefully at the front of the room, painted up to a mock flush of life for mourners to wish farewell of its journey, my father had been cremated, burnt to ash before I even had the chance to see him. I'd like to think I'd have been able to have a last moment with him, a connection, some kind of acceptance as he passed on to the next life. But even that hope was robbed from me by his heartless efficiency.

By the time the hospital called to tell me he'd passed, they had already executed his dying wish and rushed him to the crematorium to be burnt at daybreak.

When the funeral director finished, I waited for my mother's keeper to shepherd her away before retrieving the urn.

She didn't take my hand or press a kiss to my cheek. "I'll see you after school, Isha," she called, waving goodbye. Perhaps that was better for her, to not remember, to not have to melt under the harsh light of reality.

On her seat remained the picture she'd held.

I picked it up and stared down at the memory she clung to: my father and brother, the summer he died. They lounged on the dock, my brother's smile bright as the sun. Was it from the same trip he drowned in that very water in the early morning light?

I wished I remembered him, then maybe I could mourn him and forgive my parents. But I was only three when he died. Sometimes, on the edge of sleep, I could hear his laughter, but it disappeared as soon as I tried to hear it again.

I shoved the picture into my purse and walked out of the funeral home, my father's urn in my arms, my brother's memory nipping at my heels, my mother's sanity lost long ago.

The urn didn't fit on the shelf in the closet where I'd planned to keep it, so instead it sat on my mantle: a cliché out of a movie or some mockery of my lack of mourning.

How could I mourn? I wasn't even in the picture.

"Is this what you want?" I asked the porcelain vase, scratching my shoulder. "Even after death, you'll shadow my life, never speaking to me or caring that I'm the one still alive?"

The urn remained silent.

I turned my back on it and retreated to the bedroom, refusing to engage in another one-sided conversation with my father in death as I had in life.

As I undressed, my sweater caught on my shoulder and a stabbing pain ran through my arm. I reached back to find three small white feathers resting soft against my upper arm. I ran the tips of my fingers over them, so soft and silken. When I pressed against them, I felt a current run down the quill, connected to my nerves.

I considered plucking them, but couldn't bear to. Their beauty existed despite the strangeness. I needed a little beauty, something precious just for me

White and pure, they grew from my flesh in defiance of nature.

They were mine.

***

After my mother's death, I quit my job and took my parents' matching urns to the cabin I'd inherited. Shuttered since my brother drowned, it had been waiting for someone to return. Like me, it'd been locked in the memory of death. It seemed only right that I bury my parents' remains here.

I drove north, all my earthly possessions in my car or the trailer I'd bought cheap for the trip. I'd inherited their land, their money, their misery. I was all that remained. And I intended to exhume it all.

The small cabin sat on the water in Trescott, Maine, just north of Acadia National Park, and the woman who managed the land for my family owned a small bookstore in town. When I entered, the scent of well loved paper and dust wafted around me and a large three-legged dog bounded to greet me. It had white and brown curly hair and bright black eyes.

"That's Cerberus," a man with a cane announced as he entered. The dog lay at my feet and rolled over, expecting the obligatory belly rub.

I bent to pet the animal. "He hardly acts like a Cerberus."

"Well, you know, three heads, three legs, what's the difference, really?" The man rapped his cane on the ground and the dog left me to sit by his master's feet.

"I'm looking for Betty," I said standing.

"You must be Isha. Betty said you were coming by. Been a long time since we heard from your family."

"The cabin wasn't their highest priority."

"Well, I can understand, after what happened." The man shook his head and frowned. Even here, the memory of my brother darkened the air. "Come on then, I've got your keys and Betty had her boy Minh go up the other day to check things out."

I followed the man and his dog back through two more book covered rooms. This seemed less a book store and more a hoarder's wet dream. Books stacked on top of one another reached almost to the ceiling, shelves split small spaces even smaller and every available corner was filled.

We reached a back room which appeared identical to the others, except for a desk in the middle of the room. Papers cluttered the surface, but, interestingly, it lacked the presence of books. The man reached into the top drawer and pulled out a key. "Minh opened the place up for you. He made sure all the lights and plumbing still work and replaced one window which must have been broken during the last storm. We'll send a bill for the work and all that to the management company like usual—"

"Actually, I'm going to be moving in, so send it to me directly."

The man frowned and wrapped his age spotted fingers around the key. "So you won't be needing us to look after it anymore?"

"Oh, no, I will. Please, just send the monthly bill to me and I'll pay you directly."

"We don't do much you know, just keep the road clear and cut the grass some so it don't overgrow. Make sure no one sets up on your land for squatting."

"I'll still need the help, I'm sure. I've only ever lived in the city, so clearing the drive and fixing things around the place will be a huge help." I smiled, trying to reassure him that his income remained secure. It wasn't much but knowing someone would be checking on me made the idea of moving out to nowhere a little less terrifying.

"Right then." He passed me the key. "You know where you're going?"

After getting directions and promising to let Betty know if I needed anything, I headed out, Cerberus on my heels.

"He likes you." The old man smiled from his desk.

At the front door, I knelt to say my goodbyes to the three legged dog before continuing on to my new life.

***

The cabin at the end of an unnamed road off route 191 was now my home. Someone had been by and turned on all the lights and started a fire. It helped shake the ghosts away, but they lingered in the trees, watching as I made my way inside.

The small space remained as I remembered it: ugly plaid furniture, a small kitchen in one corner, a loft above where my brother and I slept and a tiny bedroom. I could see my mother standing in the kitchen, a hazy sun-bleached image of her from happier days. She said something, but I couldn't hear. Too many years had passed.

Off the living room, a deck looked out over the water. Someone had strung Christmas lights from the deck stairs down to the dock, almost like stars sparkling a path. Had that been my idea from childhood or something Betty had done? It seemed like both were true. Memory has a funny habit of changing the past.

I dropped my purse on the wood carved bench and opened the sliding door. The ocean sang in salt and silt.

I fell asleep on the couch, the lights still on.

***

In the morning, I woke slowly, half in a dream.

I made a small pot of coffee and walked out to the dock, mug in hand.

The boards were old and weathered, except for where the end had been replaced, completely rebuilt and fortified with metal supports. After it collapsed under my brother as he reached out for an elusive firefly, no expense was spared in its repair. Even if we never returned to the scene of the crime.

And that's what it had been, a crime. In that moment, my brother's desire extended his reach and he stepped out where he knew the dock couldn't hold him. His plummet into the water and the destruction that rained down on him, trapping his body under the water too long for any hope of resurrection, was no one's fault but his own.

I sat on the dock and dipped my toes in the water. The cold movement of the lake reassured me that this was now and I was not him.

The morning air heated quickly and I removed my cardigan. Feathers fluttered down the backs of my arms. The movement reached deep within me, tickling and playing with emotions I thought long dead. This must have been what freedom felt like. As the breeze played with my hair and feathers I sipped my coffee and let the sun warm my face.

"Hello?" A low voice called from the deck.

I dropped my mug and it slipped beneath the surface of the lake as I scurried to pull the sleeves of my cardigan over my arms. My feathers burned where they were pulled back against the quill and bunched under the fabric.

"Hey, are you Isha?"

I looked up to find a tall man with a wide smile and narrow eyes striding down the stairs toward me. Panic over my feathers being seen had me step backwards. I could feel the edge of the dock as my heel slipped over.

"Woah!" The man ran forward and grabbed my upper arm, pulling me back on the dock before I tumbled over the edge. "You almost fell in!" He laughed as if the idea weren't the most terrifying thing in the universe.

"Who are you?" I demanded, scowling at the interloper who disturbed my morning. One of my feathers folded forward, releasing itself from the trap of my sleeve so it could lay flat against my arm.

"Right, sorry." His bright smile faltered and his eyebrows pulled together creating an almost perfect line. "I'm—"

Before he could finish his introduction, a wild barking began back at the house, followed by Cerberus running straight for me.

"Oh my God!" I screamed and threw my arms around the stranger in the hopes that if Cerberus hit both of us at that speed we wouldn't topple over into the lake.

Cerberus loped toward us and sat with a sharp bark on my foot. His bony butt pressed into my toes in a strangely comforting way.

The man laughed again and placed an arm around my waist to keep me from falling. "It looks like Cerberus already knows you."

He released me and bent down to scratch the dog behind the ears. "I'm Minh. My mother, Betty, said you might need some help opening up the place this morning."

When he stood up, I took in the deep brown eyes, his wide pronounced cheekbones, and the sleek black hair that, when he pushed it back out of his face revealed thin, straight eyebrows.

"I'm sorry." I shrugged my shoulders, trying to unruffle. "I didn't expect you and it's so quiet out here. I guess you startled me."

Cerberus leaned against my leg and nuzzled my thigh. He made a rumbling contented sound when I scratched behind his ear.

Minh stuffed his hands in his pockets and stared at us. "Cerberus doesn't usually like anyone. He's almost as cranky as Eugene."

"Who's that?"

"My step-father. You met him yesterday at the shop. The other three-legged monster in town." Minh chuckled.

"If he doesn't like anyone why did you bring him?"

"I didn't. He hopped in the back of my truck this morning. I figured, why not let the old guy get some fresh air?" Minh reached for Cerberus, who growled softly and pressed harder against my leg. "Weird."

"Thanks for stocking up on groceries," I said, finally remembering my manners.

Minh nodded with a non-committal smile before turning back toward the house. "Did you have a chance to unload? Need help moving anything in?"

"No. I'm fine."

"You've got a trailer full of crap. I don't mind."

"I haven't decided if I'm even going to move any of it in. I kind of like the way it is."

Minh gave his smile and nod. "Well, I'm going to clear out

the gutters as long as I'm here. Let me know if you change your mind."

He walked toward the detached garage on the opposite side of the drive, like he knew this place, like this was his home, not mine. For a moment it bothered me, but he'd been here more often and more recently than I had. Any sense of possession I had about this place was decades old.

While Minh pulled out ladders of various sizes, I returned to the cabin, Cerberus close behind.

The day warmed the air, heating the tiny cabin, so I opened all the windows and doors and flipped on the ceiling fans. I worked, still shrouded in my cardigan, unloading clothes and other items I knew I'd want from the car.

I wanted Minh to leave, to give me time alone in my new home, but I was also thankful for the help. He cleaned the gutters, trimmed some of the trees away from the house, and hauled firewood from the pile into the house.

By the time afternoon had set in, sweat soaked my back and I longed to take off my cardigan. The downy feathers on my arms trapped in the heat. No matter how much water I drank, I couldn't cool down.

I unloaded some of my kitchen supplies and lost myself in digging through my mother's extra set of pots and pans that remained in the cabin. Most would need to be replaced, but the cast iron skillet was in perfect shape and made me want to caramelize something.

"Hey," Minh stood in the shadow of the front door, his tall frame blocking out the light. "I'm about done. Do you wanna grab some lunch?"

My stomach growled. I hadn't eaten anything yet and the kitchen counters hid somewhere beneath the boxes I'd hauled in. I did, I did want to grab something to eat, but what I didn't want was to spend any more time under cover.

"No, I have too much to do here."

"Well, I could run into town, grab some gyros and come back." He looked over at me and even in the shadows I could see the hope in his eyes.

"I... sure. Okay, that would be nice."

"Great." His wide smile spread across his face again, crinkling his eyes. "Do you mind if Cerberus waits here? I don't think he's going to be impressed if I try to make him leave."

I looked down at the large dog sprawled across the kitchen tile. His legs and paws twitched, dreams of chasing and running and flying free no doubt dancing through his mind. "Sure, let him sleep."

Minh's truck growled to life and I waited until I could no longer hear the crunch of his tires against the long gravel road before ripping off the cardigan. Cold fresh air blew over my arms and the barbs of each feather seemed to spread, capturing the breeze.

My upper arms were completely covered, seemingly each pore had its own quill sprouting from it. My follicles had given up the fight so that the peach fuzz layer of hair on my arms and across my shoulder blades now sported the downy barbs of a newly sprouted feather.

In the bathroom, I shed my clothes. I needed to shower, to cool off the overheating skin trapped beneath the unbreathing confines of feather and clothing. In the mirror, I noticed a small sprouting of white behind my ear. It would never blend with my hair, but after so many months, the idea of plucking any of my quills seemed impossible.

I tucked it under my dark hair and stepped under the water. The cool droplets beaded up on my feathers, sliding over them and onto my naked body. I raised my hands and turned in the water, letting it run over me, slowly making its way under the afterfeathers and down to my flesh. It rained over me, bringing my body temperature back down so I could think again. I washed my hair, careful not to scrub the new white growth too hard, and poured a small amount of dish soap on a washcloth to gently run over my arms. The suds ran down my back, over my shoulder blades and the quills sprouted there.

I wonder when my legs will sprout feathers. Some of the ones on my arms have begun encroaching on my chest, forcing me to consider what kind of neckline I can wear. What will I do when the day comes that I can no longer hide? Will I live up here in seclusion, separated from the world?

The idea depressed me, but I couldn't bring myself to part with my secret, to defile myself by removing what grew naturally.

I turned off the water, my mind lost in thoughts of hermits in caves and trolls under bridges. What did modern day monsters do to survive? Could I order groceries online all the way out here? I doubted I could live on my inheritance indefinitely. Someday I'd need to work. Perhaps I could do something online. Did I even have high speed Internet? I hadn't thought to check.

Lost in thought, I wrapped a towel around my body and gathered my clothes. The small cabin didn't have a master bath, so I walked out into the living room toward the bedroom where I'd left my suitcase.

"Isha?" Minh's eyebrows shot up so high on his forehead they disappeared beneath his black hair and his usually narrow eyes rounded as they stared.

"Oh my god!" I screamed and ran to my bedroom. How was he back? I'd been so careful, so deliberate with everything I did to avoid anyone knowing. Now would come the pitchforks and torches. I'd be tied to the dock as the rabid townspeople set it on fire and burned alive.

Cerberus barked outside my door.

"Isha, I'm sorry I startled you." Minh said through the wooden barrier between me and absolute destruction.

"Ok, you can go away now." I forced the words out as I held my breath, my heart beating so hard it ached in my chest.

"I just got back, I didn't think you'd be walking around naked." He chuckled again, but his voice was tight, not the open sound from that morning.

"It's fine, I'm not upset. No problem. Why don't you just take off though, I think we're done today."

"Isha..." The unasked question hung in the air like mist over the cove. It seeped into my pores, chilling my bones.

"Go away." I whispered, clutching the towel.

Cerberus whined and scratched at the door again.

"The dog doesn't want to leave yet." Minh said.

"The dog can stay. You can't."

"I... okay. Have a good day Isha."

I listened to his footsteps as he crossed the living room and the bang of the front door closing. The crunch of the gravel faded out and I could finally breathe.

Cerberus scratched and whimpered until I opened the door enough to let him in. He sat with me on the hard wooden floor as I stared at nothingness and waited. Eventually, in spite of the hardness of the floor, I fell into a deep, dreamless sleep.

I woke late in the evening with my stomach growling. I still hadn't eaten anything. Cerberus lay on the floor beside me, his oversized head draped across my leg and his one front paw over his nose.

"I'm a little chilly too, boy." I sat up and scratched his ears.

The house was dark and quiet. All the windows were open, letting in the cool evening air. The hypnotic lap of the sea against the dock synchronized with crickets and the other evening sounds.

I pulled on a tank top and jeans. The feathers kept my top half warm enough and I was tired of covering them. Cerberus followed me as I grabbed the gyro and soda from the table and walked out to the dock.

"You're probably hungry too," I said as I sat and unwrapped the sandwich.

He laid down beside me with bright eyes and a lolling tongue.

As I ate, I picked apart the pita and fed pieces of meat to the dog who had adopted me. Fireflies hovered over the water, beckoning me to join them in their dance.

Dusk filled the sky with blues and purples as the meager meal filled my empty stomach. I had wished for so many things and this peaceful solitude was at the top of the list.

I leaned back on my hands and Cerberus scooted closer, settling his head and his only front paw on my lap. Stars filled the sky and the moon rose, its selenophic beauty mesmerizing.

Soon, even my downy warmth drifted away and the night settled cool over the water. I thought about my brother, so daring, so willing to try to reach out for more, and how different I had grown to be from the little girl who wanted nothing more than to follow. I risked nothing. I pleased no one. I was alone.

I retrieved my parents' urns from the trunk of my car, Cerberus close on my heels. I carried them out to the dock and placed them side by side at the edge.

"This is what you'd always wanted. To be with him. To die when he did. Neither of you wanted to live after that day and you never even let me try."

I removed the caps and tilted first my mother and then my father into the lake. Their ash danced in the glow of fireflies, mingling together before sinking and drifting off into the depths.

When I turned back toward the house, I found Minh standing on the deck next to the sliding doors with his hands stuffed in his pockets. I hadn't brought a sweater or a shawl out with me and now I stood in the moonlight, my white feathers on full display.

In my terror, I wrapped my arms around myself and my feathers dropped protectively over my exposed skin as if trying to protect my flesh from his eyes, when really it was the opposite I worried about.

"What are you doing here?" I asked.

He stepped closer and Cerberus left my side to greet him. Minh crouched down and pet the mythic beast who I had come to think of as my own. "I didn't want to scare you again, but I needed to talk to you."

"Why?"

"Will you come up here? I can barely hear you out there." He stood again and, while his smile wasn't as broad as before, it seemed sincere.

I approached, hesitating before stepping into the light spilling from the cabin doors.

"Why did you kick me out? I've been thinking about it all day. Did I do something wrong?" The words tumbled from him in a pile that gathered at his feet.

I stared at him in confusion. What did he do wrong?

"I mean, I know I saw you in just a towel, but I wasn't trying to... I mean, I didn't plan that." He ducked his head.

"Are you fucking with me?" I asked, anger growing in my chest.

"What?" His head snapped up and his eyes met mine.

"Is this some kind of game? Why are you here?"

"To apologize for startling you."

"So you startle me again?" I drop my arms, forgetting my feathers until they move with me, deeply connected to the nerves along my arms and back. "Did you just want another look?" I hold my arms out, letting the longer feathers on my triceps dangle their full length.

Minh frowned. "I did. I mean, I do, I do want another look. They're beautiful. But that's not why I came back."

"Beautiful?" It was a word I'd always associated with my anomaly, my growths, my deformity, but not something I ever imagined someone else would say. I dropped my arms to my sides.

He stepped closer and I had to look up. His strong features, his broad shoulders, he was the beautiful one.

"I didn't want you to be upset." He finally said, our bodies close together.

"I'm not. I mean, I am, but not at you really."

He reached out and took my hand in one of his own. It was cool, like the night, and when he leaned down to kiss me, every feather on my body fluttered.

***

I woke early the next morning to find Minh staring at me. He had his head cradled in his hand as his eyes roamed over my naked body. When I looked down, I found my arms were covered in pin feathers. They looked like shiny blue quills and spread across my chest, stopping just above my breasts.

I sat up and held out my arms, the full feathers on the backs of my arms had grown and I could feel the air in the room as it moved across each one. The pin feathers were surrounded by small downy white sprouts.

"What happened?"

Minh ran a hand over the silky growths before bringing it up to cup my face. "You somehow became even more stunning."

I shook off his touch and climbed out of bed. The long feathers which had before only come to my elbows hung past my knees. They were heavy but I found my arms were strong enough to hold them. From by breasts down remained feather free.

"Are they everywhere?" I turned trying to see my back and Minh laughed.

"You look like Cerberus chasing his tail!"

At the sound of his name, the old dog sleeping at the foot of my parents' bed raised his head and snorted.

Outside, I could hear the birds calling, the wind rustling through the trees. Through the window I watched as the last of the fireflies began to disappear.

I ran after them, Minh following behind me, the throw from the bed wrapped around his waist.

"What are you doing?" he called.

I didn't answer. I just ran faster and faster until I was sprinting down the dock toward the end.

"Isha!" he screamed, running after me as I leapt off the end of the dock and the wind lifted me up into the sky.

***

ABOUT THE AUTHOR:

Award-winning author of multi-cultural and transgressive literature, P.K. Tyler is an artist, wife, mother and number cruncher. In addition to literary fiction and Sci-Fi, P.K. also writes erotica and romance under the name Pavarti K. Tyler.

She graduated Smith College in 1999 with a degree in Theatre. After graduation, she moved to New York, where she worked as a Dramaturge, Assistant Director and Production Manager on productions both on and off Broadway. Later, Pavarti went to work in the finance industry for several international law firms.

The best way to stay up to date with Pavarti is to join her mailing list. If you do, she'll even send you a free short story!

Sign up at http://smarturl.it/PavNews

Follow her at www.PKTyler.com

The Zealot
by Christopher Godsoe

"You know, this would go a whole lot faster if you'd talk a little."

"Maybe for you, Dru. But the more attention I pay to you, the less I pay to what's going on out there." Tobin Maldovan gestured towards the windshield of the land cruiser they were staked out in. "We're here to find out information. This isn't a date."

"Don't be condescending."

"I don't know any other way to be. I told you, I don't want to talk about my personal life. And since we're partners, and I don't have any information about our case that you don't, I don't see that we have a great deal to discuss. I hate small talk. I'd rather we do the job we were sent here to do. Is that all right?"

Dru hated not knowing anything about him. It was hard enough for her to overlook his cybernetic eyes, glinting moonlight as he turned back to the display panel on their cruiser, but to not have any real glimpse of humanity from him made her feel like she was working with an android.

She tried not to think about the bottle of alcohol waiting in her freezer, how much she missed the bite of it against her throat. Not given to confession, she wouldn't admit that the reason she was trying to get him to talk wasn't because she thought he was interesting, but because she wanted the distraction. Needed the distraction.

"Look, there he is."

Tobin was already out the door in the moment it took her to reel in her thoughts.

Dru snatched her gun from the center console and dashed after him. She hadn't seen the man as Tobin had, but owing to his augmented vision, that wasn't much of a surprise. Tobin Maldovan was cold, had a reputation for being ruthless, but Dru had learned to respect his instincts over their six months together as partners.

By the time she caught up to him, crouching behind a door frame with a decent line of sight to the office building on the opposing side of the street, her breath broke from her lungs in ragged gasps. Tobin looked at her with an expression of disappointment, and she didn't bother to defend herself. She was a police officer, not an ex Special Forces commando who continued to train as though anticipating a call to active deployment at any moment.

Dru scanned the building, every window lit in the fluorescent blue-white psychologists recommended for maximum productivity. People strode with purpose along every floor, driven more by the prospect of unemployment than the choices in lighting, the third shift of some global technology empire that never slept.

Her SideARM, a miniature processing unit connected to the displays embedded in her contact lenses, had already tagged most of them, their identities broadcasting through an encrypted wireless signal for law enforcement and rescue personnel. Translucent rectangles hovered over their heads, a menu with additional information sliding down if she focused on any of them for more than a moment. Far too many were augmented for this to be a random selection by The Zealot.

A man walked near the windowed front wall of the building, and Dru decided to pass the time by reading up on his augmentation. Tobin could deride her for reading a magazine when they were supposed to be paying attention, but he would have no way of seeing her access the information on Mr. Larry Johnson's cerebral web implant. The implant, according to the file, was a primitive design, one that had been implanted in his youth as a means to "cure" his seizures. The implant had been disabled when he reached adulthood, but it still broadcast its signature, shouting to anyone with the clearance to hear and betraying his privacy for the rest of his life.

Most of his coworkers had similar body modifications, the vast majority of them surgeries to correct some deficiency or restore function lost due to an accident. *What a broken people we must have been*, she thought, before science allowed us to cheat nature and fate. These people just wanted to live their lives, and the same implants that allowed them to do so came with hooks, legal provisions Dru had a hard time justifying at that moment.

She looked away, acutely aware that delving into people's lives in order to alleviate her boredom constituted an abuse of her power. Her gaze landed on Tobin, to the translucent tag hanging over his head, and the sadness in her grew a little more.

Tobin blinked. He never blinked, it was one of the things that bugged Dru about him. His cybernetic eyeballs had no need to be lubricated in that way, even if the shrapnel that had originally claimed his eyes hadn't also been responsible for removing his tear ducts. For him to begin again now must mean he was remembering back to before his implants.

She thought about the animosity augmented humans garnered in some circles, and wondered how they must feel having someone out there like the man they were chasing. They called him The Zealot because his modus operandi included forcibly removing augmentations from his victims prior to killing them in an attempt to rid the world of implants, which he saw as an abomination. Tobin was an FBI agent, trained in hand to hand combat and trusted with the ability to use deadly force. If it bothered him that this monster was still out on the streets, deep down on some level that only manifested in his regressing back to subconscious biological ticks, Dru couldn't imagine what day to day life must be like for the people in the building in front of them.

Many of the managers and team leaders probably lived in the building, better to be available at a moment's notice should the company need them. It felt like a cage to Dru, to have your existence so wholly owned that you could never get free of it. *Little more than indenturement*, she thought. It was no life for her.

Then, the building erupted. The blast came in stages, the first report emanating from deep within.

Tobin threw them away from the open doorframe an instant before it became a funnel for shrapnel, barely escaping behind a heavy industrial milling machine a few steps away. Hollow and low, the following blasts were more crisp and defined as the building exploded outward with fewer obstructions between the blast and her ears.

Dru blacked out.

She woke later to a concussion and ears that probably wouldn't be able to pick up silent conversation for days. She felt the ringing in them more than heard it, saw the shifting landscape more than she could understand Tobin yelling to her that they had to go.

He frowned when she didn't move and cast her over his shoulder as he made their escape.

The building listed to one side, though in her condition she couldn't tell which. Everything blurred for the next few moments, bouncing left and right, up and down, with more sound than her head could bear. Mercifully, she blacked out again for a few minutes, only waking for good when medical personnel brought her back with smelling salts.

Tobin was nowhere to be seen.

Against the EMT's wishes, she climbed from the mobile examination table, brushing aside the automated scanning arm as she made her way towards the rising column of smoke a few hundred yards away.

She found him inside the blasted out building, still holding its verticality by some miracle. Many of the walls were missing large chunks, but the overall structure remained. Tobin picked through the rubble along the first floor, walking a grid and scanning each section with his augmented vision. Seeing him, so uninterested in anything but the charred refuse on the floor, caused something in Dru to snap.

"Couldn't be bothered to see if I was all right?"

He answered without looking up. "You were fine. There wasn't anything I could do for you, so I came here to begin processing the crime scene while there are still meaningful heat signatures to pick up. I knew you would find me when you were up and around."

Dru clenched her fists, bit her tongue. She reminded herself that Tobin was ex military, tried to make her peace with how he probably saw his actions as pragmatism, but it felt an awful lot like his not giving a shit.

She swallowed her frustration, tried to think of things from his perspective. Everything he said was true, and the fury in her was clouding her judgment. She told herself that he waited around for her to wake up for a little while, then decided to work on the crime scene. She knew better, but the lie quenched her anger enough to push the red from her vision.

"Fine. Yeah, I'm fine."

Tobin looked up at her, and nodded.

"Good. I found a few things that might be important."

Dru, careful to not disturb anything of significance, made her way over to him.

"Yeah? What did you come up with?"

Tobin waved a hand in front of his face, as though swatting a mosquito. From that direction, slides of information materialized into her view, projected by her augmented reality contact lenses as though floating a few feet in front of her. She reached up, the miniscule cameras embedded into the lenses recognizing her hands and allowing her to shuffle the files as though real.

There were spectrographic analysis reports hyperlinked to referenced locations in a separate folder containing thousands of images and videos. When Dru ran her hand down, scrolling to the bottom of the stack, she saw that it was being continually updated by the neuroNet implant grafted to the base of Tobin's skull, inserting images and forensic data on the fly as he captured it with his eyes.

"Well, this sure takes all the fun out of police work." Apparently she was feeling fine. Her sense of humor had returned.

"We still have our work cut out for us. There's always a lot of information at a crime scene, but very little of this helps determine if this psycho blew himself up or managed to escape."

Dru sorted through the overlays, finding one with identified bodies. Partial dental records, facial recognition, and any other visual means of identification had already been applied. Dru scanned the identified remains, some of them little more than blackened parcels of meat. None of them matched their suspect, the man they had been tracking. The man they had seen enter the building.

The Zealot.

Dru could only skim the data due to the vast flow of it.

"All of these people, murdered. Just because they wanted to take advantage of technology to improve their lives." She shook her head at the waste of life before returning to the list. A name caught her eye, but she couldn't stop the shuffling display in front of her in time for a second look, and had to backtrack to find it.

"Tobin."

"Yeah? Have something?"

"I think so. One of the implants in this room is still broadcasting its identification tag."

"And?"

"It might be nothing, but the name is from a recent victim of The Zealot."

"Let me see."

Dru cast the document over to Tobin, who, after a glance, began stepping over refuse and corpses towards the Northeast corner of the building, near the entrance. He kneeled next to a blackened chunk of slag, and, after a moment of examination, picked it up.

"This is the piece. It matches the description of the ankle joint that went missing in the Janell Sceptre case."

Another moment passed as Tobin used his implant to pull whatever additional data the implant had to broadcast.

"It's definitely the same implant. All the serial numbers match up."

Dru made her way over to his side.

"But why would The Zealot bring the implant here?"

"Not sure. Keep looking, see if you can find any of the

other implants reported missing as part of the investigation."

Dru nodded. "Will do. I'll also see if I can locate The Zealot's body anywhere. Or, at least identifiable chunks of it."

A smirk fought through Tobin's stony expression. The Zealot had taken many lives, gaining a fair amount of notoriety for his habit of removing any augmentations or implants from his victims prior to killing them. Or, in some instances, as a means of killing them, if the implants were life sustaining. Judging by the extent of the defensive wounds found, this process most often would be performed without anesthesia, yet no DNA or clues of any kind were left. Considering the state of the art forensic tools at the FBI's disposal, this was a physical impossibility no one had yet explained.

The working theory at home office, and this was how he had been given his name, was that The Zealot believed in keeping the human body pure, and saw augmentations or implants as an abomination under whatever religious tenets he held dear. At several of the sites, crosses and other assorted artifacts had been recovered which bore out this theory.

Dru lifted the carbon composite skeleton of a human hand from the floor, bringing it into a shaft of light that had found an opening in one of the walls.

"Take a look at this."

Tobin focused on it, furrowing his brows. "Another match, but to a different victim."

Tobin breathed deeply, exhaling through his nose in a controlled manner. He closed his eyes and tilted his head down, an affectation Dru understood from their time together as his way of clearing his mind before forcing a large amount of data through his implant. He only did this when he thought he knew what had happened, a "hunch," in cop-speak.

Dru remained still, not wanting to distract him from a potential breakthrough.

The cybernetic hand in her grasp glinted amber, late day sunlight off of black composite. Something about it struck her as odd. It wasn't that the hand looked human, manufacturers often matched shapes to what they considered "classic human architecture", but the complete lack of blood or human tissue. The blast would be responsible for much of the spider cracking tattooed over each of the composite bones, but there should still be evidence of skin or blood, as the model she held appeared to be a common under-skin replacement. It wasn't a model meant to augment a human's ability so much as it replaced a lost original.

And then, making one of those *X+3.14=Colonel Mustard did it in the library with the candlestick* leaps of deductive reasoning, she had it. She turned to Tobin, about to open her mouth when she saw that his eyes were already open, wild with understanding.

Tobin spoke first. "He steals the body parts to build androids."

Dru expanded his sentence as though their minds were linked, "....and then controls them remotely. That's why he didn't hesitate to blow himself up. I thought something felt wrong about that, it didn't fit his MO."

Clapping, barely audible over the first responder bustle outside of the blown-out building, came from a darkened corner of the lobby they occupied.

Tobin turned, releasing the magnetic catches running vertically along the front of his jacket as he did so.

Dru watched, the first traces of adrenaline in her blood tripping the latent psychoactive drugs she took every morning as part of her police protocol. Each molecule of the drug was safely stored away in a membrane, only unlockable by adrenaline to ensure that the effects were only administered when the drugs might save her life. The drug, a refined version of Methylphenidate, instantly overcranked her brain, allowing her perception of time to slow. She considered herself lucky that the concussive force of the blast had knocked her out earlier, causing her adrenal glands to shut down and preserving the latent chemicals in her blood stream for now, when she could use them.

Tobin's jacket flew open with the centrifugal force of his turn, leaving a slight gap between the garment and his gun, should he need it in a hurry.

Her position in the room allowed her to see the form approaching from the shadows before Tobin completed his turn, and, in that half moment, he moved into the light enough for her to identify the robed figure that they had spent the past six months searching for.

The Zealot.

Her mind registered everything, the momentary hesitation as Tobin recognized him, then the second instant it took for him to snatch the cling-bonded handgun from the contact patch inside his jacket and level it at The Zealot. The bullet, released with a snap by the electromag slide atop the gun, did not hesitate.

The Zealot didn't flinch as the bullet passed cleanly through him, exploding the plaster on the opposing wall directly behind his head.

Tobin lowered the gun without a second shot.

Dru couldn't understand why Tobin had stopped firing.

"What are you doing? Take him down!"

Tobin's voice was calm, "Dru, check the thermals."

"Oh."

The Zealot was invisible to the infrared spectrum of her SideARM contact lenses, meaning that not only was he not before them as a flesh and blood person, he wasn't a machine, either. He was hacked into their vision through augmented reality, a digital ghost.

Once they were all on the same page, The Zealot spoke. "I recognize that you are largely an instrument of war, Agent Maldovan, so I thought meeting you corporally might detract from our ability to speak candidly with one another."

Tobin holstered his gun.

"Unless you are attempting to negotiate your surrender, I don't see that we have much to discuss."

The Zealot threw back his hood.

Dru was a little disappointed by the gaunt, unremarkable man beneath it, now that she could finally see him up close. Approximately forty years of age, with short blond hair, cropped on the sides and slightly longer in the center, only noticeable because of the difference in the way light played across it. His eyes were perhaps the only notable thing about his face. They shone a piercing blue, but more importantly, they weren't the angular, angry eyes she expected to see, but rather the intelligent, expressive eyes of an artist. Eyes that did not miss details.

The Zealot focused on her for a moment, as though attempting to read her thoughts, before returning to Tobin.

"I am going to need something from you, though your acceleration of my timetable by witnessing my presence here tonight means that you'll be waiting around a bit for your role to come into play."

"I'm not doing anything for you. You just murdered 173 people, asshole. The only thing I'm going to do for you is make sure your life is as brief and insignificant as I can."

"How terribly short sighted of you, Tobin. Sophia would have expected more. In fact, she is."

The room fell silent. The shouting of the search and rescue crews, the crunching and grinding of their excavation machinery beyond the demolished portion of the south wall faded.

He didn't move. Didn't speak. His mechanical eyes lost focus, and Dru stepped closer to catch him should he fall. Tobin quickly regained his composure, bringing with it a white hot intensity directed at the slender man in front of them.

"I will kill you if you touch her."

The Zealot smiled. It was lopsided, lecherous, and the equal to Tobin's merciless glare.

"You already threatened that. Next time, perhaps you should hold back a little, perhaps avoid blowing your proverbial load before you have a sense of how the encounter is going to go. Regardless, I've already touched her."

The 4" Karambit knife was in Tobin's hand before the analytical parts of his brain could have reminded him of its futility.

"What...did you do to her?" The sound of Tobin's voice, forced through gritted teeth, was more trash compactor than human speech.

"I took something out, and put something back in. You're going to be upset at first, but if you play along, you'll be grateful I stepped in when I did."

"What are you talking about?"

The Zealot started towards the door. "Walk with me."

Tobin looked at Dru. In his eyes, she saw a man at the tenuous end of his composure. Unable to offer any real consolation, she shrugged. The motion felt stupid and useless, an involuntary response to confusion.

The Zealot called back over his shoulder, "This projection is being served locally from Tobin's SideARM, from which I've massaged superuser status. I can quite easily go wherever you go. I'd avoid talking too much to me in the presence of others, though. Since I'm inserting my avatar into a private layer that they can't see, it might bring your sanity into question."

Dru turned to follow, closely tailed by Tobin. The voice of the robed figure striding away from them never broke cadence.

"Sophia had a dangerous heart valve condition that she probably never told you about. Not wanting to worry you while you were away, and all."

"And?" Tobin wasn't able to mask the irritation from his voice.

"And...it's no longer a problem. You see, while you may think me a monster, I'm not without a desire for the greater good. In fact, while my methods are necessarily direct, my end goal is the betterment of all mankind."

"And how does harming Sophia bring you closer to that?"

"Sophia is merely a motivating factor, a way for me to ensure your cooperation. As I already said, I need something from you. And I didn't harm Sophia. I told you that as well. I merely fixed a heart condition by replacing her defective heart with a very expensive cybernetic unit. For free. You're welcome, and try to pay attention, I do hate repeating myself."

Tobin released a slow, cleansing breath. Dru guessed that he was not used to someone speaking to him like this.

"Alright. What do I have to do to get Sophia back?"

"That's between you and her. If you're inquiring as to what I'll be asking of you before I will release her, the answer is nothing. You can pick her up any time you wish. She is not my prisoner."

Tobin eyed The Zealot warily. He appeared to be leading them back to their car. Dru stepped aside to inform the onsite liaison that they were leaving to pursue a lead, and would check in later. She caught Tobin and The Zealot as they exited the narrow walkway leading from the warehouse district. Neither man spoke until they were seated in their cruiser.

Dru drove, as she typically did, and Tobin sat in the rear of the vehicle alongside The Zealot. To anyone passing by, it must have looked as though Tobin was suspected of committing a crime.

The Zealot resumed speaking once they could no longer see the flashing lights of the crime scene. "We need to get on the highway and go north. I've programmed the navigational system to prompt you as we approach each turn, but not before. Too much information all at once can be a bad thing."

Dru made the next right, and a short distance later merged onto the highway as instructed.

Tobin, quiet during their time in the car, finally spoke. "I don't understand. Why would you do this?"

The Zealot pursed his lips, thinking. "I am a pragmatic creature, as are we all when emotion is removed from our decision making processes. I replaced her heart for two reasons. The first is that I need her to live long enough for you to accomplish the task I will set out for you in the coming weeks, and the second is that I needed a place to irrevocably install the small explosive device that will serve as leverage."

Tobin finally took the swipe at The Zealot he had been restraining, passing the hooked blade of the Karambit efficiently through the neck of the projection. The blade passed cleanly through open space, barely missing the rear headrest.

The Zealot's expression didn't change. "Do you feel better, now that you've purged that impulse?"

Tobin's expression indicated otherwise.

"As I said, the explosive device is merely leverage. I will continue to input the daily deactivation code, extending her life another 24 hours, and will input the permanent deactivation code upon conclusion of our business. At that point, attempting to remove the explosives will no longer trigger the detonation. Any attempt to intervene by medical personnel will cause instantaneous loss of life to anyone standing within several hundred feet. I will give you a task in the next week, and I want you to understand now that it is not a task you will object to, outside of the motivational methods I have already outlined."

"But you aren't ready to tell me what this task is."

The Zealot parroted his response. "But I am not ready to tell you what this task is."

Another cleansing breath from Tobin.

Dru could feel the tension begin to flow out of her. Even though the bomb still hung over their heads like a proverbial sword of Damocles, they all understood the stakes, and also that he wanted something from Tobin. While he did not have ultimate control over the situation, knowing they had a small amount of leverage left her with hope that they might make their way clear of this alive.

Tobin, seemingly on the same page, added, "I have no choice but to pursue you, even now. It will look strange if we just throw in the towel."

The Zealot smiled. "Oh, I understand that. You have my permission to make a good show of it. That said, you will share none of what we have discussed today with anyone."

"That's not going to scan with my boss."

"As far as your boss is concerned, I died in tonight's explosion. I have left genetic information in several of the implants that my simulations indicated would survive the blast. This DNA is not in any database, so there will be no means to disprove your story."

That stoked Dru's curiosity. "You expect us to believe that your DNA isn't on file?"

The Zealot turned to her, the makings of a smile twitching at the right corner of his mouth. "Oh, my DNA is most certainly on file...somewhere. You are quite right that it is logistically impossible to expunge that. However, I have found a ready source of untraceable DNA. A descriptive match for this visage, cloned from an aborted fetus. I was able to match the physical descriptions of the prospective parents to this physical description. Or the other way around, who knows? I just hope the mother was not keeping secrets from the father. That would be embarrassing for all involved."

She wanted to throw up, pull the car over, and pistol whip the hologram until she couldn't lift her arm, but the tone in his voice indicated that the process was unavoidable, and not anything from which he drew any enjoyment or satisfaction. It was just enough detachment to let her keep her lunch, but she could not let the remark go without voicing some disapproval.

"You're a sick fuck."

She delivered the line without turning around or making eye contact.

The Zealot paused, pensive, before calmly responding. "I can see why you would think that. The slaughter of a defenseless child is such a waste of potential. So much possibility, so many things that child could have gone on to do, so many years of it being cute, toddling around while everyone pretends to have its best interests in mind. I did not choose to abort the baby, Dru. I simply put its remains to my use, as opposed to the alternative medical uses that it would have gone to had I not stepped in. As I said, I'm a pragmatist."

The exchange had not made a noticeable impact on Tobin's expression, which was already appropriately notched somewhere between disapproving authority figure and a person preparing to throw the lever on a guillotine.

In the void of Tobin's silence, Dru punctuated the exchange. "Whatever you have to tell yourself."

Already focused on his face, unable to break eye contact through the rearview mirror like a person crossing a particularly dangerous brand of snake, she saw The Zealot turn his head to look out the window. A meaningless affectation meant to end the exchange, but it got Dru thinking. Since he was not there physically, everything he saw had to be from Tobin's perspective, through his cybernetic eyes, or from Dru's SideARM.

The seeds of an idea formed in her head.

A neural network, originating at the implant affixed to the base of Tobin's skull, controlled his eyes. Thin tracer wires extended deep into his skull, terminating at thousands of points in his brain. She wasn't sure, but she couldn't discount the possibility that The Zealot might be able to read his thoughts, perhaps even sense his emotions. For her plan to work, she needed it to escape The Zealot's attention. That meant she not only had to hide it from him; but from Tobin as well. She couldn't risk her partner becoming unwitting surveillance.

Tobin was ex Special Forces, and probably the most insightful and observant FBI Agent she had ever known. Hiding her plan from him would not be easy. She also needed to lock down a few pieces of information before she could say if there was even a chance to turn the tables on the psychotic apparition seated behind her.

Dru wondered why he was trying so hard to put them at ease. He never made a move that had not been previously calculated, scrutinized, and had a contingency waiting. Something about his smug expression ate at her until she couldn't stand not turning his screws for a minute.

"Why not just tell me where we're going? Why the suspense?"

When he shifted his eyes to hers, she could see the way his gaze wavered against the undulations of the vehicle. He was not watching from her perspective, but from Tobin's. Had he been watching from her perspective, with his projection able to see itself without having to guess perspective, it would have locked on to her face and remained steady. Since he watched from Tobin's gaze, he was constantly adjusting, and that showed up as his eyes tracking all over her face. Sensing her attempt to read him, he answered.

"Do I really have to answer that?"

After fifteen minutes with the man, even if only with his displaced shadow, she thought she knew enough about him to nail down a few points of his character. Many of his responses had been petulant regarding intelligence, or at least in comparing his intelligence to others. Perhaps she could use that to her advantage by downplaying her abilities. Not pretending to be useless, just consciously dropping her IQ a few dozen points in the hopes that The Zealot would drop his guard, and let something slip.

She shrugged, and his eyes unfocused. It was not quite an eye roll, but as if it pained him to look at her, that the glare of her ignorance might infect him if he looked at her too directly. When he spoke, his voice came out in a sigh.

"Fine, I'll spell it out for you. You might not be willing to risk Sophia's life, but I'm sure Agent Maldovan here would have a surgical field team and a brigade of Agents at the facility prior to our arrival."

"I'm not sure either of us would want to risk Sophia's life for that chance to catch you."

He scoffed and returned his gaze back to the window.

It was the type of slip she was looking for. He wasn't worried about being caught because he wouldn't be at the warehouse, at least by the time they reached it. Another cog of the plan dropped into place. She felt abandoned by Tobin, even though his inability to help his own cause was no fault of his own. She couldn't do anything that The Zealot could see or hear through her SideARM, which made things difficult, and slowed her down.

Dru understood what needed to happen. She needed to find a way to disable the bomb inside Sophia's chest, without disabling the heart itself. Whatever plan she came up with could go wrong in half a dozen ways, so she resolved to use whatever time they had before they arrived to find ways to minimize that risk.

The Zealot viewed everything through Tobin's implant, or was focused on his point of view. It made sense; given that Tobin's enhancements would give him more information, but Dru could not be 100% sure that he wasn't also inside of her SideARM. Active frequency dampeners lined her jacket pockets, shielding the device inside from everything except the low power, high priority quantum encrypted signals necessary for its function. The SideARM automatically raised and lowered the shielding as needed with microsecond latency. In short, the gate was never open long enough for an intrusion to get in. Even knowing this, there would be risk involved in deviating from expectation.

The danger to Sophia grew with every city block as they closed on her location. If Dru was going to do something, now would be the time to start the ball rolling.

Careful to keep her eyes on the road, she took advantage of Tobin being in the back seat and reached down to her pocket. She worked the cover to her SideARM apart, careful to keep all movement hidden from the shoulders up. Tobin might have a range of vision that could see through her seat, but she also knew he had to consciously will his implant to enable it. Or, in this case, The Zealot would need to do so.

Working from muscle memory, she traced her left hand across the surface of the circuit board inside, knowing roughly where the battery connector would be. She glanced up at The Zealot, then over to Tobin. The Zealot continued his charade of finding interesting things outside of the cruiser to look at. Tobin stared bleakly through the opposing side of the windshield.

Her finger caught the only ridge of plastic on the otherwise featureless board, and she set to work trying to dislodge the battery connector. If her SideARM went offline and The Zealot didn't react, she would know he was not actively monitoring it. It was a pretty big piece of whatever plan she might put into motion. The onboard navigation directed her to turn right, and she glanced up to see The Zealot watching her.

She didn't respond, just adjusted her arm position to ready for the turn, hoping that an exaggerated movement with her right hand would deflect any attention paid to her as she removed her left hand from her pocket. Careful to simulate her normal mannerisms for fear of discovery, Dru turned as instructed before returning to her previous position in what she hoped was an appropriately casual sequence of movements.

The withdrawals from the neurotransmitters added an unwelcome twitchiness to her hands, demanding every ounce of focus not dedicated to driving as she again felt for the clip holding the battery's ribbon cable. Feeling it, she flipped the miniscule plastic clip that locked the cable in place with her thumbnail. She placed her thumb atop the cable, the tension of the socket the only thing keeping her SideARM online.

One more glance, to verify that both men in the back seat were otherwise occupied. Tobin first, the mechanical iris' of his cybernetic eyes slightly wider than normal, unfocused. For the first time, Dru recognized it for what it was. Fear. She had never seen Tobin afraid before.

He really loved his ex wife. The Zealot knew that, knew it would be the perfect fulcrum with which to leverage Tobin's cooperation. How much did he know about her? Had he been thorough enough to discover her background as a psychology major in college, her short tenure as a reformative psychologist with the corrections system before joining the FBI? Something told her he hadn't bothered. He had accepted her earlier ploy of ignorance too easily.

Probably a chauvinist, she thought. Relief at the lack of attention overwhelmed any anger at him as she slid her thumb and separated the cable from its socket.

The heads up display in her contacts cut out immediately, and the naked feeling of detachment surprised her. It took every ounce of courage to suppress any external reactions, but losing the ability to instantly answer any question shook her confidence more than she cared to admit. A moment earlier, anything she wanted to know was only a glance away. Then...nothing.

The navigation unit directed her to make another turn, and her sense of abandonment from the internet took a back seat to her current circumstance. Moments earlier, the concept of The Zealot being in charge had terrified her, and now it was the only thing keeping her from pulling over and hyperventilating. She made a mental point to start unplugging more often, if she survived this ordeal. This dependency was a weakness of character she could not tolerate.

Slow, shallow breaths pulled her heart back to baseline before the display in the dash called out the next turn. They were making their way towards the industrial district, via the most circuitous route Dru had ever seen. The Zealot was not taking chances, fearing a tail. Dru assumed he had probably blocked the car's tracking device before they left the explosion site as well.

Wireless connectivity was everywhere, both a blessing and a curse. It made magic possible, but it also left cracks for demons like The Zealot.

After the third turn, Dru warmed to the knowledge that The Zealot wasn't monitoring her SideARM. As a security measure, the hardware necessary to remotely track her SideARM had been omitted from the design, so unless he actively tried to access it, he would have no way of knowing if it was online or not. A few years before she joined the force, a hacker targeted police during a sequence of riots, posting real time information on their locations.

By the time the riots subsided, nearly half the police force had been wiped out in ambushes. Once they discovered the problem, all police issue SideARM's were redesigned at the hardware level, and replaced with updated units for their protection. Acknowledging that any software was at some level vulnerable, they simply removed the parts necessary for that function.

If The Zealot tried to access her point of view later on, she could always offer the excuse that the battery died. As feeble as it would sound, there would be no way to prove her story false. Uncertainty was preferable to outright discovery.

The gaps in her plan surfaced again, and her mind grasped at them like a drowning person might a life preserver. She needed a way to separate the explosive from the cybernetic heart, a way to disable the explosive, and a way to do it without The Zealot or Tobin realizing it was happening until it was too late to detonate the device.

Was she 100% certain The Zealot would not be with Sophia? Dru was betting all of their lives on it. Everything in his profile indicated a severe level of risk aversion. He worked through proxies. He worked from the shadows, wirelessly pulling strings so others took the fall if things went bankrupt.

No, he would be there, but he would not be *there*.

Dru combed her mind for any angle she could exploit, any facet of the situation that The Zealot might have overlooked.

Her father's heart was cybernetic, a replacement after decades of heart disease risk finally came to fruition as a heart attack. She remembered going through the literature with him, reading all of the options, helping him select his new heart. The entire process felt like whittling down the world's most surreal Christmas list. She also remembered that he had to have a second surgery a few years later, when the device they had carefully selected needed to be replaced because of a factory defect.

The design they had initially chosen was found to be susceptible to electromagnetic radiation. In the unlikely event that a transformer blew within fifteen feet of him, or some other large scale electrical burst, there was a chance that the microprocessor controlling his heart could be permanently damaged, so her father went in for a second surgery. His new heart was, by most accounts, almost bullet proof, and guaranteed to outlive him.

Dru rolled the radiation angle around in her mind. If she knew for sure that the heart was a newer model, one of the electromagnetic pulse grenades in the trunk of their cruiser could disable the explosives. It was unlikely that The Zealot would have been able to install the explosives inside of the heart. They were tightly engineered, and designed in such as way that damaging the unit would send out a distress signal. Assuming her own memories weren't betraying her. Her habitual reliance on the recall function built into her SideARM allowed her to be lax on memory retention, since it recorded everything and kept the pertinent details from every day. Without it, she found herself doubting her ability to dredge up the unremarkable memories.

They were nearly to the industrial district now. They were running out of time, and when it ran out completely, she would have to start taking chances. They would never again know where The Zealot's attention was focused, where he was watching from. Dru wanted to let Tobin in on the plan, but there was no way to risk doing so. If The Zealot suspected her, he could trigger the implant in an instant. Tobin's hijacked senses would give him every opportunity to catch her before she had the chance.

They arrived at the warehouse a few minutes later, and the navigation system instructed them to enter the building by a small entrance door on the south facing wall. Dru climbed from the car, immediately making her way to the trunk, nearly reaching it before Tobin spoke up.

"Dru, what are you doing?"

She assumed that The Zealot had mentioned something, due to the delay in the response. He would have tried to say something to her first, and resorted to threatening Tobin to reach her when that hadn't worked.

"I'm getting the First Aid kit. If that asshole butchered the job, do you want me to have to run back out here for it while she's bleeding out?"

She walked right through her statement, positive The Zealot would object, but she would have the trunk lid open and the EMP grenade in her pocket before his command for her to stop could relay back through Tobin.

She snatched the First Aid kit as well, and the trunk lid was already coming down when Tobin spoke again.

"He wants to know why your SideARM is off."

"The battery is dead. I didn't have a chance to get a decent charge on it before you called me for the stakeout."

Tobin looked at her, scanning her for deceit. Dru understood The Zealot was probably scanning her for a great deal more than that, relieved that she had been able to get the EMP grenade into one of the shielded pockets in her jacket.

Minimally satisfied, Tobin turned to go. Dru made her way around the car and followed him into the building.

Inside, a diffused shaft of light illuminated a gleaming white Autosurgeon suite with Sophia atop it, wrapped within a sheet of antimicrobial cloth. Small specks of bright red wicked slowly outward through the fabric atop her chest, indicating recently completed surgery.

Tobin ran to her side, gingerly lifting the cloth to inspect her wound. He turned away, visibly composing himself. "I'm taking her some place to make sure this doesn't get infected."

A pause, during which Dru assumed The Zealot would be reminding him of the "no medical personnel" portion of their agreement.

"Then not a hospital, but I need someone with medical training to see her."

Another pause. Not knowing the other half of the conversation put Dru on edge, and she stepped forward to offer assistance, more to diffuse the helplessness she felt than out of any expectation of helping matters.

"Let me see."

She inspected the wound, and saw that the stitching was tight, uniform and even, covered with the protective tape Autosurgeons used as a means to quickly dress and seal wounds after sterilization. A tinge of amber around the wound indicated that it had been sterilized after surgery, carrying with it the assumption that sterilization had taken place prior to it as well.

She stepped back and turned to Tobin. "Everything I can see tells me the procedure was carried out as cleanly as possible in a place like this. The wound is sterilized and sealed like you'd expect from a properly maintained Autosurgeon."

Tobin nodded reluctantly, moving away from the surgical suite to address The Zealot. Dru tried to assemble the rest of the conversation in her mind, given the half of it that she was allowed to hear.

"So I can take her now?"

"Yes, as I said. But do not cross me, it requires more thought for me to keep her alive than to let her die."

As The Zealot spoke, his voice emanated from a hijacked speaker in the Autosurgeon. Apparently, using Tobin as a proxy had proven too cumbersome.

"Fine, then we're going. I have no choice but to play your little game. For now."

"Of course you don't. And I will keep my word about keeping her alive, so long as you continue to play along."

Dru needed to make her move. She expected Tobin to argue, but he had all too easily agreed to The Zealot's terms in order to get Sophia out of the warehouse. Maybe she could use that.

"You hate augmentations, or anything you see as unnatural. Why should Tobin believe you won't kill her down the road? Why would you kill nearly every augmented human who crossed your path, only to let that one live?"

She pointed to Sophia, still on the operating table a few feet away from a newly concerned Tobin.

"She's right. This makes no sense."

The Zealot smiled. "This 'Zealot' persona the media has cultivated has served my purposes until now, so I've allowed it to exist. If I were to be completely transparent, I would tell you that I am almost precisely the antithesi-."

Tobin cut him off.

"Stop talking in circles and answer her."

"I have." The Zealots voice was cold, imbued with the tone of a machine with its finger on a trigger.

"Then answer *me*. No more metaphors, no more half truths. You have exactly ten words before I assume you're going to kill her anyway, and I take her with me and you can fuck off in regards to everything else."

The man in the robe paused for a moment, a smirk spreading slowly across his face. "We must become ghosts in the machine to survive," and after a pause, "satisfied?"

During the exchange, Dru made her way around the Autosurgeon and checked the main power switch located on the side opposite Tobin and the Zealot. Finding it off, she reached into her pocket and triggered the grenade without further hesitation, releasing it from her hand so as not to be burnt by the discharge mechanism.

The snap of the grenade was followed by several other sounds in quick succession; every light bulb in the room immediately blew, and Tobin fell to his knees, clutching his head as he screamed in pain.

Ignoring her agonized partner, she threw the switch on the Autosurgeon and began removing the antimicrobial cloth from Sophia.

Hearing the noise, Tobin struggled to his feet. "Dru! What's happening, I can't see!"

"Tobin, calm down. I had to disable your implant and any tech in the area that could send a trigger signal to blow the bomb in Sophia's chest. I'm booting up the Autosurgeon now to remove it before he finds another way to set it off."

Tobin growled, "You're going to get her killed!"

The Autosurgeon finished it's fast-boot sequence, and laser light dappled the surface of Sophia's body from a sensor mounted above her.

"Scans indicate that the subject is recovering from previous surgical intervention, and is no longer at risk. Please state the elective measures you would like taken at this time."

Dru ignored Tobin, staggering around with hands outstretched, and shouted at the machine.

"We suspect an explosive device to have been coupled with the heart implant during the prior surgery. Please scan and advise."

Beneath the work surface, a circular beam of beige painted metal slid out past the end of the bed and rotated around to pass over and under Sophia's inert body.

"No foreign bodies detected."

"What?"

The machine began to repeat the message, but Dru cut it off. "Scan again, and display region from previous surgery."

The machine did as ordered, showing a high resolution MRI of the requested area on the side display panel. Dru manipulated the three dimensional simulation, inspecting all sides of the cybernetic heart. Nothing was implanted outside of it, and by checking the specs on an adjoining readout, she could tell that the device was indeed intact, unaltered, shielded from EMP and functioning normally.

Tobin screamed at her from nearby, his voice a growl pushed through a veil of pain. A thin tendril of smoke emanated from the singed implant at the base of his skull.

"Dru, tell me what the fuck is going on! Is she alright?"

Dru swallowed before speaking. "Y...yes, Tobin. She's fine. There is no explosive in her chest. He was bluffing."

"What? There's no explosive?" Tobin's voice, almost pleading, made Dru want to cry.

"I just scanned her twice. I'm looking at it right now. There's no evidence of anything except a fully functioning, late model cybernetic heart inside her, but let's get her in the car and take her to the hospital to be sure."

Tobin, using Dru's voice to echolocate her position, made his way to her side.

"Thank god. Let's get her out of here, before that motherfucker has a chance to bring up a contingency plan. I'll feel better having her checked by a machine not supplied by the guy who put her in this position. I'll carry her, show me the way out."

Dru guided his hands to lifting positions beneath her

shoulders and knees, and with a hand on his shoulder, aimed him at the exit. As Sophia's weight was removed from the machine, the surgery table clicked from somewhere deep inside, a pressure switch engaging.

The side display again flickered to life, and The Zealot's face appeared.

"Very well done, Dru."

She whirled around, her gun already leveled at the source of the sound. She stepped outside of the Autosurgeon's reach should The Zealot decide to send it instructions to perform more impromptu surgery.

"What do you want? I called your bluff, and I won. We're done here."

The Zealot laughed. "Yes, indeed you did. Of course, I anticipated something like this might happen. Actually, this entire game was designed to test your resourcefulness. It's true that I'm not even on the West Coast right now, as you must have suspected prior to risking Sophia's life. During my research, I discovered that she had a heart abnormality that might impugn my plans later on if she had an episode over here while Tobin was conducting business on my behalf, so I corrected it. As I said, I have a task for Tobin. While I knew there was a chance one of you might destroy the illusion I carefully crafted regarding the explosive, the part about needing Tobin's services was not a fabrication. Unfortunately, I expect that you will be along with him when he returns to Maine, and I didn't have time to research you as thoroughly as I have him, necessitating this little test of character."

Dru turned to Tobin, "What's in Maine?"

Tobin's face grew taut.

"Tobin is starting to put together the pieces now, no doubt. I can see it on his face. Ruthless move, by the way, risking permanent damage to his brain with an EMP grenade to save Sophia's life. A risk I calculated for you already.

Would you like to know if the damage will be permanent?"

"Yes," Tobin answered before Dru had the chance to turn him down, and the naked need in his voice made her feel instantly guilty. She did what she did for a good reason, but she was still responsible for his current—perhaps permanent—disability. That she assumed anything for him was wrong of her, but she'd done it for Sophia and had to believe it's what he would have wanted.

The Zealot continued, "By my calculations, the probability is that the damage would remain localized to the external portion of the implant. As you no doubt know, it is replaceable through an outpatient procedure, followed by a calibration session. Internal microfiber structures have only a 3% chance of permanent damage, though your ocular prosthetics will need to be replaced. Frankly, you needed the upgrade to help accomplish the task I will set out for you, and I knew you wouldn't accept it unless the units you wore now lost function."

Tobin took a step closer. "So, you planned all of this?"

"Well, I planned to leave you two options. Owing to the immense complexity of motivating factors that passes for human free will, that's really the best I could hope for. I feel as though I understand your motivations enough to remove most of the doubt from such an approximation, so, yes, I guess you could say I planned for you to either take Sophia, subservient to the idea that you had to do what I asked at the expense of her life, or that you would find a way to disable the bomb, and I would have to let slip another piece of information to draw you back to Maine."

"And what information is that?"

"That we've met before."

Tobin nodded, the news confirming something he had suspected for a while now. "ATLAS."

"Indeed. Now I believe you know where you need to be."

Tobin took another slow step towards the machine. "Yes. And once I get back to Maine, I'm going to find you, and I'm going to do things to you deemed illegal under the Geneva Convention."

"*Promises.* Regardless, I want you to try to do just that. It's no fun stealing money from the government without a foil who is up to the task. It's boring. Since the only joy in my life is the rush of staying one step ahead of law enforcement, I thought it might be fun to bring you back into our little game again. Now that Sophia's health problems are out of the way, you won't have any distractions."

Tobin turned to leave, daring few blind steps in the expanse of the warehouse.

"I know where to start looking. You're going to regret all of this. Dru, let's go."

Dru caught up to him. "Who is ATLAS?"

"A hacker and thief that worked through augmented reality to steal millions from Central Credit Holding last year. He's the reason Sophia is even here on the West Coast. He manipulated a transfer at the company she worked for in order to get me to follow her instead of pursuing him. I almost caught him at the Maine/Canada border, but he escaped."

"My god. All of this...fabricating The Zealot persona to steal body parts, which he used to destroy a facility for reasons that no longer seem to make any sense...Kidnapping Sophia, implanting her with a cybernetic heart, pretending to implant a bomb to force you into doing what he wanted...it's so *elaborate.* The man is a psychopath."

Dru guided them to the car, helping him place Sophia in the back seat. Tobin sat in the back with her, cradling her head.

"Yeah, and when I get my hands on him, he's going to regret ever involving my family in any of it."

***

NOTE FROM THE AUTHOR:

The preceding tale, "The Zealot" is a short story set in Christopher Godsoe's *d.o.mai.n* series. Chronologically, it takes place following the first novel in the series, *pre://d.o.mai.n*, and prior to the events of the second novel, Infinite Loop, which will be released in 2016. The Zealot spoils little about the plot of the preceding novel, but having read *pre://d.o.mai.n* will place this story in a different context. That being said, upon completion of *pre://d.o.mai.n*, you may wish to return to this story, as additional details will be noticeable not only from *pre://d.o.mai.n*, but also in the upcoming Infinite Loop.

ABOUT THE AUTHOR:

Christopher Godsoe lives in Central Maine with his teenage son. Common themes in his stories include the perception of reality, the definition of self, the proliferation of a free and ungoverned internet, as well as corporate and governmental corruption. The majority of his characters appear in separate works, showing them from various perspectives and giving a more complete account of their lives. Regular updates on his works can be found at www.christophergodsoe.com

THE WELL-ROUNDED HEAD
BY SALLY BASMAJIAN

My trophy husband, that's what he was. So handsome, with skin the color of glossy, brown acorns, and dreamy eyes of deepest russet.

But that's not why I married him, and it wasn't for his money, either. No, to me, it was all about the shape of his head. His big, fat, oversized noggin. Easily double the size of a normal man's, I would brag to my friends. And what a turn-on it was.

It was round, like a child's filled-to-popping party balloon, without a single imperfection. And so smooth – not a single hair grew there, and it wasn't because he shaved it, because he didn't. He was just blessed with a bean that looked remarkably like a brown snooker ball, except way, way bigger.

To me, he was irresistible. In bed, whenever we finished making love, I would take his head between my hands and stroke his bulbous temples until we both hummed with pleasure. So velvety, so orb-like–so *hot*.

In the early days of our marriage, my husband was sexually insatiable. We were playful in bed: he the randy stable boy to my aristocrat's daughter; the lusty doctor to my white-capped nurse. In his arms I spoke in tongues, felt the universe expand, and saw the earth's beginning and end. He made love with the zealous commitment of the converted, my satisfaction his divinity.

Until his appearance changed in a most alarming way.

Maybe I misjudged and I know I definitely overreacted. My friends swore they never noticed anything different about him at all. But, to me, my husband's transformation was unmistakable and so unwelcome that when I first detected it I felt my stomach clench in horror that quickly turned to disgust.

His head was no longer a flawless ball-shape.

No, there were ever so slight indentations on either side of his forehead. It wasn't just a trick of the light; I was sure of it. When he approached me, smiling, with those twin depressions marring his globular head I flinched and moved out of reach, staring in anguish at what I considered to be a gross disfigurement. Maybe he was still more circular than ovoid, but those little dents made him look to me almost like a normal man, and that I could never accept. I wasn't about to downgrade to Mr. Potato Head when I had married the perfect Nerf.

He babbled: what was wrong, why was I shunning him, had I found someone else, oh, please, please tell me, promise not to leave me. On and on. My husband still wanted to be with me; yet in my eyes he was ugly, ruined. His dome was dented; his cranium crenellated. I couldn't bear to look at him, let alone touch him, or–worse yet—let him touch me.

That night, when the lights were off, my husband reached for me in bed. I slapped him, hard, and told him his advances were unwelcome. He said nothing, but a few minutes later I heard him sobbing into his pillow. I think I broke his heart, but it wasn't my fault. I hadn't married him for his personality; it had all been about his impressive, Charlie Brown head.

The next day, I moved my things into the guest room, down the hall. I chose to sleep alone with good memories rather than bunk with my new and revolting reality. Whenever possible, I avoided my spouse, eating breakfast after he left for work and retiring to my separate room before he returned. I knew this was cruel, but he was too hideous with his misshapen skull. I couldn't bear to look at it.

A week passed.

Knock, knock, knock.

My husband rapped on my bedroom door.

I hunkered down under the sheets and ignored him.

Knock, knock, knock.

I stayed as still as possible, breathing shallowly. *Go away, go away*, I screamed inside in my mind, trying to psychically dissuade him from attempting to come in.

No such luck. After a while, he started to rattle the doorknob. He wasn't going to go away. And that freaked me out. What if he came in, with his caved-in head bobbling away at me? I didn't think I could stand it.

In my bedside table I looked for a weapon – anything I could use to protect myself if he entered my room against my wishes. All I could find was a riding crop and a starched nurse's cap, relics of our sexy, carefree days. Oh, God. What was I going to do?

And then, the door burst open and he was in the room and moving toward me. An agitated pulse throbbed in his disfigured temple. His arms reached out to me in supplication, but I bolted out of the bed, reached into my bedside table drawer, and brandished the riding crop. I would have appeared much fiercer, if I hadn't somehow managed to snatch the nurse's cap, too. There it perched, on top of the crop, with the combo looking like an insane medical puppet. Now, instead of looking indomitable, I just looked ridiculous.

But sheer panic can sometimes be the mother of ingenuity. I realized that the cap was attached by its rubber band to the riding crop. I could try to shoot it at my horrifying husband, like tiny David shot monstrous Goliath, and really, that worked out pretty well for good ol' Dave.

So, I aimed, pulled back on the cap, and let it fly.

Bullseye. The crisply starched point caught my husband square in one of his welling, russet eyes. One minute he was standing and begging me to tell him what was wrong; the next minute, he was gone. Dead. Kaput. Never to bother me with his hideousness again, thank God.

You may think I'm a monster, but I'm not. I'm just someone who likes a man with a round head. Go ahead: call me shallow; call me murderer – your words don't hurt. But stay far away from me unless you have a dome like a bloated harvest moon. Otherwise, I'm just not interested.

***

ABOUT THE AUTHOR:

Sally Basmajian is an ex-broadcast executive, who has spent much of her professional life selling, marketing, acquiring, and scheduling other people's artistic visions. Over the past year she has started dabbling in writing and has found some success, winning the 2014 Rising Spirits Award, publishing in CommuterLit, and placing in a recent ScreaminMamas creative non-fiction contest. Once upon a time, she was a piano major in university, eventually attaining a Master of Arts degree in Musicology from the University of Toronto. She has just finished her first novel, a fantasy for young adults.

RESERVED
BY SM JOHNSON

The second Pete Spencer set foot in the club, he knew it was a mistake. The lights, the noise, the people–feathers and glitter and skin, the crush of bodies, the strobes of lights–it was all immediately overwhelming. And he was *early*.

A push from behind forced him inside another step, and he tightened his gloved hand around the crest of his cane. He had to work to maintain his balance for a few seconds as his senses adjusted to the environment. He wasn't in pain, not yet, but he scanned the club in a hopeless quest for an empty table. The burlesque show was advertised to start at ten, which was ridiculous–who starts a party at ten at night? Pete was usually in bed by then, drifting away on pain killers and broken dreams.

He glanced at his watch. Eight thirty, which he'd planned, thinking that would be plenty early to score a seat, but apparently not. The only open table he could see in the whole place had a folded card on top announcing its reserved status. He might as well go home. There was no way he could stand even until the show started, much less for the duration. Not only would he not enjoy it, he might fall down and create a humiliating little show of his very own.

His mood hung somewhere between disappointed and resigned. There was always some glitch that ruined every outing.

A flurry of cold air rushed in from behind him, then a boy, pushing past him into the club. At least he thought it was a boy. Pete took a second look. Yes, a feminine, delicate young man, almost buried beneath a purple calf-length winter coat, a backpack, a duffel bag, a large multi-colored purse, and a metal lunch box featuring large-eyed cartoon characters. The boy's cheeks were red from the cold, his hair hidden beneath a ridiculous pink knit hat with a white pom-pom on top.

The boy shook his whole body, as if shaking off snow, though it wasn't snowing, then looked around the club, frowning. Someone called out, "Rory–you're late, slacker!" and the boy's frown grew more pronounced.

"Like there's any sense in being two full hours early," he muttered, but only loud enough for Pete to hear.

Pete, who was trying not to stare, but failing.

The boy caught sight of Pete and looked him over from face to groin to cane to boots. Pete waited for the curl of lip, the expected dismissal of *gimp*, and *old guy*, but it didn't come. Something unusual happened instead.

The boy looked him over again with a strange sort of interest. He moved a step closer, jostling against Pete with the arm that held the duffel bag and the lunch box. "So," he said, "I have a proposition for you."

His eyes were blue.

Rimmed with eyeliner and glitter.

Pete Spencer was immediately wary. Beautiful glitter boys rarely had good propositions for bitter old gimps. "I highly doubt that." Pete answered and considered slipping out the door. His instinct to leave had been the right one after all.

"Nothing indecent, I swear. Hear me out."

Pete cocked his head. Waited.

The glitter boy licked his lips.

Nervous? This beautiful creature was nervous about speaking to him? How could that be?

"I have that table over there reserved," the boy jerked his head. "Only, I'm the master of ceremonies for the show tonight, and if no one saves the table for me, people will sit there and I'll have nowhere to perch between the acts. Joey was supposed to sit there, but he dumped me last night, so now I'm kind of screwed. So would you mind? I mean, no offense, but you'd probably rather sit at a table for the show anyway, right? I mean, you have a cane. You can't want to stand the whole time. "

Pete was stuck on the fact that someone dumped this beautiful young thing and it kept him from answering right away. For too long, apparently, for glitter boy shifted from foot to foot, sighed, turned his lips into a pout and made his eyes big and beseeching. "Please? It would help me out a lot."

Pete nearly smiled. "You don't have to plead. I'd be grateful for a seat. I was thinking about leaving because this bum leg won't let me stand for long."

Great big shining smile. "Perfect! Let's go!"

And with that, the boy shifted the duffel bag to his shoulder, the lunch box to this other hand, and grabbed Pete's free hand, pulling him through the crush of bodies toward the table. When they arrived, Pete slid to the far side to tuck himself into the corner near the wall. The boy wagged a finger at him and shook his head, then spoke loud enough to be heard above the juke box music. "Sit here at the end, where you can see best. This is going to be a great show."

A voice boomed over the music. "Rory–get your ass downstairs and get ready."

The boy rolled his eyes. "That's my cue. No worries, though, I'll be back in a flash, and you'll hardly recognize me!" He disappeared in a twirl of coat, backpack, duffel bag, purse, pom-pommed hat, and lunch box.

Pete watched him go, the throb of his leg still mild enough that he might almost enjoy the evening. A waiter quite a lot more robust than Rory came by and winked at Pete. "Can I get you something? A drink, a shot, nine inches, uncut, at your place later?"

He felt his face turn red. Was that really on the menu?

The waiter must have noticed Pete's discomfort, because he said, "Dude, sorry, kidding." Warm brown eyes. Friendly lopsided grin. "Can I get you something from the bar?"

Pete ordered a soda. He felt old and broken and out of place. He didn't belong here. But he hadn't belonged in the rehabilitation center, either, and he was bored at home alone in his cave all the time. It was such an effort to go out, to push himself to new places. He didn't know what he liked anymore, *who* he liked, who would like him. But books and movies and online flirtation could only take him so far. He wanted...well. It didn't matter what he wanted. It was something he couldn't have, not anymore, not with this broken body and all its missing pieces.

The person who flounced onto the stage, tapped the microphone and hollered, "Is this thing on?" and then, "Hey! Can the music, would ya?" was, indeed, unrecognizable as the same boy who tripped in cold from the outdoors an hour before.

He'd grown four inches in height, and added at least a foot of lush auburn hair. Thick, rich, theatrical eyelashes, sharp cheekbones, luscious lips, and eyebrows from here to there. He was clearly a male in drag, making no attempt to pass as a woman. Pete couldn't tear his eyes away, and he'd hardly managed to take in the evening dress, the stunningly high heels, feather boa, and an elegant Victorian-style fan.

The music stopped, and the club went quiet.

"Well. Hello there, boys and girls," Rory purred into the microphone. "I am your delicious diva, your lickable lollipop, and your entertaining emcee for the evening. Please give a loud and boisterous bellow for the performers downstairs getting ready for ya'll–really loud, now–and stomp your feet– I want them to hear you clear down in the basement."

A wild cacophony ensued, stomping and whistling, clapping and yelling, until Rory calmed them and chattered about upcoming events, and that the proceeds from tonight's event were to benefit homeless GLBT youth, and to go ahead and toss dollars to the stage. "Or even tens and twenties–hell, write a check if you want, sweetie." He blew kisses and fanned himself. Finally he pressed his lips against the microphone in an obscene kiss, panted in a parody of heavy breathing, lowered his voice, and said, "Let's do it."

The lights lowered and soft, tinkling piano music began.

Rory bounced off the stage and landed very nearly in Pete's lap. "Hey there, big boy, what do you think of my transformation?"

Pete examined him, up close and personal.

Too much make-up. Too much glitz. A little was okay for a feminine boy. A lot was okay for a queen. Pete didn't know what to say because he didn't want to hurt Rory's feelings, and it felt like Rory was asking a bigger question. So he shrugged, tried for a reassuring smile, and realized smiling didn't come naturally anymore.

Rory leaned close. "You don't like me?" That question came in a small voice, one Pete could barely hear above the music.

Pete forgot he'd even come to watch a burlesque show. "I don't even know you, what's not to like? I'm grateful for the stool. Your get-up," he gestured vaguely from Rory's hair to Rory's heels, "is perfect."

That was enough, wasn't it? Surely Rory knew he was beautiful. He didn't need Pete to tell him that, did he? Or was he fishing for compliments?

Rory nodded. "Thank you for sitting at my table and pretending to be my new boyfriend. It's helping me get through this."

Pete felt the shock jolt through him.

He'd agreed to nothing of the sort, and was about to point that out, when Rory leaned right against him, nearly knocking him off the stool, and said, "You have no idea what a son of a bitch it is to get false eyelashes to stick when you can't stop crying. It sucks so bad."

Rory pressed his cheek ever so gently to Pete's chest, and Pete caught the scent of some perfume so erotic he vowed to never wash his shirt again. He patted Rory's shoulder and lowered his lips closer to the glitter boy's ear to mutter, "I can't even imagine."

"You can take your gloves off, you know," Rory said and patted Pete's hand. "It's plenty warm in here."

Pete pulled his hand away, afraid for a second Rory would insist. "Maybe later. I'm attached to them."

They were expensive gloves, of a very breathable fabric, not worn for warmth.

The music seemed to be winding down, and Rory leapt upright. "Duty calls," he sang, and blew Pete a kiss as he ran toward the stage and bounded up the steps on those crazy high heels.

Pete watched him go, and for some reason thought of hummingbirds, quick and busy, and hesitant to land anywhere for more than a moment.

Rory, the apple-cheeked glitter boy just in from the cold, looking at him, seeing him, and Pete reminded himself that it meant nothing, men like Pete didn't get to have glitter boys like Rory–the world didn't work like that, no matter what Rory wanted to pretend for tonight to save face in front of his friends. The minute Pete started to believe otherwise was the first step toward the fall. And if he fell that hard again, he might never get up.

He should leave the club right this minute, because having these thoughts at all was a sign of trouble. He was only safe if he expected nothing, wanted nothing, longed for nothing, yearned for nothing. He was only safe if he could be satisfied by the touch of his own hand.

He didn't even care about the burlesque show anymore. He didn't watch it. He only watched Rory, was fascinated by him. Captured. Already obsessed. He watched Rory's hands flutter, his lips move, his eyelashes bat. Watched the exaggerated emotions play across his face, his sighs, his laughter, his pout as he wiped away a tear. The cadence of his voice as he told a story, all diva, no falsetto. Breathless. Excited. Cute.

And then Rory was back at the table, standing between Pete's thighs, signaling to the waiter, and the waiter lined up two shot glasses in front of them, and looked expectantly at Pete, who felt obliged to remove his wallet and settle up. "A tab?" the waiter, the same charmer from earlier, suggested. Pete dutifully provided a card instead of cash.

Rory tilted his head up and his lips grazed Pete's ear. "Such a nice Daddy," he purred.

This time the shock of his words was electric.

Pete made sure his voice was as firm as the hands he used to push Rory gently out of his space. "My name is Pete Spencer. Call me Pete or call me Spence."

Rory stared at him, his face both defiant and hurt. "But

don't call you Daddy?"

"Exactly."

Rory's face fell into a full-on, dramatic pout.

Pete glared. This was a boundary he would not allow Rory to cross. No way.

Rory kept pouting, so Pete picked up his cane and his coat and eased himself from the barstool. He felt a kind of hollow sadness that he would never see Rory again, but it really was for the best, and he knew it. It could never be anything, anyway. Rory was just heartbroken and insecure right now. He'd needed someone safe at the table, and Pete had been handicapped, alone, and available. That was all. If he let himself be manipulated and charmed into thinking otherwise, he was an idiot.

He started to push past Rory, toward the door.

"Mr. Spencer, please don't go."

Pete turned his head. Rory's eyes were shining, as if filled with unshed tears, and his voice was loud enough to be heard, but polite. "I didn't mean to be rude."

It wasn't exactly an apology, but almost. Probably close enough, because Pete found himself turning back. "It's just...we don't know each other." He knew he'd already said that once, but couldn't help saying it again.

Rory nodded. "I understand. Cheers, Mr. Spencer." He picked up a shot glass, saluted Pete with it, and tipped the contents into his mouth. Swallowed in one big gulp. He grinned and set the glass back on the table, upside down. He turned and flounced up to the stage again.

Funny, Pete hadn't even noticed the current performance ending, so entranced was he with the drama going on at his own table.

Ridiculous.

Without allowing himself much thought, he picked up the remaining shot glass and knocked back some awful, sweet, sticky red syrup that he never wanted to taste ever again. And then he waved the hunky waiter over and ordered a Jack and coke.

**

Something was wrong, but Pete couldn't identify exactly what that something was. Alarm bells rang in his head, even though everything about the scene seemed okay, overall. Timmy lay prone across his lap, wriggling and whimpering, and Pete's cock loved it. Hard as a stone, pressed against Timmy's squirming body. He was spanking his boy for some naughtiness, although he couldn't remember the exact transgression, which was unfortunate.

Timmy clearly adored the punishment, which meant he well and truly deserved it, because that's when he loved punishment the most.

"How many spanks until you forgive me, Daddy? Can I count them?" And when Pete wouldn't tell him, just kept up the hard rhythm of the swats, Timmy's voice grew even more pleading. "Please forgive me, Daddy, please!"

Pete felt a rising burst of pride. Timmy would take as much as Pete needed to dish out to feel whole again. He was such a perfect, perfect boy. Pete's cockhead pulsed with need, and he could feel pre-come dripping from his slit, and then–

and then he remembered.

Timmy was dead. And Timmy didn't smell anything at all like the clean rain smell of the actual boy crying in Pete's arms.

Pete's eyes snapped open.

He recognized the dim glow of his bedroom. He was on his left side, fully clothed, spooning a quietly sobbing boy. It came back to him slowly. Joey or Rory or Jory. One of those. The middle one, he told himself, more convinced the more he repeated it to himself. Joey had been the one who dumped

Rory, just the night before, or something like that, which is why there'd been no one to save the table, and why Pete, with his cane and his bum leg, so desperately in need of somewhere to sit, had caught Rory's attention.

He didn't know why Rory was crying now, and wondered if it was his fault, if he'd gotten drunk and said something mean. It was possible. More than possible, it was probable. He didn't remember getting home, so clearly he'd gotten drunk, was probably drunk still because he couldn't tell if he had his shoes on.

He hoped to hell he had his shoes on.

He knew he was bitter, knew he was angry at luck and circumstance and all the world and his place in it, so asking Rory why he was crying didn't seem like a good idea. No, not at all. So instead he smoothed his palm across Rory's back. "Shh. There, there. It's all going to be all right. Go to sleep, glitter boy."

He followed his own command, refusing to think about the feel of Rory's back against his bare palm.

***

The sun streaming cheerfully into the room woke him, and the searing pain in his head guaranteed the awakening was exceptionally unpleasant. Pete squinted hatefully at the window, wondering what kind of supreme asshole would fling the curtains open at this time of the fucking morning, but he was alone, and he lived alone, so it was his own fault for forgetting to close them last night. He cursed at himself for being an idiot, then wound himself tighter into the blankets and rolled away from the brightness.

He just wanted to sleep.

Except the tightness of his jeans against his bladder was really annoying.

There were sounds coming from beyond the bedroom. Clinking noises, like dishes being moved around. And a musical half-humming, half-singing sound.

Back to the tightness of his jeans.

He'd gone to bed wearing jeans and without closing the curtains, and someone was in his kitchen. Not someone. Rory. The glitter boy who was the master of ceremonies at the burlesque show last night.

He groaned out loud.

He'd had too much to drink and a good bit of the night passed in a blur. He remembered waking to Rory crying in the night, and noticing his gloves were gone. He had no recollection of leaving the club or getting home.

Whether he'd taken his shoes off or left them on.

He was pretty sure they were off now. He slid his right hand beneath the covers. Right thigh. Right knee. Right calf. Stump.

The bottom dropped out of his stomach. Had Rory removed his shoes while he was drunk? Poor kid. That probably explained the crying. No one deserved that. Take a guy's shoes off and find out he has no foot.

He wondered if Rory had pulled his shoes off first or his gloves. Which had he discovered first, half the missing right hand or the whole missing right foot?

Pete wouldn't have blamed him for sneaking out right then. In fact, they'd probably both have been a lot more comfortable if Rory had. So what the fuck was he doing in the kitchen?

He really had to piss, and he didn't know where his prosthetic was, or his cane, and the thought of Rory walking in while he was pissing into a plastic urinal jug was just–no. That's what that was–a complete and total no.

And then the room door popped open and there he was, glitter boy, holding a plate and a coffee cup, smiling, fresh as a daisy.

"Daddy! I brought you coffee."

And before Pete's brain could formulate a single word, Rory set the cup and the plate on the nightstand and flung himself onto the bed.

"Rory–" Pete managed to sputter.

"I'm sorry. I'm not supposed to call you that. I forgot. Mr. Spencer, then."

He was all wide blue eyes and too-long hair, and Pete realized he hadn't seen Rory's real hair until now, or at least hadn't seen it while sober, because first it had been tucked beneath that ridiculous pink hat, and later it was hidden under a wig. He liked it. Long and loose, past his shoulders, with a little bit of wave. Not quite blond, not quite brown. Plenty of hair to wrap one's fists into, to pull that face right into his–he coughed, cleared his throat. Tried to clear that visual out of his head.

"How did you end up here, at my place?"

"Please don't be mad." Those eyes, they got even bigger, though how that was possible, Pete didn't even know. "I did a very bad thing and got you ridiculously drunk. And then it seemed irresponsible to send you out in the cold alone, so I figured the best thing to do was to see you home."

"I had a ride," Pete protested.

"Oh, yes, you did," Rory said, and there something in his voice, just there. Some kind of judgment.

"What?" Pete asked. "What was wrong with my ride?"

"Do you even know that guy? He's like–one of the biggest drug dealers in the–wait! Are you a drug addict? Mr. Spencer!"

Rory's whole face fell into such disappointment that Pete felt immediately ashamed. "I–"

"Seriously?" Rory slid away then, backing up until he sat on his haunches at the end of the bed. He sighed, let his shoulders hunch forward, and then lifted his face toward the ceiling. "How does this keep happening to me? How is it that I pick the wrong guys, over and over and over, every fucking time?"

"Rory. It's not like that."

"Really?" Rory asked. "Because that's what they all say. Every single one. No wonder you got shit-faced so fast. And I brought you coffee and a bagel and everything."

Tears slid down his cheeks, and Pete felt like the lowest dirt-bag on the face of the earth. He wanted to cry, too, but he'd quit crying a long time ago. "I'm sorry. I was in a bad accident, and sometimes I run out of pain killers before I can refill my prescription. I don't know what else to do, so yes, I buy them illegally."

"There are other ways to cope, you know."

"I haven't been good at that."

"Have you even *tried?* Like meditation and yoga and breathing and distraction?"

Pete sighed. His bladder felt like it was going to explode. He couldn't have a reasonable conversation when he was this uncomfortable.

"You don't want to talk about it." There was that accusation in Rory's voice again.

"It's not that. It's just complicated. And I need a few minutes of privacy."

"Why, to shoot up or something?"

Now that was offensive. So offensive it made him spit out the truth. "No. To empty my bladder. Do you mind?"

"Fine, whatever," Rory snapped, and flung himself out of the room.

"Will you close the door? Please?" Pete called after him, gritting his teeth.

Rory poked his head back into the room to grab the doorknob, rolled his eyes, and pulled the door shut with a slam.

Pete rolled to the edge of the bed near the window and found the urinal. His body protested every move even more than usual, as if he'd spent last night dancing like a maniac rather than sitting on a barstool. When he was done, he set the container carefully on the floor beneath the nightstand where he hoped it wouldn't get knocked over. He'd never imagined having a sleepover and this was why–too many things had the potential to be exceptionally awkward and embarrassing.

He got his fly fastened and zipped, wrapped himself in the sheet again, and scooched to the far side of the bed where he could reach his breakfast. He tried to call out to Rory, but discovered his voice was stuck. He coughed, and reached for the coffee mug. "Rory," he called out. "It's fine now. You can come back in."

He sipped the coffee, and it was good.

Rory didn't come back. Pete waited, listening for sounds of Rory moving around, but his little house felt silent. Maybe Rory had cut his losses and ditched. That was probably for the best, really, but the thought of Rory being gone left him feeling hollow and sad.

Ridiculous.

Idiot.

They didn't even know each other.

He took another sip of coffee. Looked at the bagel. Ugh. Too early for that.

Then he spied a shoe near the bed. Four shoes, actually, one of them containing his prosthetic foot. He leaned toward the floor and picked up the heavy shoe/foot combination and tossed it at the door. It hit with a loud thump.

Within seconds the door opened and Rory peeked in. "Are you okay? Are you decent?"

"Yes to both."

Rory looked around. "What was that noise?"

"My foot hitting the door."

Rory grinned, and peered around the backside of the door to look down at the foot-in-shoe combination. "I can't even tell you how much that scared me last night." He made his eyes go big and round. "I screamed like a little girl in a haunted house. And you! You weren't even nice, not at all. You cussed and swore and said all kinds of crusty mean things. Like it's just a missing foot, for fuck's sake, and if I was going to be such a baby I might as well get the fuck out. Man, Mr. Spencer, you got issues."

Pete stared into his coffee cup and wondered how much worse this could possibly get. "What else did I say?"

"You tore your gloves off and waved your hand in front of my face and you said, you said...well, never mind what you said, but you made me cry."

Pete looked up at him then. "What did I say?"

Rory was biting his lip, and maybe even blushing. "It's embarrassing. And not even true."

"Was it mean? I know I'm a shitty, mean drunk. I don't know what I was thinking, ordering hard liquor. I know better than that. I'll apologize a hundred times over if you just tell me what I said that made you cry."

Rory closed his eyes. "You said, 'Not everybody gets to be as pretty and perfect as you'– See? I told you it's not even true."

Pete was so embarrassed he wanted to crawl under the bed. Nothing like too much booze to make him spew his true feelings in the most humiliating way possible. He set the coffee cup on the nightstand and covered his face with his hands. Groaned. "Remind me to never drink again."

He took his hands away and looked at Rory, who'd finally sat down on the end of the bed. "But I meant it as a compliment, you know. I mean, it's even harder to be me around someone like you."

"What do you mean by that, someone like me?" Rory asked.

"Young, attractive. Whole."

"You're attractive!" Rory said. "I mean, why do you think you're not? Well, aside from the obvious."

Pete glared. "What the hell, aside from the obvious?" *Old and broken, pieces of him sawed off and sheared away and tossed into a bio-hazard disposal bin, flushed away or sent to space or whatever they do with that shit.*

"That you're so fuckin' grumpy."

Pete stared at him. "That's the obvious? That I'm *grumpy?*"

"Well...yeah. What else would it be? I don't think I've seen you smile yet, and we've spent hours together. And seriously, I'm not perfect, but I *am* adorable. I make people smile all the time."

"I believe it. And I'm sorry, a hundred times over, for making you cry."

"Okay."

"That's it? Okay and I'm forgiven?"

Rory nodded. "Sure. So long as we get back to how you aren't an addict because you use other things besides drugs to cope with pain."

"You're not letting that go, are you?"

Rory shook his head, and his hair swished in a lazy, sexy swirl around his shoulders. "Nope. Because I don't date drug addicts."

Maybe there really was something wrong with this kid. Maybe he had screws loose that weren't immediately noticeable or something. Like a...Pete couldn't quite find the right word for it. But no, now he was being an ass.

"We're not dating."

"Says you."

Pete rolled his eyes, exasperated. "I must be twice your age."

Rory blinked. "Maybe I like that in a man. Maybe that's *my type.*"

"You don't even know me." Pete said, for what, the third time?

"You keep saying that. But that's what dating is for, isn't it? Getting to know someone?"

Pete growled. He couldn't help it. This bright young thing was barging into his gloomy domain, bringing glitter and light and hope, and when he left, he would leave the place darker than ever, and Pete couldn't stand the thought of it. Might not live through the loss.

He shook his head. He didn't dare take the chance.

"Rory. Go home. I'm not the one for you. Whatever romantic notion you have in your head about me, you're wrong."

"Because you're not perfect?"

Pete didn't even know what to say to that. He was so far away from perfect it was ludicrous. He was more than a mess—he was a lost cause, beyond fixing. Too broken to deserve to lay even one finger on the perfect skin of this beautiful creature.

Rory stared at him with big watchful, wary eyes, as if he could see Pete thinking all of these things. And he didn't wait for Pete to find an answer. He said, "The thing is, Mr. Spencer, what you can't seem to see is that I'm not perfect, either."

Pete boosted himself further up on the pillows. "Tell me, Rory. Since you've seen so many of my imperfections, tell me at least two of the ways you're not perfect."

Rory sprawled across the bed, scooted close enough to rest his head on Pete's belly, and without even thinking about it, Pete let his left hand drop and his fingers tangle into that lovely hair that felt as soft as it looked.

"I'm way too emotional," Rory said. "My whole mood can change in a heartbeat, and then change back again. It makes people crazy, makes me hard to be around. If someone gives me a chance, takes a little time to get to know me, they can figure out how to head it off, or get me out of a mood pretty easily, but people usually get tired of me too fast for that. A person either needs patience to deal with me, or they need to figure out how to discipline me. I'm a lot of work."

Pete felt his pulse jump at the word 'discipline'–and coached himself to keep his breathing even. Some part of him suspected Rory used that word on purpose, probing for a reaction, but he wasn't sure. "Is that why you keep calling me 'Daddy'–you want me to discipline you?"

"I don't know," Rory said softly. "Maybe."

"I had a boy once," Pete confessed. "A lover, I mean. I've never been married or had a son. He was my world."

"Where is he now?" Rory asked.

"Ashes," Pete said, and squeezed his eyes closed. He didn't cry anymore. He realized his fingers were clenched into that soft, soft hair, so he unclenched them and started carefully petting it instead.

"The same accident?"

"Yeah. It's been almost five years. Still hurts." Petting, petting. So soft. So nice.

Rory purred. "Scratch my back, please?" A little space of silence, and when Pete didn't move, Rory nuzzled his cheek harder against Pete's belly and said, "I'm sorry about your boy."

"Thank you," Pete murmured as his hand wandered past Rory's hair and explored each shoulder blade, tapped along the bony knots of his spine.

"Both hands. And under my shirt, not over it. Please."

"But–" But his right hand was only half a hand, and it was wrong to touch such pure flesh with something so horribly misshapen and deformed.

"Scratch!" Rory shifted and wriggled and somehow maneuvered his tee shirt off his body and over his head.

Pete watched his hands descend to Rory's back, and it was like slow-motion, like a dream, his whole left hand, his other hand, missing the pinky and ring fingers and a third of the palm–Pete was used to it, but that Rory wanted this hand on his skin, well, it was hard to reconcile, but then both his hands made contact, and Rory blew hot breath into the fabric against Pete's stomach, then mumbled, "Mmm, now scratch." Pete did. Rory arched and moved under Pete's whole hand and half a hand, and seemed to not mind it.

Pete found himself in a weird place of touching and scratching and exploring the planes of Rory's back, and in between Rory's sighs and murmurs, Pete talked, telling Rory things he'd never told anyone, about himself, about Timmy, what it was like to be a Daddy, to have a boy, things he'd rarely spoken of to anyone because so few would understand. Somewhere in there Rory's hand crept beneath the sheet, wandered along Pete's thigh, and then lower, tugging at the leg of his jeans, the *right* leg. Pete felt the softness of the sheet against the rounded end of his limb, Rory's cool fingers below his knee, exploring along his calf, and his own hands went still, his whole body rigid. He said, "Rory–" in a voice that felt as strangled as it sounded. And nothing more, because he was so filled with terror he couldn't even breathe.

Rory's fingers found the sudden end of his leg, curled around the stump, palmed it. Didn't stroke or rub, just cradled that poor pathetic place where Pete's leg should have continued.

"Does it hurt?" Rory asked. "When I touch it like this?"

Pete realized he was holding his breath, and exhaled and inhaled. Made an effort to breathe like a normal human being. "Not like...actual pain. It hurts in a strange place inside my chest that I have this deformity you're curious enough to touch. Brave enough to touch. This repulsive deformity."

"It doesn't feel repulsive," Rory said. "It feels interesting. The skin is stretched and smooth, almost like a huge cock. I want to suck it."

The thought of Rory's mouth stretched around the end of his leg did something inside Pete's head and stomach he couldn't even explain, and his next thought was of Rory's ass, and then he was harder than he'd been in five fucking years. "God, don't even say that," he groaned, embarrassed and incredibly turned on, all at the same time.

Rory giggled, and curled his fist obscenely around the stump. "Oh, I feel like I should say a lot more than that." He slid down Pete's body, taking the sheet with him. Pete felt the wet slick of Rory's tongue slide along the muscle of his calf, moving down, down, and it was too much, more than he could take.

He rose to a sitting position and reached for that hair. "Oh no, come here, you naughty thing." He grabbed Rory, one hand in his hair, the other winding across his back and under his arm, until he could haul the boy bodily onto his lap.

Rory grinned into his face. "Are you going to spank me? And if so, do I get to call you Daddy then, at least?"

Pete froze for a second, then couldn't stop the unimaginable from happening. He laughed.

The laugh was cut off when Rory kissed him.

It was a sloppy kiss, wet from Rory's open-mouthed grin, messy and fast and not at all sexy, or at least not until Pete tightened his grip in Rory's hair harder, then caught his chin with the finger and thumb of his damaged right hand, and slowed the kiss into something serious.

He got lost in the softness of Rory's lips, the shivers that danced through Rory's body, and the tiny whimper that escaped his throat. Rory pulled away gently, but not far away, and he looked into Pete's eyes, and he wasn't laughing when he asked, "Are you sure you don't want another boy?"

Pete closed his eyes and pictured Timmy glaring at him, asking him why he would refuse a chance to be happy. And he also heard the insecurity hidden inside the question. Not just 'are you sure you don't want another boy', but also, 'maybe can I be your boy?' He inhaled, exhaled. He'd never been a liar. He said, "I do, but..."

"Yeah, yeah, we don't know each other yet. But let me tell you, I would be a great distraction, and I could probably help you with that drug problem."

Pete opened his eyes. "You're really worried about that."

"Well, yeah. Addiction is gross."

"A lot of things about my life are gross. Wait till you smell the rubber piece that makes my foot fit properly."

Rory wrinkled his nose. "I'll do my best to pretend you never said that."

Pete sighed. "Okay. I don't think my drug problem is as serious as you do, but I kind of like you, so I'll see what I can do to minimize the use of painkillers, and we can talk about dating. Agreed?"

The bed jostled as Rory leapt off it and did a little dance, waving birdie hands in the air, his hair flying around his face. His smile was big, his whole face almost glowing. "Really?"

"Yes, really. I give up, or give in, whatever. Now, my whole body is going to tighten up like a virgin's asshole if I don't get out of this bed, so if you would kindly hand me my shoes, and figure out where I dropped my cane, I need to take a shower."

As Pete moved to sit at the side of the bed, Rory kicked his shoes over, then plopped down on the floor, cross-legged, like he was a kindergartner and it was circle time. "You are not going to sit there and watch."

Rory's hands were already reaching for Pete's right leg, and he looked up, his expression more baffled than anything else. "Why not?"

Soft hands enclosed his right calf, sliding gently up to his knee and back down nearly to the end of his leg, and it took everything Pete had not to flinch and pull his leg away. He didn't feel pain, it was just was so unexpected to be touched that way at all. "Because it's..." *humiliating,* he wanted to say, *because I'm ashamed that I have no foot.* "I don't know. It's embarrassing, I guess."

"You're embarrassed about having a fake foot but not embarrassed about being a drug addict? Mr. Spencer. That is so fucked up I'm not even sure what to say."

He still had his hands on Pete's leg, and he curved his spine and leaned forward, sliding his hands again toward Pete's knee, lifting Pete's leg until his lips, those soft, soft lips, feathered lightly across the skin that protected the rounded end of bone. And then he gently released Pete's leg, sprang to his feet, and said, "Go ahead and put yourself together. I'll go find that cane."

Pete watched Rory's retreating back, and for a few seconds just sat there, marveling at the sensation of butterflies in his stomach, how such a strange feeling could start in that nerve-sensitive spot he'd resented every waking minute of every day for the past five years.

He was still thinking about it twenty minutes later in the shower, but the thoughts were darker, his brain fast-forwarding to the end of this, the butterflies morphing into dread, worrying already about what happens next, and what happens later, when Rory goes home, and where is home, and how long would he be gone, and Pete didn't even have his phone number, and what exactly did it mean, to date? Where would they go? Would he have to hang out with Rory's friends? Go out to clubs? Smile at stupid idiots? Good God, would he have to meet Rory's parents?

He was so anxious by the time he finished his shower he forgot to be careful climbing out of the stall, and fell with a horrific crash and a lot of cussing. So much for his insistence that he lived alone, did this every day, and certainly didn't need Rory's help.

Rory came bursting into the bathroom. "Pete! What happene-" then he slipped on the wet floor, and fell on top of Pete. It was an awkward pile of Rory's arms tangled with Pete's legs, one of Rory's knees dangerously close to Pete's nose, the other lodged tight against Pete's chest.

Pete was still swearing when Rory started giggling.

"What the hell's the matter with you?" Pete growled.

Rory managed to stop laughing long enough to choke out, "Are you hurt?"

"No, I'm pissed off because I'm a clumsy bastard."

"Okay, good," and the little twat started laughing all over again.

"It's not that funny."

"It is if you forgot to dump the urinal," and he exploded in such a fit of giggles that Pete didn't even know how he was managing to breathe.

Pete spied the plastic jug behind the toilet, and almost grinned despite himself. "I did that first thing. I always do that first thing."

"Well, that's a relief, because now I'm almost as wet as you are."

And then Pete felt a hand slip between his legs, and what definitely felt like the press of teeth against his hip, and the warm wetness of a teasing tongue swiped over the gentle bite.

"Rory-this isn't a good idea, we-"

"Hush. Mr. Spencer. I know."

Soft hair draped over Pete's hips, hid Rory's face when Pete wanted to see, and surprisingly firm hands pushed at him to roll over onto his back, which wasn't comfortable, but Pete rolled without arguing.

When Rory's lips slipped over the head of his cock, Pete thought he would come right then, like a horny teenager, and he bucked at the sensation overload, too sensitive, too hot, too good. He groaned and went still, fighting for control.

Except he wasn't still, he was trembling.

Rory's hand slid down the length of Pete's right leg again–would his fascination with that never end? His fingers curled around the stump, and he pumped it like he was giving a cock a handjob. When his mouth slid along Pete's actual cock, the two sensations were irreconcilable, and Pete had to see the boy's face. Cool air rushed across his groin as he gathered that hair into his fist, and Rory's eyes met his, dark with desire. His lips stretched around Pete's cock, and he hummed a sound of approval, maybe in response to the near loss of control that must be showing on Pete's face.

"You're being a very naughty boy," Pete said. "Taking advantage of me when I've fallen down."

"Mm-hmm," Rory hummed, and swirled his tongue around the ridge just beneath the head of Pete's cock, which made Pete's whole body twitch. He sucked in a quick, sharp breath.

Rory gave the end of Pete's leg a gentle squeeze, then brought his hand up and wrapped it around Pete's cock, slowly jacking his hand toward his mouth. He lifted his face away just as his fist reached his lips. "I am very naughty. And if I had a Daddy, he'd surely punish me for such behavior."

Pete remembered to breathe. "God, Rory, you're killing me."

"Just a little spanking, please?"

His pleading was electrifying, and something inside Pete broke loose. Why not? Why shouldn't he have this, take this? Who would get hurt, in the end, except himself?

He pushed at Rory, slid out from underneath him, and pulled himself toward the door, pushing it closed so he could sit up with his back against it. "Take off your clothes, boy."

It was as much a bark as a command, and Rory scrambled to his feet. "Yes, Mr. Spencer," he said quietly, and shrugged out of the shirt he'd stolen from Pete's closet, then unfastened his jeans and slipped them off. His feet were already bare, and he apparently didn't wear undershorts. His cock stood up, curved a bit toward his belly, and was in perfect proportion to his fine, young body.

Pete allowed himself a few seconds to appreciate that body, enough seconds that he could tell Rory became uncomfortable, waiting to be told what to do next. "How old are you?"

Rory's lips twitched. "Shouldn't you have asked me that before you told me to get naked?"

"Rory." Just his name, but Pete hadn't forgotten how to do this, and he injected plenty of warning into that one word.

Rory's eyes dropped straight to the floor. "Twenty-three. Sir."

Ah. He'd played this game before.

"If you really want me to spank you, get over here and put yourself across my lap."

There would be no going back now, and some scared place inside of Pete hoped Rory would change his mind, but Rory didn't. He dropped to his hands and knees and crawled across the floor, and settled himself into position, dropping to his elbows. Their cocks kissed, and Pete tried to remember if he'd ever spanked Timmy while they were both naked. He realized he wasn't sure, which was odd, because he'd promised himself he'd never forget a single detail of his time with Timmy. He almost got hung up on that, almost, but a vision of Timmy sternly telling him to 'knock it off' forced him to shake it out of his brain.

He let himself be distracted by the perfect roundness of Rory's waiting buttocks, clenched in nervous anticipation. He placed the palm of his left hand on Rory's back, right between his shoulder blades, and rubbed soft circles into Rory's skin as he examined his damaged right hand, wondering what it would feel like to be struck with such a hand. What it would feel like use this half hand in this particular way.

He felt Rory relax, and knew it was time to stop wondering and find out.

The first spank was half-hearted, barely left an imprint on Rory's skin, but he had more confidence with the next and despite the strange zing that flew along the sheared bone of his hand, he quickly found a balance of rhythm and strength that seemed comfortable for them both. His arm remembered how to do this, and his ear remembered, perfectly, how to listen to the sounds of a boy being spanked, and his body remembered the cues of the wriggles on his lap, and before they were done, the holes in his spirit seemed to knit themselves closed.

When Rory cried out, "Daddy, I'm sorry," Pete pulled him up, turned him so they were chest to chest, and Rory shifted and wiggled and folded his legs around Pete's waist, then buried his face against Pete's chest.

Pete hugged him tight, the hand that had done the spanking now twined into that delightfully soft hair, as he murmured, "It's okay, baby, Daddy forgives you."

It suddenly didn't matter if the darkest days were yet to come. It didn't matter that they didn't know each other yet, or if he would get to keep Rory for a month, or a year, or forever. Pete Spencer felt alive and whole for the first time in half a decade. It was time to stop hiding, to stop being scared. The time had come to step up and be the man he was meant to be, and if he only had one real foot to step up with, well...never mind. It was enough.

He used the hand in Rory's hair to pull the boy's head back, gently, just enough so he could look into his face. No glitter on the glitter boy this morning, just shiny tear streaks on his cheeks, and a shy smile curving his lips.

"That was the best spanking I ever had," Rory whispered. "Could've been a little longer, though."

Pete shook him, but just a little. "You're an insolent little brat. Did you use my shower before I woke up?"

Rory nodded. "And your toothbrush."

Pete growled.

Rory laughed and said, "I told you I'm adorable."

Pete shut him up with a kiss that lasted a long, long time.

***

ABOUT THE AUTHOR:

SM Johnson hibernates in a conservative community of northern Wisconsin, where she writes characters who aren't exactly mainstream. Her stories are erotic, romantic and often somewhat unexpected. Visit her on blogspot to feed your hunger for darkly erotic fiction, messy lives, and things that go "naughty" in the night.

http://www.smjbookteasers.blogspot.com

SCARS: FIRST SESSION
BY JORDANNE FULLER

I sat in the chair, still as can be, while buzzing filled the room. My body had long since become accustomed to the pain the artist promised to provide. I wasn't worried, pain was something I understood. Music played through a nearby speaker which blended into the background. The artist gave up on small talk around the same time the sounds faded. I cut him off short in every conversation he tried to start, leaving him nothing much to say. The silence suited me well, I only came to cover up the scars anyway. A sharp, unexpected needle pang shot up my thigh, forcing me to reflect upon my past.

***

Don't cower you fucking bitch! You're only making this worse! You have to stand your ground or he'll never stop. You're bigger than he is.

My internal monologue was almost worse than his verbal insults.

"That's right, you whore, you're the weaker sex for a reason," Garry sneered at me. It had been a long time since I felt any love toward the man. "I will see you torn apart, like you did to my heart when you started fucking my best friend."

His assumption stung worse than the actual words ever could. I never slept with anyone but him, but he'd been drinking and there was no point in trying to force reason on such an addled mind. I shook in my corner, self hating and cursing a god I was no longer so sure I believed in.

How did I stand being with this man for fourteen years? The progression of abuse is one hell of a drug. He was so beautiful and strong, although skinny in the minds of most. I was a larger girl at the time, binge eating at fault for my severe weight gain. I never meant to let myself go. My size only gave the beast more ammunition for his relentless assaults.

Besides, I never had the time to cheat on him, I was his sexual plaything more often than I thought my body capable. Nothing broke me like he had. I found myself so completely lost and within a world I no longer recognized; inhabiting a body I hadn't remembered altering.

***

"...cause you know, as cathartic as this is, you're only covering up the scars."

"Hmm?" I hummed as I fell from my day-terror and back into the chair. My body remained limp while I relived my nightmare.

"I was just saying I believe beauty comes from within. These scars you're trying to cover are badges of courage. They're there to remind you how much you've survived. Although I think making them more colorful is a great idea, it won't hide the pain under the surface."

"Yeah, well, you weren't there when I got them. Trust me, not having the scars there to remind me would feel better," I huffed. I didn't mean to be such a difficult person. I just felt like it was none of the artist's business. He was a man. He couldn't possibly know how I've suffered.

"I get that they're a sensitive subject. Anyone with scars has felt pain. No one person hurts more or less than another, everyone experiences agony on different levels," he winked. "It doesn't make any discomfort greater than the last."

I was getting sick of his happy, motivational bullshit. He was just an artist. If he wanted to be a psychologist he should have gone to school for however many years it took. That's what I had to do to get my job. I was oddly content as the familiar pain brought another uncontrollable flashback on its heels.

***

"You are not going out to the movies with her! She is poor, unchristian, and not suited to be your friend," my mother shouted in my sixteen year old face.

"She's more than just a friend," I sneered under my breath.

"What did you just say?" my mother screamed at a pitch I was surprised wasn't only audible to dogs.

"I said," I paused for teenage dramatic effect, "she's my girlfriend!"

Had I known at that age what I came to learn about my mother later that year, I wouldn't have been quite so bold. It takes years to beat a strong woman into submission. It has to start somewhere.

Thwack!

"What the fuck was that?"I screeched as my hand flew up to touch the back of my head. My mother glided to my side to slap me across the face.

"You will *not* shame us by being...one of those, and you will *not* swear in this house."

Her voice was lower and quieter than I had ever heard in the past, rising in volume only when she said 'not'. She stormed out of the kitchen, slamming the door in my face when I tried to follow. I immediately regretted my decision to be bold. I loved my mother. Why would I say things just to make her angry? Alecia and I were only friends anyway. Sure, we were close, but we never really talked about any feelings we may have had for one another.

I wasn't sure if the hurt I felt was for disappointing my mother, from the venom that dripped from her words, or the lump that formed at the base of my skull where the rolling pin had connected. I blamed myself for each. I should have known better than to antagonize my mother.

My parents had always told me homosexuality was unnatural, that it was an abomination against God. I decided to read my bible as punishment. I hoped it would make my mother happy. The headache began as I took that first step toward my room. Instinctively, my hand found the lump on my skull and snapped back to show the result of my query. No blood. I avoided the hospital that time.

***

"Most people squirm when I do this part, don't worry," Tobias, the tattooist, cooed as the needle repetitively punctured a particularly sensitive section of my ankle.

His words were meant to be reassuring, but instead, forced me back to the present. At least in the past the pain was mostly emotional or psychological. I could feel the crack to the back of my head, but it was like a dream. The sensation didn't linger the second my consciousness returned to the tattoo parlor.

I wondered, had I been born into another household would I never have been abused? Had I kept being friends with Alecia, maybe no man could have ever hurt me. I knew that was just my anger speaking. I was jaded and I knew it. I didn't believe for a second that women were any better. I really had become maligned with age. Maybe the artist was right about the emotional scars. I probably would have been better off going to a shrink.

No! You are not going to let them walk all over you again. You are strong, you are beautiful, you control your own future.

Who was I kidding? I'd never think myself beautiful again.

"Can I ask where you got this one?" Tobias was tentative as his needle gun passed around my gnarly mess of an ankle bone.

"I was shot," I shrugged.

That particular scar was the only one I didn't get from abuse; unless of course the stupidity that comes with being brought up by abusive people counted.

"Care to give details?"

The man gave an awkward chuckle. I looked at him truly for the first time. He was a very good looking twenty-something year old man. His stylishly cut hair showed off a tattoo from his temple to the back of his head. His crystal blue eyes twinkled with that excitement for life I long since dismissed, and a drive that left the first time I was stabbed.

"My dad had guns when I was a kid. I was rooting around in their closet for a bible one day," I paused to clarify, "they were real fundamentalist types, you know? Well, a box fell from above and I was curious about it. I had never seen a real gun. My parents wouldn't even let me play with pretend ones. So I pointed it at the ground, and pulled the trigger. The kickback all but flung the thing from my hands, the bullet lodged deep in my bone. I was the youngest person my surgeon had ever worked on. The man reconstructed my ankle from pretty much nothing."

I smirked. The story made me happy for some twisted reason. My ankle scar was the only one I'd given myself. It represented a token of control I hadn't relinquished. Of course, I left out the part where my mother whipped me with my father's belt until my ass felt raw before I was allowed to go to the hospital. My smile faded at the memory. How had I not realized then how horrible she was? Not that my father was the saint he would have people believe. A Pastor, yes. Saint? No.

"I find it strange that the scars we come to terms with first are the ones we create ourselves. It's a strange pride one takes in one's ability to make and learn from their own mistakes," Tobias answered.

I was surprised he had gotten so deep into my own thoughts that I had a hard time closing my mouth and popping my eyeballs back to their preferred spots in my sockets.

"I have a Bachelors of Psychology, and Masters of Social Anthropology. I'm trained in how to read people," he chuckled, reading my expressions, I gathered.

"Why are you a tattoo artist?"

Damn him! I was so prepared not to care what or who this person was. He was just another man capable of hurting me. I realized immediately my unfair assessment and took it back within my mind. I re-evaluated my stance, concluding that he couldn't be trusted because he was human. Gender had little to do with it. After all, my mother had hurt me worst of all.

"Such a genuine question from someone so hostile. Am I wearing you down?" Tobias winked at me again with that insufferably childish face of his.

I assumed he sensed my anger and continued before giving me a chance to snap at him. I was thankful deep down for the intrusion. I didn't like hating the world, it just came naturally now.

"I'm using this to pay off school. I had some financial troubles and got kicked out of my program. I can pick it back up once I'm out of debt." He paused. From the look on his face, I assumed he was taking a second to think his next words through. "I've always had a penchant for art and I thought people who wanted to change their bodies forever would be great subjects to keep my mind on my intended profession," he held his hand in the air as the gun clicked off. "I think you're the first who's been this interesting. Which, for four years of working with the gun, is saying something."

"So I'm just a subject?" I meant to ask this with simple curiosity, but the hurt from feeling used once again crept into my voice and, I assumed, showed in my features. The artist looked at me with an expression I'd seldom seen. It was like pity, but this time I didn't feel as though he thought me beneath him. I settled on reading sincerity from his features.

"No, of course not." The words thrust through his mouth, bewilderment speckled his speech. "I'm so sorry. I got used to using field terms in school and sometimes forget not to apply them in everyday life. If I were observing you from a one-way mirror, conversing among colleagues, I would refer to you as a subject. But you came into my place of work for some ink and a shoulder. I'm so sorry if I made you think anything less than the amazing person you are."

"Yeah, so amazing that I've been hurt this many times," I scoff, sweeping my hands over my body.

It had been a long time since I felt insecure. As my life progressed, I had begun to think of my scars as clothing. The more damage my body retained, the less desirable I became. I was no longer a sexual creature.

My insecurity surpassed the simplicity of being exposed before a man's eyes. I felt a different kind of bare. It was as though he could see through my body, right into my soul. I shuddered at the thought of a spirit. It always pushed my mind back to the religion I had been born and raised with. I was groomed to believe I was a lesser being than a man. My mind flipped through the implemented ideals that preached being kind to your fellow neighbor; unless of course that particular neighbor didn't believe in God. Then it was more than acceptable to accost, alienate, and ostracize them as the need arose.

Tobias cleared his throat. The sound reclaimed my attention and I realized the tattoo gun no longer buzzed. My daydream had been selfish and rude. All of my teachings had me craving to apologize, kneel, wait for him to strike me, then apologize as if I had made him do so. My experiences placed a scowl on my lips and daggers in my eyes to fight the trained urge to submit.

"I'm done the piece you wanted. Would you like something else, or is this it for today?"

"Cover me," I demanded, fists balled at my sides.

"Aw honey, there isn't enough time for that, not today at least," he thought for a fraction of a second before he continued. "How about this: I don't have anything else scheduled for the day so I can work on you until you can't take it, I get tired, both, or midnight. Maybe later if the owner lets me keep the shop open but it will take lots of sessions to cover your entire body. It took me forty five minutes just to do that," he pointed to the rose on my ankle.

When I first walked into the shop, I told him to do whatever he wanted. He said that the most common starter tattoo was a flower and he wanted to know my favorite. I had never been given flowers, and I decided my first rose would be a gift to myself.

Now that the rose was mine, my mind scrolled through all the images I could ever hope to retain upon my flesh until I die. My breaths slowed, becoming almost inaudible. I could hear the blood rush through my ears as I felt it drain from my face.

"How do you feel about a butterfly?"

"Isn't a butterfly kind of," I paused to find the word I wanted, "weak?"

"Have you ever seen how hard a butterfly works to struggle itself from its cocoon during a transformation? The butterfly is one of the strongest animals I know of. It starts as a caterpillar, something most people find ugly and strange. Slowly, it transforms into something beautiful. A butterfly's entire life is filled with unknowns and constant change, but in the end they not only become one of the most beautiful creatures that exist in our world, they come bursting with color and fly from their previous lives with the strength and courage they need to continue. Their lives are still not easy, as they are fragile creatures, but now they can fly. They leave who they were, what they were, behind them."

My entire face went slack at the description of what I previously thought were just pretty insects. It was a perfect description of where I wanted to go from where I felt I had been. My scars were ugly and I wanted to make them beautiful. I wanted to become this transcendent creature.

"Yeah. I think I'd like that," I mumbled at my feet.

This artist was having more of an effect on me than I thought possible. As he smiled, I swore I saw a jolt of understanding shoot to his eyes as one of his eyebrows lifted toward his hairline. My heart raced for a fraction of a second before I forced the excitement from my mind.

"Think of what color you want it to be before I get back. Make sure you want this. It will be on your body forever. I'm going to step out for a cigarette."

I thought of the artist while Tobias inhaled his tobacco. His imperfections swirled around his face in the smoke. The addiction could have been much worse than cancer sticks, but I knew better than to think I could judge him on first impressions alone. He could be a rapist for all I knew. The cold metal table I sat upon suddenly gave me a cold, sterile feeling. I covered myself subconsciously as my hand roamed from hanging at my side to just under my breast. A pinkie finger grazed a scar, the only one I had from my time with Alecia.

***

Her ash blonde hair, cut severe around her face, hung in wisps against her back. She used bleach, of course, but I couldn't picture it any other shade. I loved how she wore such dark makeup against her pale, Iranian skin. She was a white lily among red roses, her deep black eyes the only thing that betrayed her true ancestry. I loved her more than anyone before, or since.

Alecia was kind, gentle, and patient. She always looked at me with love in her eyes, until the end. The last time she looked upon my face was the only time I had ever seen her hurt or angry. I often reminded myself that I didn't mean to break her heart, but I would never get that expression out of my memories.

I looked deep into her eyes before we took our first kiss. Nothing had felt like that. I was nervous, anxious, and kind of upset. I was actively sinning, but didn't want to stop. Something must have been wrong with me. Nonetheless, my first kiss stolen by a girl was bliss. The love I felt for her at the time was something I would learn didn't come along often; some never got to experience pure love at all.

My religion, however, taught me I was doing something bad. After a relentless struggle and infinite patience from my best friend, I finally conceded I would live as a sinner. My decision and my new life made me so much happier than what my parents had me believing was God's will. At sixteen, I didn't really understand the bible anyway. I wish I'd known then that I could have grown to be whomever I wanted and still be acknowledged by God. I've learned He doesn't lightly decide human worth on matters of love. All sermons since breaking from my parents' church taught me to love, over all else.

Unfortunately my parents used religion to hide their abuse. Their beliefs were the excuse they used to hurt others and not help others as they were supposed to. They were fundamentalists in every horrible way imaginable. Not that anything could be done about it. They believed so heartily that they were doing God's good work.

"What in the heck do you think you're doing young lady?" my father screeched as he opened the door. To hear a grown man screech is a terrifying experience. Screaming is not manly, and my father would sooner die than stoop to a woman's level. Or at least what is perceived as such. For him to lose his composure and make such a sound meant he was more upset with me than he had ever been before.

Horror and disgust radiated from him, I could feel it from the bed where my girlfriend and I sat. We had only just pushed the boundaries of our friendship but since I had lied to my mother, my parents considered it strike two. The hand up my shirt became strike three. Alecia's long nails scraped along the bottom of my breast while trying to remove herself from my under-wire. My chest throbbed in pain but I knew better than to complain by this point. I would only be told my injury was my repercussion for my heathen ways. Unfortunately I believed this, and jumped to that conclusion before it ever needed to be stated.

God was mad I was happy.

"What are you doing to me?" I screamed in hopes that my father wouldn't punish me.

Alecia's dejection sent daggers through my heart. I wanted to take those words back so badly, but I knew even then that I wasn't the right person for her. She was so kind and I was so fucked up. I turned my eyes toward my feet when I caught a glimpse of blood pouring from my chest. The stain kicked my gag reflex into gear. I got up to rush to the bathroom. My father wouldn't let me leave the room and, in turn, ended up wearing my lunch.

"Leave," he bellowed.

Alecia sprang from my bed, muscles finally kicking into a gear after the shock of my father bursting in had rusted them into place. She fled from the room, anger radiating from her soul, masking the betrayal I knew she felt. I had hidden my parents' fundamentalist tendencies from Alecia. She never looked back on my crumpled form, nor my father's looming presence as she left. There is no way my mother would call after Alecia. Not only did mom suspect us of being together for longer than we actually had been, she undoubtedly heard the argument, as short and one sided as it was.

***

My hand lay resting on my scar when I heard the door's bell chime. Tobias smelled of spices along with the tobacco. His cigarettes were something I had never smelled in my life. It was somewhat intoxicating.

"What were you smoking?" I felt I had to know.

"Oh, they're a special kind of cigarette I order from specialty tobacco shop down the street. They put spices in them, what you smell are the cloves."

"I don't hate it as much as I usually do, the smell of tobacco smoke." I trailed the conversation, halting us to an abrupt pause. It was probably one of the few I'd felt in my life that wasn't uncomfortable.

"So you want your butterfly there," he asked, eyeing the place I forgot I had covered.

I nodded, unable to find my words. I still felt everything that was said and screamed in that last memory. My stomach turned with the thought of being sick. My color must have blanched as the artist disappeared wearing a worried expression, only to resurface seconds later with a cup of something fizzy.

"Sometimes, the tattoo process messes with people's adrenalin. This helps, I promise."

I chugged the drink back, not realizing how thirsty I truly was. My words remained trapped within as I stayed in the thoughts still clutching my soul, too pulled into my daydream to even recognize my drink by taste, but it did seem to help.

"I'll need you to take off your top for this one. Will you be okay with this?"

I couldn't believe he was a man who asked. Most would just tear it from my body in what they perceived as the throes of passion. I had never been asked before, and my face grew hot, reflecting my internal struggle. I mentally grafted my feet to the floor in an act of affirmation in my choice, and slid the garment over my head. Multiple scars were exposed, and I could see sadness reflected in Tobias' eyes as he studied the spot I requested the ink as though it were a blank canvas. To him, it must have been. Thinking of my body as a medium for art gave me the rest of the strength I needed to lay half naked on the man's table. Only when I loosened all my taut muscles had I realized I was counting my breathing; a trick I had learned to help calm my anxiety.

"How about I start with the outline and we can go from there?" He suggested. I could only guess that he sensed my unease and was trying to help.

I nodded again as I lay down. I was reluctant, at first, to let this man touch my scar. The memory attached was so emotionally charged that I felt the tears before I saw them well within my eyes. This particular wound belonged to the only person I ever really cared about. Was it wrong of me to want to cover it?

"Can we maybe ink around it? I don't want to cover this one."

Tobias smiled, it lit up his face in a way I had yet to see. It reminded me I didn't know him well. Perhaps this man might actually care?

"Of course. How about we make it the body, that way the wings are for the scar itself."

"I like that idea. Um... can..." I trailed off, scared of what I was about to admit to myself. I cleared my throat before continuing. "Can I make it rainbow?

"Girlfriend?" he asked.

"Something like that."

"You loved her?"

"Definitely," I replied seconds before I felt the familiar pain return.

I couldn't see what he was doing very well, even though I held my breast out of his way. I was much more worried about this tattoo than the last. It not only would be a surprise once I had my hands on a mirror, it meant so much to me.

"Do you have a particular style of butterfly in mind?"

I hadn't thought about it. I guessed there were different kinds, but was not well enough versed in butterfly etymology to make a proper decision. Tobias must have sensed this when he spoke again.

"I think a swallowtail will be the prettiest. Was she pretty?"

"She was the most beautiful creature I've ever seen," I replied proudly.

"Yeah, swallowtail. You'll see." Tobias trailed his sentence as he left for the other room, where he kept his drawing pads and template paper.

Just then I realized exactly how much trust I gave this man. When I first came in here I just wanted to cover myself. But I should have known that I could do that with clothing. Tattoos were permanent. I sighed in relief upon remembering what my rose looked like. Tobias was very talented. His work was so lifelike.

My body twitched as the needle floated over my tender flesh. The spots with the scars were infinitely more sensitive than those without. I was quite relieved that the artist suggested to make this one around the damage. I never thought I could be happy adorning one of my scars. It finally hit me why so many people thought of their scars as badges of honor. This pushed me to reflect upon the one I hated the most.

The curving scar went from my neck straight up my face and across an eye. Had I not closed that eye...

***

"I'm not happy about this. It's going to hurt me so much more than it will you."

My mother reached for the extension cord.

***

Tszzzzzzzzzzz. The needle pierced my skin over and over. I looked down as a tear crested my lash and splashed upon my nose. Tobias was far too engrossed in his work to notice. His hand danced along my sternum as it sketched in the antennae. The needle tickled the underside of my breast seconds before a painful jolt sparked up my side. Sometimes the transition between uncomfortable to painful felt seamless, tricking my mind into believing there was no line at all. A second jolt put my consciousness back in front of my mother.

***

"Mom," I shouted, "Jesus says to love everyone. Don't hate the sinners, hate the sins!"

"The bible also teaches children thou shalt respect thy mother and father. Being with that Jezebel is the furthest thing from respect I could ever have imagined. I should have done this the moment you told me you were dating that temptress!"

I had gotten the belt before, but my father was too enraged to be the one to do the disciplining today. My mother possessed no belts, as she had explicit rules to dress solely in frocks. The woman was not allowed take my father's garments without his permission. The priest had long since locked himself inside the bathroom, to wash away the vomit and keep distance from his evil daughter.

Tears streamed down my mother's face as she wrapped the cord, leaving loose a length that would be appropriate for what came next.

***

"Abigail!"

"Huh?"

"I've been calling you for a few minutes, are you okay?"

Tobias pointed at the tears streaming down my face.

"Yeah," I lied as my voice faltered, giving me away. "I guess."

"Do you want to talk about it?"

When I looked at the artist, his eyes portrayed a concern I seldom ever saw in others.

"No, I think I just need the thoughts to run through me. I think it helped before." He stayed quiet, seemingly reluctant to push his luck.

"I'm sorry I was difficult before. I think we should call it a night after the butterfly." I wasn't sure if I could take any more of this tonight.

I attempted a wide smile, but my reflection in the mirror behind his head and the sadness in his eyes told me it fell short.

"Some of us go through more than others. Heal at your own pace, and in the meanwhile I'll be here to provide the bandages."

A smile played on his face. He was trying to be nice and I had treated him badly. I reflected on the day, and the unexpected closeness that grew between my tattoo artist and I.

"I can trust you, right?"

My eyes widened at my own words. I hadn't meant to voice my thoughts. I was mortified by my own brazen behavior.

"I know you don't trust many people, but yes. You can trust me; at least with this."

Tobias lifted the gun in the air and I managed a short laugh. He could tell I was uncomfortable with my admission and found a way to help me cope with the fallout. My smile drooped as I remembered the first person I learned not to trust.

***

"Sit," Mom commanded as she dragged me to one of our kitchen chairs, shoving me into the chair, forcing me to straddle the thing..

I did as I was told. My mother lifted my shirt so there was nothing to encumber the belt that would soon whip against my skin. Dad was always efficient with his punishments. He did not like to hurt me, and so he wanted it over for the both of us as soon as possible. That was never the case with my mother. The anticipation was agonizing, but the mistake I made was worse. I held my breath for what felt like five whole minutes before turning around to see what my mother was waiting for.

Crack!

My face and body scrunched at the sound. I was too scared to open my eyes.

"What in the name of the Lord were you doing?" my mother screamed. "How on Earth did I end up with such a horrible child?"

I felt the warm, sticky blood trickle down my face before I had even dared open my eyes.

"I'm sorry, I just..."

"I just... I just..." mom imitated my voice right down to the last whimper.

"I wanted to see..."

"Well you got your wish, now you may never see again," she interrupted.

"I'll get ready for the hospital," were the last words that escaped my lips before the sobs.

"Do what you want, but not in this house. I can't handle a Satan-spawn like you. You have no place here. I don't care where you go. God can take care of you now."

I opened my good eye just in time to watch my mother turn around and walk out of the kitchen, throwing her hands in the air as if to tell me she'd had enough, tears long since dried. My sobbing continued, however, tears mixing with blood. All I knew was that I needed to get myself to the hospital. I decided to concentrate on that. The rest happened naturally.

A surge went through my sternum before bringing my mind back to the present.

***

"All done Abby," I wasn't sure at first if he was telling or asking. "Want to see?"

"Yes, please."

It was hard for me to utter the words. My face was drenched and I realized the tears I shed in my memories matched those in this chair. I looked at the beautiful butterfly beneath my breast. The creature looked so realistic, its wings were vibrantly colored and shaded; it was as though they stood removed from my flesh. New tears appeared where the old had left their trails.

"Thank you."

I had no other words for work the artist had done.

"There's time for another. Would you like to sit back down?" Tobias asked.

My mother had demanded I sit.

"I think I've had all I can take for one day."

Tobias seemed to know my most difficult pain that day was not caused by his gun.

"Okay, same time next week?"

The chair in the kitchen was where I lost myself.

"Yeah, sounds good," I smiled.

The chair in the tattoo parlor is where my true self emerged.

***

ABOUT THE AUTHOR:

Jordanne Fuller is a mishmash of creative talents whirling into one another, solidified into a woman. She has been writing since she can remember but didn't realize how much she enjoyed it until her poetry explosion at the age of sixteen. At twenty, she wrote her first unfinished novel that will likely never see the light of day. Now that she is thirty(ish), Jordanne has finished Night, a novel that she hopes to publish in the near future. Although Dusk (the stand alone prequel to Night) is her first work to enter the hands of a publishing company, Troy was her first work to be released as a contribution to the Love Sucks Anthology, published by CHBB. Both anthologies achieved top ten international bestseller status the day they launched. She also has works within Twisted Tales: A Paranormal Anthology and Curse of Heroines Anthology; The Flight of Phoenix and Trapped respectively. When not writing, Jordanne likes to do various arts and crafts, but most of all enjoys spending time with her son, fiancé and four cats. She has lived in Toronto for much of her adult life, but spent her childhood among many of the surrounding towns.

FROM THE PUBLISHER

Thank you for reading UnCommon Bodies. We hope you have enjoyed the stories contained within. Please take a moment to leave a review. We love to hear from readers and it makes an incalculable difference for small press collections like ours. We've even made it as easy as possible with links that will take you directly to the review page!

To Review on Amazon: www.smarturl.it/UCBAmazonReviews
To Review on GoodReads: www.smarturl.it/UCBGoodReads

To hear about more projects and writing opportunities from Fighting Monkey Press, check out our website at www.FightingMonkeyPress.com.

Printed in Great Britain
by Amazon

79320658R00208